The Bloody Bokhara

A Will Stock Mallorca Mystery

by

George Scott

"When the only tool you have is a hammer,
every problem begins to resemble a nail."
                                        Abraham Maslow

First published in Great Britain by
Eyelevel Books

Copyright © George Scott, 2000

The author asserts his moral right to
be identified as the author of this work

ISBN 1 902528 08 5

Printed in England
by
Biddles Limited
Guildford and King's Lynn

Cover design by Judy Brabner Scott and Martin Will

Dedication

To my two sisters who do not read mystery stories, and to the memory of my dear dead sister who did, and to my late, sweet Ma who'd have been proud of me whatever I wrote. And to my big daughter, an inspiration through example and a one-person fan club and cheering section. I also dedicate these words to my smaller, or at any rate younger, son and daughter. And to their mother particularly, my business partner, sounding board, and boon companion.

An Acknowledgment

Pretty much buying a pig in a poke, and certainly without knowing what he was letting himself in for, John Foley allowed himself to be coerced into the daunting final editorial task of vetting the manuscript, and did so uncomplainingly, while in the process teaching me some English – as opposed to American – grammar, punctuation, and spelling – he might say 'spellings', but he didn't vet this. Without having changed a word, his advisory contribution to the accuracy and fluency of the final text has been immeasurable. All remaining awkwardnesses, sloppiness, and plain bad writing, are mine alone.

Craven Disclaimer

This book mixes fact, opinion, and fantasy. Most of the places and a few of the people mentioned are real: some names have been changed to protect the guilty. As a general observation, the thoughts expressed are mainly a reflection of the author's own arbitrary and capricious prejudices.

Where I have mentioned hotels, I have made no judgements about them, as I've never had a chance to stay in any of them. The comments regarding my own hotel are certainly prejudiced and probably fatuously self-serving, but I beg forgiveness on the grounds of a helpless infatuation with my partner's wonderful taste.

Especially with regard to the restaurants mentioned, the opinions are both personal and current. Assessing and evaluating restaurants is a notoriously slippery business. Chefs fling down their toques and stalk out of their kitchens, enterprises change hands, staff have off days, and customers' expectations, standards, and taste buds vary wildly. Don't count on anything written here; take every appraisal only as a provisional recommendation subject to your own judgement. And don't blame the author if you don't like a meal, or indeed are disappointed with any casual recommendation contained herein.

On the other hand, the author is willing to accept full responsibility and all praise for any endorsement or experience on the island that turns out well, including the weather.

One

Oddly enough, my first thought was for the floor tiles. The blood from the corpse's crushed skull had soaked through the Bokhara rug and pooled in a low point in the floor, and was now blackening at the edges as it dried. Had the tiles been impervious *gres* I'm sure I wouldn't have had such a bizarre thought, but *barro* – terra cotta – is permeable and I knew Ninian's gore would probably leave a permanent stain. Bloody inconvenient.

I was standing in the doorway of what we call the library, but which really is an anteroom off the stairway which leads into our two best suites, the elegant Grand Suite and the more cosy and *gemütlich* Blue Suite. The body rested about midway between the two entry doors, half crooked to one side, the left leg partly drawn up and the left arm curled protectively back over the nape of his neck. Fat lot of protection it had afforded him. The wound was massive and the murder weapon obvious, a nice little Hepworth bronze I had picked up cheap in Istanbul – allegedly a limited edition strike but more probably a faked copy – which lay bloodily incarnadined next to the burr walnut tapestried lowboy. Barbara's nobbly surfaces won't have given purchase to any fingerprints, I thought.

There was a faint aroma in the air, almost savoury, not like the usual coppery acidic smell of blood.

Good God, the thought struck me. A corpse in the library of a hotel. The shade of Agatha Christie must be hovering somewhere near.

All these musings seemed to happen simultaneously. There was no emotional reaction apart from the mild irritation I felt towards the corpse for so inconveniently bleeding all over my pretty floor, the antique tile floor on which we had spent so much travail attempting to protect it against the demands of the Spanish hotel licensing functionaries who would rather have seen it chipped into shards and replaced by cement or linoleum; not even to mention the depredations and despoliations of mindless building workers, fresh from taking steam jackhammers to a *treizième siècle* church in order to make room for a car park. I looked at the corpse and sighed. Ninian Mede had been a pain in the backside in life, and had contrived not to change his spots even in death.

'Mariela,' I called out down the stairwell. 'Call the police, and it better be the effing Guardia. Don't come up. Call from the *entrada* and page me when they arrive.'

While I waited I sat down in the big Dutch shellback chair and looked at Ninian's shucked husk. Why the hell had he picked my hotel for his bloody wooden anniversary? Couldn't he have gone over to one of those German rural *finca* hotels? And couldn't his killer have been more considerate? He might have brained him on a golf course and made everyone's lives easier. They'd only have had to wait for rain to wash things up. This way I was probably going to have to do the scrubbing job myself, for it certainly wasn't something I could assign to a member of staff. 'Oh Catriona, the brass *placa* outside needs a bit of a polish. And by the way there's a lot of blood from that corpse upstairs that you might clean up while you're at it.'

Let me digress. What is a tale without an introduction? My name is Will Stock and I'm the eponymous co-owner of Stock's, a small elegant hotel in the centre of the island of Mallorca, hideaway for the 'Tatler' crowd and getting more so all the time. Lots of people, journalists mostly, keep describing our place as 'luxurious,' but that's a word I'm allergic to, as its meaning seems to vary from the schlock gilded and flocked excrescences to be found in Vegas, or even on the coast here – I name no names – to the understated decor of the best of London or the over-egged Parisian styles, or even to the glowing pantheons of marble to be found in Rome. No, I like the word 'elegant,' though 'comfortable' is what we actually try for here. Hannah, my business partner and best friend, has a genius for making spaces in which people feel comfortable. They walk in, look around, and instantly begin to notch down. I tried to explain it once to a rich friend who owns one of the new five-stars that are suddenly bursting out like mushrooms after the rain of German money that has fallen on the island in recent years. 'Look, David,' I told him. 'Your decorator decorates from his ego. He wants to impress everyone. He wants people to walk in and look at all the expensive silk and vibrant colours and dramatic drapery and oversized and overstuffed furniture and go, "Oh, wow, gee, what a terrific decorator!" But people have to *live* in those opera sets for a week or so and they're just plain intimidating, not to mention inhumanly out of scale. When Hannah decorates a room people walk in and simply go "Mmmm". They feel as though they've come home, even if they never knew quite where home was before.'

But I'm digressing, as usual. Actually, who and what I am is irrelevant. We spend, the majority of us, too much time establishing credentials that mostly nobody has any interest in. Let me just try to tell you the story plain and straight.

Let me get the corpse in on the act.

Ninian Mede, by all accounts, must have been one of the most roundly despised, if not hated, men on the island, at least by those who knew him. No doubt his reputation was better with those who hadn't yet met him. Belligerent, litigious, arrogant, unprincipled and devious, he seemed to make a career of alienating people, rarely missed a chance to be gratuitously unpleasant, and had so many lawsuits pending that it was a wonder he could keep them all straight.

I blamed it on his height.

Ninian was at least 6'7", perhaps even taller as it was hard to judge because of his pronounced stoop. He gangled in all directions, a sort of cross between a blue heron and Ichobod Crane. I suspect he'd never been able to relate to so-called normal people, having been no doubt the subject of ridicule when young, and thus had become progressively more alienated as he grew older. Some big men seem never to suffer from this problem; they simply are normal on a larger scale. Ninian, though, was an outcast, or so at least he felt himself to be, and it's what he felt that counts. The result was that he seemed to hate us all, just on principle.

I'd first met him some years ago when he'd recently come out from London. He'd made some money suing a carpeting company for product liability relating to a loose-weave shag rug they'd manufactured which had apparently leapt up and encircled his ankles, causing him to fall and twist his back, creating unspecified but painful and persistent injuries which prevented him from engaging in useful work – or so at least he said – thus comprehensively and irremediably blighting his life. It must have been true, the lawsuit documents said so.

He was represented in this endeavour by Sherman David, one of the new-style American lawyers who at that time were just beginning to practise in London, and who had imported the modern American legal notion that no one should ever take any responsibility for anything, that everything wrong in the world is somebody else's fault, and that the new way to get rich is to focus on that person, or more preferably a large, rich corporation, and sue them. Product liability litigation or insurance costs probably add at least $500 to the price of every car sold in the USA since if some dumb turkey gets drunk and runs his car into a tree, it is without doubt the Ford corporation's fault for having built the car in the first place.

This meretricious nonsense was just sufficiently novel enough in those days in the UK so that the combination of Sherman David's slick histrionics on Ninian's behalf, and Ninian's own speciously exaggerated grimaces of pain, somehow mesmerised the jury into an award far in excess of any rational application of common sense or fairness. *Chutzpah* baffles brains. The defence was so nonplussed by the size of the award that they fumbled the appeal and Ninian took the money and limped to the bank with his two-thirds share.

Shortly afterwards he departed for warmer climes. He was beginning to forget to limp and feared the consequences of a photo showing him mamboing his way along the West Ken tube station platform in the company of the only people with whom he felt comfortable, the Croatian second string basketball team, a collection of prognathous-jawed and hirsute demibarbarians who didn't take offence at Ninian's remarks about them as they had the useful advantage of not speaking English.

In due course a cramped and draughty Spanair plane brought him to Mallorca – 'Majorca,' as he called it in those days – the flight full, the noise level almost intolerable, and with Ninian's knees tucked up so neatly under his chin that he had to decline the nosh on offer because it wouldn't squeeze past his Adam's apple.

His history here was undistinguished for the first few years, though the climate seemed to have an instantly salutary effect on his back pain, which disappeared upon landing at Palma airport. He bought some property, then bought some more, then sold some, and carried along and buoyed by an ever-rising property market, finally found himself the owner of a largish restaurant strategically located along the Paseo Marítimo in Palma.

Buying the restaurant was a stroke of genius on his part. Each night he had a new crop of hungry diners to insult and alienate, degrade and deprecate. And because of the constant turnover of tourists, it didn't matter that virtually no one ever came back to the restaurant for a second visit. The establishment was in a number of guidebooks, courtesy of the culinary skills of the former owners, so Ninian never had to worry about filling the place. Basil Fawlty had come to Mallorca and gone into the restaurant trade.

And his chef's name – I kid you not – was Manuel, a man who even mimicked his namesake in kowtowing to the boss, bending to his lash, licking his boots. Manuel could have worked anywhere, for he was, and is, a fine chef. Regrettably, his father, a Francoist disciplinarian, had made a masochist of him, and his relationship with Ninian seemed dedicated to fulfil some dark agenda that had been programmed into him from birth. The food business makes for strange bedfellows, though not literally in this case, as Ninian had five years previously married Hazel, a tiny, assertive woman from Slough, of few distinguishing personal characteristics apart from her small size, her doll-like prettiness, and her zealous avarice. Adding their two heights together and dividing by two gave the stature of one normal person, so perhaps that's what appealed to each of them separately, and although they seemed to have little in common, they were nonetheless apparently mutually devoted. The only strange thing was that they hardly talked to one another, though come to think of it perhaps that was the secret of how they got on so well. Days could go by with only monosyllables exchanged between them, a sort of prehistoric grunt language. They did observe form, however, and amply celebrated public holidays, their birthdays and their anniversaries, by taking short hotel breaks, going out to dinner, or sitting in nightclubs or bars, regularly moving the venue for their grunts from one place to another.

Which brings me back to the present situation. Ninian had rung me the previous week to book our Blue Suite, the smaller one that people tend to book for next year as they go out the door this year. As it happened, it was free for the weekend and since business is business I refrained from declining the booking on the spurious grounds of being full, something that Hannah no doubt would have done and sod the income. She cannot abide the man, and now will no doubt never forgive him for sullying her

Bokhara, even if it does wash clean, which it probably will. Anything that can stand up to camel dung surely won't blink at human blood.

Just as I'd begun to give up on them, a clamour in the nether regions interrupted these musings and signalled the arrival of the Guardia Civil. Spain has three major police forces. The *Policía Local* are the ones who wear blue and are the rough Spanish equivalent of the old English bobbies on their bicycles. Local men, for the most part, stationed locally, they tend to know everyone, and often are adept at adjusting the law to fit the vagaries of human frailty. They rarely project the aggressive macho authoritarianism which now so characterises most policemen in most countries. In small towns like ours they are a welcome anachronism, and even the little cars they drive around in are straight from Noddytown. If you ever felt the urge to hug a policeman, it would be a *policista local*.

The Policía Nacional and the Guardia Civil, however, are another matter. They aren't from here, wherever here may be. They always come from somewhere else, and hate everyone here on the simple principle that if we weren't here then they wouldn't have to be away from there. Come of think of it, I've hardly ever met a Catalan-speaking member of the Guardia here, an island that is becoming ever more chauvinist – however misplaced that notion may be – about its Mallorquin/Catalan-speaking identity.

I can remember my first visit to Spain, which seems a long time ago; I first arrived in Barcelona as a newly-minted U.S. Navy midshipman, aged eighteen. One of the things that impressed me then was that the Guardia were too poor to have cars; they simply patrolled the roads on foot carrying submachine guns. So if they signalled you to stop, believe me, you stopped. Much has changed since the days when they were the extension of an intolerant Franco regime, but some of the bullyboy tradition lingers on. If they tell you to do something, it's a damned good idea to do it. Right now.

As this was going to be a matter principally for the Guardia Civil, they were the ones I'd have to deal with. They tend to come in two general categories: the macho young ones, sort of slightly maturer versions of those thug adolescents who torture cats or pluck the wings from butterflies; and older ones from virtually the same mould, just with more experience and subtlety, who have found it's more fun to torture people, these days generally by way of officious bureaucracy. I knew that whichever type turned up, my next few hours were destined to be less than full of frivolous gaiety and riotous laughter. Some situations are both unavoidable and lose-lose, whichever way the dice may fall.

'Send them on up, Mariela.' Might as well get it over.

It was a young one – on his own as a change from the usual custom of travelling in linked sets of two, seemingly joined at the hip. I could tell by the first question that we were in for a long session. His Spanish was positively – how can I render the feel of it? – Liverpudlian.

'Who did that?' he said, pointing to the body as though it were a splash of graffito. I'd no doubt he'd lost his capacity for revulsion practising on the cats. Better play it dumb.

'I just found him there,' I said blandly.

'Why didn't you call us sooner?'

'Sooner than when?'

'Sooner than before. We'd have come immediately.'

This was becoming mildly surreal. I didn't know Pinter was familiar to the Guardia Civil, though on second thought maybe that's where he collected his material, even down to the long pauses.

Fight fire with fire. 'I *did*.'

'Did what?'

'Did call you sooner.'

'Ah. That's all right then.' Long pause. 'I see he's become dead.'

There's something about the Spanish language that makes the avoidance of personal liability or responsibility very easy. You will never hear anyone ever say, for example, 'I broke it.' The phrase is, *Se ha roto*, 'It has become broken,' as though there had been no human intervention in this process of the thing arriving at a state of permanent dissolution, merely the manifestation of some divine wish somewhere that this thing not continue to remain intact.

But sometimes one can use this to one's advantage.

'Yes. He seems to have become defunct,' I remarked. 'Maybe you can arrange to take him away. We have some impressionable guests in that other suite.'

'First I'll have to refer this to higher authorities,' he said, retreating from any modicum of responsibility. He hadn't even asked me if I could tell him the corpse's name. This was unsurprising, as he could see by Ninian's clothes and size that he probably wasn't Spanish and thus would sport what would be, for him, an unpronounceable name; and second, it is the Pavlovian response to anything more complicated than an ill-parked car for a Guardia man to refer matters to higher authorities. I knew I would soon be visited by one of the older ones. My young friend jabbered into his walkie-talkie, which had been squeaking and muttering to itself all this while, and then, this task accomplished, walked over and picked up the Hepworth bronze.

'Fingerprints!' I cried, anxious to get one up on him. I knew there couldn't be any, but hoped he wouldn't realise it. He put the thing down like a hot potato and I knew I had him. Ah, implied blackmail, the unspoken threat of ratting on someone. My mood cheered up immensely. I smiled sweetly and motioned him over to the heavy Jacobean carver where I thought he would be least comfortable.

Prolonging the mood of unreality, I called for tea. Mariela, our Bulgarian beauty of the azure eyes to die for, was summoned yet again, though yet again forbidden to rise beyond halfway up the stairs. She clearly was curious, but equally clearly knew that whatever it was I had to relate, I would tell her in my own good time. Intelligence is Mariela's middle name, or at least the only middle name she has that's pronounceable.

The nameless, gormless, clueless young policeman and I hadn't much to say to one another. Ninian was as good company as the Guardia man, perhaps in his inert state even better. We sipped our tea in silence, observing the corpse with the same polite regard one might bring to the observation of a particularly incompetent game of bowls or, given my background, cricket. I perhaps should have mentioned earlier that I am American by birth and general fealty, though half my life has been spent in various countries in Europe, and much of that in the company of an Englishwoman, an experience which has turned me into something of a cultural nomad, caught between several different cultures, at home in none of them, though generally comfortable in most of them. I'm one of the New Strangers, Colin Wilson's uprooted, dispossessed people of this century, too worldly to settle in one single place and yet lonely for roots and a place to call home – culturally exiled after many years of wandering. I'm still waiting for that T. S. Eliot experience – to end my exploring by arriving where I started, knowing the place for the first time. Why is it that I somehow don't think that notion applies to people from Chicago?

But maybe that's why I so much like Mallorca; it's a mixture of cultures, and only two hours by air from practically every interesting place in Europe. It seems caught between and among the various influences from its history – from the peninsula, from Catalonia, from Germany, from England, and from all the various folk who visit each year in their millions. It's a place with its own identity, but an identity which is being constantly challenged by those who wish to impose a different set of values on it. Perhaps I connect with the internal stresses here, as they're stresses I know about and with which I can sympathise.

The silence drew out until there were other noises from below that betokened a further visitation. This would be the older one, and I didn't kid myself that I was going to get off so lightly.

The man who appeared at the top of the stairs, however, put paid to all my preconceptions and previous experience with the Guardia. Tall, lithe, well turned out in his green and patent leather uniform – his was obviously bespoke-tailored – he was something of a larger and better looking version of Antonio Banderas, even to the charisma, which he manifestly radiated. I noted that in accompanying him Mariela rose four steps further up the stairs than she should have, and placed herself eighteen inches closer to him than she normally would have with a strange man.

He smiled with perfect teeth from behind a deep tan, extended his hand and charmed me instantly. I could tell from his accent that he was Mallorquin, and I quietly choked on all the words I had heretofore used concerning the Guardia. He glanced back at the younger man slightly dismissively and switched over to perfect, accentless – unless one counts a Sloane drawl – English.

'What can you tell me about this – *unfortunate* – affair?'

'Not a great deal. I came back around five this afternoon, was heading for my room – I'm the night porter here a few nights a week – and there he was.' I recounted the facts as best I could, skipping the deeper knowledge I had of Ninian. He'd find out soon enough if it turned out to be relevant.

'Who had access?'

'Any guest, any member of staff. We don't keep the

front door open, all of our guests have keys and come and go as they please, treating the house as though it were their own home. We have no front desk, no reception, no bellhops or concierges or time share reps or twee shops selling plastic souvenirs and saucy postcards. Our guests prefer it that way.'

He took in my propaganda without blinking. 'Any ideas?'

'Sorry. None at all.'

'Right then. Let's get the forensic chappies along.' With that he rose, instructed the gormless one to make the call, and extracted a tooled-leather card case from his pocket.

'I'm Fausto Milagro,' he said. 'And no,' with a twinkle, 'the street in Palma was named for my grandfather, not me. Here's my card. Come by tomorrow morning and we'll sort out the paperwork. Or ring me anytime until midnight if you think of anything relevant.' With that he disappeared down the stairs. I was clearly dismissed and couldn't have been happier for it. I heaved a sigh, waved in a desultory way to Ninian's corpse, and made my way up to the bar to see if Pepa could fix me up with some smoked salmon and creamed cheese on a slice of good Mallorquin bread. And a double brandy. Yes, there are still some perks to owning a hotel.

I decided not to go back to the library until the body had been removed. The crime scene squad from Palma closed it off for an hour or so to take their pictures and dust for fingerprints, Catriona's tactful Scottish touch made moving Lady Bisquith and her daughter to the Amadeus Room an easy task, and around eleven one of the girls called up to the bar to say the room was finally clear. True to my intentions, I got a bucket and mop and duster and went on up to tidy. Apart from the blood there were some curious bits of what looked like some sort of food, as though someone had been eating something, definitely a no no upstairs in our hotel. The library table, too, needed tidying, as all the books and the chessboard had been shoved over to one side to clear a space, and more crumbs were in evidence. Probably it had been the forensic team, bringing their sandwiches in to munch while examining the corpse. An imperviously nerveless lot, they. Altogether, though, the cleanup job wasn't that bad. Ten minutes with the duster took care of the fingerprint powder and then I lugged the carpet down to the laundry room for a soak. A household hint from Dracula's housekeeper – soak bloodstains in milk before attempting to wash them out.

I also had a bright idea about the nasty bloodstain on the tiles. I fetched some BioKleer from the laundry room and made up a strong solution. No doubt some of those enzyme-eating organisms would just love the taste of human blood. I rubbed it gently into the stain and it seemed to work. Maybe I had stumbled on something here. It might even be an inspiration for a whole new advertising approach. 'Troubled by unpleasant pools of blood around the house? Tired of sticky red patches on your floors and walls? Try BioKleer!' I determined to get in touch with the company the very next morning.

Just as I was leaving, I turned back to survey the room for one last check to see if I'd missed anything obvious. Through the door of the *salita* I could see the longcase clock, the hands forever stilled, like Rupert Brooke's church clock, at ten till three. My hand was already on the knob of the library door, about to close it, when I spotted a faint gleam of silver underneath the air conditioning unit, the only ungraceful element in an otherwise exquisite room. I bent over and fished the object out, a small key. Though it looked familiar I didn't think it was one of ours. It might have fallen from Ninian's pocket when he was hit and somehow the police had missed it. I thought it best to turn it over to Captain Milagro in the morning. That weighty decision taken, I dropped it in my pocket and drifted back to my room, where I spent the balance of the night in benign and dreamless sleep, undisturbed by memories or concerns or even a whisper of a visitation by Ninian's ghost.

Two

Next morning, I descended to the kitchen and found my usual cup of *café con leche* steaming on the table. Maribel, our morning ray of sunshine, listens out for the sound of my shower – I bunk directly over the kitchen – and prepares my coffee accordingly. As I arrive, it does too. As I said, one of the perks of hotel life, and something to offset the inconvenience of having Americans ring at 3 a.m. to make a reservation because it's 9 p.m. their time and they're under the impression that we're six hours behind them, not ahead. 'Oh, I always do get it mixed up. Silly me,' one said brightly. I couldn't have agreed more. I asked for her number and rang her back the next day at 3 a.m. her time to confirm the booking. 'Oh, silly me,' I said, as brightly as she had. 'I always get it mixed up too.'

I could make a fortune, I sometimes think, just teaching Americans how to do business with the rest of the world. Lesson One – is anybody listening? – put an airmail stamp on letters you send out of the country. Yes, it's that stamp with the picture of an aeroplane on it. It saves having the brochure arrive six weeks after the special offer has closed. So is that clear now? Lesson Two – programme your damned computers so that they accept addresses and phone numbers other than those in USA form. I can't tell you how many times I've wanted to buy things on the Internet only to have my address refused because it didn't conform to the matrix laid out on the computer form. Lesson Three – oh, to hell with it, this could go on forever.

After coffee and some fresh-squeezed o.j., a triangle of delicious Mallorquin pastry, *ensaimada*, and a couple of plums, I ambled over to the post office to pick up our post. We now have an *apartado*, a postbox – No.11 if you really want to know – since we never seemed to get the hang of the local method of delivering letters. For a long time, back before we had the postbox, we received our letters in various ways, depending upon which of the charming people in the post office was in charge of deliveries. Sometimes they were stuck under the front door, which was fine save when there were letters too bulky to fit, so that they just lay in the street. Some post was introduced, usually on Wednesday or on Saturday (especially on the latter day) through the *persianas*, the louvred shutters on the front windows: our task in the game to guess which one. Or at times a neighbour would be given our post for onward transmission, more often than not Jordi, who lives elsewhere and only comes to visit his house next door once or twice a week. Or we might be flagged down as we left on the school run, to have a pile of letters cheerfully thrust through the car window at us. Or one of our cleaning staff might be given our post to deliver, or indeed, any of a number of other creative variations on the theme of hide the parcel. Call me old-fashioned, call me conservative, even call me a curmudgeon; I like to be able to lay hands on my letters in a consistent way. It even seems to help with little things like reservations and such.

In any event, I was just introducing my key into the postbox when I realised what I'd found the night before. I took out the key from the library and compared it with mine. It was indeed a postbox key, though there was no indication as to which box in which town it might possibly fit. No doubt the police could find that out easily however.

As it was a lovely day – it's virtually *always* a lovely day on Mallorca – I decided to walk to the Guardia Civil headquarters. They're located up along the strip of the old main road between Palma and Alcudia, less used now that the *autopista* has gone through to Inca, and by far the least salubrious part of the town. There are those of us who are grateful for this ugly strip, for it seems to have protected the town against an excess of investigation by tourists or developers. People have just seen the long ribbon of rundown factories, seedy apartment blocks, Mafia-front-looking improbable wholesale fish food stores, or nondescript bars, and have assumed the rest of the town to be more of the same. Not so in reality. We have the second largest number of 18th-century palaces and seignorial houses after Palma itself, and the town is regarded by cognoscenti as an architectural gem, even described as a 'symphony in stone' in one of the more lyrically fanciful Mallorquin history books. We are the wine centre for the island, the focus of the stone and carpentry trades, but an as yet undiscovered haven of tranquillity only twenty minutes from the bustle and noise of the capital. Long may we continue to flimflam passersby with our unappealing and charmless facade.

When I arrived at police headquarters I began to get a strange feeling about this case. Fausto Milagro wasn't there, and the sergeant on duty was evasive regarding his whereabouts. He was usually based in Palma, I was told. He'd only happened to be there last evening and was the senior man on post. I was ushered to a dusty cubicle and given some paper on which to write out my report of the incident, after which I was closely questioned by one of the older officers – a man much more in the line of the kind of Guardia I'd been expecting the previous evening – ill-mannered, marginally hostile, suspicious, literal, pernickety, and without a hint of sensitivity, much less humour. What raised little whispers of concern was that he kept coming back repeatedly to what I'd told Fausto Milagro, what he had said to me, and if Captain Milagro had mentioned knowing Ninian. All a bit strange. For some reason that wasn't clear to me at the time I omitted mentioning the key. I couldn't have said why.

That afternoon I had various errands to do on a run up to the north coast, about a half hour away. I climbed into Balthasar, our battered 1982 Volvo estate, preparing to fill the capacious cargo space with an order of wicker baskets, dried flowers, and *pot pourri* that Hannah had ordered from some talented and able handicraft people she knows up there. She and I argue as to which of the three kings brought the gold in the nativity story, but settled on Balthasar, as neither of us wished to drive a car called Melchior or Gaspar, nor travel in a vehicle with associations with smelly frankincense or cloyingly pungent myrrh.

If you go in this direction, and have the time, I recommend the hillside route. You don't take the main road, which is fairly straight and boring, but rather cut up in the direction of the mountains and follow a network of smaller roads that move generally, disjointedly but inexorably, towards the coast. One has to weave about a bit, sometimes guessing the direction in which the next appropriate road may be found, but after all, that's half the fun of it. Although signage has improved since the old days – anything longer than three years ago qualifies as the old days – it is still the case that on the really small roads very little is marked, for we all know where everything is, don't we, we who live here? And it's *our* island, isn't it, not yours, and if someone puts a sign up in horrid Spanish we'll tear it down or replace it with one in unreadable Mallorquin, won't we?

Anyway, the views are wonderful from these roads, looking up to the mountains on the left and down to the *pla*, the flat bit with lumps, on the right. Along here you get two crops of wildflowers every year, and two crops of lambs, and lush flowery fragrant foliage most months of the year, save of course that it all goes brown and dusty and desiccated during the months of July and August when all the tourists come to the island. But what do *they* know? We were in late January segueing into February weather and the blossoming almond trees gave the whole countryside a confectionery dusting of white interspersed with patches of pink.

As I drove along and ruminated about the matter, I

felt more and more a prickle of unease – something wasn't right somewhere in this affair and I thought I'd better ring Captain Morell at my earliest opportunity to find out if he might be willing to enlighten me as to what was going on – why the Guardia were behaving so strangely. It wasn't really my business, save that I was annoyed by Ninian's lack of consideration in managing to get himself topped in my hotel, and I wished to be reassured that it wasn't something that was likely to blow up to anything larger. We would not benefit, I felt, from the publicity. Some nitwit once said that all publicity is good publicity, and certainly it was probably true that there would be people who might want to visit the hotel simply to relish some morbid connection with the grisly and the macabre, but many of our more esteemed guests shun publicity, hide from the press and the paparazzi, or are simply too well brought up and good mannered to wish to associate with corpses, even at second hand. No, on balance this was publicity we could do without.

At Moscari I stopped by the English artists' colony to pick up some cushion covers we were having hand-embroidered for one of the new rooms along the back wing, next to the indoor Roman-style swimming pool where the old stables used to be. The front of our building is late 18th-century, but the bit at the back is Moorish and goes back a thousand years, making it difficult to get modern amenities like air conditioning or smoke alarms in without messing with ancient walls that hate being messed with. Something damp and musty had taken up residence in the pool cushions and it had taken us six weeks to locate where it was coming from, drips from an old lead roof-drainage pipe. I'll never ever again undertake to reform an old house – better to build a new one and then face it with stone so it looks period.

The next two hours were all business – zip up to Pollença and then down to Alcudia, those pleasant Roman towns, along to the wildlife preserve at Albufera – very much worth a visit – and then a quick nip along to Muro, still keeping to the little roads. Muro's not much to look at, but it has a cracking museum, El Museo Etnológico, which provides a genuinely professional look into Mallorca's history, and which is head and shoulders above the overtouted touristy and commercialised La Granja. Of that ilk, Es Calders, near Sineu, is better.

Back home I picked up the phone to ring Captain Milagro on the number on his card. Once connected with the Guardia I was passed to an apparently senior man who seemed to be informed. I got even more of the interrogation.

'Who wants to speak to Captain Milagro?' I identified myself. There was a pause.

'What do you want with him?'

I suggested, most politely, that there was something to do with the murder case at Stock's Hotel that I wished to discuss with him.

'How did you get this number?'

What a stupid question. This was, after all, a police station.

'He gave it to me.'

'I'm sorry to tell you he won't be available on this number.'

'Can you give me a number where he can be reached?'

'I'm afraid that won't be possible.'

'It's about the murder case,' I explained, 'and he'll surely want to talk to me again.'

'He's no longer associated with that case. Let me have your number and someone will ring you if necessary.' I wasn't getting the impression this was likely.

'He's been taken off the case? Can you tell me why?'

'I'm afraid that won't be possible.'

'Listen, I really need some information here.'

'Let me give you a piece of advice, Señor Stock. Just forget this whole matter. We're sorry it was an inconvenience for your hotel, but now it's a police affair and is nothing to do with you. You should, if I may put it politely, mind your own business. Goodbye.' The phone went dead.

Now if there is anything likely to pique my curiosity, awaken my stubborn streak, and get my dander up, it's being warned off. Sod you, I thought. We'll see where this thing leads.

I felt my first port of call should be Hazel, Ninian's wife – widow, as I reminded myself. She'd been working yesterday afternoon and was supposed to meet Ninian at the hotel, the appointed time being about two hours or so after I'd found the body. He'd been planning a surprise dinner for her – the food imported from their restaurant, of course, since Ninian never spent money in anyone else's kitchen – so we'd simply prepared a table upstairs in the bistro, decorated with a dusty rose tied with silk ribbons. Mercifully, Hazel had been spared the shock of arriving here unawares when Ninian was lying dead in the library. A Guardia man had given her the sad news before she'd had the opportunity to get over here, so she'd avoided the chance of being the one who found him. There was a remote possibility, of course, that she was the perpetrator, but I doubted it – not only did she seem to have an alibi, but she'd have had to use a ladder to hit Ninian on the head, even if he'd been accommodating enough to kneel. Besides, whoever had mashed his noggin had done a thorough job; it wasn't any love tap that brought him low. I doubted Hazel would have had the strength, even if she'd had the inclination and the opportunity.

My intention had been to visit her later, but knowing my way with good intentions – I've paved much more than my fair share of the Road to Hell – I thought maybe I'd better do it sooner. So off Balthasar and I set, along the road to Santa Eugenia, which is next to one of those lumpy escarpments I mentioned that stick up from the plain. It's another of those timewarp towns that pock the middle of the island, largely unaffected by the ten or twelve million visitors who descend on the coasts every year. As late as two years ago Santa Eugenia still had a street named after General Franco, who has been largely consigned to the dustbin by the rest of Spain in the almost quarter century since his demise. In fairness, I have the feeling that the name was kept on in Santa Eugenia out of inertia than any lingering loyalty to the Caudillo's memory.

Santa Eugenia isn't *not* pretty, if you know what I mean, but isn't long on character either, though that just may be a prejudice on my part since I think it's too close to the flightpath to the airport. In the summer months this island can get up to 800 flights a day – that's almost one plane a minute during all the hours of daylight we get. If the wind blows the noise in the direction of the town, it's *not* peaceful.

I also think of Santa Eugenia as a deeply Mallorquin sort of town of the interior, and that notion set another train of thought in motion. As one cliché has it, there are two kinds of people in the world – those who divide all the world into two kinds of people, and those who don't. Glibly speaking, one may divide Mallorquins into two main varieties: those of the coast and those of the interior, and one needs to distinguish between their vastly different characters.

Every couple of weeks, I write a travel and commentary column for a publication called The Mediterranean Travel Newsletter, run by a feisty, grumpy little man named Hector Blankenship. I'm not sure any more how I got myself roped into this commitment though at the time it seemed a relatively painless way to promote our hotel whilst simultaneously inflicting my opinions on a faceless audience of fifty or sixty, as I judged the circulation of the magazine to be. Regrettably for me, I'd reckoned without Hector's dedication to the form of anodyne, fact-laden, boosterish travel writing, and his intolerance of sloppy, slipshod, off-the-cuff opinion, the very kind of journalism at which I excel. He continually badgered and harassed me, prodded and – yes, *hectored* me – and now had me cringing and cowering to his whip to the point where I actually tried to write him something acceptable – acceptable to him, that is – to put in his tiny rag-mag. So, the thought having been triggered, I began, in my head, to write about the differences I'd observed among and between the Mallorquins on the island. I began to crank up my modest byline, the tone impersonal and objective, as dry as I am capable, but of course omniscient.

Lurking Around Mallorca
by
Will Stock

The Mallorquins of the interior might be generally described as rural conservatives, with traits in common with farmers all over the globe. They are phlegmatic, hardworking, reluctant when confronted with novelty, circumspect and prudent, honest, incurious, and acceptant of foreigners in an unexploitative way. Family is of paramount importance, as the interconnectedness of the web of relationships among and between the inhabitants of the interior sets the tone for all social life. Every Mallorquin born in the interior begins life with a patrimony of aunts, uncles, cousins, nephews, nieces, et. al., who may serve as network, bush telegraph, entrée, information base, or safety net for a lifetime. If a rural Mallorquin can't do something himself, he has a cousin who can.

The Mallorquins of the littoral are different. Their blood has mixed with traders, invaders, conquerors and visitors for thousands of years. One epithet dismisses them as the result of thirty centuries of commerce between sailors and whores, but that is to undervalue the essential courage, flexibility, persistence and endurance those two ancient vocations require. It is also an observation that could be made with equal truth about every other port town around the Mediterranean. The coastal Mallorquins have resisted, capitulated to, but eventually profited from, invading Phoenicians, Venetians, Romans, Moors, pirates, and now tourists. An impressive track record over the centuries.

Coastal Mallorquins, however, more readily demonstrate the traits of opportunism, ambition, and an eye for the main chance that were bred into them by the circumstance of being vulnerable to raiders and assailants from the outside. They can charm you, but in treating with them you might want to count your change carefully, perhaps even your fingers. They can at times promise much, deliver little, and then take offence if you complain.

In sum, I've found most Mallorquins to be warm, though sometimes distant; mainly straight, though with a few curves along the coast; supremely uninterested in outsiders as people, though generally helpful; unaggressive save on the road; and paradoxically generous in spite of the seeming inwardness of their family-orientated society. They can be very considerable people, worth investing time in cultivating. They may open up slowly, but often as not there are pearls inside.

These ruminations percolated through my skull as I made my way through the dusty streets of Santa Eugenia's sunwarmed stone, over the brow of the lumpy knoll, and along to the stand of pine trees on the reverse slope of the hill. That text would never do, of course. Hector would jump on my opinions in a New York minute, cut the criticisms, implied or otherwise, and turn my descriptions of the Mallorquins into colourful caricatures worthy of a 1930s musical production: costumed peasants gambolling in fields of flowers accompanied by rainbow-dyed sheep and Disney cows. Yuk. I tried again, seeking something potentially less likely to invoke Hector's volcanic wrath.

Were I to write about this town, for example, he'd want something like:

Visitors to the island's unspoilt centre may pass the delightful village of Santa Eugenia, nestled in the picturesque *pla*, or plain, that runs from the slopes of the Sierra Tramontana mountains to the east, to the coves and caves that dot the opposite coastline. A large hill, or mount, backdrops part of the town and provides its gentle inhabitants with painterly settings on which to build their rustic stone homes. For the physically active, there is a pleasant walk from the tranquil town centre up to a commemorative cross on the top of the escarpment. Not a strenuous climb, and the reward is capacious views from the peak. Visitors passing this way will find this walk a fine two hour diversion.

That was much more Hector's speed, though he'd cut 'escarpment' as being too challenging a word for his audience, and substitute 'beautiful' for 'capacious' just on principle. But I can only dumb down so far, or so at least I like to flatter myself. There are those who would dispute that opinion.

I parked outside the pinkish chalet the Medes had built in the pine trees and rang the bell. In due course Hazel appeared, looking smaller and more shrunken than I'd ever seen her, her eyes bleary and bloodshot, her makeup smudged and her hair dishevelled and greasy. For probably the first time since I'd known her, I felt some crumb of compassion. Perched on her stool behind the cash register in the restaurant, she had only ever inspired comparisons to those daunting *mamans* who run family bistros all over France, intimidating equally their families, their staff, and their customers. This time, all the toughness was gone, all the stuffing blown away in the draught of grief that gripped her. I'd never had thought Ninian could have mobilised so much emotion, although – unkind thought – I didn't yet know how much she was grieving for him and how much for herself.

'Hello, Hazel. I wanted to come by. I think you know I found him.' I felt stiff and awkward and out of place.

'Thank you. It was kind of you to visit. I'm sorry for how I look. Can I offer you a cup of tea?' I could see she felt as awkward as I did.

'If it's not too much trouble, yes please.' I crossed the threshold, took a step down into a sunken entrance hall, and followed her into the sitting room. I'd not been in their house before.

'Wait here,' she said. 'I'll just pop along and put the kettle on.' Tea, the English panacea. I examined the decor. It wasn't like anything I'd seen for most of a lifetime – a wall-to-wall salmon pink shag rug, a white sateen three piece suite covered with transparent plastic to protect the material, some Lladro figures alongside huge round terra cotta lamps with starbursts carved in them highlighting painted coloured motifs under crinkled shiny yellow plastic shades, and some 1950s-style expressionist abstracts mainly in orange and green. The wallpaper was peach and light chartreuse, lightly raised in rows, and flocked. The effect was stunning, if that's the apposite word. I was sitting trying to decide which of the various hideosities I would like to give my lawyer as a Christmas present – an exercise I undertake from time to time in the wake of receiving of one of his bills – when Hazel returned.

We sat and sipped quietly for awhile. The tea was good.

'Did he suffer, do you think?' she asked tremulously.

'Not likely. It must have been very quick.'

'Have the police told you anything, found anything?'

'That's a question I was going to ask you.'

'They've not said much. I got a call from one who spoke posh English but then another one called me who didn't speak English well at all, and my Spanish has never been up to much, especially now.'

'What did the first one say?'

'Not a lot, but he seemed nice. I didn't like the second one very much but he said he was in charge now.'

'You mean he said the first one was off the case?'

'Not in so many words, but that's the idea I got.' She hunched over her tea, poured us both some more, then offered me a biscuit.

'Listen, Hazel, I really don't want to intrude at a time like this, but do you have any idea who it might have been? Did he have any enemies that might have done this? Can you think of anything at all that could have brought this down on him?'

'You know it's odd, Will. The police didn't ask me that, though I expected them to, or at least the second one didn't. The first one didn't get that far – he just offered condolences and said he was going to make an appointment to visit. But the second one acted almost like he knew something. I know people didn't get on with Ninian – he was always fighting with somebody – but he wasn't a bad man. He didn't deserve being killed.' She broke at this point, put her face in her hands and rocked backwards and forwards, shuddering, but silent. That was worse than sobs or tears. I felt paralysed. I didn't know her well enough to move over and put an arm around her, but I felt equally like a lily just sitting there. Predictably, I was unable to find appropriate words. I suspect we are often as much put off by other people's grief as we are moved by it. Few of us seem to know how to offer condolence in a genuine, unembarrassed, considerate and sensitive way. I certainly don't. I stayed silent.

'I'm sorry,' she said, as though it had been a gaucherie on her part to show grief. Oh, Albion, I thought, you have much to answer for in how you hold your people ransom to the stiff upper lip.

'That's all right,' I said, equally inappropriately, as though I might be offering her some benign absolution for the crime of showing excessive emotion. I tried to change the subject.

'Where do you have your postbox?' I asked, grasping at a straw. I thought I might return the key.

'What? A postbox? We have no postbox,' she said, looking at me as though I'd taken marginal leave of my senses. 'We have our post delivered here, or directly to the restaurant. Why do you ask?'

'Ah, well, no reason really,' I lied. 'I thought Ninian had mentioned one sometime.' It was lame, but she was too distressed to pay attention or care about my response. But just as with the police, some instinct told me not to tell her about the key. Besides, I quickly rationalised to myself, it might not have been his key at all. It could have been under that unit for months, though somehow I didn't think so. I'm in that room fairly often, and look into it almost at floor level from the staircase on my way to my bedroom. I was certain that if it had been there I'd have seen it previously.

'So you don't have a postbox then,' I said mindlessly, bestowing her with a somewhat ingenuous grimace. How dumb could I get?

'No postbox that I know of,' she said.

'Do you think Ninian had any – uh – *private* business you might not have known about, that might have a bearing on what happened?'

'You mean a girl, or something?' She reddened a bit. 'No chance. He lost interest in all *that* years ago.' In your dreams, Sweetie, I thought to myself, but wiser counsel held my tongue.

'So there isn't anything you can think of that might help the police solve this thing?'

'Are you stupid?' she flared. 'That's *all* I think about, and there's *nothing*, nothing at all.'

I didn't – couldn't – reply.

'I'm sorry,' she said. 'I didn't mean that. I just don't know what to say or what to do. I need time to work things through.'

'Yes,' I said, 'I really shouldn't have intruded. And I really should be on my way now.'

'That's probably for the best,' she replied. 'I'm no use to anyone in my present state.'

Relieved to be off the hook, I mumbled a few more soothing inanities and got out of there as quickly as I could. I felt she was telling the truth, that she really didn't know anything about the who or the why in this case. Suddenly I felt it was even more important than before to try to track down Fausto Milagro and talk to him. And while I was at it I thought I'd have a crack at looking for that postbox. It was a long shot that it had anything to do with something other than Ninian getting pornographic pictures through the post, or for the exchange of *billets doux* with some popsy in Essex, but it was a loose end and I had a hunch about it. Somebody had felt strongly enough about something to have done Ninian in with extreme, as they say, prejudice. And they did it in my hotel, which both narked me and involved me. I had the feeling there had been huge emotions behind that blow. I'd seen Ninian's head, and whoever killed him hadn't just hit him to put him out and mistakenly hit the wrong spot – his skull had been caved in with one crushingly decisive blow with immense strength behind it, a blow intended to fell him instantly. Perhaps *intended* isn't even the right word. Perhaps it was hate and anger that could only be expressed with a blow so massive there could be but one outcome.

I fingered the key in my pocket. Where to begin?

Three

One thing you can count on about Mallorca: there are few secrets. Think of a small town writ large, and not even writ so very large at that. There are, after all, only 700,000 permanent residents, almost half of them in Palma. So the rule is, if you don't want it to be found out, don't do it, or at least don't do it here.

But I figured that was what I had going for me. Ninian's secret, if it were a secret, wouldn't be hard to find out. I'd find his postbox. Maybe I could turn something up to tell Captain Milagro. Besides, I was intrigued; everybody wants to play detective once in his life.

Starting with the premise that Ninian wasn't the world's most energetic man, I thought I'd check the various post offices along the route to his restaurant. He'd have driven back and forth two to four times a day from home to the restaurant, so my bet was he'd have used whichever post office was most convenient for him. I wound down from Santa Eugenia to the *autopista* turnoff, followed it in towards Palma as far as the Via de Cintura (literally the 'beltway'), swung left for a half mile and then turned off down the exit to the port and the coast and the Paseo Marítimo, the road that runs along beside the sea and the marinas in front of the city.

I have to admit I'm a sucker for Mediterranean cities about the size of Palma. You can walk from one side of Palma to the other in less than an hour, drive the whole, mostly beautiful, length of the Paseo in ten minutes, gawking at the several billionsworth – you name your currency: pounds, dollars, marks – of yachts in the marinas, ogle the cathedral, which I find lovely on the outside and disappointing on the inside, and nip up for a restful few minutes to Castell de Bellver, a singular round castle dating from the early 1300s, vertiginously situated over the city and looking down on the bay, the inner patio now a worthy venue for the concerts held there. For me, Bach has never sounded better than in the acoustically-beneficent arched circular central open cobbled courtyard.

Palma's old town, too, is impressive if you don't mind having to step over a few *drogadictos* in your wanderings, and there is a whole array of sophisticated restaurants, *soigné* shops and smart boutiques for those who like that sort of thing. The galleries tend to be a bit modern for my taste, but then I'm a fairly fusty sort. Once I got to be forty I decided I didn't have to pretend interest any more in most modern art or music, experimental poetry, avant-garde theatre, or haute couture. It was wonderfully liberating not to have to be intellectual and fashionable and just grow my middlebrow straight across.

Mostly I like Palma, I think, because it's a city, a real *city*, but on a human scale. And despite its pocket size, it supports opera and ballet seasons, an abundance of concerts and exhibitions, and – I think the cliché term is 'a host' – of other diversions, cultural and otherwise. The gratifying advantage to having all these things happen more or less sequentially is that I actually go to them. When I lived in London the sheer plethora of opportunity was so great I ended up not going to very much at all. Oh, what the hell, there's so much to do that it can always wait until tomorrow. In Palma it's easier to bite the cherry of opportunity, grab the brass ring of diversion, and *carpe* the *diem* today instead of tomorrow.

I followed what I thought would be Ninian's most likely route to his restaurant, noting any post offices I saw along the way. There were only two, and I more or less discarded the idea of one of them because the parking in that area was so impossible. Palma suffers from one particularly abominable and abhorrent affliction: its drivers. Streets that should have at least two lanes of traffic flow in both directions generally only have one because they are lined with double-parked cars. One inconsiderate driver can thus inconvenience hundreds and hundreds of other drivers, and he will – he *does* – seemingly at every opportunity. And because a bad example seems almost irresistible for many people, the double-parkers proliferate, thus somehow conveying a sense of legitimacy to what is patently an uncivilised practice. It's like the 'one-piece-of-paper-thirty-minute-rule' promulgated by the folks who take care of the greenswards around the monuments in Washington. As long as the lawns stay pristine, nobody throws trash on them. If one piece of paper is left for more than half an hour, it gives permission to everyone to throw their trash down, and they do. I've long thought that if we could simply summarily hang the first double-parker of the day from the nearest lamp-post in Palma, the problem would go away fairly quickly. I'd even volunteer to hold the rope. Or, as a somewhat less extreme option, I'd love to have one of those James Bond cars with, I don't care which, the laser beam or the Boadicea-style extendable revolving scythe blades. When a sufficient number of drivers returned to their double-parked cars to find two mutilated tyres on the traffic side, eventually they might catch on to the notion that someone, maybe even a whole city full of someones, was trying to send them a message.

One must always ask oneself in Spain whether or not the dictatorship was a completely negative experience. After all, under Franco the crime rate was virtually nil, prices were low, the health system worked, and artistic representations were more lifelike than excremental. In Singapore one can be fined $500 for dropping a single piece of paper on the ground. Has the quality of life for ordinary Spaniards truly been improved by its illusory democracy?

Hector would love that. The frightening thing was that even as I mocked and parodied his views, some bits of me agreed with these ideas. What had become of the liberal principles of my youth?

So discarding the idea of double-parking and nipping in to the big post office in the crowded area, I parked – legally – near the other one and ambled in to ask around. Piece of cake. The great advantage I had was that Ninian had been anything but nondescript; he was eminently 'descript' in any language. But no, none of the employees had, or would admit to having had, seen him. And a man 6'7" on an island in Spain is not inconspicuous.

I drove as far as Ninian and Hazel's restaurant, turned around, and headed back along the Paseo. Their place is located down close to the Yacht Club, and enjoys formally tidy views over the marinas and port. This time I spotted a parking place as I approached the main post office just off the Borne. My parking angel had been sulking earlier but finally decided to give me a break. She gave me a space right outside the front door. Once inside, I tried every single window, even waiting for the surly sub-manager to finish with his consequential tasks of smoking his cigarette, rooting some wax from one hairy ear, inspecting it at length and then wiping it in the fold of his trousers behind his knee. In due course he lit another cigarette – the Spanish smoke all the time and everywhere – grudgingly trudged over to me, inspected me up and down before I could speak, and then opened his mouth, pointed to his tongue, and shook his head. This was meant to signify that he didn't speak my language, regardless of whatever language I might speak.

I spoke to him in Spanish, called Castellano on this island, as distinct from Mallorquin, which is allegedly in turn distinct from Catalan, though there are many who will argue the toss. He answered me in Mallorquin. No doubt he'd have done it the other way around had I essayed my question in Mallorquin. Virtually all Mallorquins are bilingual, the middle-aged ones having been educated in Spanish under Franco, who suppressed all regional languages, and the younger people having access to all the national radio and television programmes in Spanish. But one thing that drives me wild is their nationalistic – regionalistic, to be correct – tendency to deprecate Castellano, a noble language spoken by almost 500 million of the people on the globe, this condescension from the fewer than six million people in the Catalan language region, who can't even agree on the names of things from village to village, much less on a common grammar. From time to time I'll hesitate over the gender of a word, and ask a local whether it's a *la* or an *el*. Maddeningly, the answer is as often as not a shrug and an '*es igual*, – it doesn't matter. But for a foreigner attempting not to sound terminally maleducated it of course *does* matter. In any event the sub-manager and I did not get very far towards success, as he claimed never to have seen such a person as Ninian, though I suspected he might have been saying that simply to be obstructive. There are those people in every walk of life, and we all know them well, who are uncooperative just out of spite.

I'd try another tack. Occam's razor – when in doubt, consider the obvious. This time, instead of taking the fast road, I headed off towards the old main road running parallel to it. Once past the creeping *urbanisaciones*, all those pretty fields being ploughed up for suburban developments, I struck out along the original Roman road up to the north coast. Now that the motorway is through, this ancient way is quieter and more fun to drive. The first major town is Santa Maria, which is attractive, but has, at least for my taste, too many foreigners. (I never said I didn't suffer from the now-that-I've-arrived-let's-pull-down-the-portcullis syndrome.) For some years Santa Maria was at the end of the first completed stretch of motorway and foreigners just used to drive to the end of the motorway, get off, look around, and go buy a house. It was almost that straightforward. In terms of convenience for people coming to live on the island it's one of those things that cuts both ways; on the one hand the inhabitants are used to foreigners, so it's easier for those who don't speak Spanish – sorry, Castellano – but the down-side is that things are inevitably more commercialised, less authentic, and more expensive here than they are in some other, equivalent, towns around the island. One exception is the tile and ceramic shop a few yards off the main road on the Consell end of town.

At any rate, I had the notion that Ninian might have opted to keep his postbox here. It was on his way home, parking near the post office is relatively easy – *relatively* being the operative word, and as there are usually foreigners about, Ninian wouldn't have been quite as overly conspicuous, despite his height handicap.

My next transient worry was whether I'd be able to find out Ninian's box number if it turned out he indeed had one here, though on second thought I considered it unlikely anyone would question me, unless of course by some chance the Guardia had got here first. If you ask permission to do something in Spain, the chances are you'll be refused, at least at first, just as a kneejerk bureaucratic response. In practice, things are different. With a bit of gentle persuasion, it will turn out that in spite of the obstacles, many of them in the form of paper, a solution can be found, and this does not necessarily imply any under-the-table grease, though it can. A bit of quiet dosh seems to go a long way on the coast, or so I'm told, but in the interior things can be positively sanctimonious. I once acquired, as part of a job lot in a local auction, some chairs in the Alfonsine style – that sort of bastardised imitation art nouveau – and decided to donate them to the town art collection because they weren't in keeping with our general decor, were consistent with the periods represented in the museum, and because – well, mostly because they were manifestly ugly. But we also happened to have a small planning application pending at the time, and in the ripeness of bureaucratic time I was called before the mayor to be questioned as to whether I saw any connection between the possible approval of our planning application and my donation. Frankly, it had never occurred to me that anyone might consider chairs of such surpassing unsightliness as candidates for a potential bribe, but in the end I had to write a letter to the town hall disclaiming any intent to subvert the council with woodworm-ridden Alfonso XIII furniture.

Mostly as regards being queried about my interest in Ninian's box number, I simply counted on the deep lack of interest with which most Mallorquins regard us. We are, by the way, generic *extranjeros* – foreigners. There is usually little or no distinction between and among Germans, Swedes, Swiss, English, or whomever; we're just foreigners, though that perception is beginning to change a bit under the pressure of German money flooding onto the island. Now, if the natives are selling, they may hope you're German, or at least hope for what they call a 'German price.' And even they are beginning to show some signs of resentment towards the Germans, albeit that resentment is an emotion largely foreign to the Mallorquin psyche.

At any rate, when I arrived at the door, the post office was locked. It wasn't a holiday and I was well within working hours. Glancing at my watch, I saw it was coffee-break time. Whole national offices will lock up like this. Regardless of what it says on the door about opening times, when break time comes the staff close up and troop out for half an hour, sometimes locking the door right in the face of an incoming customer. This drives northern Europeans wild, though the locals don't seem to mind. Either they are simply used to being downtrodden and abused by petty officialdom – a fair bet given Spanish history – or else they are just more acceptant than we are. Or resigned. Whichever it is, they tend to live longer, so there must be something to it.

The same thing can be said, by the way, for bread queues at the bakery. Foreigners must learn to accept that the bakery is not only a place to buy bread, it is also the central gossip exchange, and the process of buying a loaf of bread would not be satisfying and complete without the retailing of the latest information and speculation, sometimes even about us, the foreigners, though as I have noted previously, we are usually regarded with deep uninterest by the locals. (As opposed to *dis*interest, a word coming into wide currency to describe lack of interest, when in fact what it properly means is objective, impartial, or unbiased interest.) Am I getting too pedantic here? Let me get on with things.

Actually, I couldn't get on with things as I had at that point, at a guess, twenty minutes before the office would reopen. Luckily, not far down the street there is an old-fashioned, narrow, tobacco-smelling bar with outside tables cunningly arranged to block the pavement against its use by pedestrians, and I chanced to have with me an unread copy of one of the island's English language newspapers.

The paper is charming despite its somewhat erratic spelling and eccentric typesetting, its random locutions in Spanglish, or its sometimes puerile preoccupation with celebrities and stars. That's all part of small scale journalism – few provincial papers do much better – and it's part of the price we readers pay to have a shadow of an idea about what's going on. I do not wish to sound elitist here, as I read the paper thoroughly every day and am especially a fan of the picture editor, who will use any pretext in order to shoehorn in a picture of a celebrity. There will be a picture of Claudia Schiffer over a report of a dogfight, just because it took place within a mile of her house and she may once have met one of the dogs. If I am ever to be hanged for throttling a journalist – or even some serious crime – no doubt he will head the story with a picture of some celebrity who stayed at my hotel in the dim past.

Not long ago, the paper increased its size, which means it now has more pages to fill than previously. This also means more filler stories are picked up off the wire and reproduced as is, seemingly without regard to anything that might have any relevance here on the island. 'Humphrey, go tear a story off the Reuters printer – no, I don't care which one, but it has to be at least three columns long.' And thus it is that we are treated to a long exposition regarding the motor trade in Singapore, and I – more fool I – will like as not mindlessly read it all.

So it was that several Singapore-style stories later I saw the postmistress and her little coven return and made my way to the door. 'Ninian Mede's box, please, which one is it?' I said, waving the key. Now this is supposed to be confidential information, but I thought the key would do the trick. 'Number 111,' replied the boss lady. 'Over in that bank of boxes on the far wall.'

There were only two envelopes in the box, neither of which had a stamp on it, which made me pause momentarily. Then I twigged it. They hadn't been sent to Ninian, he was keeping them there much as one would use a lockbox in a bank – safe, private, ignored by the postal personnel, and readily accessible. He probably didn't even receive any post there, so there was little reason for the post office people even to look in his box, though he had an excuse to visit the box whenever he wanted to. I slid the envelopes out, pocketed them, and made for the door before anyone could have a second thought about my presence.

Thinking it best to be out of sight and gone, I took the back road that meanders out of town up towards Alaró. Just at the top of a hill coming into the view of Alaró, there is a wide place where one can park and ingest glorious views of the *puiges* – two big three-thousand-foot igneous extrusions along the chain of the mountains, that reflect the sun from their peachily oxidised sheer cliffs. They're tall enough to hold back the clouds that form lenticular shapes at the top, so they're almost always a pleasure to watch, as there is inevitably some vivid interplay between the reflections of the light and the roiling shapes of the clouds. The road is lightly used, so it's a good place to sit and ponder.

First I opened the fatter of the two envelopes, both brown, each with a waxed cord wound round a flat plastic wafer on the flap. Both had mucilage on the flaps, though only one had been licked and sealed. It was the sealed one that interested me.

I already had a hunch what I'd find inside. Money. There was a pile of pesetas, all in 10,000 notes, a pile of dollars, mostly hundreds but some fifties, a smaller stack of deutschmarks, hundreds again, and finally a slim packet of pounds, mostly twenties but a few fifties. It didn't look like a huge sum, but then it wasn't inconsiderable either.

I wondered about its provenance. It didn't seem like restaurant skim money – tax dodging is the national sport that ranks just after football here – as the bills were wrong, unless Ninian had changed his contraband pesetas. A moment's thought rendered that possibility unlikely as it's fairly complicated to change money *into* foreign currency here, even though the banks take a lot of it in. The Bank of Spain still keeps stringent control records on foreign money and nonresident, as opposed to resident, pesetas. A mystery. But a mystery I could put on hold for now.

I opened the second envelope. This time there was just one single sheet of paper with a typewritten list:

Pto Soller, 221b	£	45,000
Orient, 3	SwF	30,000
Puigpunyent sm	US$	100,000
Arenal, 6	DM	30,000
Deya, 119	Pts	37,750,000
Portals, b	US$	25,000
Pto. Alcudia, 57	DM	100,000
Pollensa, 66	US$	25,000

And down at the bottom, in ballpoint, the note, 'Stella to Antigua.'

This time, a lot of money, in total. And an even more significant amount if in the form of cash, untaxed. I did a quick calculation on the sums and came up with an amount well over half a million dollars. But what did it mean? And who was Stella?

The only thing that was obvious was that the names were all towns on Mallorca. The money amounts were meaningless. Payments to people? Payments *from* people? Property? And what did the other numbers mean?

I watched the mountains for awhile, seeking, but finding no inspiration. They're too beautiful in any event to engage the intellect; they simply offer a purely sensual experience, rarely failing to give me a *frisson* of pleasure. But as I tried to learn from a Buddhist friend, if you wish to solve a problem, don't think of it piecemeal; shape it in your imagination into the form of a crown and place it on top of your head. Then forget about it. Your wiser bits can then work things out at their leisure and in due course they will figuratively tap you on the shoulder and tell you the answer, or at least *an* answer. Just trust the process.

But I wanted some more immediate help. The person I really wanted to be in touch with was Fausto Milagro. I had instinctively trusted him, though I've been fleeced more than once by people I've instinctively trusted, not that it seems to make me any wiser. In his case, however, I took heart from the impression that at least one senior Guardia officer didn't want him near the case, didn't want me in touch with him, and seemed to want to sweep this murder under the rug, and a bloody Bokhara it was. Something stank.

Just then, a Guardia patrol jeep passed by me, and one of the policemen looked at me intently, deliberately. Talk about instant paranoia. Rationally I knew they patrolled this road routinely and came along here on their way down to set their regular alcohol, tax registration, and general harassment trap for drivers coming around the big roundabout adjacent to the motorway at the Santa Maria turnoff. But emotionally I felt as though they certainly must have been following me to keep tabs on my movements. For here I was, sitting with an envelope full of a dead man's money, illegally acquired, and with a dead man's puzzle sheet referring to an even more considerable sum. Just to round things off, the dead man had been killed in my hotel; it was I who had discovered the body, and I hadn't even a gossamer tissue of an alibi for the previous evening.

Mierda. Maybe they suspected I did it. Or maybe somebody wanted to pin it on me. I thought I'd best go home and hide under the covers.

Four

I drove slowly back to the hotel, using the back roads. There are usually sprinklings of wildflowers at most times of the year, but early in spring and late autumn there can be whole sweeping billows of them, like multi-hued kaleidoscopic surf breaking in slow motion over the fields. One of the positive by-products of the local farmers' mean reluctance to use pesticides is that they don't kill off all the flowers. You do see insensitive practical philistines ploughing under whole fields of poppies from time to time, but at least you know that in six months the field will again be an impressionist's dreamscape. And you can eat the fruit and vegetables here without having either to wash them like a hygiene-obsessive raccoon, or suffer those nasty pencil-prick pesticide headaches over the eyes. And of course the local honey is marvellous.

Up with Hannah on the top terrace, the one with the roofscape views, I sipped a cup of tea and prepared to bounce some of my paranoia off her.

'I'm beginning to suspect they may think I did it,' I said. 'They told me to go away and forget about it, but I think that was meant to mislead me, or lull me into a false sense of security. After all, the body was still pretty warm when I found him, and I'd been out in the office for an hour or so before, so as far as I know no one saw me. My alibi is pretty flimsy.'

'Well,' she said cheerfully. '*Did* you do it?'

Hannah is so helpful at times. Paradoxically, if I *had* expunged Ninian, Hannah is probably the only person in the world I could tell. She and I used to be a couple, and then a few years ago the skeins of that relationship began to unravel. But as we had various joint responsibilities, and as we had always had a solid friendship, we didn't do the usual split-up-and-separate routine; we sat down to talk things out, to see if we could find some mutual accommodation. It was hard work, but eventually we succeeded in separating out and putting aside our former relationship as a couple, retaining the best of the rest. So here we still are, with our business and parental partnerships intact and operating, and working together as friends. Most of the other cracks seem pretty much mended, though we each carry some old sorrows, now fading. Isn't there some fact, though, to the notion that healed fractures are often stronger than unbroken bones?

'Shit, Hannah, this might be serious. Let me tell you what else is going on.' And I told her about the postbox.

'You're a fool,' she said matter-of-factly. 'If somebody is trying to pin anything on you then you've given them the perfect opening. Do you really think the post office people won't remember you? Do you think the Guardia won't check Ninian's records and see that he's got a postbox? You *know* everything is recorded in some file somewhere in this country. You should have simply handed over the key and walked away.'

Hannah has an annoying habit of being right. I wouldn't have a leg to stand on if they followed up on the postbox. So my nosiness had really dropped me in it this time. I could see only one way out, and that was to find out myself who did it. I floated the idea.

'No, Will, you'll just get yourself in deeper. Just tell them the truth and don't mess with things. It's *their* job to solve the crime.' Hannah was beginning to get upset. But this time I felt it was she who was being naïve. I had a deep instinct that if I couldn't sort out the mystery, they'd end up hanging me out to dry simply because they didn't have anyone else to fit up for the murder.

'I think it's too late for that. Or maybe it's still too early, I don't know which. All I know is that I think I have to find Fausto Milagro, talk to him, and see if he knows what's going on.'

'All very well, but you accuse *me* of being too trusting. Now you want to rush off and bare your soul to a man you've met only once. How do you know he isn't involved up to his ears in whatever's going on? Just because he's charming doesn't mean spit about his trustworthiness. In fact it often means quite the opposite. Ask any woman about that.'

She was, of course, right again. I didn't see any clear way forward. All I knew was that I couldn't just sit still and let the mills of the Guardia grind exceedingly fine; it was I who might be the grist.

Just to be certain of my lack of an alibi I called Mariela and asked her if she'd seen me in the office in the hour or two before I found Ninian. No, she hadn't, more's the pity, and Mariela's the last person I could think of to commit perjury on my behalf. I wouldn't ask her to, but even if, out of misplaced loyalty, she were to try, she's incapable of telling a lie without going all pink and shifty. I asked her once to put off a salesman I didn't want to talk to by telling him I was in a meeting, and she came back looking as though she'd been caught red-handed lifting the Crown Jewels.

It was time to take out a little bit of insurance, though it seemed to be much too little, much too late. I calculated the number of hours it had been since I'd found the body – no more than seventeen. I went to my room and got the clothes I'd been wearing last evening. Thankfully they were visibly soiled. I popped them into a big plastic bag and walked them over to the notary's office on the side of the square. In Spain you use a notary for everything. Virtually every transaction of consequence you'll ever undertake will need to be countersigned by a notary, and of course they take a fee for doing so. It's another one of those closed-shop rip-offs that abound in the Spanish bureaucracy. You buy a house, sell a house, take a loan, pay off a loan, start a business, wind up a business – you name it and it involves a trip to the notary, more often than not a long period of sitting around, and then a five-minute clown routine of the notary reading the legal papers out loud and then signing as a witness. These days you can pay an absolutely enormous amount of money for this totally useless ceremony, as the notary's fees are calculated as a percentage of the face value of whatever document is being processed. As inflation and property value increases have multiplied these sums, the notaries of Spain have become some of the richest people in the country. But they can have their uses, or at least so I hoped in this instance.

I asked Margarita, our local notary, to seal and date and time-stamp the bag with my clothes in it. Frankly, I'd been surprised the Guardia hadn't asked for them last night, but I didn't think I'd been a suspect then. Now I figured they'd get around to hitting on me as soon as they'd run out of any other obvious candidates. I wanted my clothes, despite the fact the blow to Ninian's head hadn't seemed to splatter very much, to be able to be checked for bloodstains. And I thought any decent forensic lab would be able to deduce that my clothing had been worn for a couple of days previously and not just been hurriedly washed and dried last night. I figured there might be a stain or two from when I'd first found him and rolled him over to confirm who he was, but that wouldn't leave the sort of splash pattern the killer might have acquired. Thank goodness I'd had the wit to change my clothes last evening before tidying up the bloody mess of the rug and the stains on the floor. There'd been a few drops on the door architrave and on one wall above the dado, but nothing much. Mostly, what I wanted to do here was protect myself from easy accusations. People had seen me wear those trousers and that pullover both the day before and at the time of the discovery of the body. If I covered myself by proving the clothes hadn't been cleaned after the discovery of the body, I might cut off one avenue of accusations, though actually I knew I was probably putting myself in another lose-lose situation. Merely by going to these lengths to prove these clothes hadn't been worn by the killer – possibly assumed by the police to be me – I'd be indicating to at least some of the more suspicious of them that I'd put on a special costume to do the job, presumably my restaurateur-killing outfit, the sexy black number. Lord knows, there have been plenty of times in my life after a particularly bad meal when I cheerfully would have dispatched the owner of the restaurant, but Ninian, despite his aggressive lack of charm, had never been one of them. Thanks to Manuel, the food at his place, if not the welcome, was dependably excellent.

Trundling back across the square I was almost mown down by a very small girl on a kamikaze tricycle, who moments later hit an uneven patch in the cobbles and tipped over, landing in a heap with a thump, pause, wail. I picked her up, dusted her down, wet a forefinger in her tears to wipe away a smudge, and sent her cheerfully on her way again within a minute. One of the joys of living in a town which is a throwback to more innocent times is that one can respond naturally and spontaneously to children in need without pause for consideration as to how it might be viewed. Here, one sees small children playing more or less unsupervised at all hours of the day and surprisingly late into the night, roaming free on their parents' assumption that any adult in their vicinity will function *in loco parentis* if necessary. And they do. Children not only are comforted on occasions such as the one I had just experienced, but at times you will see a surrogate parent scolding a child for errant behaviour. Contrast that with the experience I had in an international airport a few years ago. As had happened today, a small child had fallen over close to where I was standing. As I instinctively reached to pick him up, a great stentorian voice boomed out, 'Don't touch that child!' I looked up to see myself advanced upon by a human version of a Volvo eighteen-wheeler lorry, who bent over – with some difficulty I observed unkindly – and unceremoniously, even roughly, snatched the child from the floor. Pitiful, what we're coming to, and it seems to get worse all the time. We're becoming one vast suspicious, litigious, alienated, cynical, greedy antheap. It's part of the reason I love this old-fashioned town. People here haven't got that way yet. Yet.

Back in the hotel, there was a message waiting for me to ring Fausto Milagro. The number wasn't either of those on his card. I rang. There was a click on the line but no one spoke. Then the line seemed to go dead. I tried again. No answer. I went and did some of the hateful administrative chores which all seem to land on my desk, dead-headed some of the flowers in the patio – it's an almost all-year task; the jasmine blooms even at Christmastime here – made a few other calls and then tried him again. This time he answered immediately.

'Captain Milagro?'

'Yes. That's Señor Stock, isn't it? I was waiting for your call.'

'Well, I rang about fifteen minutes ago and someone picked up, hung up, and then on my second try there was no answer.'

There was a pause. 'That's odd. I've been here. Listen, perhaps we should meet personally. Are you free at the moment?' His voice was evenly modulated but I thought I detected a hesitant note, a hint of disquiet.

'Yes. As a matter of fact I wanted to talk to you.'

'Good. Could you come into Palma right now?'

'No time, as they say, like the present.'

'Fine. Half an hour at – do you know the Casa Gallega off Plaza Weyler?'

'Yes. See you there.' I rang off.

Twenty minutes moved me from one world into another. It's a hop and a skip and not even a jump from our town into Palma, but they're at least one century apart in attitudes and two in sophistication. And that's even taking into account that Palma is hardly the most urbane of cities by world standards today.

I parked in the underground car park near the Teatre Principal and walked the couple of hundred yards back to Plaza Weyler where there is the recently renovated and restored art deco Gran Hotel, which is no longer a hotel, but houses an excellent art bookstore, a public gallery, and a stylish modern bar. It's a splendid building, of its genre unmatched in Palma. Passing the Forn de Teatre bakery, with its swirly art nouveau front and artistic displays of toothsome *hojaldres* – baked savoury quiche clones – I negotiated the busy zebra crossing where you play dodgem with the drivers who are apparently stripe-blind, walked back 100 feet into the side street and entered Casa Gallega. The entrance isn't obvious, so you have to be careful not to confuse it with the Meson Gallega, which is cattycorner across the street to the left and which has big tanks in its windows full of live lobsters and crabs. Not that the food isn't good there, too, but I prefer the ambience of Casa Gallega. They serve, among other things, crispy *chiperones* – baby cuttlefish deep-fried – an excellent Galician cheese, the best *jamon serrano*, mountain ham, I know of on the island, and a young white wine from Galicia, slightly cloudy, slightly effervescent, and wholly satisfying.

Captain Milagro was tucked into one of the booths on the ground floor opposite the long bar. Upstairs is more formal, with tablecloths. He half rose as I approached and I waved him back down to his seat. We shook hands and then I slid in opposite him. A waiter appeared and we ordered the house wine and *pa amb oli*, country bread rubbed with tomato and garlic and drizzled with olive oil, a pleasing accompaniment to rough country wines.

He was wearing a wool and silk mixture tweed jacket, a buttondown blue Oxford cloth shirt, well-cut flannels, tassel loafers – a charmingly old-fashioned touch – and a foulard silk scarf carelessly knotted at his throat. He certainly did not look like a policeman. 'Let's not bother with chitchat,' he said. 'I rang you because I wanted to warn you.'

'Yes,' I sighed. 'I think I know what's coming.'

'I'm sorry now I didn't take you in last night and do all the reports. At least you could have got your side down on paper while I was in charge of things.'

'You're off the case? Is that official?'

'I'm afraid so.' He grimaced slightly and looked away. 'And the new man has a bit of a bee in his bonnet about you. The only reason he didn't pick you up this morning was that he had one or two other people to interview and he had the late Señor Mede's wife set up a meeting with them down at the restaurant. But from what I've heard, all of them are in the clear and now he's circling back in your direction.'

'But why are you telling me this? It's not your case, even. And besides, you don't really know I'm not guilty.'

'Well, possibly you might be, but I very much doubt it. Frankly I don't think you're that good an actor. I saw you last evening, within about – what? – two hours of the crime? You didn't fit any of the profiles of people in any kind of post-traumatic or post-emotional state, and unless you're a lot more cold-blooded or a lot more stupid and reckless than I suspect, it just doesn't fit that you bludgeoned him. At least that's the way I'm betting.'

'I thank you for the vote of confidence,' I said dryly. 'Now all you have to do is convince your replacement. What's his name?'

'Francisco Vega – Paco to everyone. And he's not a man for turning. I thought you'd best be warned so you can prepare to defend yourself.'

'I've already taken a couple of steps in that direction,' I said glumly. 'But I don't have a puncture-proof alibi. If I'd done it I'd have arranged one. Even I am not that dumb.'

'No, I didn't think you were either, which is why I put credence in your story.'

I couldn't resist the obvious question. 'A Spanish

policeman using a word like "credence"? Sorry to be nosy, but how does that fit?'

'It doesn't, actually,' he chuckled. 'I come from a family of lawyers but didn't want to be one. And we had an English tutor, my brother and I, instead of going to the local school. In those days it was hard to get a good education here on the island and our parents didn't want to send us abroad. Hence the accent and the vocabulary, and hence the job as a policeman, as it's the closest I could be to the law without being a boring lawyer.'

'Just as well, too,' I remarked. 'They're probably my least favourite profession so don't get me started about them. I'm lawyer-allergic. And this from a man who may need a good one fairly soon.'

'Let's hope it doesn't come to that.' He smiled, albeit a touch grimly. 'Let me see what I can do, though I can't guarantee anything.'

'Let me in on a secret,' I said. 'Why are you off the case?'

'I was afraid you'd ask that.' He paused and rotated the stem of his wineglass. 'There's an off chance I could be involved.'

'Involved? How? What does that mean?'

'As I said, it's an off chance, but it has to do with another investigation – one I'm still involved with, that may turn out to involve someone close to me. I know I'm being cryptic but I can't say any more just now. You'll simply have to trust that I can't touch this one for personal reasons. On the other hand ...' He stopped, looked down, sighed and shook his head.

'Now you're really baffling me. What does *that* mean?'

'It means there are things I can't talk about, things I don't understand yet. My motive for ringing you was simple; I just wanted to warn you that Paco will probably be picking you up, and that you should be prepared. I'd normally never do anything like this, especially if there were a remote chance I could be aiding a criminal, but I don't think I am, and I'm concerned by Paco's drive to get this case wrapped up and get someone – apparently you – in the dock and behind bars. I joined the force for idealistic reasons, maybe because I thought I could make a difference. I didn't join up to see people railroaded into the nick on the basis of circumstantial evidence. So perhaps you're my good deed for the day. Let's hope the warning will be helpful.' He drained his glass, reached in his pocket, and threw a couple of bills on the table.

'Hang on a minute,' I said, putting a hand on his arm to stay him. 'There's something you should know.' I told him about the list. He listened quietly, not reacting, just assessing. When I'd finished he shook his head and gave me a rueful half smile.

'You'd better give me that list. If anything happens from here on out it will look better if I can say you gave it to me voluntarily.'

'That's what I thought too,' I said as I reached in my pocket and handed over the piece of paper.

'Did you make any copies?' he asked.

'No, this is the original.' I didn't tell him I'd memorised it. I have one of those funny eidetic memories for some things. I can't remember ten percent of what I hear, can't remember the words for songs, can't remember, seemingly, what day it is half the time. But if I see something in print, and especially if it has numbers on it, then I can usually reproduce it verbatim.

He took the list and looked it over. 'I think I know about some of this,' he said. 'But not all. It could be useful for me. It's probably related to that other investigation I was talking about earlier. But I'd like you to keep what I've told you under your hat, if you'd be so kind.'

'All right, I'll do that. Is there anything else can you tell me?'

'Strictly speaking, I shouldn't tell you anything, but you're involved now, so I'll give you what background I can. We've been investigating Ninian Mede's restaurant as a centre for some kind of racket, though we don't yet know what kind. It could be drugs, or counterfeiting, or a hot money scam. We haven't – or *hadn't* prior to his death – got that far yet, though we're probably looking at drugs here.' He paused. 'Will that do you?'

'Well, it's tantalising, of course, but is that it? What more can you tell me? How did you get onto it?'

'Most of it's not relevant to you, but I can tell you we had a tip via customs. Señor Mede ordered some bugging equipment from abroad and we're always interested when that sort of thing comes into the country and so we follow it. We sent a man into his restaurant with a scanner to do a discreet sweep through the place. Apparently it's installed at a table he uses to entertain personal guests. There wasn't any reason to follow up on it – he might merely have been recording for more or less legitimate business purposes – so we left it alone. Now that he's dead the matter takes on a more sinister aspect.'

'You people still do that kind of thing? Checking on bugs, I mean? I thought Franco was dead.'

'Don't go all sanctimonious on me,' he replied. 'He bought the equipment from your country, you know. We've got a job to do and we do it anyway we can. This country – this island – is very close to North Africa and is a clearing point for drugs coming into Europe. It also is a focal point for hot money coming down from northern Europe – all those Germans, among others, who want to get their money out of their country before the euro comes in full force.'

'What's the significance of the euro changeover?' I was puzzled.

'It means that within a fairly short period of time all the people in the Euro Zone are going to have to turn their marks and francs and pesetas and other currencies into euros. Don't you know about what used to happen in South America in the Sixties? The hyperinflation countries like, say Brazil, would simply declare a new currency and give people a two-week period to turn in all their old cruzeiros for new ones. Then there would be a taxman standing behind the teller at the bank. If someone came in to exchange his money and he had more money than he had declared on his tax statements, the government would want to know where it came from. It's the same principle operating here. There are huge amounts in undeclared monies hidden in mattresses or biscuit tins all over Europe. What will happen when that money has to be taken to the bank to be exchanged for euros? Don't you think questions are going to be asked when allegedly poor people turn up with significant sums of money? What do you think is fuelling the big property boom here? If someone can bury the money in property, and especially if he can underdeclare the purchase price, then he's ahead of the game all around. And so are the sellers.' He sat back, folded the list and put it in his pocket.

'True, but why don't they simply change their money into dollars or yen or something else? In South America their currencies weren't convertible, over here they are.'

'We're not talking about logic here, we're talking about emotion. This is money that's illegal, even that which was earned from legitimate businesses. As long as tax hasn't been paid on it it's money that frightens people, and basically honest people get much more frightened about breaking the law than crooks do. I can tell you that from experience.'

'All right, I suppose I understand. That computes, emotionally speaking. But coming back to our problem, what do we do now, or rather, what do *I* do now?'

'Actually, I think you can help. This is a small island and people know me. You can go to places I can't go to, and talk to people without raising suspicion. If I were to do it people would immediately know what I was up to. And besides, there's an element in this I can't talk about, at least not yet.'

I was flattered by his candour but was beginning to hear alarm bells ringing faintly in the distance. With a touch of reluctance I asked, 'Where do I start?'

'In the old days it used to be *"cherchez la femme,"* but these days it's *"cherchez l'argent"*. Ah, money and women, women and money.' He sighed, rolled his eyes towards the ceiling and spread his fingers, palms up. 'At any rate, see if you can put some names to those sums of money. If you can do that, we'll be in a much better position to try to tie things together.' He again pushed back in his seat as if to get up, and this time I let him. 'Keep in touch on the number I left,' he said. Then he paused. 'But you say you rang and didn't get an answer the first and second times? And you're sure you dialled the right number?'

'It had to have been the right number. The third time I just used the redial button on my phone and got through immediately.'

'Well,' he said. 'It may not mean anything, but let's try something different. Here's my private mobile number. I generally keep it switched off unless I'm out, so you can leave a voicemail message in the *buzon de voz*. I'll pick it up and get back to you.'

We shook hands and he left. I sat for awhile pondering what he'd told me. Bugged tables, or at least one table, in Ninian's restaurant, possible connections to hot money scams, or fraud, or worse, and now I could expect a going over by the Guardia in connection with Ninian's death. This was turning into a real fun week. And to top it off, all Fausto wanted was for me to go and be a clay pigeon. My observation, when I used to shoot skeet, was that whatever clay pigeons made it intact past the flying loads of shot ended in pieces anyway as soon as they hit the ground. A blithe prospect, I thought.

Well, I'd best get on with it.

Five

They picked me up later that afternoon, after I got back to the hotel. Two of them, predictably, and equally predictably, young thug types. We headed for Inca, never my favourite town on this island, and less so at the moment. Thankfully, the hotel wasn't full to overflowing as we tend to be during spring and autumn, so I could be absent with a clear conscience. I've never been able to figure out why there aren't more visitors to the island in the stretch from the end of October to the end of January. Yes, it's true there's rain during that trimester, but the light can be enchanting with the sun low in the sky, the most enjoyable attractions aren't crowded, one gets more attention and better service in restaurants, and the temperature is usually up to shirtsleeve weather during the day and at light jacket level in the evenings. Ninian had at least chosen, though no doubt more from my point of view than his, a convenient time to get bumped off.

I didn't think they'd hold me long, but these things aren't predictable. Nobody chatted with me on the way, so obviously my escorts had been told I was a suspect. We drove through the entrance to the headquarters building, a depressingly institutional stone heap with fraudulent crenellations over an improbably ill-proportioned archway leading to a kind of backyard no-man's land. We parked in a corner of the dusty lot and then went on through to the ground floor offices between the street and the car park. No cuffs or weapons or anything like that, just close surveillance and no fooling around. I've always reacted the same way when being questioned by the police, even when I know full well I'm innocent or only a witness. I begin to get a creepy feeling in the pit of my stomach and an insistent niggle of insinuating guilt. One must resist these responses as much as possible, of course, as they lead to giving off the very emanations of culpability one is trying *not* to generate.

As a coping strategy I have generally resorted to one of two basic responses – neither of which has proven to be effective, though I never seem to learn any better techniques. Either I affect a stance of outrage that anyone would have the temerity to suspect me of whatever the particular wrongdoing is – evoking the small child who lives inside me and pouts and shouts 'Unfair, unfair!', or else I retreat into a posture of amused superiority, which is usually the furthest thing from what I am actually feeling, and which is particularly ineffective, as archly superior supercilious amusement is not a trait likely to impress policemen or move them to release you forthwith.

I did what I could, answering all the straightforward questions as best I could – how long I'd known Ninian, what he was doing in my hotel, when I'd last seen him, where I'd been the previous afternoon, who had seen me, how I might establish my whereabouts at the time of the killing, why I'd been going up the stairs to my room, what I did when I found him, what I did next, what I did after that – and on and on.

It lasted for about two hours: polite, very formal, very correct, everything written down, no heavy pressure. There ensued the unavoidable further hour's delay while my statement was written up, and then we all signed it, after which I was finally free to go. The silent duo drove me back and dropped me off in the square outside the hotel. As these things go it wasn't bad, though I didn't kid myself it was over; this was clearly only step one in the process. I hadn't yet graduated to being interrogated by the Palma crew, and Commandant Vega hadn't yet involved himself. I'd know it when he did.

Poised with my key actually in the lock of the front door – we're a private hotel and keep the door locked, giving guests keys so they can come and go as though in the home of friends – I suddenly found myself overcome by hunger, a not uncommon stress response. Instead of raiding the fridge up in our bistro, I thought I'd pop across the square to the place we refer to as 'The Plaza,' a very typical Mallorquin village restaurant, open all hours seven days a week. I knew I could huddle in a corner, turn my back to the ever-blaring television set, and stuff my face while I recapitulated the situation that seemed to be sucking me down into a slough of frustration, if not yet despond.

For those who are not familiar with Mallorquin village restaurants, let me detour into a quick disquisition on their merits and their failings, very generally speaking. Maybe, whilst noshing and ruminating, I could work something up for Hector's travel journal.

First of all, regardless of where you go, in general terms you will probably find the food excellent, and the decor, ambience, and aesthetic sensibility – well, *local*. Or let's call it 'authentic.' Most village bar/restaurants are open at least six days a week, virtually all hours, and the lunch 'Menu' served from 1 p.m. (and almost never before) is usually an absolute bargain. Entree, main course, dessert, water and wine for less, it seems, than it would cost you to buy the ingredients. Coffee is extra. The listing, often on a blackboard outside the front door or just inside, usually offers two or even three choices of each of the courses. You may need a translation, but at those prices you can at times afford to be adventurous.

Apart from the daily Menu there are often tapas, which are arrayed behind the bar in flat chafing dishes. This is a sort of point and nod operation, though there are some basic recommendations: *croquettas* are the little lumpy oblong cylinders of what looks almost like pastry dough, deep-fried. One type is ham- or chicken-flavoured – it varies depending on what they have – and is lighter in colour; others can be slightly greenish and are spinach-based. Both types are usually excellent and filling. A few of each is normally plenty if taken with other items. Then there are *albondigas*, spicy little meatballs. Generally very good. *Frito* is a famous local dish and widely on offer. Not to everyone's taste as it's basically potatoes and some vegetables fried up with lots of oil and a variety of unmentionable animal innards. For those who can ignore the ingredients and concentrate on the flavour, a treat is in store. *Frito* is a tapa for the broadminded, as are callos, or tripe, also good. There are various other tapas that resist ready description and identification, but any of the deep-fried vegetables are wonderful, and usually recognisable. Especially to be recommended are the sliced and deep-fried *calabacines*, courgette, or *berenjenas*, aubergine. Just point. And to round things off, a bit of *ensaladilla* is always a blander foil to the concentrated flavours of the fried tapas. It's the white potato-salady sort of thing and is made with home-made mayonnaise, capers, and hints of lemon around the other veggies they throw in.

One tip. Don't order the house wine in the local restaurants. It's almost always poor quality, and I've never understood how the owners of these restaurants, who are generally discriminating when it comes to food, and who buy only first-class ingredients, can offer their clientele such bad wine. Sometimes it's because a brother-in-law makes it, which is how the Mallorquins operate, but that can't always be the case. No, order the best on offer. It won't cost much by international standards. The local rosé, *rosado* in Spanish, is excellent and easy on the head the next day. The tinto, or red, is also good. Generally speaking, don't bother with white wines from this island; there are only a few worth drinking and those that are tend to be overpriced because of misplaced pride.

So don't be put off by local restaurants simply because they lack kerb appeal. Hygiene standards are high, since one tourist bellyache can translate into nine columns of space and two pictures in *The Sun* or *News of the World*. The authorities are stringent about storage, cleanliness, and freshness of ingredients, and most of the time the food in local restaurants is reliable, tasty and affordable. If you're just hungry, you'll rarely go wrong.

I took a piece of paper and, with the murder gnawing at my innards almost more than my hunger, began making one of those mind map thingies, a sort of thought tree with lines from the various different elements of the trunk and branches to connect the ideas they represent. I didn't get far because I didn't have enough information. One thing was beginning to make itself clear – if I wanted help I'd·have to provide it myself. Fausto Milagro seemed positively disposed but I couldn't help feeling he had his own agenda operating, and then there was that funny interruption on his phone line when I'd rung him. I'd normally not have given credit to the free floating suspicions that were beginning to present themselves to me, but I reminded myself that a man had been murdered, not in a particularly nice way – is there a nice way? – and that there were those who wished to lay him, figuratively speaking, at my feet.

On that cheerful note I took myself off to bed. One thing I can usually count on is a good night's sleep. We buy handmade oversized beds, use lovely long staple cotton percale sheets, goosedown pillows, and quilted cotton ·mattress covers. You have to have something wrong with you not to get a good night's sleep on those beds. Am I being too self-aggrandising about my hotel? I don't care; I'm proud of it.

Six

Mornings, I try to do some exercises. Over the years I've managed to whittle them down from a dozen or so stretching, strengthening, and yogically relaxing routines, to my current regimen, which consists of 'The Lifetime Five Minute Five Step Exercise Programme.' These five exercises are guaranteed – it said so on the cover blurb – to keep me svelte and flexible, strong and dynamic, energetic and enduring. And my loyalty to the programme will be absolute until such time as someone constructs an even more efficacious 'Lifetime Three Minute Three Step Exercise Programme.'

Over coffee – we usually use a Spanish blend and filter it – I thought about the sheet of paper I'd nicked out of Ninian's box. It would be sensible to make the rounds of the towns on the list and snoop about a bit. Nothing's very far from anywhere else on this island, so it wouldn't be a daunting undertaking to cover several locations in a single day, depending of course on what I found. The task might also have the advantage of keeping me away from the long reach of the Guardia.

I thought I'd go first to Orient, as it's only a twenty minute drive from here. Just as a treat I took Stanley, my venerable black Beemer, which may be almost twelve years old, but has the big BMW 3.5 litre injected engine and goes like you-know-what off a shovel when I put my foot down – though I can almost watch the petrol gauge decline reproachfully if I do. It's my treat to luxuriate in the worn-in leather seats, tune to the crystal clarity of the sound system, and feel the solidity of a precision machine. And also, unlike our other two hotel jalopies, Stanley doesn't have dents – at least not the massive tree-hollow-sized ones suffered from rubbish bins blowing across the square in the biannual gales. Also, in sharp contrast to our other cars, everything works: the locks, the windows, the tape system, the windscreen washers, and the dozen little gadgets one enjoys but are not essential to getting from A to B. One of my other cars is so disreputable that one day a delegation of our cleaning and serving staff, all of whom drive shiny new cars, approached me to suggest that the time had come for me to change the car, that I was in fact, in their view, lowering the tone of the establishment by parking it outside. One of them even pointed out that my car has moss growing on it, which I'd never noticed as I rarely go around to its north side. I dutifully hung my head in feigned shame, but never felt strongly enough about it to get around to doing anything about the poor old rustbucket. One of these days I really will have to do something positive and decisive, maybe even go see about that moss.

You reach Orient by driving up to Alaró, a few miles above Consell, then skirting the town, ignoring the mostly unmade road up to the Castell de Alaró and continuing into the gap between the two towering *puiges*. Another five or so winding minutes will bring you into the long valley leading to Orient, passing fields full of apple trees, which do well in the cool moistness at this altitude, and which create a picturesque foreground for Orient itself, a candidate for the title of prettiest hamlet on the island. Sadly, it's a dead village now, as the houses have virtually all been sold to wealthy Palmesanos as weekend retreats, or to foreigners who come out to Mallorca for a few weeks of the year. There's not even a bakery, which on Mallorca is the death knell for any town. But the tumble-down-the-hill houses are staggered together in pretty clumps, and the church is attractive, all in a bijou setting with decorative cats.

I wandered about a bit, feeling more and more like a Charley, not knowing what I was looking for, not really even knowing what I was doing there. I kept looking for the number three, as that was the number next to the indication for thirty thousand Swiss francs on Ninian's list. There aren't many streets, so I figured it wouldn't take me long to cover the place. Helpfully, as in all good Mallorquin towns, many of the houses don't have numbers, either because they have names, sometimes indicated, but generally not, because identification isn't deemed necessary – after all, everyone knows where Jaime and Kati live. Of course in other towns, like our town, houses can have *two* numbers on show: an old one, often left over from Franco days, and a new one, assigned in recent years. They did it in spades in our town; not only did the authorities change all the house numbers, they changed most of the street names too, just not all at the same time, lest it become too easy for the burghers. And as an extra little fillip to the puzzle, you must bear in mind that many houses go through to the next street, and so have double frontages, or, more accurately, a frontage and a backage, which means that up to four different addresses can apply to the same house. Older inhabitants, moreover, don't use numbers at all, since they remember the days when there were no numbers, only a designation based on the owners' nicknames: 'Pedro's House', or 'Anna's Cottage'. There are thus – since our house goes through to the street behind and had the nickname: 'Ca'n Ximmaró – Jimmy's House,' – five address designations that will get a letter to us, though I knew we'd really finally arrived when we received a letter addressed simply to 'Stock's Hotel, Mallorca'.

I passed a restaurant and it occurred to me that the owners, like the currency noted in the list, were Swiss, but couldn't imagine any probable connection between them and Ninian. Among other things, he hated all other restaurant owners on principle, deeming them to be 'competition'. From his point of view, the most satisfying situation would have been for him to have owned the only restaurant on the island. It was useless to point out to him that good restaurants breed other good restaurants, which – in their turn – breed more and more discriminating diners, thus increasing business for everyone. He'd have none of it. The notion was too subtle.

My search continued, though things were not looking encouraging. Orient was by far the smallest town on the list, and if I couldn't turn up any clues here I'd be even less likely to find anything in the larger towns.

Having about given up, and becoming convinced I'd need to go on to the next town, I started to descend towards the main road via a small street I hadn't yet traversed. I looked for a signpost and found I'd stumbled into the *Calle de los Reyes*, the Street of the Kings. The number three, in Orient – something to do with the Three Kings of the Magi? 'We three kings of Orient are…' swam into my head – a tune that's hard to get rid of. I kept to the steep flagged path on the more open side of the street, checking the houses. Might there be a house with a No.3? There was. Might there be an obvious clue? There was not. Still, I wanted to satisfy my curiosity about who lived there. Banging on the door probably wasn't my smartest option. The whole street was pretty blank, so I merely eyeballed the house – a small two-storeyed, two-windowed, dressed-stone typical row house – in what I hoped was a discreet manner, and kept on meandering down the hill.

There's an overpriced bar/restaurant/hostel at the bottom of the village along the main road, with a waiter who could insult and ignore and ill-serve for Spain in the Rudeness Olympics, though the girl in the bar is normally cooperative and often will serve you what you want as long as you order it in fluent Mallorquin. But she wasn't there, so I settled for the Rude One's understudy, who actually thawed a bit when offered a drink. Did he live here? No. No surprise there. Did he know the village? Of course, what was there to know? Did he know who lived up in the *Calle de los Reyes* in the third house along? No, he couldn't remember. Who did live in that street? Didn't know. Never noticed. Any foreigners live up there besides the restaurant people? Maybe one or two. Not sure. Maybe one in that street, maybe not. What kind of foreigners? Not sure. Swiss? (Objection, M'lud, leading the witness) Yes, that's it. Swiss – something to do with boats. (Really? Ex Swiss Navy?)

I decided to stop there. Maybe paydirt, more likely fool's gold. I thought it best to ride out of town on the horse I rode in on, while the gittin' goin', as it were, was still good. Besides, if I went to the *ayuntamiento*, the town hall, in Alaró, I could probably find out who owned the house.

If you carry on through Orient you come out on the road to Bunyola, not to be confused with *bunuelos*, the tasty deep-fried doughnuts you often see being prepared during religious holidays by elderly ladies who stand over a half oil drum full of almost boiling oil flicking little nuggets of dough into the oil, letting them puff up and brown and then fishing them out with a wooden paddle. Rolled in sugar – usually too much sugar, so shake some off – they're delectable.

The narrow road from Orient to Bunyola is little trafficked and meanders through the valley that parallels the 3,000-foot Sierra de Alfabia range. It transits some of the prettier parts of authentic old Mallorca, as the area is just inconvenient enough in terms of access, and just close enough to the mountains, to have been protected from overexploitation. It passes ancient farms, *possessiones*, that have been operating since Roman times, and one still sees the vestiges of the irrigation networks created by the Moors in the 10th century.

Snuggled against cliffs at the end of a long valley, Bunyola is picturesque and just about worth a detour, though there isn't much of touristic interest inside the town itself. A couple of miles south of the town are the *Jardines Raixa*, gardens laid out in Moorish times but with a generous sprinkle of Renaissance statuary. I turned the other way, though, and headed up the busy road towards Soller.

There are two basic ways of reaching Soller – road or train. The restored 1890s train from Palma can be a fun journey and worth the investment in time, though the timetable is odd, giving you the option either of turning around almost immediately to go back, or else having to spend the whole of the afternoon in Soller and Puerto Soller, which come to think of it isn't really a hardship, as Soller is one of the most pleasant towns on the island and is located at the head of an exceptionally attractive valley.

If you are touristing, and decide to go by road, take the old, free, serpentine road up over the 500 metre sidehills to the valley, curving back and forth more than thirty times before reaching Soller itself. Coming back, when you're tired out by walking around, the new toll tunnel is probably a better option, as it cuts under the hills and saves time and driving effort. Not being in sightseeing mode, I took the tunnel up.

There is a old-fashioned Toonerville trolley down to the Port of Soller, but unless you get on at the starting point, up left from the train station, you'll have to strap-hang as it's almost always full. The port, which was built much later than Soller itself, isn't as interesting, nor does it have much history. Why didn't they build down by the water to begin with, people ask. 'Well,' answer the Mallorquins, 'would you like to build your house where it might be vulnerable to the next set of pirates who happen along?' We moderns tend to forget details like that when we visit the cities of the Mediterranean. We simply ignore a couple of dozen centuries of history, oblivious to the reality of how exposed the coasts were back then, and how much safer it was to fortify oneself up in the rocks behind the coasts, shelter in the hills where there was protection, or away in the interior where it was the invaders who were more vulnerable.

As recently as a few years ago one could observe the

stresses inside Mallorquin families when the whole system of inheritance went awry because of economic forces from outside the island. For generations the Mallorquins had followed a variation on the tradition of primogeniture, with the eldest son inheriting, not all the land, but the choicest land, the next son the less choice, and so on down to the least arable or conveniently-positioned fields, which were allocated to the daughters, who, it was presumed, might marry a man with better land, but who in any event were not equipped to work the land by themselves. An unfair genetic lottery, perhaps, but one that had been the norm in many countries around the Mediterranean for as long as history records, and presumably beyond.

But on Mallorca, in the late Sixties and during the Seventies and Eighties, everything changed. The best land had always been, of course, the land in the interior – more valuable as it was more protected, closer to sweet water, and more fertile. The land along the coast was rockier, harder to till, thin and partially scoured away by the sea winds, exposed to invading pirates and therefore generally regarded as less desirable. Then the tourists came, first in their thousands, later in their millions. Land along the coast began to skyrocket in value as tourist facilities were built – hotels, restaurants, shops, and an infrastructure of roads, water lines and electricity cables. The youngest sons and the daughters of the great Mallorquin landed gentry, those who had inherited the dregs of their parents' estates, suddenly found themselves heirs to land worth five, ten, even twenty times more than that of the first-born sons, and as they sold off their rocky patrimony with sea views to big hotel chains and developers, the intrafamilial jealousy and tension caused feuds that still go on today. Ah, such sad stories there were. My heart is always sorely taxed by the pitiable problems of the very rich.

Down in the port, I found myself somewhat at a loose

end, much as I had in Orient. There was perhaps a clue here, but I didn't even know where to begin to look for it. For almost an hour I drove aimlessly about, up and down the streets of the port, looking for a number 221b. The 'b', I had assumed, referred to '*bajo*', the Spanish indication for ground floor. In half an hour I didn't see a single one. The house numbers in the port tended not to rise above fifty or so. Finally, I parked and went into a nearby bar for a *cortado*, one of those strong little coffees cut with a dollop of milk. Coffee is supposed to make you more intelligent, if only in a transitory way, and a boost of intelligence was something I needed right now.

Happily, it must have worked, for I found myself looking at the problem from a different angle. 221b. An obviously familiar number. Sherlock Holmes's address in Baker Street, London. I'd read it hundreds of times as a teenager when I first discovered the stories. Maybe the clue was as transparent as that.

I got in the car and circled the town again, looking for anything connected with London, Baker St., Conan Doyle, or Sherlock Holmes himself. At the far end of the port, where the ferry lands and where the boatyards are, I found it. Across the water I spotted Holmes Boatyard, a small enterprise from the look of it, with a six-slip jetty projecting into the bay and a large enclosed, corrugated-metal workshed designed to be used, presumably, for painting or whatever work needed to be carried out in a place protected from the elements. It was big enough to accommodate a twenty-metre yacht, with a central openable slot in the roof that would slide to one side to allow the masts of a sailing boat of considerable size to protrude beyond the already tall roof, which rose almost three storeys in height. The building was painted a dull silver. There was only one boat tied up in the slips, which seemed surprising, given the shortage of anchorage and berthing space here on the island. Most boatyards and marinas are usually full to overflowing.

Gaining access to the site from the land side wasn't easy. I wove my way down towards the water through a warren of small streets, several dead-ending as they neared the bay. Finally I found a somewhat wider access road that led down to the yard itself, which was protected by a stout chainlink fence with chainlink double gates with a hefty lock on them connected to a buzzer access system. There was one of those private-property-keep-out-we-have-a-security-system signs mounted on the right hand support pole for the gates, which seemed slightly odd for what was presumably a business open to the public. Everything looked firmly closed and buttoned down, though lights visible through a high-up window of what I presumed to be the office suggested occupancy.

I tucked the car along the side of the street about fifty yards from the gates and contemplated the enclosure, with its hoists and cradles and rusting oddments of abandoned spare parts. Nothing seemed out of the ordinary save perhaps the scarcity of boats and the higher than usual level of security. It was, nonetheless, named Holmes, and though I felt I might be reaching a bit, the only hook I had to hang anything on was the sort of schoolboy's code on the list for the name Holmes. It may have been too patently obvious a connection to take seriously, but it was the only idea I had to go with.

My first obvious choice now was to see what I could glean from a conversation with whomever would talk to me. If that attempt didn't bear fruit I thought I might try to get in and look around when the place was unoccupied, which would be in another half hour or so. Most Mallorquin businesses close for lunch around 1 p.m. and their workers take a break of at least two hours, more usually three – a civilised practice, though inconvenient if one is trying to cram a northern-European schedule into a Mediterranean day.

Given that I didn't wish to expose myself, I thought I'd try first by phone, and extracted my mobile from the glovebox. After only two attempts I managed to wheedle the telephone number of the yard from Telefónica's directory enquiries, the operators for which qualify among the most ill-gracious and least competent telephone service people one will ever encounter. Telefónica offers, generally speaking, third world service and efficiency at first world premium prices.

When I rang, the phone was picked up on the first ring with a snap and a plangent snarl, 'Holmes!'

I began in Spanish, just to see how the scene might play.

'Speak English, mate!' The voice was Australian, phlegmy and rasping, as though twenty cigarettes were only a morning's quota. Had he picked up immediately on my accent or did he not speak Spanish?

'I'd like some information about renting a berth. I saw from across the bay that you seem to have some space free.' I hoped he wouldn't ask too many questions as I hadn't prepared a cover story and my responses would doubtless be unconvincing.

'Forget it, mate. We only do limited private work and we're booked up.' A quicker brushoff than I'd anticipated.

'I simply would like some information, perhaps for the future. Am I speaking to Mr Holmes?' I was getting nowhere and running out of options. Maybe I'd have to take a chance on a face-to-face meeting. 'Might I come by?'

'Naw, don't bother. Let me tell you straight – we're not taking on business, we're not renting space, we're not interested, and I'm about to close up and leave. Got it, mate?' The phone went dead.

I got it. I punched the cutoff button on the phone and stuck it back in the glovebox. Mr Holmes had succeeded in kindling my curiosity. I started the car and backed twenty yards up the side street that led off into the trees that ringed the nose of the bay. I was still able to see the gates but my car was less obvious to anyone inside the yard. I turned on the radio and settled in for a wait. There are two good classical stations to choose from here, the Spanish national station and the Catalan station out of Barcelona. The Spanish national network also has the single best pop-rock station I've heard anywhere, and we even have a frequency, 95.8, which is shared between the English station, which broadcasts some truly ancient pop music from 8 a.m. to 1 p.m., and the German station, which occupies the frequency from 1 p.m. around until 8 a.m., broadcasting a wider range of fare, even including at times heavy Teutonic economic discussions in the evening.

Radio Tres, the pop station, was broadcasting *Adiemus*, that pulsating Carl Jenkins composition with the London Phil's percussion section beefed up three-fold, and with the six Finnish sopranos, three brassy, three sweet. Certainly not pop music in any usual sense, and though normally I'd have given it my full attention, today I was more concerned with working out my next step. I settled down to watch.

After about fifteen minutes I saw the door to the office open and there emerged a beefy redhaired man with a built-up right shoe that didn't seem to ameliorate a prominent limp. I didn't like him on sight. His great grandfather was probably a convict, I thought unkindly. He stopped outside the front door and squinted across at the closed shed before locking up. He was one of those Celtic types who should never live in sunny climes; his skin would only ever redden and burn, never tan, and probably develop melanosis if he stayed in the sun too much. Why is it so many of these physical types seem to end up as sailors?

He had a lantern jaw, a bulbous nose on which I could see the broken veins even at this distance, and wore a Peruvian-style embroidered shirt over a more than incipient paunch. He limped around the corner of the building out of sight, and a minute later a potentially classic 1950-something four-holer Buick sedan lumbered around the corner in a low gear, approached the double gates, and slowed even more while he zapped the automatic gate opener with a remote control.

After they'd opened and he'd driven through, he swivelled around, activated the remote again, and waited while the gates trundled closed. I slumped down in my seat out of sight until I heard his car pass by on the way up the hill. Decision time.

I thought I could probably get in over or around the fence, and that course of action had some appeal, though I had to offset any possible advantages against the difficulties that might arise were I to be detected breaking into the yard. If this were a straightforward boatyard operation, however – and I had no real indication so far that it might be otherwise – then I could be fairly certain the workmen wouldn't return before at least three, so I had plenty of time in hand. I thought I'd have a go. Apart from my instant visceral dislike of Holmes, and my curiosity about the place, I was distinctly eager to turn up something – anything – suspicious.

Now I have few skills as a burglar. I read paperbacks peopled with private eyes who can get through a lock as soon as look at you, but my escapades in plundering have largely been confined to rifling the refrigerator in the middle of the night for leftover apple cake, or, when terminally strapped for change, breaking into the flimsy tin box the girls use to keep the petty cash in the kitchen. Sometimes I even have problems getting into that. Overcoming the lock on this fence was clearly out of the question.

Avoiding the gates and following the chain fence along, I clambered across some rocks that descended in the direction of the sea. The barrier continued about ten feet into the water before terminating. Whoever had put the fence in originally hadn't reckoned on it being used to back up a medium-high security system. However daunting it seemed up at the entrance, it dwindled into schoolyard level protection down by the water. It might be awkward to climb around the terminal post but I figured I could do it almost without getting my feet wet. If caught I supposed I could spin some tale about having been dropped off by a boat and ask a lot of questions about how much they would charge to splice my gillets, or frennet my sopwiths, or some such nautical nonsense for my nonexistent yacht.

In the end, it was easier than I had thought it would be. I found two lengths of plank lying near the fence, propped them in the water and leaned them at an angle against the links. That way I could step into the join and get purchase for one foot, hook my fingers into the links, then lean down, replace the next board further on, and in four operations I was around the corner and heading back for dry land inside the yard. And I couldn't even be seen, save from across the water, and that was a pretty fair distance.

Once onto the edge, a rubble and rockstrewn beachhead, I started for the closed shed, curious to see what might be inside. There was a big door on the water side, but it was closed and locked, with a formidable padlock on the hasp. Pointless to try there. My hope was to find a breach in the walls so I could see inside. Circling around to the left I found a loose place between two of the corrugated panels and prised them quietly apart. I didn't know who might still be inside, as the shed connected to the offices, so that if someone were still in the offices I possibly might be heard, or seen, from inside. The man I assumed to be Holmes hadn't turned the lights out when he left.

Through the gap I could make out the hull of a sleek ketch or yawl – hard to tell which at this angle – in the process of being repainted. There were rubbed bits and undercoated areas patchworking the whole length of the side I could see. From the look of her fittings, she was luxury class. The hole I was looking through was about a third of the way along the boat, and although I strained to see some identification, I couldn't make out a name. Cranking my head as far around to the right as possible, I could make out the far wall at the stern end of the boat where the doors led to the ramp into the water. Down in one corner there were a couple of cracks of light, indicating perhaps a gap where I could get a better look inside. Gingerly, I let the panels spring back into place and made my way back the way I'd come, walking as silently as I could on the gravelled and rocky surface. Once at the corner, I could see what I'd missed previously, a suspended two-foot-square door at ground level, hinged like a large cat flap. Getting down on all fours, I inched the flap inward, raising it enough so I could see the stern. They'd put on the first coat of primer over the whole of the transom. The name was obscured but there were what looked like spaces where brass letter plates had been attached – six of them. The name of the home port was illegible, completely painted out, though underneath I could just about make out what I thought was a small French flag. Why was a French boat being repainted here? That didn't compute. As a lead it wasn't much, but maybe something. It may not have been a jackpot, but I'd got one of those little payouts that keep you plugging in the coins.

Then I saw a change in the dim light at the far end of the shed. A moving shadow was accelerating gently in my direction and all of a sudden – a belated awakening – I understood what the large cat flap was for. Trotting towards me and beginning to pick up speed was a *Mastín Español*, a short-haired mastiff, one of the nastier of the breeds the Mallorquins use as guard dogs. It had heard me, probably was now scenting me, and clearly knew I wasn't supposed to be here. Mallorca is full of yapping dogs, but this one was ominously silent.

Retreating hastily, I let the flap fall, grabbed a brick lying at the base of the wall and jammed it into the opening, hoping to wedge the panel closed. Then I got up, silently cursing my right leg for having started to go to sleep, and began a retreat to the fence. Behind me I could hear the dog pawing at the flap, and then I heard a tinny thump as the brick came away. I was a hundred and fifty feet ahead of the dog, but he could go lots faster than I could, and I still had the fence to negotiate. I could hear the scrabble of his paws as he gained on me, but what choked my throat and loosened my bowels was that he was completely silent. I glanced back and saw him running full out, jaws open, milky flecks of saliva dropping from his mouth, his tail tucked under.

I wasn't going to make it to the fence.

Lovers of dogs should now look away, skipping the next paragraph.

By this time I'd reached the shaly margin of the rocky strand, close, but not close enough, to the perimeter of the fence. I'd have to face the dog and sweet reason wasn't going to do the trick. When young I'd been a baseball pitcher, and as I bent to seek a suitable rock I hoped the old rubber arm hadn't lost its cunning. I scooped up two fist-sized sharp rocks, went into a quick windup and loosed the first at my target, by this time fifty feet and closing. Missed. I adjusted my windage, rocked back and fired again, feeling a griping twinge in my rotator cuff as I let go. The missile hit the dog over his left eye and sent him spinning, though still without a sound, not even a yelp. Stooping quickly, I gathered up three more rocks and threw again, advancing towards the dog before he could get himself orientated towards me. Sideways he was a better target. The first rock struck him spot on the shoulder joint, making a dark mark where its sharp edge dug in. He raised that leg and this time I heard a guttural growl as he tried to put weight on the front paw. Closing even more I threw twice more, missing once and hitting him in the ribs with the second. There were no more handy rocks on this patch of ground and I retreated a few feet to pick up two more. When he saw me cock my arm for yet another throw the dog wheeled away and began a limping retreat back towards the shed. For a moment I had a fine target of his hindquarters, and the scared part of me dearly wished to hit the bastard yet again for having so terrified me, but the rational part, having established that the rock is mightier than the dog, suggested in urgently reasonable terms that it was time to leave. Where there is one dog on Mallorca there are often two, and I didn't fancy a bout with big brother. Besides, my shoulder was beginning to hurt like bloody blazes.

The return scramble around the fence was uneventful, and I gained the refuge of my car with no more visible evidence of my adventure than dusty knees from kneeling outside the dog flap, and big dark rings under my arms where I'd sweated my shirt through. I felt inordinately proud of my triumph over a dumb, though dangerous, animal, and all my atavistic hunting instincts seemed to be honed and acute. Can we take pride in hurting things, killing things, acting in a savagely primitive way? You bet. When it's us or them we just love coming out on top.

This time I took the long way back, enjoying the car as it bit into the serial bends of the tarmac road over the valley top, delighting in the golden transparency of the late January sun as it picked out the details of the tiers of walls going back to Roman times, two thousand years of domestic Mediterranean history graven into the hillsides. A few people still build walls here, just as you can still sometimes see a man in a field walking behind a mule, ploughing, looking like a Daumier etching.

Well, I had a lead. I didn't know what I'd do with it, but I had it. For a moment I felt like the proverbial happy puppy with two tails, but then struck the dog image as being inappropriate. What I needed now was a long hot shower and a cold glass of wine.

Seven

'So now I suppose you're going to tell that Milagro man everything.' Hannah was curled up on the cane sofa in the bar in front of a toasty fire of olive wood. Outside howled one of those operatic storms we get from time to time between November and February – tempestuous winds, improbably theatrical lightning, Wagnerian thunder, and buckets and sheets of unbridled rain. I love these storms. For some years I lived in Devon where it merely greyed over and drizzled, lugubriously and unimaginatively. To live in a place where Ma Nature really ungussets her girdle is a great treat.

'I told you. You're too trusting.' She lowered her head and looked at me over the horn rims she wears for reading and sewing. Hannah is shortish, topheavy in a curvy *zaftig* way, warm, immediate and bright. As far as people are concerned, I generally defer to her judgement, though not always and sometimes to my cost. But in this case I felt I had to follow my own star, benighted as it can sometimes be.

'Well,' I said, 'who can I talk to about this stuff? Sometimes if you only have one ace you have to bet it.' Although I've lived in Europe for more than half my life I sometimes like to play on my American, good-old-boy side. When I grow up I'm going to buy myself a white linen suit and take up saloon poker and say things like 'What a phoney. Big hat, no cattle.' I'd reincarnate as Mark Twain in a minute.

She gave me her ironic smile. 'Just as long as you keep your own counsel,' she said. 'In your position I wouldn't trust anyone.'

'Anyone?' I asked, eyeing her wryly.

'I'm the proof of the rule,' she said, rising and tucking her book under her arm and bussing me on the top of the head. 'See you in the morning.' And off she went.

I sat and watched the fire for awhile. Olive burns with a lambent blue-green flame from below, where the fat in the wood concentrates. Pretty, but like the mountains, not conducive to rational thought. After awhile I traipsed up to read some more of *Cold Mountain,* that fine book.

In the morning I decided to have my second cup of coffee at the Sportsman's, the bar on the corner opposite the side of the church, between the shop – and this is no foolin' true – that sells birdseed and men's underwear and the shop that sells cigarettes in the left half and health products in the right half. The bar isn't actually named the Sportsman's, but we call it that because it is peopled almost exclusively by the senior seniors, at least seventy-five years plus, who spend the day watching sports on the mega TV in the corner – football, *always* football, but also skateboarding, dog racing, ski jumping, mud wrestling, sumo, three varieties of hockey, basketball, you name it. Some of the faces are there all day long every day, save for one week in the year when they go out to shake their olive trees and harvest their year's income. I like going there because I am invariably the youngest man in the place, which feels odd, but cheering.

After coffee I went to the bank to do my daily battle with the green-eyeshaded sharks. In the absence of freedom under Franco, I'm convinced that all of the creative energy that might otherwise have been concentrated into making films or writing books or creating other works of art became focussed on designing ways for the banks to screw their customers. I've simply never – and I've lived in six countries and dealt with a variety of financial institutions worldwide – encountered organisations so singularly and zealously dedicated to separating the customers from their money. My most recent theory is that all those pirates who fell overboard during coastal raids simply swam ashore and started banks. And the awful thing of it is that the Spanish have been exploited for so long they don't know anything different. They lie down and accept the most outrageous hammerings without a whimper. I pray there is that eighth ring of Hell where the Devil will consign the bankers together with the lawyers and – oh, I have my list.

I rang Fausto Milagro. We arranged to meet in Puerto Portals, a posh little marina port down on the southwest coast. Portals is one of the primary arenas here in which to play spectator. There are boutiques that sell the kind of clothes one otherwise only ever sees on the ambulatory sticks who walk the runways at clothes shows, and moored along the interior of the marina are the kind of boats that normally sit on chocks at boat shows to impress the plebs like me. And then, at least for the edification of all the men within sighting range, there are the apparently escaped showgirls – ah, such improbably cartoonly curved women – who adorn the yachts owned by the grizzled guys my age who've had tummy tucks and hair transplants and sport gold medallions, Rolexes, and bronze lamé thongs. I can't think of a more delightful way to spend a late afternoon than to find a ringside seat at one of the outdoor cafes and indulge my inner voyeur. And do I envy the *dueños* of the yachts their delectable quail? Well, I'd have to admit that an expandable part of me certainly does. But afterwards you'd have to *talk* to them, and that's a daunting prospect. So would I really want to *be* like those guys, trade lives with them? Most emphatically not. There is something pitiful about that anxious grasping after a season of life now past, a search for spring when the sun is already low and descending. Not me. Autumn has always been my favourite season – the bright crispness of it, the pungent overripeness and the cool threat of winter yet to come. It makes you savour what you've got, and reaching back to try to roll back Nature's Law is a fool's undertaking.

So I thought about the house up in Orient. Possibly Ruth might know something, or if Ruth didn't know,

Ruth would know someone who did. Ruth's like that. Small, intense, funny, and irredeemably Philadelphia in style despite many years in Spain and an improbable former career as a flamenco dancer, Ruth is now a single mother who earns her keep as a simultaneous translator and all around know-it-all. Ask anything – she'll know it or find it out. Better than a library. Faster than the Internet. Able to get to conclusions in a single bound.

I rang her on my mobile and, as a rarity, she was at home. We swapped banalities for awhile and flirted in a desultory manner. Ruth and I have lowered our eyelids at each other in a speculative way for years, knowing that in reality we'll never do anything about it. We tend to run into one another once or twice a year at school barbecues and the like, and stand around and chat while our respective children participate in the chaotic ferment of whatever activities are on tap. I suppose we enjoy it because we're both American and there are few of us Yanks left on the island, so it's a bit of a fix of home to use an almost forgotten vocabulary, let old intonations creep in, and make references to the cultural trivia of our youth. I asked her if she could find out about the house. Discreetly of course.

'Sure. I know a guy up there who does rentals. If he hasn't got it on his books, his cousin probably does. And I'll spin some yarn about a possible fatcat German buyer so they'll keep their traps shut.' That's Ruth. Got it in one.

'Can you do me a favour and follow up on it "toot sweet?" I'd really like to know who lives there.'

'Okay, I'll get on it. You're so mysterious sometimes, Will. You don't want to live up in that moribund movie set, do you?'

'Listen sister,' I said, putting on my improbable imitation of a Bogey accent – the one that usually comes out sounding like Vincent Price doing John Wayne – 'just cut the gab and get me the gaff.'

'Sure Chief, anything you say. I'll call you back.' She hung up.

Heading into Portals, I started looking for a parking place at the top of the hill, well before I got down into the marina itself. Punta Portals has been overtaken by its own success, and the proliferation of restaurants and shops around the marina has brought in far more traffic than the limited parking areas can bear. I feel sorry for those who live nearby, as half the time their access to their own homes must be blocked. I shoehorned Balthasar in between a Mercedes convertible and a pristine Porsche, which looked to have about nine miles on it. Last time I was down this way the Rolls/Bentley concessionaire had set up along the dock and was flogging his wares as though they were souvenir T-shirts. A little bit of the French Riviera come to Mallorca.

Fausto Milagro was seated outside the bistro at one of the restaurants with pretensions – fine food, numbing prices – again wearing civvies: suede jacket, polo shirt, light brown chinos, but soft riding boots this time instead of the loafers. He looked as if he belonged here, which is a talent some people have that I've always envied and never mastered. Maybe it's because I feel like such a phoney when I dress up that I never quite seem to have got the knack of blending in. Actually, truth told, I think I just lack style.

'Good of you to come.' He was even more the English gentleman today. 'Take a pew.'

'Nice to see you. Have you ordered yet?'

'No joy on that front so far.' I was mildly surprised. Waiters can ignore me for twenty minutes when I'm right under their noses, but Fausto looked the kind of money I'd have thought they'd immediately gravitate towards. I settled in and waved casually though without much hope at one of the black-suited minions lounging under the awning. Astonishingly, he came and took our order. Fausto must have paid our waiting dues. Waiters on this island are generally professional and helpful, but some in the tourist areas have become tainted by their exposure to us, and are inattentive or surly, which actually doesn't surprise me in the least when I see how some tourists treat the waiters, shouting at them in English or German, snapping their fingers, or complaining about perfectly edible and palatable food and then leaving without tipping. Sometimes I'm surprised so many of the serving personnel are as tolerant and longsuffering as they are.

'Do you have any news for me?' he asked, taking out a small leatherbound agenda and what looked like a gold Cross pen. He tugged a suede cuff, glanced at yet another gold accoutrement, a slim Piaget chronometer – at those prices they are no longer plain old watches – and glanced over my shoulder before looking at me and raising an eyebrow in an interrogatory way. I filled him in on my activities over the past day, leaving out my encounter with the dog, which had twinged my conscience as much as my shoulder. He listened attentively, made a few notes, and asked several questions about the boat. 'I'll ask a friend about that,' he said. 'He's a nautical type. Got a smashing bit of hardware here as a matter of fact. One of his companies brokers yachts, so I'll ask him about Holmes.'

'Without mentioning me, I hope.'

'Set your mind at rest, dear boy. Discretion is my stock in trade.' The public school accent seemed even more pronounced. I wondered how he fitted in with the general run of Guardia types. Spanish doesn't really have degrees of poshness or educatedness in terms of accent, only in usage and vocabulary. I wondered about Mallorquin. We finished our coffees – double the price they charge in my town – and parted, or rather I left and he stayed.

I walked along the quay, past the big indoor/outdoor bar restaurants that are fine venues for peoplewatching, and down along as far as the seawall. I wasn't sure why I was dawdling, but I'd picked up on something in Fausto's demeanour and without even thinking about it consciously I found myself circling back up to the walkway between two of the restaurants to a spot where I could look down unobserved at the table Fausto still occupied. Even as I watched, he glanced again in the direction in which he'd looked when we were talking, bent down to take a mobile phone from his briefcase, dialled a number and spoke briefly into the phone. Then he rose and walked out onto the quay that extends to the lighthouse. The next to last boat was a big schooner with an unusual seagreen paint job. Fausto waved to someone and went aboard up the gangway. I couldn't see much more from where I was and I didn't want to be seen hanging about. I figured the boat wasn't likely to sail away this very night and that I could probably satisfy my curiosity later, so I headed towards home, stopping briefly at the top of the hill to buy one of those scrumptious carrot cakes from the coffee shop there. Then I popped next door for a couple of dozen of the incomparable Cumberland sausages Tony Dunn, the English butcher, sells. They would cheer the children up.

By the time I got back Ruth had indeed rung and left her mobile number. I dialled her as I leafed through the pile of faxes that had come in. I love fax and email reservations; they make life so much easier. Not that I don't enjoy chatting with people who ring to book or make inquiries, but they always seem to ring when I'm just going out the door, or heading for the loo, or hungry. That's one of the few disadvantages of being a small, personal hotel with relatively few rooms; we don't have a large staff to put potential guests on hold for five minutes on an international call, or mix up their reservations, or forget to book their hire cars. It's all down to me to do it. Like the sign on the Chinese laundry: 'We don't tear your clothes with large machines, we do it carefully, by hand.'

'Well, did you find out? You've had two hours.' I like to rag her a bit about her vaunted efficiency.

'As a matter of fact I did, smartass,' came the tart reply. 'Jaime rented the house on behalf of a Mallorquin whose name he didn't mention to a Swiss sea captain name of Armand Martillo. Isn't that a lark – a *Swiss* sea captain. Must have trained with the Swiss navy. Anyway, he didn't know much more than that Martillo skippers a boat that's moored down at Portals. And apparently he's gone a lot in the winter, which is kind of odd, since most of those boats pretty much stay put wintertime and are out in the summer.'

'Nice job, Ruth,' I said. 'I'm grateful and no kidding. He didn't – I know it's a long shot – know the name of the boat, did he?'

'Come on, Will,' she shot back. 'Remember who you're talking to. I grilled him well-done and if he'd known, you'd know.' With a feisty snort she rang off.

So, as one of my old military instructors used to say, food for thought, old buddy, food for thought. Martillo skippers a boat in Portals, Milagro knows *somebody* on a boat in Portals, Holmes is in the boat business in Puerto Soller. Wouldn't mean a thing if Ninian's list hadn't sensitised me to the possible connections, the nautical connections. As for Captain Milagro, I'd follow Hannah's advice and try to get as much as I gave in future. Meantime, it would probably be wise of me to prepare for another encounter with the Guardia.

Son Ben had put together one of those unlikely teenage snack suppers of Mexican nachos with hot sauce and melted cheese, some cream cheese and *guindillas* – those curved green pickled peppers – toast rounds, a slice of pizza, spicy sausage rolls, and rice cakes, they being the only healthy element in an indigestible panoply of fartmaking comestibles. Wonderful! Nux Vom. here I come. I went to bed and, contrary to all the old wives' tales about the effects of such food, slept like a baby.

Eight

True to expectations, the Guardia rang at 8 a.m. to *invite* me – their ironically stressed word – for an interview with Commandant Vega promptly at 10 a.m. at their Palma headquarters, a palatial building I had known heretofore only from the outside. Some of the government buildings in the city are sumptuously opulent palaces dating mostly from the 18th century, and I've always supposed simply having the chance to be in them every day must constitute some small perk to the workers as an offset against the drabness of their pencilpushing jobs.

My imagination overtakes me each time I enter one of these ornate edifices agleam with polished sculptured marble, magnificent pendant chandeliers poised overhead as though awaiting only the lighting of the thousand candles that will illuminate the grand ballroom and set the turned brass balustrades glowing gently alongside the wide curved staircase seemingly constructed expressly to show off the broad trains of the silken gowns worn by the raven-tressed obsidian-eyed porcelain-skinned swellingly-bosomed Señoritas as they descend to extend diamond-dappled hands to their equally dark-eyed and handsome, dashing and sabreclad escorts.

You can tell I spent a large portion of my youth in cinemas.

So it comes as a slight jolt, even shudder, to have that vision, that dreamlike ghostly evocation of bygone splendour, dashed by the reality that now stands behind the lustrous portals – a drab brown metal desk personed by a slight, balding man in a nylon shirt, polyester tie, and an ill-fitting uniform above scuffed synthetic leather shoes. The void of discrepancy between what was before, what must have been so scintillatingly brilliant, and what exists today in these palaces – a reality so flat and pedestrian and dull – depresses and unnerves me.

Having presented my passport – just as in the old

dictator days one should not move a step in Spain without carrying adequate personal identification – I was directed along a seemingly interminable hall to Commandant Vega's office, where I knocked, was summoned, and entered.

The office was smaller than I had anticipated, lit by a single window far up in the rear wall, which is to say that the Commandant himself was in shadow but anyone he interviewed would be clearly framed in the light. This was obviously intentional, since the overhead fluorescent lamps were turned off. The room was strictly functional, almost bare of nonessentials. Apart from the plain pine desk, with two discoloured and distressed deal chairs in front of it, there was only a side table with a stack of files and an old-fashioned green metal filing cabinet. A square-framed photograph of a chesty horse was the only adornment.

I extended my hand as I came in, but the Commandant ignored it and stayed put in his chair. He was slim, in his indeterminate forties, olive-skinned with slicked-down dark hair and the ubiquitous Spanish moustache. His uniform was natty, his hands neat and well manicured. He looked at me appraisingly with intelligent eyes and waved me to a chair. He lit a cigarette but didn't offer me one, either because he already knew I don't smoke, or else simply to establish ascendancy.

'Señor Stock,' he said, without inflection. And then he just looked at me.

Two can play at that. 'Commandant Vega,' I said, copying his tone.

Then we sat and looked at one another. Many years ago when I was working my way though university selling encyclopedias door-to-door I learned a couple of sneakily effective tricks. My old sales boss used to swing his gold watch chain in blurry circles as he advised us, 'Ask a closing question and then SHUT UP! Whoever speaks first *loses*!'

So I just shut up. And we looked at one another. The second trick I learned is that when someone looks you in the eye with the intent to intimidate, to stare you down, never look back directly into his eyes. If you pick a spot in the middle of his forehead you can look at him all day long without strain. And so I did. The pressure in the room began to increase palpably. I didn't move, didn't shift my eyes, didn't speak or even twitch. Nor did he. But something had to break.

And break it did. 'So,' he rapped out. 'We must talk about this murder.' He had used his cigarette as an excuse to be the first to speak. It had burned down to the point where the ember had broken and dropped a grey furrow of ash onto his papers. He had dropped his eyes and flicked the detritus away, seemingly casually. My old sales manager would have been proud. The Commandant had lost the first round. Nevertheless, I thought it wise to be magnanimous.

'How can I be of help?' I asked, benignly.

'You can answer my questions fully and truthfully,' he said with an edge. I think he was used to winning these little games and it probably didn't sit well to have his ploy turned back on him, his gambit trumped. I'm sure there's some other kind of bridge term for doing whatever I'd done, but bridge has always been beyond me.

'Fire away,' I said, maintaining my sweet equanimity.

'Right.' he said, 'This is what I want to know.' He took me through the drill.

'How long did you know the decedent?' Nice word for a bloody bludgeoned corpse.

'About five years.'

'And you owed him money.' Attempting to be provocative.

'No.'

'Were you in dispute with him about anything?'

'I may be the only person on the island who wasn't.'

Watch your mouth, Will. You'll antagonise him. But he let it go.

'Do you know of any serious enemies?'

'No, actually not. Just lots of seemingly small disputes he was involved in.'

'What does that mean?'

'It means, as anyone who knew him will tell you, and some people probably already have, that Ninian had disputes with everybody, that he was ill-mannered, disputatious, litigious, and thoroughly unpleasant – God rest his soul.'

'Could you make a list of these people?'

'Yes, probably at least some of them, but other people could likely give you an even more complete list. I really didn't know him well.'

'But well enough for him to stay in your hotel?'

'As an exception, yes, but he'd never stayed with us before.'

'And he was never murdered before, either,' he said, demonstrating a touch of mordant dryness I hadn't given him credit for.

'Touché,' I said, lifting my eyebrows. I've always wanted to be able to raise just one of them, but only succeed in looking like a surprised chicken when I try.

'Did he owe *you* money?'

'No.'

'So you didn't owe him money, he didn't owe you money, you weren't in dispute with him about anything?'

'No.'

'But he came to your hotel while you were there, with seemingly few other people about, and within a few hours he was dead and you have no witnesses to give you any sort of alibi for the apparent time of death? Is that a fair summary?'

'Regrettably, yes.' I had tried to be jocular about the whole matter, tried to be above it, tried to act as though it really had nothing to do with me, but now I was beginning to realise how vulnerable I was, how flimsy were my defences, how bleak my prospects might be. If this man really wanted to put me away he could probably make a convincing circumstantial case, whether he could prove motive or not. Means and opportunity were certainly there to be stacked against my feeble protestations about lack of motive. My feelings must have shown on my face. The next question was surprisingly softly pitched.

'Señor Stock, who do you think killed this man?'

My answer was heartfelt. 'Please believe me, Commandant Vega, if I had the faintest idea I'd tell you. If I had a theory I'd try to persuade you. If I even thought I could deflect you to someone else, I'd probably try. I take it that seriously.' The Guardia doth make cowards of us all.

The intelligent eyes glittered. 'I'm going to choose to believe you. Let me tell you what I am going to do, Señor Stock. I am going to let you go free for now. I am not even going to take your passport away, or book you on suspicion, or fingerprint you, or question you further. But I want you to listen, to ask around, to find out what you can. It is, after all, in your own interests, and you can go places in the foreign community where I cannot. Will you do that?'

Will a thirsty man refuse water? He was asking me to be a spy for him, much as Captain Milagro had asked. I grasped the lifeline.

'I would be pleased to cooperate. I realise I can only help myself by helping you.' And never were such hypocritical words more genuinely meant.

'*Trato hecho*,' he said. 'It is agreed. You will call me if you have anything to tell me. And you will also realise that this arrangement,' he paused and cleared his throat, 'is just between us. You see what I mean?'

'Yes, I see what you mean.' Weasel words on my part. I saw what he meant all right, but I wasn't strictly, technically, agreeing to it, was I? Or was I simply asking for trouble by playing cute with him? I'd decide later. I covered by extending my hand and this time he took it.

'You realise you are still our prime suspect,' he said. 'So far you have no alibi, nothing to exonerate you, and I must warn you that despite my conviction of your probable innocence, I shall not hesitate to arrest you if the exigencies and requisites of this case so predicate.' Educated Spanish people actually talk that way. Being closer to Latin roots than we are via old French, they use what we think of as fancy words in a generally everyday – they would say 'quotidian' – manner.

'Be in touch,' he said.

'Yes, of course,' I replied. I turned and left, and as I cleared the door a weight of tension dissipated that I didn't even know I was harbouring. But I still felt piggy-in-the-middle.

Nine

Before heading back I decided to take a walk and think things through. The new pedestrian path along the sea now runs for several miles from the west side of the Bay of Palma, that is to say the far end of the inner city by the ferry port, all the way out to the old fishing port of Molinar, and beyond. It's a good walk, usually for me a tranquillising walk, with the sea nuzzling at the rocks below, murmuring and soughing, exercising its pacifying influence on the mind. My internal decision tree was sprouting a number of buds – mine sometimes seems like a Busy Lizzie – and I needed to think about my next steps.

Commandant Vega had given me a respite, but I was under no illusions that he wouldn't carry through on his threat to incarcerate me if no other credible suspect came to light. I was mildly surprised, in view of Fausto Milagro's characterisation of him, that he had turned out to be, from my point of view, so very reasonable. But then, perhaps Milagro didn't know him well, or perhaps he had – more in keeping with Hannah's theory – his own agenda.

What was perfectly clear to me was that I'd need to do what both Milagro and Vega were pushing me to do – get out and get more information. With something concrete in hand I could follow my own dictates with regard to whom to give it and how I would proceed. What also seemed clear was that both policemen felt out of their depth in trying to tackle the task of squeezing information out of the foreign community. Despite Fausto Milagro's polish, perfect English, and wide acquaintanceship in the English sector of the island, he seemed to feel I might be able to go places and pursue avenues of enquiry that were possibly closed to him. Commandant Vega obviously felt the same way. In that sense, all of our interests overlapped.

The most important goal for me right now, this very day, was to find someone with a strong motive to have eliminated Ninian. That would take me off the hook. It would cut my risk immensely of being caught without a chair when the music stopped if I could halfway credibly direct the Guardia's attention elsewhere. Unless, of course – a fretful internal voice piped up to remind me – I began to get too close to the real killer, and he found out about it and decided to eliminate *me*. Sometimes I wish that paranoid inner person would just shut up and go away, though in this case I couldn't fault his logic. No doubt he had my best interests at heart. Anyway, I'd do a Scarlett O'Hara and think about that one tomorrow. Right now what I needed to do was track leads.

By this time, with ample pauses for woolgathering, rubbernecking at the comely boats in the bay, ogling a pair of equally comely German blondes who passed on bicycles, and consulting with my stomach regarding lunch, I found myself on the outskirts of Es Molinar. There are two fine fish restaurants in Molinar, and possibly more; I haven't yet discovered the others. Both are famous among a small circle of cognoscenti, if that isn't some kind of contradiction in terms. Both are small, unpretentious, and simply serve simply prepared simply wonderfully fresh fish. For the most part you can have it either grilled or grilled – no fooling around here with fancy sauces or artful garnishes. Simple, you might think, just to take a fish and grill it, but it ain't as easy as it seems. Different fish require different treatment, different cooking times, temperatures, degrees of moisture, proximity to the fire. Simple is sometimes the most difficult, and both cooks know what they're doing.

I opted for a light lunch at the first one I came to and was rewarded for my decision, though no doubt I'd have felt the same way if I'd opted for the other. Which reminded me, whimsically, of an experience I'd had once when travelling in Ireland. Finding myself hungry in a tiny hamlet, I was confronted with a choice between two alehouses offering lunch. A local stood nearby and so I asked which of the two had better food. 'Well,' he said, scratching the stubble on his chin. 'Put it this way. If you eat at the one you'll wish you'd ate at t'other.'

I'd pretty well decided I needed to solicit help from Hazel. If Fausto Milagro's surmise regarding Ninian's purchase of bugging equipment was true, it just might be he'd stumbled into something that had turned out to be inconvenient for whomever he'd bugged, and in turn fatally inconvenient for Ninian. A knock-on effect, so to speak. I rang her and set up another meeting, this time at the restaurant, during the break between lunch and dinner. She'd apparently gone back to work as a way of taking her mind off things. Of course, I didn't say why I wanted to meet with her – better, I felt, to bring it up in person. At this point I didn't even know if she knew about the bugging operation. Ninian didn't strike me as the sort who would have confided in her about such things, though I could be wrong.

About this time another present thought tapped me on my mental shoulder. The police – a glaring oversight on their part – hadn't asked about any telephone calls Ninian might have made from the suite. The records, if there were any, would be in the hotel computer.

I rang the hotel and got Semiramis, our able relief manager. She's a bountiful gift from heaven for me, as she's totally overqualified for the job we have for her and really only does it for fun part-time and because she loves the hotel. One of the great luxuries I have is an able staff to take the pressure off when I'm away, or out chasing rainbows. Or murderers.

I asked Semiramis to see if Ninian had made any calls after arriving, and waited on the line while she checked our computer call monitor. She came back to say, yes, he indeed had made two calls. My little black heart went pitty pat at the news. Then I asked the 64,000 dollar question: were the calls to his home or to the restaurant? Or somewhere else? She of course didn't know, nor did I recognise the numbers offhand when she gave them to me, so again I waited while she looked them up in the telephone book.

As a digression, I must remark that I usually try to get Semiramis, someone who grew up on the island and knows the system, to look up numbers in the phone book. I can never find anything. The alphabetical listings are by town – common practise and not unreasonable save that the island is so relatively small – and so you need to know not only the names of the people you are ringing, but where they live. But that's not all you need to know, as it may be that the listings are in the name of whomever originally contracted for the telephone back in 1958, or whenever. It's inconvenient and costly to change a listing, and since everybody knows Paco is actually listed under his mother-in-law's maiden name – at least anyone who *possibly* might want to get in touch with him – there is clearly no point in Paco taking the trouble to have the listing put in his own name. And to confuse things further, the towns on the island may or may not be listed under their own names; they may in fact be listed under the nearest larger town in the district. So the result of all this is that sometimes when you need to call a mechanic to fetch your broken-down car, an experience I've had more than thrice, you need to know that Tomeo's Garage isn't listed under Tomeo, or even Garage, but rather under Pedro's Tyre Repair Centre, which it was originally, some years ago. Of course all the locals know these things, and they look at you with some degree of incredulity when you complain. Why would anyone even use the phone book, they no doubt ask. Why not just ask Miguel next door who has it all written down on his calendar because he, too, has a dodgy old rustmobile and needs to call Tomeo regularly? Drives me crazy and enchants me in equal measure, depending on how urgent is my need.

Semiramis knows the system, however, and always gets the number.

It turned out that Ninian's calls had been neither to his home, nor the restaurant. So now I at least had a couple of numbers to investigate, and perhaps they'd provide a thread to tie to a string to attach to a lead to hitch to a hangman's noose.

There was an hour before my meeting with Hazel. I walked back into the old town and across the winding pedestrianised streets to the Sa Nostra foundation museum, where there was an exhibition of Rembrandt etchings. Another thing I love about this island is that you can actually see what's on show; nothing is ever so crowded you can't get close enough to enjoy it. Some years ago I was in Tokyo and heard there was to be an exhibition of paintings from the Hermitage in St. Petersburg – Leningrad, as it was in those days. In my innocence I thought I might amble along and take a gander at some of the pictures, but when I arrived there were more people than I think actually lived in Tokyo. Organised by those uniformed pushers they clearly had recruited from the underground stations, we went past the paintings in a lockstep queue, crushed breathless, never pausing, like baggage on an airport carousel. What a way to look at paintings. And I even had some height advantage. At 6'1" I at least could see something. There was a tiny wizened woman nearby who probably only had a view of armpits.

So I've given up on all the blockbuster art shows in the great capitals of the world. Better a half hour with some lesser works, comprehensively viewed, than two hours in the scrum in Washington or Paris, trying to get a minimal view of a Vermeer admired in reproduction for a lifetime but now with all possible enjoyment spoilt by the jostle and the noise and the distraction of hundreds, even thousands, of other people intent on the same thing. Unmitigated snob that I am, of course, I want them all just to go home and let me enjoy the pictures all by myself. Dream on.

Promptly at 4:30 I rapped on the glass front door at Ninian's – now Hazel's – restaurant and Manuel shot the bolt back and let me in. Manuel was looking tired and strained, probably because so much of the weight of responsibility for the restaurant had passed to him with Ninian's demise.

'Hallo Meester Stock. Hew are good today?' Manuel always insists on speaking English to me, and although we've been trading pleasantries for several years, and I know he does the same with other people, his command of the language never seems to improve. Or perhaps I'm being unkind. It may be his accent. Some people manage to make a foreign accent charming, some just sound like a caricature. Poor Manuel is among the latter group.

'Hi yam getting Missus Meeed for hew,' he said, ducking his head and disappearing into the back, skulking away like a dog caught chewing on the Sunday roast. I wondered if he'd got himself in hot water with Hazel. Probably now that Ninian was gone the dynamic between them had changed. Well, 'whatever,' as my cyberteen daughter says. I didn't feel like speculating about other people's equivocal relationships.

Hazel came out in a minute or so. She looked slightly better than when we'd last met, but still had a pinched look as though two large hands had taken hold of all the hair and skin at the sides of her head and drawn them sideways, squinching her features into a reflection from a fun fair distorting mirror. I apologised for disturbing her, but told her I needed to talk about something that couldn't wait. We adjourned to a table over by the wall.

'Have the police been here yet?' I asked.

'No, why would they come here? They talked to me at home.'

'So no one's been here nosing around the restaurant?'

'No, Will. No one official anyway. Why?' There was

a note of impatience in her voice.

'Look, Hazel, this will sound stupid, but Ninian apparently was involved in something – something the police know a little about, but not enough yet to justify swooping in here with a search warrant. I hate to break this to you so soon, but I want to help, and I think I may be in a better position to try to fend them off than you are.' This was only halfway misleadingly hypocritical on my part, I thought. I truly did want to help, but didn't see any reason to tell her it was more to get myself off the hook for Ninian's murder than to prevent inconvenience to her.

'Well, of course I assumed he was involved in *something*,' she said with a sharp note of asperity. 'Why else would anybody kill him?' A valid point, and one which highlighted the fatuousness of my comment.

'I have to tell you something I didn't tell the police. I found a key to a postbox and I thought I'd best check it, and … well, here. This is yours now, I guess.' And I handed her the packet of money.

She looked shocked when she realised what it was. 'Money?' she said, colouring. 'He hid money? That bastard didn't need money. And this is what he got himself killed for?' She threw the envelope down on the table with a gesture of disgust.

'*Calma, calma,*' I said. You don't know for certain that was the reason he was killed. He skimmed money off the take here, didn't he? I thought everybody in the restaurant trade did.'

'Yes, I suppose he did,' she said, in a way that led me to conclude she knew damned well he did. 'I just didn't know where he kept it.' My private assumption was that it was *she* who did most of any money skimming that had been going on.

'So this could be *legitimate* black money, then,' I said. 'As opposed to *crooked* black money.' In countries in the Mediterranean this is a recognised distinction. Not paying tax on income is one thing, theft or fraud is something else.

'Yes, I suppose so.' She said it grudgingly. I suspected she was surprised that Ninian would have been able to hide so much from her. By now, I was beginning to be convinced that in fact the money, given the variety of the notes and denominations, must have come from some other source, blackmail perhaps, but I wasn't going to mention that to her, nor was I going to mention, at least just yet, the list.

'So you don't know what he was involved in?' I asked.

'No, I don't,' she grated angrily, but with tears forming at the same time. 'Do you?'

'Let's simply take it from what I *do* know, but don't know if *you* know,' I said, trying to get down to practicalities. 'Do you know about the bugs in this restaurant?' The look on her face signalled that I'd put my foot in it.

'What bugs?' she began to splutter, looking down at the floor. 'And what in the world…?'

'Not *those* kind of bugs,' I cut her off. 'The listening kind.' Now it seemed I had totally baffled her. She was struggling to catch up. 'You know, the *eavesdropping* kind,' I finally said, and saw light dawn.

'Oh those,' she said. 'What about them?' What did she mean by that? That she knew about them generally, or that she knew about the ones Ninian had put into the restaurant?

'Did you know there's one operating here?'

'What? Here? A microphone? Where?' Either she genuinely didn't know or was a better actress than I gave her credit for being.

'Yes, here, a mike. And the police know about it. I think the only reason they haven't come around yet is that they can't tie it specifically to Ninian's death. They'd probably need a warrant for a fishing expedition like that.' I was using my tough guy know-it-all voice, the persona that had seen the movies and read the thrillers.

'But – but what should I do?' There was a sudden switch in her tone. She looked up at me from under her lashes. Now *this* was a Hazel I'd never seen before, the fluffy little girl appealing to big strong Daddy. No thank you. I wasn't buying in on that one.

'Let's go look for it,' I said, rising. Action Man would be all right, Daddy never. I headed for the back of the restaurant. 'Which table did Ninian generally use?

'Oh, he didn't have any particular favourite. No, actually, he liked that one by the window.' I somehow didn't think that one was it.

'What about those two booths over in the corner?'

'Yes, lots of businessmen have meetings at those. They're a bit quieter.' Either of them looked likely.

'Which one did Ninian seat people in more often – those businessmen you mentioned?'

'Usually the right hand one.'

We practically bumped heads as we both got down simultaneously to look under the table. There was a moment when we both scanned fruitlessly, and then – bingo, we both saw it at once. A round black button stuck to the bottom of the tabletop all the way back against the partition wall, with a thin white cord that went out of sight through a small hole in the wall. There wasn't much light, but we could plainly see the device and the wire leading from it.

'Where does that go?' I asked, pointing to the wire.

'Back into the kitchens,' she said. 'Near the cupboards.'

We walked to the kitchen door, pushed through it, and followed back along the wall on the opposite side. I paced off what I thought was the approximate distance and then checked the wall. Sure enough, the slim white lead came through and then down and then ran along the skirting board until it reached a set of cupboards. It was plain enough to see, but anyone noticing it would probably assume it was a telephone wire.

Hazel opened the cupboard. It housed pans. We could see all the way back to the wall on the upper shelves, but when we went to check the bottom shelf, removing two big aluminium pots, we could see there was a panel between the shelf and the wall. I bent over to see if it was loose, and sure enough, it lifted right out, revealing a paperback-sized silver recorder and a small electronic console, both attached to the wall with dull brown masking tape secured by drawing pins. A bit of a bodge job of mounting, but seemingly secure enough for Ninian's purposes. There was no indicator light illuminated on either the console or the cassette recorder so I assumed they were off. Maybe they were activated by voice, maybe with a remote. I popped the lid and thumbnailed out the cassette. The machine had a label on the bottom identifying it as an Olympus L250. It looked like an unamplified model, and had a jack for an earphone monitor on playback. There seemed no immediate way to try it out, but I didn't want to play it here anyway.

'Do you have a cassette player?' I asked Hazel.

'Not here. At home,' she said. And then she burst into tears, but tears of anger, not grief. 'God damn his eyes!' she hissed. 'God damn his greed and his stupidity and his selfishness! And God damn whoever killed him!' She turned and strode away. 'You take the God damned tape, Will. I don't want to know anything about it.' And she left me standing there, the cassette in my hand.

I felt eyes, and looked up. Manuel was on the other side of the kitchen, looking at me expressionlessly. We hadn't noticed him, or at least I hadn't when Hazel and I came in. As our eyes met, there was a fleetingly hostile cast to his expression, fear or even anger perhaps at having been deserted by his *ersatz* father, the abusive dominant figure who was now gone from his life. Then, hurriedly, he turned away and busied himself with a bowl he had on the counter next to him, shutting me out. I pocketed the tape, shoved the panel back in place and restored the pots to the shelf. I didn't think there would be any point in trying to talk to Manuel so I simply left the kitchen, let myself out the front door, and drove home.

For once, I put my curiosity on hold and decided I'd had enough intrigue for the day. I rang the children to confirm, with pedantic fatherly reiteration, that they had indeed finished their homework. 'Yes, finished,' goes my litany. 'Everything done, nothing left to do and nothing you're hoping to do in the car tomorrow morning on the way to school. Finished means finished, OK?' But after the heavy father routine I then went over to the flat to curl up with them to watch, yet again, *Singing In The Rain*. And yet again, we all laughed in all the usual places.

Ten

Schweitzerdeutsch! Bloody *Swiss* German. I was listening to the cassette we'd recovered from Ninian's recording device. For most purposes my German is pretty good – grammatical and fairly educated even if a tad thin in the vocabulary department – but I couldn't make diddly squat out of the Swiss dialect I was hearing, or rather not even hearing very well since the mike was muffled by the thickness of the table and there was obviously a lot of ambient noise in the restaurant. I barely could make out the odd word here and there.

Not that I had expected to hear state secrets, mind you, or at least not many *important* state secrets, but the presence of the bugging equipment had argued for the possibility that Ninian had been eavesdropping on something seriously shady, that he had tried to put the squeeze on the wrong people, and that he had been mutated, as his comeuppance, from being a busybody into being a dead body.

The problem of the *Schweitzerdeutsch*, however, was capable of solution. Kurt, a Swiss friend, runs a nearby restaurant – called 'El Suizo', the Swiss Chef, (and very good, I might add) – and he no doubt would be prepared to interpret for me, though of course there was a moral dilemma involved. If it turned out to be dangerous knowledge – perhaps that *little* knowledge that's supposed to be so dangerous – then I'd be wrong to involve him. It might have been Ninian's knowledge of the information on this tape that had led to his death, though somehow I doubted it, as he hadn't spoken a word of German, much less its gnomic derivative. Nevertheless, the tape might contain a piece of relevant information, and if I were able to parse even enough to know what the subject matter was, then I could make a decision as to whether to involve Kurt or not. To my unhappiness and discomfiture, no matter how hard I listened I couldn't even remotely guess whether they were discussing the weather, or dinner plans, or stock market prices. Or when and how to kill Ninian.

Of course, foreign languages can do that to you – create curiosity inappropriately. I can remember when I first came to Europe and encountered all these people who said things I couldn't understand, and so I thought whatever it was they were saying must be of great pith and moment, trenchant wit, huge interest and penetrating wisdom. So I worked hard and studied some of those languages, only to find, once I was able to eavesdrop with reasonable ease, conversations like this:

'So I said to her, "Well I never," and she said, "Well you wouldn't believe it, would you?" And I said, "Not in a million years," and then she said she'd tell her mother-in-law, and I said, "Oh no, you better not," and she said she would anyway.'

To which her friend replies, 'Well I never.'

Blah, blah, blah.

Still, it's nice to be able to order in foreign restaurants and know you haven't just ordered tripe and ice cream, or to be able to ask the way to the train station when you've worn out your welcome wherever you've been.

On reflection, I thought I'd go ahead and ask Kurt to give me some help with the tape. It might be putting his head on the block, but I was sure he'd understand. In both senses.

Meantime, I could follow up on seeing who might be on the end of the phones Ninian had rung just before he met his Untimely. Semiramis had printed them out from the computer, so I had them even if the police didn't.

I contemplated my options. The tape had recorded a Swiss man, two Swiss-speaking men in fact, and that pointed to the distinct probability one of them was Captain Martillo. I now knew he lived in Orient, but I couldn't figure out what to do with that information.

Staking out the house would be pointless and time consuming, though at least I might find out what he looked like. But in that tiny hamlet it couldn't be done at all discreetly, so the notion was a non-starter. Taking a look at that boat Fausto had gone aboard was a more appealing idea. At least hanging about in Portals would be more entertaining than watching the house in Orient, and I'd be lots less likely to be detected.

Ultimately, neither possibility appealed. I wanted some action, not just to be a passive observer. I dialled the first number on the slip Semiramis had given me. A bloody sports results recorded service. Just like Ninian, probably checking on the Croatian basketball team's results. So I tried the second one, apparently an Alcudia number from the prefix. It was answered on the second ring.

'Gewürz Associates,' said the female voice.

'I'm not sure I have the right number here,' I said. 'It's handwritten and hard to read. What does your company do?'

'We're a printing company,' she said. 'Speciality print and design.'

I wasn't sure where to go from here. 'And the man in charge? Who's he?'

'Señor Gewürz. What are you asking, actually?' She wasn't suspicious, but beginning to run out of patience with dumb questions.

'Well, it's a personal matter. Friend of a friend sort of thing. I'm not actually sure I've got the number right. Where are you?'

'We're in Alcudia, in the Vistamar building near the port, just down from the Roman theatre.' I knew where it was, a bland, dreary, white concrete block.

'Yes, I've been there.'

'Do you want to make an appointment?' she asked, warming into helpful mode.

'Actually, I think maybe I have the wrong phone

number after all. I'm not sure if I've got the right person written down. I'll need to check it out. Maybe I'll let you know tomorrow.' Like hell, I'd be down there like a shot.

'Well thank you for calling Gewürz Associates. Have a nice day,' on an upward, lilting note. She must have learned that one in America. We rang off mutually.

I buzzed Hannah over at the flat and asked if she could cover for me at the hotel. We have wonderful staff, but don't like to leave them completely to their own devices, so we keep at least one senior person here all the time. Then I drove by Kurt's restaurant to drop off the cassette, a copy I'd made. The original I'd put in the safe along with my written-out copy of Ninian's list. Not that I didn't trust my memory, but if somebody decided to rip off my arm and beat me over the head with the bloody stump, as my sweet Irish grandmother used to threaten, then I at least wanted somebody else to have the clues, most especially if Fausto Milagro turned out to be other than what he appeared to be.

It's about a twenty-five minute drive from here to the north coast if you keep on the main road. No dawdling about today. I pulled up on the narrow street that ran above the tasteless, characterless Vistamar building and strolled around to the front. Happily for me, Gewürz Associates was on the ground floor, with a large plate glass window that allowed me to see inside in spite of the vertical blinds hanging to shade against our 335 days a year of sun. I strolled on by.

The layout was fairly standard – display window on the left, entrance door on the right, a customer counter inside, a half dozen or so grey metal desks with computers on them, presumably Macs if they were doing any kind of sophisticated graphic work. Four fresh-faced and wholesome young women and a plump fortyish man were at the desks, and a stylishly-turned-out young blonde was seated behind them at a desk in front of a glassed-in private office with its shades drawn. I thought she was probably the girl I'd spoken to. At the back of the room I could see two further doors, one of them leading into a workroom where a press was rotating monotonously, and another to a room where I assumed they stored their paper and supplies. Rounding the corner to the right into the alleyway that ran alongside the building, I saw a heavy, oversized door for deliveries. I crossed the street and sat on a low wall watching the building for awhile, munching an *empanada*, one of those savoury meat and pea pies the Mallorquins make so well. The pastry is light and flaky and the innards peppery and filling. I opened the paperback thriller I'd taken as a prop to justify my presence on the wall.

Gewürz's shop seemed reasonably busy, though in my first twenty minutes of observation I saw few walk-in customers. Probably most of the projects were for small businesses. I was trying to work out a safe approach to get inside and look around, maybe spin some tale about a new brochure or price list. My absolute dream option would be to have a private snoop, but there didn't seem much chance of getting that opportunity; they weren't just all going to go out to lunch and leave the door open for me, were they? As for breaking in, I didn't even know how to begin thinking about it. Force was out of the question and I'd tried once in my life to use a credit card to open a locked door and had only succeeded in ruining the card. And though the idea of picking locks has always appealed to the romantic renegade side of me, a locksmith had told me once it was stacks harder than the fictional private eyes make it out to be, and besides, I hadn't even a nail file with me, much less a picklock. I thoughtfully gnawed on my hangnail until I got it to bleed, another smart move.

The whole journey was beginning to seem like something of a footless waste of time when a van pulled up in the alleyway to make a delivery. The driver walked around to an intercom box on the wall outside the door, pressed the bell, muttered something into the box and was buzzed inside. The door swung out and he propped it on a kickstand that was mounted on it, as they are on motorcycles, or on those horrible buzzy motorbikes one hears everywhere on the island and which so remind me that in a few small ways we are still in the third world here, despite the superficial facade of first worldness everyone tries to cultivate.

I had an idea. The Watergate burglars had taught me at least one trick. Quickly, I got up and walked back to my car. In the glovebox was a roll of duct tape, that indispensable adhesive material that holds the universe together. I tore off a strip and palmed it. Then I nipped back along to the end of the alleyway where the van had entered and sauntered down, trying to time my arrival at the back of the van just as the driver entered the building wheeling another trolleyload of stacked paper. Then, the moment he was safely inside, I circled around to the edge of the door, slapped the piece of tape over the catch, and swiftly retreated back around the van and on along to the street. I didn't think anyone had seen me.

Back on the low wall, I kept my head down but an eye on the side door. As I'd hoped, when the driver finished he just nudged up the kickstand and let the door swing shut of its own weight. Now all I had to do was hope there weren't any more deliveries before lunch, hope that no one stayed in for lunch, hope that the tape held, hope that no one saw me go in if I could get in, hope that no one saw me once I was inside, and – small matter – hope I could find something instantly incriminating among all the paper in a print shop. Some hopes.

It seemed to me a small coffee was called for. A small coffee is often called for. The television set in the bar nearby was showing a bizarre programme in which people in blue costumes lined up to try to carry buckets of water along a rubber walkway underneath which people in red costumes lay on their backs and tried to kick the people in the blue costumes through the rubber so they would spill the water before reaching the other end of the walkway to empty the buckets into a barrel. This process involved much slipping and falling and sliding and tumbling and at times some wincingly brutal kicks from below when the bucketcarriers fell onto the walkway rather than down four feet onto the hard floor. Only a sadist and a masochist in tandem, I thought, could have dreamed up the game, though the studio audience apparently found it hilarious. I didn't notice much hilarity in the bar, however, part of that larger audience for whom the programme ostensibly was made.

Finally I couldn't avoid the moment any longer. It was ten minutes into the shop's lunch break. I walked back down the street, checked the inside of the shop through the glass of the door, and then rapped hard on the glass as though I were a late arriving customer hoping to find someone still on duty. No response, all empty and deserted in there. Ignoring the effervescent tingling in my stomach and a persistent dry lump in my throat, I walked quickly around into the alleyway as though I were impatient with the lack of response from inside, went straight to the door and tugged on the handle. It opened easily. I slid inside, calling out as I shut the door behind me. Still no response. It seemed I was alone.

Bypassing the stockroom and the machine room, I went directly to the small private office. Surely if anything were to be found, that's where it would be. It was, thank goodness, unlocked. I checked to see that the blinds were all the way down, turned on the light, stepped back outside to see how lightproof they were – sufficiently, I thought, if I didn't waste too much time – and went back inside to rootle around.

Opened envelopes on the top of the desk were addressed to Herr Heinz Gewürz, so now I had a full name, though I still wasn't sure he was the man I was after. Theoretically, any of the people I'd seen, or indeed someone I hadn't yet seen, might be the person whom Ninian had rung, but somehow I didn't think so; the staff all seemed to have that faintly apparatchik look about them that appeared indicative of a lack of involvement or commitment. I couldn't precisely articulate my reasons but I'd have bet against any of them being involved in whatever had led to Ninian's murder. About Gewürz I had another feeling entirely. There was something of money about the various envelopes on the desk, thick watermarked paper for the private communications and an array of substantial bills from fancy shops. His American Express bill was truly impressive. Gewürz also seemed to be doing some building somewhere on the island, and if I know anything, I know how stupefyingly expensive building work is here. It somehow didn't seem that this small shop, busy though it might be, could support the lifestyle implied by these bills. I looked in all the drawers, all of which were open and manifestly disorganised. Gewürz was not a tidy soul. Then I checked the file drawers, also unlocked, also disordered. If he was hiding something I began to fear that it wasn't here. I checked my watch, twenty-seven minutes and counting. Theoretically I had plenty of time, but I've been undone by theory before.

I pushed back from the desk and looked underneath. It was a kneehole affair and there was a space at the front with a shallow shelf. An antique-looking wooden box reposed innocently on the shelf. I drew it out. Locked, but for once my luck was in regarding locks. It was one of those old-fashioned locks requiring only a single or double web key. Maybe I could fool it with that universal tool, the paperclip. Probably there would be nothing of interest, for who would leave anything valuable or incriminating in a box so easily breachable? But then perhaps Gewürz was sloppy, or arrogant, or overconfident. Or, on the other hand, maybe he had nothing to hide.

It took about two full minutes, longer than I'd thought it would, though I was being ultracareful not to scratch the lockplate or damage the ward inside. I ended up having to braid three paperclips together to get something strong enough not to bend. When I finally lifted the lid I could see a neat pile of a half dozen so separate bundles of papers and certificates. I lifted out the top one. Ship's papers – certificates of sale, of seaworthiness, of engine tests, of registration in the Turks and Caicos Islands, of insurance through a bank in those same islands, and a certification that the boat was free of liens against it. I glanced quickly through the other bundles, all the same, just different boats. I scanned the names of the boats and then put the papers back without examining them further. I was beginning to get a feeling I ought to be out of there.

Thirty or so seconds was all it took to relock the box and get it back in place. I had a quick go at tidying the desk but abandoned the effort as pointless since it had been so untidy to begin with. Excessive neatness would be a tip-off that someone had been there. Then I flipped the light off, took a quick peek to see that the front door was clear, and walked briskly back through the stockroom and out the door, ripping off the strip of duct tape as I went. Again, no one seemed to see me. That area's a fairly quiet place in the off-season. Thank you, Lady L.

Once in the car and a mile away, I pulled over in a quiet turnoff to mull things over. I was feeling pretty chuffed with myself. Will Stock the cat burglar. But when I put my hands out in front of me they were shaking with delayed reaction. Maybe I wasn't quite as cool as I thought. But then again maybe I had a few answers, so perhaps I could indulge myself with a mini-pat of pride after all. Gewürz seemed to own – though in fact I hadn't actually seen his name on any of the ship's papers – at least six boats of some substantial size, all registered in a tax haven. Maybe he had them chartered out. That would explain the income he seemed to have. And if they were registered in the Turks and Caicos Islands I had few illusions he was declaring the income from them. The next question was where he might have got the money to buy them, assuming it wasn't inherited wealth, which I figured to be another long shot. But how did any of it tie in to Ninian, unless he had somehow found out about the illegal boat income and decided to cut himself in on some of it, a form of extortion of which I could believe Ninian capable. Sight unseen, I moved Gewürz to the top of my suspect list.

Now all I had to do was prove he was the perp, as they say on TV.

Before heading back, I decided to drop in on Dorrie. She lives in Puerto Pollensa, which is my favourite of the towns in that area. The bay was misty today, with a pale sun golden through haze, the few boats on the horizon looking like Lowry smears against the water.

Dorrie has lived in Puerto Pollensa for many years, in a greenshuttered square sandstone house almost at the water's edge. I parked along the quay opposite the La Lonja restaurant and walked past the row of little shops and restaurants in the pedestrianised section, up along the path under the pines that hem the shoreline. Dorrie's house is a third of a mile or so along.

I'd never really believed in love at first sight, despite growing up on a diet of the sort of unadulterated kitsch that Hollywood ground out in my youth – still does, actually. But when I met Dorrie I was instantly smitten. She looked at me from humorous eyes set over wonderful bones, soft wavy hair piled up on her head Gibson Girl style, and I felt something I'd never felt before – a sense of understanding and being understood, a sense that I didn't need to talk too much to explain myself, or justify myself or aggrandise myself. I only needed to *be* myself, and in not needing to be other than myself, I was of course all the more the best of myself.

And to add to this revelation, she clearly felt the same way about me. Dorrie had never married, though when I met her I was still in a relationship. She has never ceased to surprise me, and not always just relative to our shared tastes in music and literature, art and architecture. About the time we met I'd recently completed my training for a private pilot's licence, and was feeling pleased with my newly certificated aerial prowess. 'Oh, I used to like to fly, too,' said Dorrie, and hauled out some photos and press cuttings. It turned out that when she was younger she'd been a real life helldiving barnstorming shoot 'em up aerobatic champion; the kind who do those horrifying corkscrew twisting stomachchurning loopdeloops and kamikaze dives. And that was before breakfast. Well, it'd better have been.

Dorrie had done it all: travelled the world, lived in a tent in the Arctic, broken bread and various unmentionables with nomads, shared confidences with the mighty. But never did she reveal any part of her former life for purposes of self-advertisement or ego inflation. She's never tried for moral ascendancy in our relationship, nor indeed played any of the other small games that so confuse and complicate human relationships, especially those between men and women. She is simply true and real and warm and giving and quintessentially herself.

I took her hand and we walked slowly down, as we usually do, to the bench set under the pine tree that leans over the edge of the bay. Cats' tongues of miniature waves licked at the stony shin of the shoreline. The low sun warmed us without overheating. The path behind us was largely deserted save for a few intrepid older winter holiday couples making the gravel-crunching walk along the bayside. As usual, we said little, just enjoying the changes in the light, the shapes of the boats, the mirroring reflections on the water and the profile of the headlands. After a half hour or so I felt the sensation of empty tranquillity Dorrie evokes in me, as though I'd meditated for a long time in some holy place. She needs do no more than be and I am hers. I love her.

Each moment we spend together is precious to me, though the shape of my life dictates that these moments are too few. So I treasure them and hug them to my heart, since I know the relationship is finite, for although we both would have it otherwise, we cannot stand aside from the central overriding reality that Dorrie is eighty-seven years old.

Eleven

'Wake up, Stupid!' The inner voice was my own, a more awake and aware self scolding the sleeping one trapped in a dream, struggling towards consciousness through cobwebs and treacle. The phone kept on ringing. Finally I flung an arm out from the duvet, fumbled the receiver onto my upper ear and managed a cheerful voice totally discrepant from my true state of awareness. 'Stock's Hotel. How can I help you?' It was probably another bloody American, calling from Chicken Prairie, Iowa, or East Overshoe, Ohio. I get 'em all.

'Will? Is that you, Will?' Hazel's voice. Reality began to sink its fangs into my mind.

'Yes, it's me. What time is it?' It was still pitch black and the clock is on the other side of the bed.

'I'm sorry to wake you, but I had to talk to you.' She didn't sound the least bit sorry.

'Right. Give me a second to get myself *compos mentis*.' I shook myself half out of the cover, snaked a hand over to switch on the light, sneaking a look at the clock – 4 a.m. – and suddenly became aware of a strong urge to pee. 'OK, *que pasa*, what's going on?'

'I found some more tapes.' *That* got my attention.

'Where?' Dumb question. Who cares where?

'I was going through his clothes and things – you know – starting to tidy up, and…' her voice broke and I thought I'd get another dose of tears, but then she got herself back under control. 'There was a cardboard box tucked back behind some boots he used to wear for fishing back in England and – I guess I knew what must be in it as soon as I saw it.'

'Well, what is it then exactly? You want me to take them and listen to them, or what? What do you want me to do, Hazel?' I was still struggling to wake up, and trying to figure out why she was calling at four in the morning.

'That's the point, Will – why I called. I've been

listening – listening and listening for five hours now and I can't make any sense at all out of them. I just got fed up and frustrated and angry all over again, so I called you.' There might be some logic in there somewhere but I was too tired even to begin to look for it.

'Tell you what, Hazel. Will it be all right if I come by and pick them up in the morning?' Morning. You know, Hazel – a time before noon, but in common parlance substantially later than 4 a.m.

'Yes, Will, you're right. I'm sorry to have called so early. I'm being inconsiderate.' She must have picked up something in my tone. She'd have had to be made of stone not to have.

'That's all right. I know you're upset.' I wanted to be conciliatory too. 'Tell you what. I'll come by around nine thirty and we'll have coffee and a chat about it. Maybe I can shed some light.' Fat chance, I thought.

I didn't really get back to sleep, or rather I didn't get back to anything I'd call *real* sleep until about 7:15 a.m., a whole generous quarter hour before the alarm went off. By then, of course, my body was all prepared to make up for the rude awakening by giving me two more hours of luxurious bathypelagic delta sleep, the deep restorative stuff that heals and refreshes. But Mr Responsible, that strict authoritarian persona who lives inside me, and who chides and browbeats all the other indolent, lackadaisical, playful personae who are also in there, nagged me into vertical function. I had to do the school run, and what kind of an example would I be to my children if I were late? Mr R is a martinet and I don't like him (and neither do the children), but I have to put up with him. He puts food on the table and makes the trains run on time.

At 9:30 I presented myself once more at the Mede's front door. Hazel had thoughtfully already brewed the needed coffee and we didn't say much until we'd got through the first cup. Everybody talks about Italian coffee but the Spanish blends are quite as good, just as everyone raves about Belgian chocolate, whereas I prefer Spanish. This country was so closed for so long that there are a number of Spanish products that simply don't have the reputations – or get the press – they deserve. Maybe it's just as well for those of us who live here. Keeps the prices down.

'So where are these here tapes, then?' I didn't want to spin things out.

'I've got them here,' she said, and leaned down and picked up a plastic shopping bag that was down next to the sofa where she was sitting. It looked big.

'All those are tapes?' I asked, as she extended the bag to me and let it rest on the coffee table between us. It seemed to have dozens of them piled in helter-skelter, unlabelled.

'That's what I've found so far. I don't think there're more, but I haven't looked everywhere.' She shrugged, helpless or hopeless, I wasn't sure which.

'And you've listened to them? *All* of them?'

'No, of course not *all* of them,' she said, with a touch of justifiable exasperation with my slow-wittedness. 'I didn't have nearly time enough for that. I just picked them out at random and listened until I got so upset I had to ring you.'

'What upset you? Something on one of the tapes?' Maybe she'd stumbled on something.

'No, Will, nothing like that. It was just the same mumble, mumble, mumble – some of it in Spanish, some of it in German, some of it in English, but it doesn't *mean* anything, and half the time it's impossible to hear. I just got so angry and depressed and afraid – and for what? For this!' And she shoved the bag towards me with such force that it toppled off the coffee table and strewed its contents over the carpet. 'And they killed him, and we'll never find out why!' She squeezed her eyes closed, threw herself backward against the support of the sofa, crossed her arms and hugged herself, sinking her chin into her chest. She rocked back and forth, not crying, not making any sound at all. I thought of, but then thought better of, moving over to comfort her. She was giving off *no me toca* emanations, don't touch me vibes, and I didn't know her well enough anyway to be a shoulder to cry on, nor did she seem to want that kind of support. The best thing I could do would be to carry on with the hunt for Ninian's killer.

'I'll take the tapes,' I said, trying to ignore her distress. I leaned over and started scrabbling them back into the bag. She didn't answer. 'I'll go and listen to them and see if I can make any sense out of them and then I'll get back to you. Did you by any chance mark the ones you've already listened to?'

She let her shoulders drop and raised her head, looking at me with empty eyes. 'No, I just dipped in, listened a bit and went on to the next one. No method, no order.' I sighed inwardly.

'All right then,' I said evenly. 'I'll start from scratch. You say there're no markings on the tapes. There wasn't a piece of paper in with them by any chance?'

'No, nothing.'

'Just our luck. Well, I'd better be off, then.' I rose and put a hand awkwardly on her shoulder. 'It looks like a big job.' I moved to the door to let myself out, leaving her sitting on the sofa. She reminded me, incongruously, of a child's balloon the second day after the birthday party – shrunken, shrivelled, crumpled in on itself. I felt a pang of helpless compassion.

The feeling didn't last long. Part of me was pleased to have something to get my teeth into, part of me was cross with the prospect of having to spend hours listening to what she had described as unintelligible gibberish. Possibly she'd only found the reject tapes, the ones that didn't have anything important on them. If Ninian had had one hiding place, no doubt he could easily have arranged for another, and the tapes, in any event, would have been too bulky and obvious to sequester away in the postbox. Nevertheless, the job of checking them had to be done. I'd better get to it.

Hannah and Catriona and Semiramis all agreed they'd cover for me while I took a couple of days away in order to – well I didn't actually tell them I was swanning off to listen to tapes. I just used that hoary old phrase, 'something has come up.' They're lovely, and they all indulge me in their various ways. I also rang Commandant Vega and told him about the tapes, though of course I didn't mention my little breaking-and-entering escapade of the previous day. He seemed grateful that I was doing something substantive, and remarked dryly, when I moaned a bit about having to listen to so many tapes, 'Better you than me. I'd probably need a court order to listen to them.' Fausto Milagro was next on my list but wasn't there, so I left a noncommittal message on his machine and took myself into Palma. I have a cosy bijou attic flat in the old town that I use as a kind of pied-à-terre cum escape hatch whenever I need to get away from the hotel, or want some private space to listen to music, or when I have something weighty to think through.

Once up there, with the provisions stowed in the fridge and the heaters taking the chill off the place, I sprawled on the squashy leather couch in a track suit and began the long task of going through the tapes. First I put sticky labels on each one and numbered them. There were sixty-one, most of them hour-long cassettes, some of them ninety minutes. The calculator inside my head figured there could be up to seventy-five hours of what the adverts always describe as 'your listening pleasure' – three whole days of non-stop *Quatsch* if Hazel's preview was anything to go by. I inwardly quailed at the prospect.

Separating the tapes into the three language groups took about two hours. To begin with I thought I'd start with the German tapes, since we already had one tape of German speakers, or at least a variant on German. Then I thought I'd go on to the English group second and leave the Spanish for last. Though I actually *speak* better Spanish than I do German, probably because I use it every day, I still find German easier to understand, at least at speed. Something to do with some of the impenetrable Spanish regional accents that elide everything down to a verbal blur, sometimes missing out, seemingly, both vowels *and* consonants.

But then I had a second thought, trying to make my life easier. I knew Ninian didn't speak German at all, so I figured I could set those tapes aside for now, and his Spanish, though workable, wasn't quite up to Cervantes or García Márquez, so I rationalised myself into setting that pile aside as well. And besides, as my cunning work-avoidance mechanism was quick to point out, what little I'd heard when I was classifying the three groups seemed to bear out what Hazel had said – the sound quality was generally piss poor.

So now I was well ahead of the game: only about twenty hours to do until I had to make the decision as to whether or not to embark on the other two piles. I slotted in the first tape, picked up one of the long yellow legal pads I import from the States to make notes on, and pushed the play button.

The next two days, Gentle Reader, do not bear description. I filled four yellow pads with notes of a sort, few of which, if any, looked promising. I was beginning to get the feeling Ninian hadn't done all of his fishing in England. A lot of this just sounded as though he was recording people out of a warped curiosity to find out what they were saying, regardless of whether or not it might be grist for what I'd come to think of as his blackmail mill. A lot of the conversations, I found, could be skipped once I'd got deep enough in them to ascertain they were merely irrelevant chitchat, and my goodness, there was enough of that to make a month of idle gossip.

And throughout, the sound quality was dire. No sound engineer had Ninian been. The conversations were muffled and indistinct, variable in level and quality. He'd obviously misused that monodirectional minimike we'd pulled out from under the table. It was neither sensitive enough nor sufficiently encompassing to pick up all of the sounds he was trying to record on the tapes. Listening to them was an exercise in terminal frustration, like trying to read a dictionary through a Coca-Cola bottle bottom.

But one brief conversation stood out.

There were two voices, neither of which belonged to a native English speaker. One was clearly Spanish, the other possibly German, though the intonation could have been something else. Swiss? I hoped so.

The Germanic voice complains about work running late. He says a boat – *the* boat? – will be leaving very soon and they'll never get done. He tells the Spaniard – did he say a name? – very indistinct here, that someone, again a frustratingly impenetrable reference to a third person, must hurry up the crew because the paint will never dry on time. The Spanish voice – in fluent and cultured English – tells him to stick to his own business, to get the papers ready on time, and that he, the speaker, will take care of the rest. He tells him to bring the papers down to the boat in Portals. Was one of the voices familiar? I couldn't quite place it, though I played that small section of the tape five or six times.

'Verrry interesting,' I thought. Who is the Spaniard? Is the boat in Portals the one that Fausto went aboard, and if so, how is it tied in? What papers? And what's all this about paint drying? Related to the boat in Puerto Soller? Is the plot thickening or am I simply being spread too thin? Most of all, is this snatch of dialogue worth two days of my time lying here on the sofa going cross-eyed with boredom and ear fatigue?

I decided to quit for awhile and get out and follow the slender lead to see where it might go. I was getting so stale I feared I'd miss something important unless it rose up and smote me like a hammer. And much as I love my cosy attic hideaway, I was getting a bit cabin feverish.

Kurt wasn't there when I rang him but I left a message with Maria, his waitress. Maria astonishes me. She's perfectly amenable and competent as a waitress, milk-mild and agreeable as a person. It's just that she has a total resistance to the acquisition of any foreign language, even the basic few words most tourists pick up within a day or so wherever they go. Kurt is charming in at least five languages but Maria has been serving English and German customers for a dozen or more years without having learned as much as Thank You or *Danke*, Hello or *Hallo*. It's – well – unusual. I left word I'd pop by around 7:30, a half hour before opening.

Of course when I arrived Kurt was busier than I'd hoped he'd be at this time in the evening. A foursome had ordered his fish baked in salt for 8:15 and I landed on him at an inopportune moment. Nevertheless, he told me he'd heard at least one fact that might be of interest to me. One of the voices was likely a ship's captain. Kurt related this with some modicum of surprise, since he, too, considered such a creature to be something of a *rara avis* in Switzerland. And the other voice, though less definitive in terms of his function and role, though also Swiss, mentioned having to leave early because he 'had to drive all the way back across the island.' I thought we might have a small break. It now seemed as though one of those voices almost certainly belonged to Armand Martillo, the ship's captain with the house in Orient. As for the other, as far as I knew only one of the *dramatis personae* operated from the north of the island. Could this be Gewürz? Was he Swiss as well? I cajoled Kurt into letting me hear the voices, just to remind myself. We walked upstairs to his flat above the restaurant and he played about thirty seconds of the tape for me. It was of even worse quality than I remembered, but the voice clearly matched that on the other tape I'd listened to earlier that day: the voice that had complained, in accented English, about the speed of the preparation of the boat and the advancement of the painting process. If this were Gewürz, who had he been talking to, and what were the papers earlier referred to? Kurt was busy so I didn't detain him, telling him I'd come back if I needed to hear more, or when I could tell him more. While he trotted off to the kitchen to carry on with his food preparation, I accepted his offer of a drink, and chose a Spanish brandy. Spanish brandies are yet another example of what I was referring to earlier – underrated Spanish products. In my view the majority of Spanish brandies, star for star, are superior to their French competitors, and cost about half as much. And like their Greek counterparts, they are easier on one's head the next day, too, as they seem to have fewer congeners, those wicked trace by-products formed during fermentation that cause, or exacerbate, hangovers.

That night I decided to go back to the hotel. We were getting a delegation of aristos in and I felt I needed to be around to fly the flag, so to speak. Somehow we've got into the address books of seemingly half the minor royalty in Europe – the ones who've kept their titles even though their countries abolished all forms of royal aristocracy years ago. Some weeks the hotel looks like *Hello* magazine brought to life. One vignette will always amuse me, though I'll change the names so as not to offend any aristocratic sensibilities. Three well-coiffed ladies approached the fresh-squeezed o.j. simultaneously one morning. The first paused, smiled somewhat patronisingly at the other two and announced, as though asserting her right to first refill, 'Good morning, I'm the Countess Dantona.' She reached for the jug, only to be cut off by the second titled milady, who exposed a smirk and declared, 'And I'm the Duchess of Aruba.' Then they both looked at the third woman, who shrugged minimally and said softly, 'I'm sorry. I'm Princess Grandia.' But then, to their mutual and collective credit, they all burst out laughing. My day was made.

Tomorrow, I decided, I'd go back up to the north coast and see if I could get a look at Herr Gewürz. So far I'd only actually seen the man I assumed to be Holmes, and I was beginning to need to put faces to the voices I'd been listening to. Later on, I'd see about identifying Armand Martillo. And then if I had time, I'd go down and stake out the boat in Portals for awhile.

Before retiring, I rang Fausto Milagro and brought him up to speed on what I'd been doing, though I didn't mention the tapes. I felt I needed to get something concrete from them before I could decide how to proceed. He was noncommittally encouraging about my other activities, but also conspicuously inquisitive on one point.

'You've been interviewed by Commandant Vega, then?' He seemed curiously insistent, though I'd already told him about the interview. 'And he didn't want to arrest you?'

'No. He didn't even take my passport. He doesn't seem to find me a likely suspect.'

There was a pause. 'Well, that's good news then, isn't it?' He sounded neither convinced, nor convincingly pleased on my behalf.

'Maybe he believes my story. *You* seemed to.' I couldn't resist giving it a bit of provocative emphasis. I wondered how he'd react.

'Yes, well, jolly good, well done! Couldn't be more pleased.' He'd cut me off and retreated into Sloane mode.

'I'll keep you posted then.' I rang off. Odd, that exchange. It was almost as though he had expected Vega to be tougher on me than he had been. On the other hand, perhaps Vega was taking the give-'em-enough-rope-and-they'll-hoist-themselves-on-their-own-petard approach. I frankly couldn't be bothered thinking about it. Even just lying on my back, it'd been a long couple of days. As the call girl said to the bishop.

Twelve

I woke up with a headache. Those bloody congeners again. I'd only had one of the local *rosados* last evening, but thirst overtook me and the wine was cold and smooth and went down easily, and I just kept on pouring. Compounding my desire to alter my state of fretful consciousness was the realisation that I was discontented and devoid of inspiration as to where to go next. But that sounds like an excuse. As I always tell the children, extend your arm, make a pointing finger of blame, now bend your elbow until the finger is pointing back at you. *That's* who's responsible. *That's* who's to blame. And if you can learn to do that every time you want to blame someone else, then you'll be on your way to growing up. Move over, Kipling, we can add another verse.

So I hoisted myself up, had a hot and cold shower – I *hate* the cold bit – and slowmotioned my way down to glom onto a large mug of Maribel's restorative coffee. This was going to be the day when I pushed this investigation forward one way or the other.

Problem was, I was still suffering from terminal indecision. Several avenues lay open, each one as promising – or to be more accurate and honest – unpromising, as the next. The last couple of days had made me stale – too much lying around and being passive. It was time for some movement again. First, I felt I should check in with Captain Milagro. I'd thought about it and decided it would be a good idea for me to tell him about the tapes before he found out via some other route. I'd best be seen to be ringing him before he rang me.

'I've been able to get access to some of the tapes you mentioned Ninian was recording in his restaurant.' No preamble; I thought I'd just cut to the chase, as I didn't want too many questions. It had also occurred to me it might be useful to give him some information I hadn't yet given to the Commandant. I didn't know enough to play them off against each other; it would be foolish even to try. But at least I could ration out the information I got hold of, and just hope I gave it to the right one. Each clearly had an agenda that involved me, but I'd yet to parse what they might be, individually or collectively.

'What's on the tapes?' He didn't want to waste time either.

'As far as I've heard, not a lot. They're in three languages and I've listened to the English ones and some of the German ones, but none of the Spanish cassettes. I was going to wait to give you a full report but decided I should let you know about them now. The only thing I've found of interest so far is a couple of names I'm trying to follow up on. Most of the material is useless, and there's a lot of it and it hasn't been edited, so I'm listening and still hoping to hear something significant.'

'Do you need some help?' Surprise. An unexpected offer. Suspicion rose up inside me.

'What sort of help did you have in mind?'

'That's up to you, isn't it? But maybe we could listen to the Spanish tapes. We don't have too many people, or at least not too many people I have confidence in, but I think I could spare a man. The German and English tapes I'll have to leave to you, but if there's something else we could do …' He paused and let things hang.

'Well, maybe I'll think of something. I appreciate the offer. May I let you know in a couple of days when I've had a chance to check out a few more possibilities?' I was mistrustful and a bit lost – trying to sound competent when I felt anything but. This stuff was over my head.

'Fine with me. Keep me informed.' We traded a few more irrelevancies and then cut the conversation short.

I had been dying to ask him if the police knew anything about Holmes and Gewürz – if perhaps they already had them in their files. I'd little confidence he'd tell me if they did know about them, and felt I'd be giving too much away if they didn't. At this point, I figured, the worst thing I could do would be to compromise my usefulness to him. He might simply decide he didn't really need me and could just as well go ahead and turn me over to whichever of his colleagues wanted to stick me in the pokey for Ninian's murder. After all, the Guardia had to be seen to be doing *something*, didn't they? The murder was beginning to get some wider attention in the tabloids in the UK, and if the yellow journalists decided to get their slathering mandibles into it, and play it as something other than merely a friendly intramural murder, then it might even begin to back up on the tourist industry, and I knew that once the tourist moguls decided they needed the case solved and began to put pressure on the Guardia, I should harbour no illusions that either Commandant Vega or Captain Milagro would leap to my defence to keep the case open. They'd put me in the hoosegow – our slang corruption of the Spanish *juzgado* – soon as look at me. No, my interests were best served by me, and nobody else. I'd dole out whatever information I could glean in the way I felt was most likely to advance my own interests. I've heard about Spanish prisons and would just as soon not have the experience at first hand, thank you very much.

Before heading up to the north coast I had to go into Palma to run a couple of errands. Whilst there, and just to calm my mind (I said to myself, rationalising wildly), but also because I was getting behind on a feature for Hector, I stopped at the Casal Solleric museum in the Paseo del Borne. It's an intriguing building, combining as it does some typical 18th-century Mallorquin architecture with strong influences from the French and Italian Baroque. Well worth a visit when you're seeking tranquillity. I find it an antidote to some of the other museums here that concentrate so relentlessly on the contemporary, or rather the contemporary as it was circa 1928. Call me a fogey, call me a fuddy-duddy, but at the cost of risking my invitation to the fashion review of the emperor's new clothes, I must admit I have to take a pass on much of Miro's work, native son though he may be. It's not that I don't like *some* of his work, but a steady diet of it, like a constant exposure to Renoir or Roy Lichtenstein, Olivier Messiaen or Mike Oldfield – or pistachio crunch ice cream with marshmallow toffee topping – exhausts the senses and palls after awhile. As an alternative, it's good to have cultural centres like the Sa Nostra foundation, which doesn't have a permanent collection as such, but gets in consistently high-quality temporary exhibitions.

Once I couldn't put off the boring task of staking out Gewürz's place any longer, I retrieved the car from the underground car park – Palma has a number of them, and they're much more user-friendly than most tourists assume – and headed north.

One way to get from Palma to the north coast is via Sineu, the old capital under King Jaume II. There is a long straightish road built by the king for his convenience, as he had to ply back and forth to Palma at regular intervals. It's the only road on the island that goes from Palma to the centre of the island without going through any other town. No doubt this road was created the way the Romans used to build their famous roads – simply by taking a straight line, or as straight a line as the topography allowed, and putting the road down, regardless of whatever previously existing serfs' hovels or other buildings might be in the way. Smallholdings were clearly less of a problem for monarchs back then, as the concept of private property was pragmatic enough to support the proposition that the gentry who owned the land also owned the people on it.

In any event, the net result of the king's whim was a mainly straight road, with good views, though limited in character. However, it's narrow enough in places to be character building for contemporary drivers. At times, behemoth lorries career along this road at speed, some of them extremely w-i-d-e. Meeting one of them head on in a narrow stretch with stone walls tight up against each edge of the road can be a stimulant to instant and total penitence for all sins past or even contemplated, especially if one is cognisant that the driver of the oncoming house-sized hurtling chunk of roaring metal was possibly the driver one saw in the bar at 7:30 this morning knocking back a double brandy with his coffee.

Even so, I can recommend the journey, taking you, as it does, parallel to some of the lesser travelled byways of the island. It is along the lightly trafficked twisting narrow roads here that one can sometimes become blocked behind donkey carts still in daily, practical use. And the roads hereabouts certainly have to be an improvement on some of the more touted scenic routes. I recently saw the north coast road from Pollensa to Soller described in a guidebook as one of the most beautiful drives in Europe. Rubbish. It's constantly curvy, vertiginous in places, sunk deep in pine trees for great portions of the way, affording, save in the stretch at one end, only occasional and fleeting glimpses of the sea. The driver dare not raise his eyes from the road lest he miss a bend. His passengers are hardly better served as they hang onto their seats and fight off incipient carsickness while the car sways from side to side through the endless curves, their enjoyment reduced either to contemplating pine trees – a dismal occupation – or trying to catch the ephemeral vistas of purple mountains' majesty that appear and disappear in instants from between the trees. No, really, don't bother.

Bypassing Sineu, about which, I reminded myself, I'd also have to write a piece for Hector one day, I headed towards Ca'n Picafort and then bent off to the left to follow the coast road up to Puerto Alcudia. I once again installed myself on the wall across the way from Gewürz Associates – I wondered about those associates – turned my back on the shop front to shield myself from sight, and rang from the mobile to see whether he was available.

He was, and the same girl I'd spoken to the other day asked if I'd like to be connected. Indeed, I opined, I would.

'Is that Herr Gewürz? My name is Mudd and I'm looking to get a brochure and some mailout materials done for an art gallery I'm planning to open.'

'And how were you recommended to Gewürz Associates, Mr Mudd?' Very smooth, very Swiss. Instant English lightly accented. But did he also refer to *himself* in the third person?

'I wasn't actually recommended by anyone. Just an impulse, actually. I kind of picked your name out of a hat.'

'I see. So this is my lucky day.' Smug bastard.

'Well, if you're not interested in the business ....' I let it hang.

'Forgive me, Mr Mudd. My little joke was misplaced, I see. Of course Gewürz Associates is interested in your business.' There. He was doing it again.

'Good. I'm pleased we've established *that*.' I thought I'd be prickly and seem to take offence.

'Perhaps we should meet to discuss your needs. You can look at our work and Gewürz Associates can work out a *presupuesto*, an estimate.' No, I didn't think I was ready to meet up with him yet. I'd given him a false name and a phoney story, so I wasn't ready to risk the possibility of his having seen me somewhere, or of his connecting my face with my hotel.

'That sounds a wonderful idea,' I lied. 'I know you're near Puerto Alcudia but I'm not certain exactly where. I'll ring for an appointment in a few days and come by to view Gewürz Associates' work.' I could do it too.

'You do that, Mr Mudd, you just do that.' And he rang off. Why was that last phrase implicitly threatening? What did he mean with that emphasis? Oh, shut up, Will. You're beginning to see dangerous dogs behind every bush.

134

Not a lot happened during the next couple of hours. The weather had shifted a few degrees cooler and I hoped I wouldn't become conspicuous sitting reading my book on the wall. It's one thing to become part of the outdoor furniture on a warm day, quite another if it's not credibly warm enough to be sat outside. I figured I could stay for another half hour or so without becoming a sore thumb; after that I'd need to move to the car, though I really didn't want to be seen in it either. Too many people know my distinctive old bangers. Why is it that TV detectives never have these practical problems? All they have to do is show up someplace and all the action begins.

Clearly that was a prayer masquerading as a complaint, for just then some bored angel took pity on me and sent some action, or at least what appeared to be a harbinger of action. A snazzy white Mercedes snaked around the corner, braked aggressively in front of the shop and stopped with a protesting squeak of rubber and a short slide. Almost simultaneously, the driver's door flipped open and a bulky heavily-muscled red-faced blondish man in his mid thirties, wearing jeans and a T-shirt, some impressive tattoos and a billed mariner's cap, leapt out, flung open the front door, and advanced directly to the enclosed interior office, ignoring the receptionist as he stalked past her. I couldn't hear the door slam shut, but it looked to close with authoritative aggression. Now is when I wished I had a mike planted in there. There was something in the visitor's manner that suggested a problem, an argument, a falling out of some kind between – 'associates', maybe? Or maybe it was just a disgruntled customer and I was jumping to conclusions out of hope and boredom. Whichever, the bulky stranger was the best bet I'd had all day. I walked back to my car and positioned it up the street in such a way that I could follow the Merc when it left, though I had no illusions about Balthasar being able to keep up if the visitor drove away in the same hurry in which he'd arrived.

I drifted back down the street towards my watching post, and as I did so, the front door of the shop opened and the bulky mariner type stepped out, accompanied by a man I immediately took to be Gewürz – tall and tan and young and tubby, but square-shouldered, with sleekly coiffed reddish hair, an Italian draped suit, pointy shiny shoes, and, paradoxically out of keeping with all the other taut grooming and slickness, a deep inkstain on the back of his left hand, which he kept rubbing with a handkerchief, Lady Macbeth style. The bulky man had him by the elbow and was gesticulating emphatically with his free hand, all the while snarling aggressively into his face, breaking his space, dominating him with the sheer ferocity of his expostulations. Gewürz was pretty big himself, but he was being handled like a small child by the bulkily-muscled man. I was too far away to hear anything, but I could tell simply by the shapes his face made that he was speaking German. German is a great language for being vociferous in.

The weightlifter type guided Gewürz to his car, opened the passenger door and put him inside, police style, with a hand to the head. Then he strode around to the other door, yanked it open and threw himself in like a bobsleigh pilot mounting his sled at the top of the run. By this time I was almost back to Balthasar and had my key out, ready to follow if I could. Bulky got away first, but headed directly for the Palma road, and so although I was a couple of blocks back and losing ground, at least I had an idea of the direction they were taking.

By the time we hit the main road I was considerably further back and I put my foot down to try to keep up. I couldn't compete with the Merc for acceleration, but if he stayed within the speed limit I might at least keep pace, and I had the advantage of knowing that once headed for the other coast he probably had few reasons to stop anywhere else.

In point of fact, I overhauled them in a surprisingly

short time, the Mercedes having slowed to the flow of the rest of the traffic. I allowed myself to get up closer behind them than I'd originally thought prudent, as I could now see that both men were involved in antic argument, making an intriguing dumb show of air punches, headshaking, and obviously fervent debate. I didn't think I needed to be concerned about being noticed, and though I didn't want to push my luck by getting too close, I didn't want to trail back any further than absolutely necessary. Keeping a tail on someone, like all those other things we see in the cinema, is harder than it looks. It only takes one wrong traffic light and your quarry is blocks ahead, lost to you in a maze of streets.

We continued without incident, and as I had hoped and surmised, on into Palma and through to the commercial docks down opposite the cathedral. There is a checkpoint as you go out into the customs area, but mostly you get waved through by the sentinels, who only stop you to grill you when you're in a hurry, they having an unerring sense of who's late and who has all day to chat. Today, both of us were ignored as we entered, I having cunningly squeezed myself behind a tall fish delivery van – out of sight, I hoped – of the occupants of the Merc.

We proceeded almost to the end of the quay, with me hanging ever farther back after losing my cover van as it turned off towards a fish-fragrant loading terminal. They were headed, it turned out, for one of those monster boat transporters that dock in Palma a half dozen or so times a year to pick up or offload the yachts of the mega-rich who split their time between Mallorca and the Caribbean, sending their boats across like brown-paper-wrapped packages – at around £10,000 a trip – so as to have them at their convenience when they feel like using them for a day or so. Some of these yachts are quite big enough to make the journey by themselves, but most are under the size for comfortable transatlantic crossings, so their owners casually shove them aboard these transporters, fly the crew across, and pick up at the other end, following the best weather in all seasons. I've never known whether Fitzgerald's remark about the rich being very different from the rest of us was true or not – I fancy not – but their lives sure as hell are. It only takes five minutes to get used to flying on a private jet, but it takes years to come to terms with being poor.

We see a lot of money at our hotel – not the very rich, of course, who don't stay in hotels out here, having either friends' houses or various of their own to shelter in, but we do get a disproportionate share of the grand and the titled, the landed and the loaded, and though most are in touch with everyday realities, and generally are unpretentious and civilised people, there are at times a few who exist in a world that most of us wouldn't even recognise, and behave as though they were modern masters of the universe.

And then, too, there are some few of the wealthy people we meet who are miserly and parsimonious to the point of absurdity. I recall one peer of the realm, whose estates would equal the size of a quarter of a small county, who emptied out the breadbasket and the charcuterie plate each and every morning he was here, smuggling the rolls and croissants and the ham and cheeses to his room under his jumper, *literally* under his jumper. It drove our serving staff quite up the wall. And even when they attempted to stand guard, as it were, over the breakfast table, he baffled them with diversionary tactics, sending one for more coffee and the other to hunt up a paper for him while he staged his raid. 'Nowt as queer as …' and all that, as they say where he comes from.

I parked Balthasar alongside a casual huddle of yachtworkers' vans, where he blended in reasonably well with the port's population of battered vernacular vehicles and lumbering lorries, their workaday commonality punctuated and emphasised every fifty yards or so by the presence of a lowslung glittering egomobile belonging to a yacht owner.

Bulky was quick for a big man. He was out of the car again as soon as it stopped moving. He and Gewürz seemed to have settled their differences, or at least cooled down, for they seemed amiable enough as they made their way to the man by the sally port who was directing the arcane operations that take place in, on, and around a big ship when she's – well, almost anywhere. The vocabulary to describe those operations is always so vivid and sharply evocative. Right now I could see a warp-grade hawser being ducked up towards the dumb-chalder, where a rigger who was balanced on the wing transom waited to tally on and trice it up to the rabbet. There seemed to be a problem with the pintle, as it looked to be damaged just where it entered the gudgeon on the sternpost. From a hundred yards away I could hear the stridulation of the lower cheek block as the line was reeved through. If I hadn't read Patrick O'Brian's seafaring novels from stem to stern I wouldn't have known what I was looking at, though maybe I still wasn't sure. Lots of people mistake vocabulary for understanding.

Bulky and Gewürz fell into quick conversation with the man, another tough type almost along the physical lines of Bulky himself. He, too, looked as if he could bend a quick cunt splice – yes, that's its real name – out of your two arms soon as look at you. Bulky seemed to be pleading a case with the man, an attitude wholly in opposition to the way he'd treated Gewürz. His deference was almost servile. The man didn't waste time on them. He shook his head, pointed at the ship, and made a flat, crossed-handed waving motion, his palms down and parallel with the ground. The brief conversation was over.

Gewürz was the first to react. He resignedly turned and walked back towards the car. Bulky made one last comment to the man and then he, too, began the trek to the Merc. Neither of them looked happy. I bent over and busied myself flemishing a handy hawser so as to look innocuous. Not that I was dressed for the part I'd assigned myself, but neither Bulky nor Gewürz looked likely to be taking careful note of their surroundings. Clearly they had weightier things on their minds.

As soon as they were clear I scampered to the car and took after them. I figured I'd probably lose them but again my luck seemed to be in. There was a bit of a queue at the outgoing checkpoint and they ended up three cars ahead of me. I could see they were back at the arguments. After the blockage at the gate cleared we were all waved through without incident. They seemed to hesitate at the T-junction where the quay butts up against the Paseo Marítimo, but then Bulky pulled across and into the Borne, stopping behind the cab rank closest to the cathedral. The door opened on Gewürz's side. I dawdled past and pulled up in the slow feeder lane that goes up into the old city. If they didn't make it a long goodbye, I could still pull out of the right lane and get in behind Bulky as he came past, assuming he didn't want to get into this lane as well. He didn't. He came past, headed for the traffic circle around the fountain, then back down to the Paseo where he turned left out towards the airport. I fell in behind him two cars back. After all, I knew where Gewürz was based, and I could come back to the ship later. Bulky was the only one I had no address for.

We headed out on the airport fast road, past the ugly high-rise apartments in the no man's land between the road and the sea, past the smelly patch where you are almost always assaulted by the pong of the city's effluent, and on out past the airport itself. For such a lovely city, Palma's approaches, save on the west side or from the sea, are unprepossessing. We took the Arenal turnoff, Bulky and I, and headed back down towards the sea. Arenal is pure tourist land, in summer a roiling, seething mass of sunburnt flesh, smooth or hairy, flabby or firm, arrayed lumpily on the beach or else decoratively buffet-style around the sapphire pools of the concrete block hotels. Many of these hotels are surprisingly good at what they do, which is to process tourists and give them what they came for: efficiently-organised clean basic accommodation and ready access to sun, sand, sea, alcohol, and sex if they're lucky. There are endless bars, fast food outlets, souvenir shops, car rental enterprises, restaurants, restaurants, and more restaurants. These days, this area has mainly been taken over by German tourists, and one sees signs everywhere in German. There were even prices posted in German marks until the Spanish authorities put a stop to it. As Magalluf is to the English, so are Arenal and Peguera to the Germans. We once had a German guest who asked me about a recommendation to a good fish restaurant. As I knew of one in Arenal I mentioned it to her. 'Oh no,' she cried, 'I don't vant to go zere. It is voll mit Chermans!' I suppose Hannah would react similarly if anyone tried to send her to a restaurant in Magalluf.

The Merc slowed near a big apartment block in the second line from the beach, waited while the door to the underground garage slid up, and then disappeared inside. I went on around the block, looking fruitlessly for a parking space. Balthasar is patently too big to drive on this island. Even when some petite Fiat or Opel Corsa or Ford Fiesta pulls out of a space, more than half the time there isn't enough space to shoehorn Balthasar in, even with his wonderful Volvo steering lock, which allows me to get him into a space literally three inches longer than the car. But I did finally find a spot a few hundred yards away and walked back. I didn't figure on seeing Bulky again today, but with luck and a following wind – I was feeling overtaken by sailing metaphors – I might be able to put a name to him.

The array of bell pushes on the building wasn't helpful. There were a few with names, but only a few, and most of them German. Either the building was largely tenanted by people who wished to remain incognito, or else the other occupants were just following the Spanish tradition of not bothering to put a name outside because anyone who might wish to come to visit would already know which bell to push, and anyone who didn't know was probably someone they wouldn't wish to meet anyway. Village logic on a grander scale.

So, no joy there. I walked around and eyed the garage door hopefully, but no one drove in or out. I thought I'd scout the neighbourhood a bit, though neighbourhood wasn't exactly the appropriate word, as it seemed more a ragged extension of the tourist crust along the sea, the arcades and shops and hotels that parallel the strand. This time of year it was fairly tranquil, with most commercial endeavours still closed, though there were still a number of people walking along the wide boulevard that's off limits to cars, and a few of the German *Bierstube* were in action. Then I spotted it. Of course. We were only a few hundred feet inland from Balneario Six, also called Ballermann, the famously infamous gathering spot for young German tourists, an outdoor beer dispensary so non-stop riotous that a whole film was based on it. This surely must be the number six in Arenal that related to Ninian's code. Bulky had to be the person it referred to. All of a sudden I didn't care if I found out his real name today or tomorrow or the next day. Another piece of the puzzle had dropped into place. It was time to go home. Playing at detective was a hungrymaking business.

Thirteen

Next morning I bit the bullet and began to assemble receipt and invoice data. 'Tio' Tim was coming out from the UK and he would spend the next couple of days putting our financial house in order again. Neither Hannah nor I are good at that sort of detail, and used to get our fiscal knickers in a terrible twist through neglecting to get VAT invoices, paying cash when we should have paid with a credit card and vice versa, failing to pay some taxes, usually because we didn't recognise the forms as tax demands, or overpaying others – some of which, I became convinced, had been designed by the Spanish tax authorities especially for us. My worse offence, according to one stern official, was using the form CZ977 to import goods from abroad when any fool knows it should be CZ977-K. We were hopeless.

And then Tim Steele appeared. 'Tio' – Uncle – Tim is clearly an angel in mufti, and however much he attempts to masquerade as a plain human being, his beatific smile and endless patience betray his true identity. About two years ago Tio Tim became our financial guru, mentor, organiser, ally, partner, cohort, redeemer, or whatever word describes a miraculous being who came into our lives and made order of our chaos. 'I can sort those things out,' he said, as he looked at the convoluted mess that was our financial situation, and then proceeded to do so. He spent three weeks at the outset simply filing a thousand unmarked receipts, revamping our computer system, opening and closing bank accounts, revising direct debits, reclaiming overpayments and paying off underpayments, painstakingly extracting some semblance of order from the wreckage wrought by two well-intentioned but financially clueless people. And now he comes out from Blighty about every six weeks, sequesters himself away with the computer and our plastic shopping bags full of tatty bits of paper, till receipts, handwritten notes, and indecipherable communications from the government, and – voilà! – seventy-two hours later we are again in business – legal, organised, and worryless. Sheer magic.

My assembly of receipts done, and with those few words I gloss over three hours of diligently fastidious drudgery, I was once again ready to put on my deerstalker hat, wrap my cape around me, head for the nearest phone booth and transform myself into SuperStock of Scotland Yard, or at least his near equivalent. I thought a trip back down to the transport ship might be in order.

Before leaving, however, I got out the copy I'd made of the list I'd snaffled out of Ninian's postbox. So far, Fausto Milagro was the only person privy to this information and though I felt I could trust him I'd decided to create an insurance policy for myself by having a copy in the safe for Hannah to find it in the event of ... well, just in case. Hazel clearly hadn't known about her late husband's secret hideyhole, and the other policemen I'd talked to hadn't – or at least as far as I knew hadn't yet – cottoned on to it. I'd wondered about telling Commander Vega, but just for now I felt it could be my secret weapon if only I could figure out how to parse the code and relate the numbers and places to other suspects.

I looked at it again.

Pto Soller, 221b	£	45,000
Orient, 3	SwF	30,000
Puigpunyent sm	US$	100,000
Arenal, 6	DM	30,000
Deya, 119	Pts	37,750,000
Portals, b	US$	25,000
Pto. Alcudia, 57	DM	100,000
Pollensa, 66	US$	25,000

Some of it was obvious in light of what I'd found out. Ninian's code wasn't something it required an enigma machine to crack. I'd got lucky with the first one simply by establishing – at least I thought I had established – that 221b related to a man by the name of Holmes. Now I knew where he was and what he looked like and what he did, even if I didn't know what the sum of money referred to. But that could come later.

I'd also tracked a man in Puerto Alcudia and discovered his name was Heinz, which seemed to me to be an obvious reference to the number 57 – Heinz's 57 Varieties. Even his surname was right, though I was surprised Ninian might have been aware of it, 'Gewürz' being the German word for spice, or seasonings. So that made two of them, if I'd read things right.

Moreover, the man I'd tracked in Arenal, the as yet nameless musclebound bulky man, lived, it seemed, near Balneario 6, the only 'six' I knew of in Arenal. And, to go back to the very beginning, I had a 'three' up in the town of Orient in the guise of Captain Armand Martillo, the Swiss sea captain, whom I hadn't yet laid eyes on.

So far, then, I'd seemingly sussed out four of the code numbers in the locations on the list, though I had to admit I wasn't feeling a whole lot smarter for having done so. I still felt I had a way to go if I were to escape the clutches of the Guardia. Self-congratulation and pessimism vied in my innards with equal strength. Although I'd found out things the police as yet hadn't, there were still names to find, people to be located – *localised*, as we say in Spanglish here – and a mystery to be solved. The Guardia weren't going to wait forever.

I decided I'd sniff around the transporter ship in Palma. After that, there was the boat down in Portals that needed checking out. Either or both might lead to something.

Before leaving, I went up to inspect the possibilities in my wardrobe. As any successful fraudster will tell you, clothes maketh the con. As ye appear, so shall ye be treated. Perhaps regrettable, but true. Of course some people have a knack for looking to be of substance, or at least well-heeled, almost whatever they wear, but I've never achieved it. My normal attire is anything but fashionable, though actually I prefer it that way. In my view, old money has always had it right – quality threads well broken in.

In the end I settled for a black Pringle cashmere rollneck pullover, a pair of tan moleskin trousers I'd had made years ago by a good tailor in Cork St – two-thirds the price of Savile Row – a soft Spanish leather jacket of the sort that are wonderful value here on the island, peccary-skin slip-ons from Kurt Geiger of Bond Street, and – as a discreet touch – my gold Patek Philippe, the only surviving accoutrement from a former life when I thought I was going to have more money. And of course I took the big BMW, which possibly might make it as a superannuated-but-quality statement. Whatever money I have certainly isn't old, but I've always aspired to the careless éclat of the silver-spooned from birth. Flaunt that understatement!

The same overseer was on duty as yesterday, this time supervising the victualling of the ship. It seemed they wouldn't be moored here for much longer. He had been working somewhere dirty, was covered in soot and looking like an irritable Vulcan as he rapped out directions in fluent Spanish. I couldn't place the accent, possibly from somewhere in northeastern Europe, somewhere Baltic – hard to tell for a non-native speaker. He was a tough looking *hombre*, about my height, but heavier through the shoulders and back, with bigger bones and slabbier muscles. And a fairly typical man of the sea judging from his weathered skin and the crow's feet around pale, almost faded eyes, with that barren gaze sailors acquire after staring at a sea horizon for twenty years. He even still moved as though countering the heave of a deck under his feet. There was power and charisma there. No doubt as to who was in charge here. I sidled over and asked anyway.

'Who's in charge here?'

'Who want to know?' A question for a question and an impatient look that travelled up and down me, registering my apparel. I was glad I'd dressed up. It made me feel less intimidated.

'Stock is my name.' Better the truth at this point. 'I wanted some information about your vessel there. Headed across the pond, then?'

'You want to send boat? We have agent in town.' He was busy, irritated, wanted to get rid of me, but maybe had empty space to fill.

'Well, it's an idea we're toying with. Maybe a few months away in the Carib. Nothing fancy.' I was putting on my Brit accent, the one that always sounds so phoney to me but seems to impress non-Brits. Or so I tell myself.

He clearly wasn't impressed. 'You have to see agent. Over there is sign with number and address.'

'Well, I just thought I'd drop around. Aren't you shipping one of Gewürz's boats?'

That got a reaction. He turned slowly towards me and his eyes hardened. For the first time, he seemed really to focus on me. 'Who tell you that?'

Where did I go from here? As I dithered, he seemed to be getting bigger, his already considerable presence expanding to fill the gap between us. 'Oh, I really can't remember, something I thought I heard somewhere.'

'No, not something you just hear, Mister.' He moved towards me, leaning into my space, keeping eye contact. I'd lit a fuse, and was suddenly grateful for all the activity around us, not that I thought any one of that stevedoring lot would lift a finger if he decided to quiz me more physically. 'Where you get that name? You sure not one of his lot. And you not police.' Flattery would get him anywhere.

For a moment more I didn't say anything, mulling over possible cover stories, and evidently I wasn't quick enough for his liking. He reached out a horny, nicotine-stained hand and grasped my lapel, at the same time beginning to draw his other arm back and curl his hand into a fist.

'I just saw him here yesterday. I know him by sight.' I blurted quickly. He paused and seemed to relax a degree or so. 'I only remembered it as you seemed to be having – how shall I put it? – a bit of an altercation.'

'How you know him, then? Only by seeing, you say.' He was backtracking marginally, maybe beginning to reclassify me as harmless. I could but hope.

'Oh, just seeing him coming and going from his place in Puerto Alcudia. When I saw him here talking to you I assumed he was sending a boat with you. I was going to ask you yesterday, but everyone seemed so upset I decided to leave it.' Butter wouldn't melt. Harmless is my middle name.

'So you see us. You hear things?' He was making sure.

I had a quick flashback to my visit to Gewürz's office. Maybe I had the bait to fish for more information. Even if I didn't want this monster on my line, maybe there was no harm in trying out a dry fly. 'No, I was too far away. Just something about papers, wasn't it?'

'Yes!' It was out of his mouth before he could edit. Then he scaled it back. 'I mean only small problem with papers. Not to worry about.'

'So they're sending a boat?' Where? Why?

'No, this time they not send nothing. Technical problem with papers. And we sail early this time. You see? Almost finished loaded.' He gestured back at the ship.

'When you come back?' It was catching. You Tarzan. Me harmless question monkey.

'Oh, month maybe. Depend weather. We go slow sometimes, sometimes fast.' He was getting positively voluble.

'And you'll take Señor Gewürz's boat next time

then?' In for a penny. Nothing ventured. Faint heart never, and all those other old saws.

The amiability didn't last. 'Listen, Mister. You get nose out from other people business. You want send boat you go see agent. You better forget Herr Gewürz.' And he turned away and shouted at one of the victualling crowd, dismissing me in the same way he had dismissed Gewürz and Bulky yesterday.

I walked back to the car with a jaunty step, still smelling the lion's halitosis from when I'd put my head in his mouth. I remembered – wasn't it Churchill again? – the comment about how there are few things in life as satisfying as having been shot at and missed. My encounter wasn't quite as dramatic as all that, but for one clear moment it was obvious I'd hit a nerve. My internal balance tilted in favour of self-congratulation, though only some of the votes were in and there were many precincts yet to be heard from.

All the way along the road to Portals I kept the volume up on the Haydn Great Organ Mass. Where can it come from, music like that? Smack dab in the middle of the shittiest bits of life anyone could imagine, suddenly there are these vibrations in the air that make your hair stand up on end. And it all came from – surely not just old Joe by himself? Sometime I must make a list of the things that make believers of us all, whether we are or not.

Road bloody works, all the way down into Portals.

Once there, Puerto Portals, uncharacteristically, was almost deserted: a combination of the road works, time of year, but probably mostly the time of day. It was still a bit early for the beautiful people and the wannabe beautifuls, though no doubt the pace of things would accelerate as they gradually surfaced. No matter to me, I was only here to check out that boat.

Wellies, the English bar/bistro on the front, was quiet, and the coffee was good even at a price that would leave my neighbours at home gasping. One has to keep a sense of proportion, however, and compared to Rome or Tokyo, Portals is still inexpensive – bits of it anyway.

As I was eyeing the port I saw one of those vivid snapshot vignettes that add dimension and ironic humour to life here. Shuffling along the front were two elderly Mallorquin widows all in black, muffled up to their ears with scarves and mittens and wool hats, hunched against the icy 60-degree 10 mph wind, clearly suffering from incipient hypothermia. But right behind them, overtaking them, was a young German couple in matching lederhosen and thin T-shirts, striding along, beaming and gesticulating, soaking up the sun and revelling in the semi-tropical 60-degree 10 mph wind.

When I finally wandered out to the boat it was buttoned up tight, nobody in sight and probably nobody on board. I noted the name, Anita, out of Palma. Somehow, given the preponderance of foreign flags here, I'd expected her to be another *estranjera*. Swiss, perhaps?

In the end it was, as these things often are, easy as pie. A slightly bleary, slightly tousled blonde female head emerged from the cockpit on the next boat down, followed by a lissom body in scruffy track suit bottoms and a University of Chicago sweatshirt. I didn't even begin to believe in the university connection, given Chicago's lofty intellectual reputation. But I thought I'd try anyway.

'Good morning. Are you really from Chicago?'

She looked down as though I'd told her she'd spilled beer all down her front. '*Nej*, Køpenhavn,' she said. That was more like it. And she put the spin on the 'havn' part only real Danes can. She was perhaps somewhere in her late twenties, with clear – though still sleepy – grey eyes, and a short, straight nose. Though we were in winter, she had a residual tan.

'I'm looking for the man who owns that boat,' I said. 'Do you know if he's around?'

'Pascual?' she replied, looking mildly puzzled. 'No, he live there,' gesturing in the direction of Palma. 'He normally don't sleep on the boat. Maybe just sometimes.'

'Does he have another name? A family name, I mean?'

'Oh yes, his name is Milagro, Pascual Milagro.'

And that was it. Little tumblers clicked into position, all based on my luck in having taken a short stroll the last time I was here and noticing Fausto come aboard.

I thanked the still sleepy Danish pastry and walked away.

Fourteen

That afternoon I went to Ninian's funeral, which had been delayed by the post mortem autopsy mandatory for all murder victims. We were but few, for Ninian's friends, as previously noted, did hardly make a quorum. The service was abrupt to the point of haste – no music, a scattering of fatuous words from a well-meaning but obviously unacquainted younger cleric, and then his earthlies were sped into the fire. The closed coffin was of standard Mallorquin length, which is to say pretty short, and I found myself speculating ghoulishly as to how they might have got him into that coffin in one piece, if indeed they had.

One surprise was that Captain Milagro was there, eyeing the attendees discreetly. It was still my understanding he was off the murder case officially, so unless Commandant Vega had asked him to look in on his behalf, Milagro must have come for his own purposes, no doubt relating to Ninian's bugging activities. He was in tasteful, understated funereal attire, and clearly practised in exhibiting the sort of sombre demeanour appropriate to these occasions. We exchanged glances and with a mutual look towards the door, arranged a meeting for afterwards.

These things are inevitably tedious and anticlimactic, hardly stuff to compare to a proper Viking immolation. No longship, no swords and shields, not even any *aquavit*. Two iron doors slide open, and the coffin, seemingly of its own volition, trundles into the fire, after which the doors close sans fanfare. All that's missing is a uniformed policeman to tell us to move along. 'Go home folks, there's nothing more to see here.' And that's all she wrote. It was done.

After the service I gave Hazel the obligatory buss on both cheeks, mumbled a few well-meant but awkward words, overworked clichés that seemed to come out like hypocritical platitudes. Then I fixed with her that I would stop by the house later on to catch her up on my non-progress, or at least those bits I felt ready to divulge. My real agenda, to my discredit, was to find out if she had come across any further evidence, a subject it would have been crass to raise in the context of Ninian's funeral.

The encounter with Captain Milagro was going to require a bit more finesse. With his customary polish he had observed form with Hazel, embraced her warmly, said all the right words, and behaved as though an old friend. Now he was waiting for me by the second tree from the corner, next to a convenient bench.

'You did that very well,' I remarked as I joined him. 'I fear that however virtuous my intentions, the result usually seems fraudulent and dishonourable. I have no touch for that kind of *politesse.*'

'Ah,' he said archly, 'I believe it was your Mr Jefferson who said that politeness may be artificial but that the practice of it ends by being a substitute nearly equivalent to the real virtue.'

I refrained from observing that I had once read a piece by Miss Manners quoting that very remark, and practised good manners by keeping stumm.

'Listen,' I said, sitting down on the bench and abandoning all vestiges of flippancy, 'I think the time has come for you to tell me more about what you know. I'm out there being point man, but don't know what I'm pointing at, or even worse, what may be pointing back at me. You told me the police were keeping an eye on Ninian because of the bugging equipment, but you really didn't tell me anything more. Is there any firm evidence he was involved, or his place was involved, in the drug trade, or – what? Are we talking white slavery here? Pornography? Counterfeiting? Give me a clue.'

'I can't,' he said, shrugging minimally. 'It's not that I won't, I just can't. All we know is that he bought a clandestine microphone set. Importation of these devices is prohibited in Spain, but sometimes when we detect one coming in we let it go, just to see where it leads. That's number one. Number two is that his restaurant was regularly used by some unsavoury fellows, types who could be involved in virtually anything you mentioned, or more. Did he buy the microphone to record conversations in which he took part, or did he record information in the hope of blackmailing someone? Or did he have yet another motive? We don't – as I keep saying – know for certain. You've heard some of the tapes, so you know as much, or even more, than anyone. And much as I do not wish to turn these queries back on you, isn't it your role to find these things out? Isn't it in your interest more than mine?' He gave me a measured smile, not entirely benign.

I felt myself begin to flush, and I was on the point of bringing up his brother's name when Hazel suddenly appeared from behind us and I nipped my tongue, as it were, in the bud.

'In whose interest more than his?' she demanded of Fausto. 'I heard some of that. You police people are simply looking for a scapegoat, and I think you want it to be my husband. Yes, he put a microphone in the restaurant, but I don't for a minute think it was for any of the reasons I heard you mention. Did you ever think he might have been protecting himself? Could it be maybe it was *he* who was being blackmailed for some reason we don't know?' She was much more the Hazel I'd always known – truculent, shrewish, defensively aggressive. I wondered what tack Fausto would take.

'My dear lady,' he began ….

'Don't you "dear lady" me,' she spat. 'I've been that route. Just be straight for once. What evidence do you have against my husband?' She stood over him and glared. I sat still. She was doing all my work for me.

'Now that you mention it, *dear lady* …' He refused to be fazed. 'In truth we have none. But you must understand that the police always proceed on the worst case scenario. One swallow may not make a summer, but two swallows are summary evidence. At least for us. I regret having to say it so bluntly,' he spread his palms open in Gallic fashion, turning down the corners of his mouth, 'but there are too many circumstances to ignore.'

'Oh, bullshit,' she hissed, having given up all ladylike pretensions, 'I knew you'd say something like that. You just want to blame him for some scam because it's easy, because he's dead, because then you can blame it on a falling-out among thieves – close the case because there weren't any what you call "civilians" involved. But he damn well was a "civilian", not a thief or a blackmailer, and whoever killed him is still out there and you can't make that fact go away. Or are you going to blame it on Will here? He'd make a good fall guy. I'll tell you what *I* think, I think you people are being paid off. If there's a scam, it's a police scam, and I'll tell you one other thing, if anybody asks me that's what I'm going to say. So, go tell that to your crooked buddies Mr Smooth Operator!' And turning on her heel, losing her balance a bit, which slightly spoiled the effect, she stomped away across the gravel, crunching it aggressively underfoot.

'Hmmm,' said Fausto. 'A mite touchy, that lady. But then that's to be expected. Do you have anything to add to her thoughts on the matter?' She was right. He was a Smooth Operator.

'Pass,' I said. 'You know my position well enough. Commandant Vega could haul me in any minute now. She was right about that. And I know you aren't telling me everything, but I just have to take your word there's a good reason for it. Apart from that, I'm simply trying to do some of your work for you – or to put it your way – do some work I'm in a better position to do than you are, and so I'll simply keep on doing what I can until either you arrest me, or until something breaks to take the pressure off me. I can't say I'm enjoying the process.' I loosened my tie, the black one I've used more often as I've grown older, and examined the nasty hangnail I'd been refraining from gnawing. I'd changed my mind about mentioning brother Pascual. 'I take it you're still telling me you can't tell me anything more.' I tried for a tone halfway between statement and interrogatory.

'Sorry, old man. Not a thing.' As I'd expected.

'Well, I'd better get back at it then.' I got up a little stiffly, some old sports injury twinging. 'Let me know if you change your mind.' I gave him my demibasilisk stare, half power, but still enough to let him know that Hazel wasn't the only one who was pissed off with him.

'Anything I can do,' he said ingenuously. Teflon couldn't compete. Then he rose briskly, far sprightlier than I had, and departed with a cheery wave. And wouldn't you know, the cocky bastard had come to the funeral in a drophead Morgan. British Racing Green, no less.

When I arrived at Hazel's about an hour later, I was mildly surprised to find her in quite a different mood. She came to the door in jeans, barefoot, wearing a MacLeod tartan flannel shirt, and with her hair shaken out of its usual tight arrangement. A slash of fiery red lipstick made her look like a vampire after a hard day's night, and she was carrying a tall glass of a brown liquid tinkling with ice cubes. She was already half cut.

Not that I'd actually expected to find her clad in widow's weeds, clutching a bible and sobbing into a lace handkerchief, but seeing her as a refugee from a barn dance was somewhat unexpected. She could have just walked off the set of *Annie Get Your Gun*. She beckoned me in and we sat down at opposite ends of the plastic-clad sofa.

'That son-of-a-bitch,' she said in a conversational tone, but with a bitter twist on it. 'He thinks we all should kiss his arse just because he sounds so effing toffy-nosed. But when all's said and done he's just one more bent copper.'

'Do you really think so?' I enquired mildly. 'So far I

haven't had a whiff of corruption, but then maybe I haven't been sniffing close enough.'

'Oh yeah,' she said. 'Take my word for it. They're all alike. They wouldn't be there if they weren't. This country's full of corruption.'

'It seems to me that *all* countries have a corruption problem, it's simply a matter of degree and tradition. For myself, I wouldn't be here if I thought they were all bent.'

'Grow up, Will. You're so effing naïve you don't even know when you're being shafted. I'm only helping you because I know damned well they won't get Ninian's killer. You probably won't either, but at least you've got a vested interest in trying. So that gives me a vested interest in giving you a hand.' With that, she slid along the sofa, put a hand on my knee and looked up at me, eyelids slightly drooping. Oh shit, I thought, this is the last thing I need right now. Under no circumstances was I going to play Comfort the Widow. For every good reason I could think of, plus a few more.

'Listen, Hazel,' I said, rising and moving towards the bar. 'I could use a drink myself. Mind if I join you? And can I freshen yours at the same time?' There were glasses, ice, and an open bottle of Scapa, an Orkney single malt, good stuff, on the sideboard. I poured myself out a short slug, passed on the ice for a malt of this quality, then reached for her glass, topped it up with a bit of whisky and started to hand it back.

'Add some ginger to that,' she said, a little loosely. A single malt and ginger? Heresy. But I did it, may my Scottish ancestors forgive me. I pushed one of the chairs up opposite her, trying not to be too obvious about it, and sat down, keeping the coffee table between us.

'Oh you're a sly woodpecker, Will,' she said, eyeing me speculatively. And then she changed to a lisping little girl voice. 'Does poor Will think big bad Hazel's going to eat him all up?' She leered lasciviously and gave a dirty chuckle. Then she reverted to the coolly bitter tone she'd been using. 'Forget it. A product of the moment, a passing impulse.'

I shrugged. 'We've got enough problems, you and I, without asking for even one more. Agreed?' She nodded. 'Friends?' I said. She nodded again, but with a shine of unshed tears in her eyes. And just having seen that crack in the carapace, glimpsing the vulnerability in her, I found myself liking her more than I'd thought possible. Warming to her, even. For perhaps the first time since I'd first met her, I was beginning to think of her as a real human being, someone to take seriously in spite of her execrable taste.

Once when I was young I went for a job interview and the employer sent me off for three days of psychological testing, at the end of which I was sat before the chief psychologist for counselling. 'Well,' he said, 'I've read your tests and I'll tell you the same thing I told my own son, not that I have any illusions it will do any good. You're a pretty bright lad, and things come easily for you, which makes you arrogant and impatient with other people. But just because some things come easily now doesn't mean everything's always going to be easy. And I'll tell you another thing – until you learn that you have to respect and consider everyone you meet in life – that you have something to learn from the dumbest person you'll ever cross paths with, then you'll just be a worthless self-congratulatory arrogant shit.' And then he smiled warmly, shook my hand and sent me on my way. I passed it off, of course, didn't in truth give it any merit or weight, and continued to behave pretty much as I always had. Now, looking back, I figure it took me about twenty years to learn that lesson, though no doubt there are those who will aver that I *still* haven't learned it.

'Let's talk some business, shall we?' I said. 'Did you find any more tapes? That's actually the single thing that might help this so-called investigation along. I didn't get anything of value – hardly anything anyway – out of that pile of cassettes you gave me last time. Frankly, I suspect they were discards.' I took a big sip of the whisky and let it bloom on my tongue, slightly numbing the tip, then swallowed it all at once, savouring the peaty burning sensation it made as it went down my throat to make a pool of warmth in my middle.

'There're no more tapes, Will. I'm sure of it. I've been through every place I could think of, both here and at the restaurant. Unless he had some hiding place somewhere else, I just don't think there are any more.'

A pity, I thought. I knew about his hiding place and they weren't there. 'Hmmm,' I said, and shook my head. 'Then I don't know where to go from here. Can you think of *anything* he might have left here that could be a clue?'

'Nothing, nothing, and the bloody sons and daughters of nothing. No fucking thing!' She stumbled on the last word and I realised she was well on her way to being totally blitzed. She had developed the tell-tale weave and head roll people get when they're pretty far along the path to oblivion. And although a straggle of hair had come loose and was falling over one eye she was ignoring it. I felt the time had come to leave. There wasn't anything more here. I glugged the last inch of whisky and stood up. 'I'd better be off, then.' I leaned over and was going to give her a double-cheeked Spanish farewell kiss, but she grabbed my hand and hauled herself up. She wanted to walk me to the door. We managed to arrange ourselves hips together, though actually her hip came only halfway up my thigh. Lurching along, with one of my arms around her to steady her, we headed for the entrance hallway.

'Wait a minute,' she mumbled. 'Just wait one fucking minute. I just had an idea,' and she guided me in the direction of a dropleaf cherrywood hall table, by far the best piece of furniture in the house, or at least the bits of the house I'd seen. See? There I go again, being what she'd call a 'fucking snob.'

She leaned on me as she rummaged in some papers

piled in one corner of the table. 'I saw something here. It was out of place and I wondered about it, and then I forgot about it. Where the fuck is it?' She knocked a few of the papers on the floor, but ignored them. 'Ha! There you are, you little son-of-a-bitch!' and she handed me a small green slip of paper. 'That's it.' She smiled with self-satisfaction and waited for my response.

'It's a postal receipt,' I said, vacantly, still playing catch-up with her intent.

'You bet it's a fucking postal receipt,' she said. 'It's what you get when you *send* a parcel. And I haven't sent any fucking parcels, have I? And if *I* haven't, who did? *Ninian* fucking did, that's who.' She continued nodding. And then of course I did get it, and felt a jolt of excitement. Ninian had sent a package to someone. To whom?

'What's the date on it?' I said, even though I was the one holding the slip. I squinted to see the stamp, pale and under-inked as is usual with post office documents. It looked like Thursday a week ago, two days prior to his death. Just maybe, it could be he had a confidant, just maybe, it could be he'd sent some of the more – what? – incriminating tapes to someone else. A lawyer, perhaps, to hold as evidence? Whatever it was, it opened up possibilities for me. I smiled and folded the little square of paper in half and tucked it into my top pocket. I gave Hazel a big squeeze. 'You're a genius. How would you put it? – a gen-u-ine, unreconstituted, authentifucking *genius*. Thank you!' And I gave her a quick but heartfelt kiss full on the lips, leaned her against the near wall, and was out the door almost before she could react.

That small square of green paper just might be my ticket to ride.

Fifteen

'Vy are you followink me?' The big thumb and meaty fingers had hold of the top of my left shoulder, the trapezius muscle that runs along from the top of the neck to the tip of the shoulder, and I was caught in one of those paralysing grips only experts use, the incapacitating kind that we read about, but only experience if we're singularly unlucky. I was being unlucky at the moment. 'I haff seen you now two daze behind me. Vut do you vant?' I'm not giving you the full flavour of the accent, Scandinavian rather than German, but then my attention was distracted by the pain in my shoulder. It doesn't seem as though it ought to be all that agonising, just a rope of muscle being squeezed, but the squeeze was inexorable, as though permanently locked on, and more than that, had a promise of increase in it that I wished to avoid at all costs.

'Ease off, please. Let me explain,' I grunted out between short breaths, 'there's an explanation.' The hell there was, or if there was it was something I was going to need to construct in a hurry. He'd caught me plain and simple. Spanish has a wonderful verb, *confeccionar*, meaning to make up, to concoct, to embellish and spin into reality something that may be only a fairy story. It has overtones of spun sugar, spider webs of gossamer fragility or teetering houses of imaginary cards, apparently substantial though in reality ethereally fragile and vulnerable to the least zephyr. It was something like that I was going to have to come up with, and I'd have to do my creative web-spinning with a shoulder that was burning and cramping and hurting like blue blazes. He stared down at me with implacable, boiled egg eyes, in which I could see even the smallest of broken red veins against the milky white offset by crystal blue. They were the kind of eyes I couldn't bear, the kind of eyes that had won large parts for actors seeking roles as villains in a thousand Hollywood Third Reich movies. What was conditioning and what was instinct? I didn't like his eyes.

Didn't care much for the rest of him, either.

But let me digress and tell you how I got myself in this pickle.

After I'd left Hazel's house I was on a high, a feelgood optimist roll. It was like the story my big sister once told of a man who was in Las Vegas and had lost almost all his money and was on the point of leaving town. As he walked out of the casino an urgent little voice suddenly whispered in his ear, 'Go back, go back.' He stopped, dumbfounded. Clearly the voice of destiny had decided to speak to him. So he went back. And as he approached the roulette table the little voice whispered, 'Number 27, number 27. Bet it all.' And so the man, by now in thrall to the little voice, took out all of the rest of his money and pushed it forward onto number 27. The croupier spun the wheel, counterspun the ball against it, and the man watched as the ball hopped and jumped and bounced from number to number, slowing bit by tantalising bit, and finally, agonisingly, ultimately, settling on – number 14. And then in his ear, the man again heard the little voice. 'Oh shit.'

But that's another story, not my story.

I started, as I said, to head home after leaving Hazel's, but an urgent little voice whispered in my ear, 'Go back to Arenal. Go back to Arenal.' And so I did. I parked near the bulky man's block of flats and took up watch. And in fact the little voice was spot on about one thing – within ten minutes the automatic garage door ground protestingly upward and the white Mercedes emerged, swinging to the right and heading for the *autopista*. I fell in behind him.

We backtracked past the airport, in on the fast road until it started to peter out in the scrappy transitional wasteland around Palma, and then bent right along the beltway that loops around the city and then right again out onto the Valldemosa road, the Merc unhurriedly loafing along. Outside Valldemosa we had to slow and crawl past several bands of frighteningly fit senior citizens heading on walking tours up into the mountains, their brown and wizened faces turned towards the sun, their knobbly knees rising and falling as their sinewy legs drove them vigorously upward. There seem to be whole tribes of them that gather around Valldemosa – English, Germans, Dutch, and Scandinavians. You don't seem to see them elsewhere on the island, but I never pass that town without being awed by their robustness.

From there, it became increasingly clear that our goal probably was Deiá, arguably the most famous small village on the island, and certainly one of the better known hamlets in the Mediterranean. Long the haunt of artists and writers, Deiá has suffered an unfortunate influx of tourists in recent years, largely compromising the very qualities that made it so attractive in the first place. I recently saw the town described as 'unspoilt' and 'untouched,' in a travel brochure, but clearly whoever penned those words hadn't been in Deiá recently, hadn't seen the tour buses inching their way nose-to-tail through the town. Not that the place is ruined or compromised exactly, but 'untouched' is not a word one could use to describe it any more. Still, there are some lovely eateries there, though in my view the one that recently lost its Michelin star is overpriced, especially as now they've added more tables and pushed them so close together you don't have much privacy anymore. Try Sebastian's instead, or El Barrigón for tapas. Both good, as of my last visit. Semiramis lives up here, and her family is well connected and socially active in the area, so she keeps me up to date on what's up and coming and what's down and out. Useful, that.

Traffic was sparse along the winding road, and so I tried to hang back out of sight, keeping at least one curve in between me and the Merc. I wasn't always successful, but didn't think I was becoming conspicuous, as I was maintaining a fair distance between us. Generally the road is well trafficked, but not today. Of course if I'd actually planned this foray I'd have taken the BMW instead of Balthasar again.

We were getting close to the village itself when suddenly the Merc cut a quick turn and headed up a stony narrow drive towards a substantial stone house in the Mallorquin style set into a flattened bit of the terrain and surrounded by cypress trees and the ubiquitous pines and olive trees one sees in this area. The facade of the house was well weathered by something like two hundred years of sea winds, and the building had settled comfortably into its niche in the mountainside, with a mature flower garden, a small scatter of outbuildings, and lovely views to the sea. Sold these days it would probably command a cool million and a half sterling. As property prices go, Mallorca is becoming like central London.

I slowed abruptly, found a wide bit of the road and pulled over. From my vantage point I could just see the reflections off the white top of the car as it ascended the track. Then it pulled out of sight behind the house. I'd have to wait it out. One thing I could do, however. I rang Semiramis on my mobile and asked her if she knew who lived up there, describing the house and its position. Of course she knew it by sight, but could only say that it had been sold a year or so ago to a man from the Peninsula – Mallorquins manage to make the word 'peninsula' sound like a pejorative term; there's little love lost between them and the rest of Spain. Anyway, Semiramis said she hadn't heard his name. 'But give me ten minutes,' she said briskly. 'My brother-in-law will know. I'll ring you back.'

And so I whiled away my time fiddling with the radio – reception is terrible in this area – and waiting for the Merc to reappear, though I wasn't entirely certain whether it made sense to follow him further. All in all, I thought I'd best wait for him to come back down from the house, since for all I knew he might be just stopping to see a friend before going on to Puerto Soller. That, in fact, was where I had hoped he was headed, for there is a part of my mind that cherishes order – though those who know my office would never believe that statement – and likes to have things tidily neat and rounded off. Were he to go on and tie up in some way with the people up at the Holmes boatyard, then I'd be able to confirm my suspected maritime link and follow that thread.

The mobile rang. 'The house belongs to a man by the name of Roberto Fosas,' Semiramis said. 'He's some kind of money man, maybe retired, nobody knows for sure. He doesn't work, doesn't go out a lot, and has no family living there with him. Some people think he's gay, but since nobody knows one way or the other it could be idle village speculation simply because he lives on his own. That's about it. Anything else I can track down for you?'

'No,' I said gratefully. 'That's brilliant. I'll let you know if I need anything else from your gossip bureau.'

'*Ciao*,' she said, and hung up.

And it was just then that I decided to get some air, rolled down the window, and the hamlike hand reached through the gap and took my shoulder in its inexorable grip. He had spotted me, walked down the hill circling around behind me, and had come up behind the car when I wasn't paying attention, more fool I.

'So. I ask you before – vy are you followink me?'

'I wasn't ....' I started to say, and the grip increased in power. 'That is, yes, I was following you, but it isn't what you think.' Vacuous bullshit. You'll have to do better than that, Will.

'So vot you sink I sink?' he said, maintaining his boiled egg gaze. He was having a good time. I sink he liked to hurt people.

'Look,' I said, improvising wildly. 'I need a job done and I need a heavy. Somebody said you might do the job.'

'Who? Vot job?' He wasn't buying it.

'I can't say who.' The grip tightened again. This was getting like biofeedback gone awry. I tell a lie, I get a dose of pain. I tell the truth, I probably still get a dose of pain. Something wrong with that formula. 'I mean I don't know who. It was just a guy. We were drinking at Ballermann and we saw you and – shit, I don't know. Word gets around, and word has it you're pretty good with your dukes.' Now I was quoting from movies I'd seen when I was twelve. I needed a dialogue coach, quick. It was one thing to joke, but this monster had my shoulder in a grip like a steam press.

'Who is dis guy?' he repeated, not one to be dissuaded from simple home truths.

'Really. I don't know. I met him – you know – I was looking for somebody and you got pointed out. It's as simple as that. For God's sake, ease off a bit will you?' I don't know what's the matter with me, I'm a total coward when it comes to having muscles crushed by large Vikings. Call me unreasonable.

'Vot do you vant done?' Now things were improving.

'I told you already. I need a job done. You know what I mean.' I hoped he did.

'I don't kill people,' he said gloomily, as though this were some sort of terminal shortcoming in himself.

'No, no,' I cried brightly. 'Not kill, just – you know – maim or disable.' Now at least I knew he wasn't talking about putting up storm windows or painting ceilings.

'So. Vy you follow me?' I thought we'd been here before, but at least the grip stayed steady.

'As I said, there's this man, and I need a job done on him.' Who? What man? I was digging myself in deeper at a rate of knots.

'Vot you mean? Legs? Arms? Sometink special?'

What was this? Like a Chinese restaurant? One leg from Column A, one arm from Column B? 'No, no. Nothing special,' I said. 'Just a jolly good going over so he'll leave me alone.'

'So I tell him it's from you?' He was beginning to like the idea, I thought.

'Yes, that's it. How else would he know to leave me alone?'

'But you know vot Machiavelli wrote,' he said in all seriousness, taking on an advisory look. Wait a minute, wait a minute, this guy is quoting *Machiavelli* at me?

'No. What did he say?' Preposterous. Surreal. I wasn't having this conversation, and might have convinced myself I was dreaming save that my shoulder hurt so damned much.

'He write, if you punish your enemy you make sure he don't survive and come back and kill you. Or sometink like dat.'

Yes. He was right. I'd read something like that myself. 'Yes, well, that's why I need a good hard man to get the message across.'

'But I don't kill people. Not for money anyvay.' A fine ethical line was being drawn here.

'Maybe you could just beat him up and not mention my name. Maybe he has other enemies.' He seemed to mull over that proposition.

'Maybe,' he said, and I thought I felt his grip loosen a teeny tad.

'So will you do it?' I asked, pressing home what I thought was my advantage.

'Maybe,' he said again. He was considering.

'How much would it cost?' I asked, as much out of genuine curiosity as a ploy to distract him.

'Oh, dat depends,' he mused, and his eyes slid upward as though consulting a table of charges. So much for the broken nose, so much more for a jaw, maybe some price weighting based on the victim's size or age or physical condition.

'But that's not the important thing,' I said hastily. I didn't want to get hung up on haggling over money. He still had my shoulder in his grip and although the pressure had lessened, nearby muscles were cramping into concrete. 'I'll pay whatever you think is fair. You tell me afterward.' Can't say fairer than that, Squire!

'Sure. OK. Maybe I vill.' He'd come to a decision.

'So let go of me,' I said hastily, before he changed his mind.

'Sure. OK.' And he let go and withdrew his hand. I suspect even he was getting tired of squeezing on me. For one fleeting instant I had the impulse to hit the door lock, roll the window up, crank up the engine and peel out of there. But who was I kidding? Balthasar takes at least a dozen turns to start, he could probably put his leg of lamb arm through the window in two of those turns, the lock has been dodgy for at least four years, and anyway, with his Merc he could give me a mile start and catch up with me within three miles, even taking into account his time to stroll, or even crawl, up the hill to his car. No. On balance not one of my more intelligent impulses, though at least it indicated that the 'flight' part of my 'fight or flight' instinct was working correctly.

'You'll do it then. That's agreed.' I thought I'd best try to tie things down before he had second thoughts.

'Sure. OK. Who is it?'

That put me on the spot, but then I had a brainwave. 'His name is Fausto Milagro,' I said, and pushed the door open and got out so at least I was slightly less disadvantaged. Even when I was standing up he still made me feel like a birch next to a redwood.

'Who?' he said.

'His name is Fausto Milagro,' I repeated. 'I want him done. Duffed up, worked over, rubbed *on*, but not out.'

'So vere does dis Milagro guy hang out?' he asked. We stood there like two refugees from a new age seminar, he massaging the fingers of his right hand while I was massaging the top of my left shoulder. I hesitated to suggest we work on each other.

'I don't know for sure. I don't exactly know him socially.'

'You gotta pitcher or sometink?'

'No, no picture, but we could meet and I could point him out.'

'When?'

'Well, why not tomorrow?'

'OK, vere's he gonna be?'

'We could meet in Palma. There's a cafe right across from the Guardia Civil headquarters. Maybe midday or so – have you got a mobile number? I could ring you. By the way, who's that guy you were visiting up there? I think I might know him.' I thought I'd give him several things to chew on at the same time.

'You know dat guy?'

'Well, not really, but I think we met at a reception or something. I only know him casually – Roberto Fosas – but I know he's not from here and he's only been around for a year or so and does some finance work, doesn't he?' I'd just told him everything I knew and hoped he'd add to my slight fund of knowledge.

'Yeah. Financing tinks. Like dat.' This was really telling me a lot.

'And he's doing something for you?' I probed casually.

'No, not for me.' A pause.

'I mean I just wondered how you happened to stop by, is all.' I was still hoping – well I actually didn't know what I was hoping for, since I didn't really think he was suddenly about to bare his ample soul to my interrogation. And indeed he wasn't.

'Vy you ask all dese questions?' His brow was darkling once more.

'Just making conversation,' I said merrily. 'Idle curiosity. Passing the time of day. It's just that I didn't see you delivering anything or picking anything up.'

'You vould not see me deliver sometink from here,'

he stated ponderously and so answered my implied query, or at least I hoped he might have. Question was, what had he delivered?

'No, of course I couldn't see from here, but I thought you probably had the papers with you.' Was I going too far? Yes.

'Vot papers? How do you know about papers? Vot's goink on?' And with that he began to limber up those shovel-sized hands and moved perceptibly closer to me.

'Whoa. Nothing, nothing. I just thought I heard you talk about some papers yesterday – you know, from when I saw you with that man and followed you from Puerto Pollensa – and I thought maybe you were delivering papers. Not that I care. None of my business. It's just that you went into your building so fast yesterday and I couldn't find out which flat was yours, and ....' I began to wind down like an old Victrola.

'Yeah. OK. I thought you vas spyink on me'

'Spying on you? Not a bit,' I laughed hollowly. 'Perish the thought. I just want a job done.'

'Yeah. All right. Let's talk about dis guy. Vere does he vork?'

'Well,' said I, maintaining the brittle brightness. 'That's a bit of a catch, actually. He works for the Guardia Civil.' I smiled in what I hoped would be a disarming way.

'The Guardia?' He was slow to catch on. 'You mean he vorks in dat police building?'

'Yes.' Flat. Factual.

'Vot does he do?' Some doubt creeping in here?

'Well, he's a policeman, actually.'

'A police. You vant me to beat up a police?' He didn't seem angry – just puzzled.

'Well, yes, actually. But I don't want you to do it when he's on duty or anything like that. I mean at home would be just fine.'

'You vant me to beat up a police?' This was

apparently a difficult concept for him to grasp, but I was hoping he wouldn't become engaged by the novelty of the notion.

'I'm not angry with him as a policeman, if you know what I mean. I'm angry at him in a civilian capacity. Doesn't that make a difference?'

'Not if dey catch me.' No, not so dumb after all, perhaps simply a mill that grinds slowly.

'But I'm sure they wouldn't catch you,' I assured him.

'But maybe dey do,' he replied, still mulling and pondering.

'You could wait until dark. Nobody would see you,' sounding like a boxer's second trying to cheer his man on in a losing cause.

'No. I'm too big. Everybody sees me. I tink maybe I don't do dis job.' He'd finally got where I wanted him to go. It was time for a bit more Br'er Rabbit and the Briar Patch.

'You mean you won't do it?' I exclaimed, feigning some incipient indignation. 'You mean I followed you around for two days and now you don't want the job? Are you chicken or something?'

I'd overstepped the mark. 'Vait a minute. You be careful, Buddy,' and he started to swell like a Volkswagen-sized bullfrog.

I practically tripped over myself backing down, almost dropped my handbag even. 'I mean I'm just so disappointed. I'm really vexed with this man and I wanted someone to hurt him for me.'

'So vy don't you do it yourself?' The logic, from his point of view, was no doubt irrefutable.

'Just not my style, really,' I said, floundering a bit. 'Besides, he knows me.'

'So you could vait until dark. You said dat.' I was beginning to think he was playing with me.

'Yes, but I could never do the kind of job on him that

you could.' An appeal to his pride as a craftsman.

'No, dat's true, but still I sink maybe no. I don't beat on police.' And you don't kill people for money, either, I thought. All these petty little hang-ups.

'All right then, I'll just have to find somebody else. Do you think Señor Fosas might know someone?'

'I sink no. He don't do dat stuff.'

'Ah, I see. Well, maybe if you think of somebody who could help me out you could get in touch with me. I'd pay a good price.

'Yeah. I'll do dat. I'll call you. For sure maybe.' And he turned away and started back towards the drive going up to the house. He didn't look back.

I heaved a deep sigh of relief, pulled my shirt away from where I'd sweated it sticky under the arms, got back into Balthasar and got him cranked around and into motion along the road leading back. I'd learned a couple of useful things, though mostly what I was feeling was relief that I currently wasn't a reddish smear sullying the verge of the road back there. During that entire interchange only about three cars had gone by. He'd have had plenty of time to use those huge grapplehook hands to put me through his own personal Moulinex processor.

Just as I was feeling pretty good about all this, something crossed my mind. He'd said he'd ring me if he thought of someone to do my dirty work. He'd said it without any hesitation and didn't seem to be humouring me or putting me off. And he didn't strike me as a man given to subtle persiflage. So how did he know where to ring me? How did he even know who I am?

Sixteen

A time for reflection. This is where I exploit Hannah shamelessly. My sister Anne once said she never knew what she thought about something – a film, a book, a play – until she went to discuss it with, or describe it to, someone else. And so am I, too, about many of the things I need to consider that are important to me. I sit Hannah down and just tell her what's going on. Sometimes I want her responses, comments, or criticisms; sometimes I just want a listening ear, a perceptive human intelligence to lend attention while I think out loud. Sometimes, even, it's a sort of blend of the two – a listening person on one level, but one whose sharpness of mind I respect enough so as to focus my own thinking to a level of clarity beyond its normal sloppy-fuzzy-lazy-minimum-effort output.

We were sitting up in the terrace bar, the late afternoon winter sun slanting through the window in the far wall, glinting off the copper kettle in the wall niche and glancing along the pearled marble of the tabletops. We had just come in from having perched for awhile on the balustrade outside to watch the reflections from the lowering clouds make a light show of Nicholas's house across the garden. The front part of our property dates only from 1832, but the buildings at the rear go back a thousand years, at least for the first storey above foundation level. Nicholas's house, similarly ancient, is a big smoky-pink edifice of Moorish origin, and his family's lineage here goes back into medieval times. The portraits that line the interior hall reflect an unbroken occupation of the property back into the 13th century. Nicholas holds a sinecure post in the court that has come down to him from some distant great grandancestor and which pays him a small fee for every piece of paper that moves in the law courts, merely for adding his seal to the document. He has a clerk to do that for him, of course, and so attends court only once every month or so to collect his fees. He chose his antecedents wisely.

I settled onto a squashy cushion and began to pick at Pepa's offering of the day, a plateful of toothsome morsels of local cheeses, mountain ham, and a variety of *sobresadas*, sausages, on *integral* country bread, with a garnish of garlic oil, tomato, and a twist of freshly ground pepper.

'So it's a Mexican standoff in some ways,' I said. 'I've found out things about them, but I now have to assume they at least know who I am and where I live, and they must have serious doubts that I'm as all-fired innocent as I say I am, since I assume the Viking will pass on word of his encounter with me. Which is to say that if he knows who I am, and he knows where I live, and if he knows where Ninian was killed, whether or not he actually did it himself – which is still an open question – and he puts those simple facts together, then he won't bite on that story about my wanting to have Fausto Milagro dusted up. He may not have known all of the facts about me at the time we had our encounter, but he could now. More to the point, his associates might put it all together. And of course if I were in their position I'd assume the worst about me, too, especially now that I was caught following them. They probably will assume Ninian and I were in it together, and that I must be an accomplice in his blackmail plot. Which is further to say that if they really are the ones who did Ninian in, they probably won't hesitate to cover themselves by taking care of me as well.

'But that again leads to the conclusion that they have to assume not only that I know about them, but that I'll have taken steps to protect myself against them, especially after Ninian's murder. And so their knowledge of my knowledge of the reasons for Ninian's killing again implies a stalemate between us. Assuming, of course, that I do know enough about them. Unfortunately not only do *they* not know if I know enough about them, *I myself* don't know if I do either. There may be things I know, but don't understand well enough so that I can draw the right conclusions from what I know, if that makes any sense.'

'You're practically putting me to sleep with this stuff,' she said. 'Who was that scientist,' she asked, 'who figured out the structure of the rings of benzene by dreaming about snakes swallowing their own tails?'

'August Kekulé. And, yes, I know it's convoluted. But the problem for me is that I don't yet have enough on them to protect myself. Not only that, but there would be no redress if they decided to take me out, because no one would be able to prove anything. Which, of course would leave me pretty frustrated, posthumously speaking. Unless of course you were to choose to track them down and make sure they got put away.'

'I thought I was just here to listen,' she said dryly. 'Nobody ever said anything about throwing myself on the funeral pyre.'

'Though of course the wild card here is Fausto Milagro,' I said, paying her scant attention. 'He could, or could not, be involved, and his involvement could, or could not, be significant. On the one hand, he's encouraging me to chase the bad guys down, on the other he could *be* one of the bad guys and wants to keep tabs on how close on their tails I'm getting. Which means I have to be careful as to how much I tell him. If I tell him I know nothing, he could pass it along and they could decide to eliminate me as a preventative measure. On the other hand, if I tell him I know what I do know, which isn't enough, he could pass it along and they could decide to eliminate me before I learn any more, and finally, if I tell him I know almost everything, and he's involved, then he'll know I know, or soon *will* know, about *him*, and he may decide to join in with them to eliminate me before I have a chance to tell anyone else. God, this is getting to be like those conundrums in which you keep having to meet some people who only tell lies, some who only tell the truth, or, as in this case, a majority who keep shading it one way or the other to their maximum advantage. Is this making any sense to you?'

'Not really,' she said, pouring herself another dollop of wine. 'But it's fun to see you so passionate about it. Tell me more.' Hannah can be a real pain at times.

'So now we come to Commandant Vega. *He* may be the key. He has to find somebody to swing for Ninian's murder, and he's more or less told me it'll be me by default if I can't come up with a better suspect. I'm sure he's getting pressure from the tourist bigwigs to prove to all those millions of potential visitors out there that Mallorca is safe and civilised and that we keep our murders among ourselves and never, ever threaten the nice tourists who leave so much dosh here on the island. So he might have to put me away just to tidy up the books, so to speak. Lots of people more innocent than I am have been martyred for causes much more worthy. I trust the man, but I can't trust the system.

'Besides, as I've mentioned to you before, I think there's something strange in the relationship between Vega and Milagro. Don't forget, Milagro was to run the investigation originally, but then was summarily replaced by Vega, and I was given an explanation that seemed pretty thin, even at the time. Now, in view of newer information, it seems downright transparent. And equally, since both of them seem to have their own agendas, and both seem bent on using me, which of them, if either of them, should I believe or trust? Milagro comes out on the short side of that decision, of course, since it seems his brother may be involved in all this – whatever *this* actually is or turns out to be – and by extension Fausto may himself be involved since his brother is involved – *if* he is involved – which it seems he is, or at least *may* be. Hell, this thing is disappearing up its own backside.

'So my instinct is to trust Vega in a general way,

though I think I have to be on my guard against the tendency for policemen to close ranks when one of them is threatened by outsiders, which is to say that I now presume Vega suspects Milagro in some way, but may not be prepared either to admit it to an outsider like me, or follow up on it officially. In other words, he may have taken Milagro off the case because he thought he was involved, however tangentially. But even worse for me would be if he suspected Milagro of being connected to the person who killed Ninian and that suspicion prejudiced him against following up energetically on catching the rest of the gang, since if he were to catch them, he might, by extension, have to arrest Milagro as well. Which leaves me a bit out on a limb, as I can't even trust the man I now trust most in the case.

'And you notice I keep on – and yes, I know, on and on – about "they," and "them," and a gang, but the truth of it is that I don't even know for certain that they – there I go again – are connected in any nefarious scheme as such; hell, they might simply be nefarious individually. So that means I need to find out more about the others: Holmes, about whom I know next to nothing; Gewürz, about whom I know a bit; Martillo, if he figures as anything more than a walk-on character, as I suspect he is; and now Fosas, our newest man of mystery. I kind of like the look of him as the puppeteer. Not even having seen him, he seems to have an air of the manipulative about him, whereas the Viking seems pure muscle, Gewürz some kind of technician, and Holmes just too emotional a type to put together an organised gang. But even without knowing what they're doing, it has the feel of something coordinated and professional. And I'm including that mariner type down at the dock, who clearly knows something even if he's only their transport – though again I'm assuming transport to be a key element. I'd like to find out a bit more about *him*, too. He's certainly a pro at his job. And more mysterious than any

of them, maybe, is Stella, about whom I haven't a clue.
Who the hell is she and why is she going to Antigua?
Most of all, what I'd really like to know is where all of
this leaves me.'

'Still knowing sod all, it would appear,' she said. Her
tone was gentle, but the words were coolly realistic.

'Yep. I think you're right. Time to get on my bike
again.' I started to get up but she stopped me with a gesture.

'Hold on. Let me say something, Will. *En serio.*
Deadly serious. I've been listening to you and not saying
much, because I know that's sometimes what you need.
But I want you to bear something in mind. I know you
love a challenge and I know this mystery intrigues you
intellectually. I know you'd love to solve it for lots of
reasons, one of them perhaps even being to prove you're
smarter than the police, which I don't rate as a
particularly admirable motivation, though that's neither
here nor there and I'm willing to accept that your primary
motives are more mature than that. But what I don't want
you to do is reduce it to an intellectual puzzle. A man is
dead, defunct – just like the celebrated parrot. Ninian may
have been an S.O.B. but now he's an ex-S.O.B. And you
ought to remember that almost better than anyone; you
cleaned up his blood. So don't lose sight of the reality that
there are people out there capable of violence – vicious,
terminal violence. And don't lose sight of the reality that
you have children here who love you and to whom you
owe a responsibility, as well as a friend who would miss
you if you were stupid enough to get your ticket punched.
So in all your running around and being a cleverclogs and
having a good time trying to solve the mystery, please
just remember to be careful. Don't get yourself killed.
Will you promise us that? Please?'

I nodded mutely, touched. And went to bed to think
on it.

Seventeen

Next morning, I felt worn and weary. The Sisyphus effect. Not that the rock had rolled back on me, metaphorically or otherwise, at least not yet, but I certainly didn't feel I'd got it anywhere nearer the top of the mountain. Still, better Sisyphus than Prometheus. Having your liver torn out by an eagle *every day!* Once a week, maybe, but ...

Daughter Chessie had to go to a party near San Joan and so I drove her over, getting lost in the process in the wrinkles of tiny tracks between Sencelles and San Joan. This is an area I can commend to anyone to get lost in; shallow bowls of fields alternate with angular stands of dense trees, mostly pines, and there are prominent rocky outcrops that – wonder of wonders – crop out rockily from time to time, as though designed just to break up and lend interest to the view. As a general tip, don't take any way that is signposted, but as a subcommentary to that advice, do be prepared to turn around in small spaces when the road narrows and finally feebly peters out in a farm entrance or against one of those picturesque rocky outcrops. Practise your seventeen-point turns. And on one of these roads you'll see a wonderful local example of the triumph of form over function. There is one track that's hardly wider than the width of a normal car, but nevertheless has a white line painted neatly down its centre. Or maybe I'm daft and it's for bicyclists.

Adding to the chocolate-box picturesqueness were the wildflowers. At this time of year, early February, the almonds hadn't yet shed their blossom, the orange trees were beginning to drop their fruit to the ground, and the early pioneers of the first crop of wildflowers were busily edging all the green lines of transition with colour – dark orange, bright yellow, and the soon-to-be ubiquitous carpet of tiny white flowers overlaying the grass. Some people actually know the names of these flowers. There are even some superhumans, English people usually, who know their Latin names, though I sometimes wonder if they just make them up when they talk to me. I've always been, to the despair of my more knowledgeable family members, a blue-flower, yellow-flower, white-flower person. Just can't retain their names in any language, especially Latin.

After dropping Chessie off, on the way back I took a detour and went to see friend Pedro, a *caballista* who hires out horses to those of our guests who wish to go riding. I'd had a sneaky idea for getting the drop on Fosas, whom I considered to be the most inaccessible of the people I'd so far run to earth, and wanted to see whether I could get Pedro to help. More to the point, I'd thought I'd best try to do something quickly, as I suspected I might be the subject of speculation among the principals of the group, and didn't want them to start scrutinising me too closely, for all the reasons I'd outlined to Hannah, not to mention the one she'd raised with me.

Pedro's place always smells enchanting. I'm no horseman myself, which pretty much limits my riding to gentle nags of an understanding nature, of which, I'm grateful to report, Pedro has several. Anyway, I was standing by one of the horseboxes, watching him adjusting a shoe and taking in that pungent smoky mixture of aromas – straw and manure and leather and wood and the damp sweat of the horses themselves. I'd outlined my plan and he liked it. Pedro wears a fierce Cossack's moustache and affects a sort of oversized Buster Keaton hat which he wears straight across his brow. He likes action, so I knew he'd probably like this scheme, even though I'd warned him it could lead to a violent confrontation were it to go wrong. Truthfully, I suspect that's what he liked best about the idea: quite the opposite of my thinking on the subject. We arranged a meet for five that afternoon, so we'd arrive at our destination just as the light was waning and our quarry likely to be at home.

After that, having checked with her by phone, I did a quick run to Hazel's place and picked up the package I'd asked her to prepare. She was looking pale and sickly and wan; I had the feeling she hadn't quit on that bottle after I'd left. Her complexion had the look of frozen béchamel sauce – *old* frozen béchamel sauce. Almost wordlessly, we exchanged a few grunts, Ninian style, and then I left.

After leaving Santa Eugenia I drove over to see friend Buster, a big, bluff, charismatic Englishman who is an expert in esoteric electronics. He took my package into the back room and fooled around with it for about half an hour, soldering and splicing wires and muttering epithets under his breath every so often. I whiled away the time by leafing through a local German property magazine and being appalled by the prices. In due course Buster was finished with the device, gave me a quick briefing on his handiwork and sent me on my way.

Once back at home, I began the task of transforming myself. The art of disguise divides into two general categories: disguises of invisibility – camouflage, actually – and disguises of distraction, the latter category dividing yet again into distraction by masquerade as something else entirely from what you are, or distraction by exaggeration. As I'm no actor, I'd chosen the latter.

I worked on those elements that the Viking, or Gewürz, or even the man down at the docks might likely remember about me – the features that might form part of a verbal description. First I darkened my skin with some of that rub-on tanning lotion that can be washed off. Nice effect, that. If I cared to cultivate skin cancer a tan is what I'd go for. Of course the problem with a real tan is that after wasting all that time out in the sun it isn't even permanent.

Next I bulked myself out with layers of clothing, topping them off with a down vest, which I might regret if it stayed warm, but which might have credibility if the temperature dropped late in the afternoon. Finally I put on the silly cowboy hat Pedro had lent me and the big tall boots he'd also given me, the ones he kept for parade use during fiestas. By covering the top of my head, adding almost four inches to my height, and by bulking myself out so as look much broader, I thought I'd put myself clearly at variance from any descriptions that had been passed along by those who'd seen me. Then I opened the package Hazel had given me, tucked the contents up one roomy sleeve, and headed for the car, the Beemer today, and thence to the coast.

At five o'clock straight up, I found Pedro in the sparsely forested section about two miles along the road from where I'd been the previous day. He'd brought two horses in the trailer behind his six-wheeler and already had them out and saddled. His was a stunning bright bay gelding – I've never seen him with anything less than a magnificent mount – and mine was a pleasant old mare I'd ridden before and who must have had the car equivalent of two hundred thousand miles on her, twice around the clock as we said when I was growing up. She nickered in a familiar way, but I knew it was a con job; it had been at least six months since I'd been up on her and there was no way I was about to believe she remembered me among all the dozens, hundreds, of tourists she'd carted about since then. Besides, I was wearing my disguise.

We hid the cars, more or less, at least to casual eyes, mounted up and trotted along the road towards Fosas's house. That is to say Pedro's charger gambolled and my old lady trudged. But we got there. Once we'd arrived about two hundred yards away from the entrance drive, we headed up into the woods and then aimed for the house on a line parallel to the road. This area isn't good horse country, too steep and rocky, too many old stone terraces with olive trees on them. I hoped we might pass as neophyte riders who'd made a wrong turn. Just as we hit the property line we paused, dismounted, and circled down to look for signs of life. It was coming on to the time when anyone in the house would probably want to switch on a light, as it was considerably darker here in the wooded area than it was down along the coastal road.

Sure enough, as we watched, various illuminations appeared on the ground floor as someone inside walked from room to room letting there be light. That was our cue to get back to the horses and start our little charade.

I started by getting quite close to the house and then lying on my back and shouting out as loud as I could: 'Ow, son-of-a-bitch! Ow! (This last even louder) 'Ah thank Ah've broke mah goddamn ankle!' All of this in as authentic a Texan accent as I could muster. 'Get me some goddamn help, you dumb wetback spic!' Pedro had to suppress a guffaw. Was I over the top? 'Hurry up. Get me a doctor, get me an ambulance. Get me some help!'

At that point, having calculated I'd made enough noise to get Fosas's attention, I signalled to Pedro, who loped down to the house and started pounding on the door. '*Socorro, socorro, el dueño necesita ayuda!*' he cried. 'Help, help!' We knew Fosas was a native Spanish speaker, and of course I knew he spoke English with grace and fluency, so I wouldn't speak a word of Spanish when my turn came.

After only the shortest of pauses the door opened and a man I presumed to be Fosas appeared: middle sixties, white-haired, lean, tan and polished-looking, every inch an older counterpart to Fausto Milagro. I had positioned myself so I had a view of the door but was mostly out of sight from the entranceway. 'Tell him Ah need to call mah driver,' I shouted in English. Pedro conferred briefly with Fosas, who then turned away and disappeared inside. There was a long pause and I began to get worried. Maybe he'd just call a damned ambulance and leave us out here to rot. But then he reappeared, carrying, by God, a first aid kit. *That* I didn't want either.

'Listen, you dumb turkey, you come get me now, you

heah?' I shouted at Pedro. And he, falling nicely into character, called back, 'Yessir, yessir, Mr Vanderbilt, sir, I come now.' Maybe he was overdoing it a bit. Next he might call me Rockefeller. And the accent – Pedro speaks fluent colloquial English – had thickened to something approaching Manuel's murderous mangling of the language. 'I come now.' And he did. Next thing, he grabbed the stick we'd set to one side earlier and supported me solicitously while reassuring me volubly in Spanish that I was going to be all right and should calm myself and not lose my wool. Meanwhile, I was cursing vociferously and berating him at every other step for the transgressions of his forebears.

We arrived close to the door and I changed my demeanour.

'Ah'm most apologetic, sir,' I enunciated with the overweening dignity of a drunk as I addressed Señor Fosas, 'for any transgression on yoah property. Ah was only havin' a quiet ride with mah guide heah when he was so careless as to ride into mah path and frighten mah horse. Ah fear, sir, that Ah have badly sprained mah ankle and Ah crave yoah indulgence that Ah might call mah driver and have mahself taken from these Godfohsaken woods. Ah wonder, would yo' be so kind as to let me use yoah telephone, since this heah so-called guide does not have his mobile unit to hand.' And with that, using the stick, I hobbled towards the door with the confidence of one who is used to having doors open in front of him as though by magic. And, lo, magic there was, and Señor Fosas stepped aside to let me pass into his home. I'd reached, as we say where I come from, first base.

'And what a noble home yo' have, sir,' I exclaimed. 'Ah have rarely seen such taste on this side of the wahtah, pardon mah pride in ouah Texan sense of decor and hospitaliteh.' This was laying it on a bit thick, as so far I'd only seen the entrance hall.

'I thank you for the compliment,' the accent was

light, Spanish, but polished and cosmopolitan. I'd heard it before. 'My home is humble, rustic, without merit, but at your disposal.' He could lay it on as thick as Ah could. 'But do please seat yourself. Tell me the number and I will dial your servant.' He walked towards a phone on the other side of the room.

'Oh no, sir, it is something that Ah must do mahself. He surely would not simply accept the word of a stranger, howeveh well spoken and refined he maht be. Theah are those who would do me hahm, Ah fear, mah good sir, and mah driver is more than – yo' will understand as a man of the world, sir – *just* mah driver.'

'Of course, of course,' he said hastily. 'I understand completely.' And with that he attempted to bring the telephone to me, only to be frustrated by the length of the cord, which, of course, as with everything else that Telefónica provides, was of minimum length and quality. 'Could you make it comfortably to this chair?' he asked solicitously.

'Ah'll surely try,' I said, gyrating nimbly – but not too nimbly – into the proffered chair next to the telephone desk.

Just at that moment another man appeared in the doorway, a small, nattily dressed but rumple-browed, slightly rotund fiftyish man with half-glasses and sparse dark hair combed back and slicked down on a round skull. He blinked, as though surprised to find a cowboy loose in the parlour, but recovered quickly and smiled shyly in my general direction, though in the impersonal way one smiles at an errant seal one unexpectedly encounters in the bathtub.

Fosas didn't miss a beat. 'May I introduce my esteemed colleague, Solomon Meliá,' he said. 'Solomon does the books.' And that was that.

'I've done the books,' rejoined Meliá, getting the message. 'I'll wait for you in the other room, then,' he said, retreating back through the door. I couldn't catch the accent, but it wasn't Spanish, somewhere *mitteleuropäisch* I'd hazard as a guess.

'Ah'm so, so sorry,' I boomed. 'Ah have interrupted a business meeting, and we all know that business must come fuhst. Y'all go along now and take care of yoah important thangs. Ah'll just make this quick call and get mah ankle seen to. An' please may Ah ask may mah man theah bring me a glass of somethin' refreshin?' I added with a broad wink. 'Ah'll make mah call while y'all are investigatin' the drinks cupboard. Pedro theah knows mah tastes.'

'But of course,' said Fosas. 'Forgive me for being inhospitable,' and he motioned Pedro into the other room.

Quickly, and I felt I only had a moment, I fumbled Ninian's bug out of my sleeve where it had nestled so comfortably and fitted it back underneath the telephone table. Almost simultaneously, I jammed the flat silver transmitter up as far as I could on the back leg of the table nearest the window, securing it with the Velcro strap we'd attached to the case. It might not be the neatest and most professional of mountings, and it surely would be discovered next time the maid dusted back there, but I could do no more in the time I felt I had, and only hope Fosas employed a lazy and shortsighted maid. Besides, I thought, what more could one expect in terms of bug-mounting from a man with a painfully sprained ankle?

Nor was my timing far off, for no sooner than I'd tucked the last wire up out of sight, straightened my sleeve, and pushed myself back into my chair, speaking loudly and imperiously into the dead phone, but Fosas appeared again, with Pedro at his side carrying a short glass with a dark brown liquid in it. 'And be heah in fifteen minutes!' I commanded imperiously, slamming the phone back down.

'Kentucky bourbon and branch water,' said Fosas. 'I was in the States a few times myself and I've had a residual taste for it ever since.'

'Which only speaks volumes fo yoah constitutional good taste,' I affirmed, and beamed at him, Texan to the root and branch. 'But Ah cannot drink alone, good sir. Do please join me.'

'Oh, I am so sorry,' he said hurriedly. 'As you noted with such perspicacity, I am otherwise engaged just at the moment, and I do need to keep a clear head for the tasks before me.'

'Why, Ah do declare,' I pronounced, in what I hoped would be a suitably shamed and hangdog manner, 'Ah am keepin' yo' from yoah dutiful obligations. Ah truly cannot say how contrite Ah feel,' and I set down the glass with a thunk. 'Ah cannot stand on yoah kind hospitaliteh even one minute longah. Ah'm actually beginnin' to feel bettah and Ah don't even think mah ankle may be so sprained Ah cannot walk. Mah guide heah will surely support me down to the horses and we can make ouah way to the highway where mah man will pick me up.' And with that I stood, albeit unsteadily, and reached out for Pedro to support me, teetering towards him and letting him catch me, which he did as though we'd practised it a hundred times.

'No, please,' he said hastily, though I had the feeling he was beginning to tire of my charm – I couldn't possibly think why. 'Do please feel free to wait here for your man. You'll surely be safer as well.'

'Not a bit of it,' I said manfully, though taking the opportunity to drain the excellent bourbon, which I guessed might even have come from Fairfax county. 'Ah will not have yo' discomposed by mah inconvenience. We'll wait bah the road.'

'Well, if you insist,' he said. By rights we should have gone one more round of insistence and denial, but he clearly was in a hurry. Anyway, form had been served.

'Ah do insist,' I insisted, and leaned into Pedro in such a way as to set him in motion towards the door. 'It's no trouble whatsoevah.'

Fosas fell back a step and allowed us free passage to the outside world. I winced and grimaced but smiled at him pluckily as we passed into the darkness beyond the threshold. 'Ah do thank yo', sir, for yoah most excellent welcome and kindness, and if yo' ever find yoahself in Saluditarian, Texas, Ah hope yo' will not hesitate to call on me at Crossed Lines, mah ranch and oil field.'

'I etch your address in my memory,' he said graciously, but with a surreptitious wink at Pedro. I felt better already. If he was patronising me I'd pulled it off, at least for now.

'Farewell, goodnight, may legions of fireflies guide yo' to sweet dreams,' I boomed. Or something like that. I think the bourbon was taking effect, though it was more likely relief as I'd only had a short tot of the hard stuff. At any rate, we hobbled out of there like two A-types in a three-legged race.

Just into the safety of the darkness, we got the horses heading back along the road and reached the cars without incident, checking back over our shoulders from time to time. He'd seemed to buy my story, but he was also clearly a sharp cookie and he could well be a better actor than I gave him credit for being, though it's hard for a bad actor to judge a good one. Anyway, I didn't trust the situation, and wouldn't until we were well away from there.

Pedro got the horses tucked up in his travelling circus wagon, patted me on the shoulder, relieved me of his hat and boots and was quickly on his way, chortling to himself over our escapade. I put on some running shoes with great relief, chucked about half the pad clothing in the back seat, and decided not to waste any more time. The rest of the retrotransformation I could do later. I just hoped nobody would see me come into the hotel looking like a refugee from a rodeo. As I headed back along the home road I began to hyperventilate lightly and then broke into arias from *Oklahoma!* in celebration of what felt like an escape. Only time would tell. I'd have to go up into those woods again to get the tapes out from next to the mouldy stump where Pedro and I had cached the voice-triggered recording device after fitting the new transmitter to the bug to make it wireless. According to Buster, there was about ten or twelve days' juice in the batteries, so I'd need to come back several times. But what did I care? I could do these woods blindfolded now. I carried on at top volume. 'And the la, la, wheat, will something, something sweet, when the la, la, something-or-other rain ....' I never get the words right. But then I stopped anyway. A *Texan* singing about Oklahoma? Blasphemy.

I tried again, starting on in 'The Yellow Rose of Texas,' until I got as far as, 'She's the sweetest rose of colour that Texas ever knew ...' I stopped again. The words to that one, at least the original Civil War words, were definitely *not* PC.

You can't even open your mouth to sing anymore without offending somebody.

Eighteen

I was wondering if there was such a thing as repetitive strain injury syndrome of the brain. I'd been outside Holmes's boatyard six times during the last week and hadn't seen him even once. Not only that, but I'd also swung by Gewürz's place the same half dozen times without detecting a trace of him in evidence, fruitlessly had checked the tape machine every night up outside Fosas's house, gone up twice to Orient to see if Martillo was at home, looked in on the quay in Palma – the transporter had sailed but her sister ship would be along in a week or so – and had gone three times to check on the Viking but with nary a glimpse. He was, however, my only even partial success. I'd described him and asked about him at various bars in the area until eventually I'd been told by a lugubrious German barman that his name was Sven, no second name known. So that small fact, if indeed it was a fact and not simply his *nom de guerre*, was all I had to show for days of constant travel and travail. They'd clearly all gone to ground and I was fed up.

Commandant Vega was also getting fed up and his temper was fraying. Probably he was getting pressure from above. As for Milagro, I hadn't been in touch with him, nor he with me. The business with his brother was nagging at me and since I didn't know what to do I did nothing, which is sometimes an efficacious way of handling problems, though more often it simply stores up trouble. The more activist element of my temperament wanted confrontation with him on the subject, wanted to shake and rattle and prod and provoke, but the passivist, pacifist elements remembered young Albert at the zoo as described by Stanley Holloway – Albert *would* persist in provoking the lion and so of course got eaten. Deservedly. Part of me felt the same way about Milagro; he was only safe as long as I didn't provoke him.

Which left me pretty frustrated, doing daily rounds of checking on the contenders, with the clock running out and my batteries running down and nothing to show for it so far. I was in danger of losing the *insouciance* I'd always felt was a hallmark of my character. Grim days.

But needs must when the Devil drives, and it belatedly occurred to me I'd left one avenue unexplored, a loose end dangling. I'd not kept any sort of watch on Pascual Milagro's boat, which I had to assume would be part of the transport system for any contraband that was being moved, presumably drugs, they being the most obvious choice for quick profits. A boat like his could easily sail the short distance to the North African coast to pick up, say, hash or even one of the hard drugs, and then equally easily sail to offload at ports along the opposite coast, either in Spain itself or in France. The distances were negligible in both directions and such trips could be disguised as short pleasure jaunts.

Even though I'd heard of police spot checks on pleasure craft, or tours of the marinas with sniffer dogs, I'd also read that sophisticated smugglers didn't let drugs anywhere inside their boats these days, preferring to stick them to the bottom hull of the craft in limpet pods, or tow them behind in subaquaplaning torpedo casings. It was all part of the unceasing game of leapfrog played by the police and the smugglers. No sooner did the police figure out how to cut off one avenue of transport than the smugglers raised the stakes by adopting an even slicker way of evading their pursuers. My gang seemed fairly sophisticated to begin with, but also had the advantage that it would be an intrepid policeman indeed who would descend on a boat belonging to the brother of a well-placed Guardia officer without some hard evidence to justify his swoop. Pascual had built-in protection.

So once more down to the ships to see I went, and soon was strolling out along the quay, heading for Pascual's boat. The wind had shifted into the north and the day was cool by Mallorca standards. The sky had that bruised look it gets when the mountains reflect the low and sombre mist-filtered sun. Even the gulls didn't like the weather, and had taken their raucous clamour to roost. I wasn't sure what I'd find down here today, or even what I was looking for, but it sure beat the hell out of peering at Holmes's wire fence or the front of Sven's building. On this side of the marina where the sailboats were there was the insistent ringing of that bluegrass steel guitar music of halyards twanging against masts as the wind blew, and the choppy plash of the water along the caissons of the quay. As before, and as I had broadly expected, Pascual's boat was buttoned up like a winter overcoat. But the young Danish woman was in evidence on the deck of her ketch, baring various rounded bits to the intermittent sun, being intrepid about the wind. I hailed her.

'*Hallo, goddag, tusind tak for mad!*' I don't speak Danish, or Swedish or Norwegian for that matter, but it made her smile. A pearly-toothed dentifrice ad smile, teeth all even and straight.

'Hallo, yourself. What you are doing down here again?'

'Taking a stroll. Trying not to shiver. How can you not freeze wearing just that – those' I said, gesturing at the scanty scraps of cloth that stood between her and a state of nature.

'Warm blood. A thousand years of ancestors who sail cold seas and live on fish and those round yellow cheeses.'

'And raped and pillaged among *my* ancestors, no doubt.'

'If they was lucky,' she grinned. 'Come aboard if you wish.'

I did wish. I was impressed with her in an awake state, impressed also with what had previously been hidden under her sweatclothes the other day. My assumption then had been of less cerebral substance, which I know is a form of sexist prejudice, but there is so much conditioning we receive to assume a low level of intellectual prowess among blondes with prominent curves that it's hard to resist pigeonholing them. I began to think that maybe there was more to her than met the eye, though what was already on view was considerable.

'So you're just lying here thinking about Kierkegaard,' I said. When I get distracted I get dumb and corny. And pretentious.

'Actually,' she said seriously. 'I am lying here figuring how much more days I can stay here with the money I got left. It's my boat my father leave me, but I was here with a boyfriend and we break up and he's gone and so without him now to help I'm almost broke, *nej*?' And I owe some money. So maybe I must sell the boat and I don't want to. By the way, I'm Petra, Petra Struve.' And she extended a hand.

'Will Stock,' I said, shaking her cold little paw. *Che gelida manina.* 'Nice to meet you. Sorry to tell you I'm not one of the dozens of sugar daddies who hang out around here. Otherwise, believe me, I wouldn't hesitate to make an offer to help.' And I raised my eyebrows twice, Groucho Marx style. I told you I get corny in the presence of such expanses of lightly tanned flesh, though said flesh was beginning to take on a goosebumped aspect, and she reduced the level of distraction by reaching back behind her, grabbing the tracksuit top and slipping it on. Now there we were again, just friendly University of Chicago colleagues.

'Yesss,' she said, following up on the sugar daddy remark. 'I do see them, but I think I am too old. Most like the girls of no more than twenty-two or three, I think. You see that boat there,' she said, pointing across to where all the stinkpots and gin palaces and cigarette boats were moored, and specifying a particularly sleek Sunseeker. 'That one belongs to that nightclub man, Pedro Thongfallow or something. I see him all the time with new young girls, always different but always the same. He says he sleeps with a thousand or more women. Isn't that pitiful?' Oh, yes, pitiful – very very pitiful, I thought, trying not to look like the Mock Turtle. 'But all those women and no relationship, no friendship. That's what I think is pitiful. And he must be,' inspecting me more closely, 'maybe your age or only a little more. *Pitiful*,' she repeated, consigning me firmly to my place.

Anyway, I thought I'd get down to what even I couldn't characterise as work. 'How about your neighbour? Not around then?' When in doubt belabour the obvious.

'No,' she looked mildly puzzled. 'I have not seen Pascual for some days. Why you are so interested in him?'

Could I trust her? Of course not. I didn't know her from Eve, whom she'd so closely resembled before putting the tracksuit back on. Part of me thought me a fool for even contemplating telling her anything, but the other part of me, a large part I fear, is a sucker for attractively-tousled blondes, and even more so when they seem to have no axe to grind and claim to be broke, or close to it.

'He may be mixed up in something, and it may be something that could get me in trouble.' There. I wasn't really telling her anything.

'What kind of something?' Logical question.

'Maybe drugs.' Now the cat was out of the bag. I waited for her response.

'Drugs? Pascual? No, I don't think so.' She hadn't even blinked. 'No, Pascual don't do drugs, and I'm pretty sure he don't deal drugs either. Now Martillo, that's maybe another story.' She shrugged.

'Who?' I was laid low by the reference. 'Did you say Martillo?'

'Yes. You know him?'

'No, but I've heard the name. Why do you mention him?'

'I'm sorry. I thought you know. He's Señor Milagro's captain.'

Mystery solved. So obvious I should have seen it as soon as she mentioned the name. Martillo would have the use of the boat from time to time. I was certain he could always rig an excuse to take her out – test the engines, doodleflap the spinnaker, whatever. Or he could wait until Pascual wasn't around. A boat captain usually is given a fair amount of leeway by his owners. Opportunities were his for the taking.

'What do you know about him?' I asked.

She shifted around to look across at the boat, and snuggled down into the big sweatshirt, out of the wind some more. 'Not too much, but I see things and I'm not stupid.'

'For instance? What kind of things?' I was trying not to be impatient.

'Oh, it's more a feeling than anything, you know – solid. Like there are people who come to visit him who only come when Señor Milagro is not around. People who look flash, one or two like cheap crooks, but one or two not. You know what I mean.'

I didn't, but I nodded sagely. 'Do you know any of their names?'

'No, they don't talk outside. They just come and go aboard and stay down in the cabin.'

'What languages do they speak? Spanish? German? English?'

'I don't know for sure all the languages. One of them speaks a kind of German but I don't speak well German and I only hear them maybe twice.'

'Swiss German?'

'Probably. Martillo is Swiss. Did you know that? A Swiss sea captain! Crazy, *nej*?' This was getting to be a running joke.

'How about a Spanish man, maybe a Guardia

officer?' I described Fausto in broad brushstrokes.

'Oh, him. Yes, I see him a few times, but I can't remember if he comes when Señor Milagro is here or only when Captain Martillo is on board. They get lots of visitors sometimes and I'm not always here or I don't always pay attention. If they are doing something crooked I don't want them to see me paying too much attention, *nej*?'

'I suppose you're right. Anything else you can tell me?'

'Yeah. You got a nice voice,' and she winked.

'Thank you. You gotta few nice things yourself.' I think I even blushed. 'And I thank you for the information. But please just don't mention to anyone that you told me. This could be a serious business and I wouldn't want you involved.'

'It looks like I am already involved a little bit, *nej*?' She smiled, clearly not one to faze easily. 'But what am I involved in, that's maybe the big 64 question?' She looked at me expectantly.

'Fair comment,' I admitted. So I gave her the quick version, edited highlights. The clear grey eyes got big and round. Like me, she'd obviously been brought up on a diet of thrillers and mysteries.

'So what you want me to do, actually? I want to help.'

'All right. If you want to help, here's what you can do.' I fumbled around for a card. *Everybody* in Spain has a card. The petrol station attendant has a card – and a mobile phone and a palm pilot computer. My cards are from fifteen years ago and another life, but I like the engraved script on them and they're good quality so I just cross out all the obsolete numbers and write new ones, though now that we have a website I'm thinking of getting something else printed; it's hard to write out all that web stuff in tiny neat script. 'Just keep a eye on that boat – discreetly, mind you, I *really* don't want you to get pulled into this situation. Is that clear? If you see something you think is worth reporting to me, ring either my number at the hotel or my mobile number. Do you have a mobile?'

'No, I don't.' Just my luck. The only person in Spain without one.

'But you can use the phone over at Wellies or Flanagan's, can't you?'

'For sure.'

'Fine. But is there a way I can reach *you?*' I thought it would be a good idea to keep an eye on her, though maybe my motives were mixed. In any event, it would make sense.

'I eat breakfast every day at the French Coffee Shop. Usually between nine and ten. You maybe can call me there.'

'All right, that's agreed. I won't call every day, but perhaps every other day to check in. At the same time, you can call me if there's any news. Just be very careful of one particular man, a great big Swedish man with arms as big as my legs. You've seen him?'

'Yes, him I know. He is here lots of times. I don't know he was Swedish but yes, he look like a man who could hurt people maybe.'

'I think so, too. So don't let him see you watching the boat, OK?'

'OK. Oh, this is exciting. Just like the movies!' And she leaned over and gave me a moist but glancing kiss, missing, dammit, my mouth by about two inches. 'But don't worry. I'll be careful.'

'You do that. Now I'd better go before somebody sees me on your boat.' I got up and gave her a farewell half pat, half hug. 'I'll be in touch.' Then I swung down the gangplank and walked briskly back towards the inner harbour. I felt about twenty years younger. Something to do with the hormones, they say.

Nineteen

What is it I always tell the children? The Buddhists say there are three important rules to life, three paramount guiding principles. The first of them is Attention. So is the second. And the third? Big surprise. It's Attention. Pay attention. Focus. Keep your eye upon the doughnut and not upon the hole, as they used to say on the Burma Shave signs along the roadside when I was young and green.

And what had I been doing? Acting without thinking, substituting treadmill motion for forward movement. I felt stupid. Precious time I'd wasted because I hadn't stopped and considered, had rushed off in all directions at once. It wasn't just that I'd failed to check on Pascual's boat during all the time I was lolloping around pretending to play masterspook, but rather what I'd done with Hazel's little green slip of paper, the post office receipt.

Having made the assumption that Ninian had either an accomplice or else was trying to protect himself by sending evidence to a lawyer, I had immediately gone over to the Santa Maria post office to ask about the receipt, to see whether or not they could tell me to whom the package had been sent. This information is always recorded for official post office purposes, whatever *they* may be, and predictably is confidential. And because it is confidential the woman in charge was standing firmly on the principle of confidentiality, which was totally correct and justified on her part. For my part, of course, I just wanted to bypass the system, so I hinted at a sweetener, but she was having none of it, and of course the more I persisted the more adamant she became in her refusals.

Obviously I couldn't tell her Ninian was dead and cremated, or she'd probably ring the police to give *them* the information I was after, and so far they didn't know about my little green slip of paper – nor did I want them to. And if she hadn't already read about Ninian's murder, which had been all over the papers, then I wasn't going to enlighten her. Most likely it would put the wind up her even more, make her even more disposed to call in the Guardia or the Policía Nacional. So I just sort of stood there for a long time spinning out the conversation until it finally occurred to me to ask the most obvious question, the one I should have asked when I first came through the door.

'But he did send the package from here, didn't he? What I mean is, do you have any specific memory of him sending it, maybe a recollection of what it looked like?'

'Oh, no. He didn't send it from here. You can see,' said she amenably, opening a drawer and getting out her own book of green receipts. 'The one you have is a much darker green than mine. Yours came from Palma where they're using the new forms,' and she pointed to tiny numbers printed on the top right corner of the slip.

So now at least I had something to do. I stopped wagging and sniffing around her like an ill-trained dog and got in the car and went to Palma, where I spent another three or so fruitless hours making a nuisance of myself at the post offices along the route from the restaurant, the ones I'd visited in my quest for the post office box. *Nada, nada*. And *nada*.

Having given up, or pretty much given up, I took the old road back and then detoured up to Alaró, that bonny town that nestles in the shoulder of the mountains above Consell like a double handful of spilled dice. I needed to drop off some brochures with a posh private travel agent who does accommodation arrangements for heavy-duty celebrities and politicians and captains of industry and rock stars, though we usually don't accept bookings from rock stars. She endeared herself to me forever when she first visited us and looked at our Grand Suite, which consists of a double bedroom with a king-sized four-poster bed, a formal drawing room with a noble carved mirror, graceful silk hangings and an elegant painted ceiling, plus a smaller single room with a French sleigh bed and an English 18th century armoire. It was into this room that she peered and said, 'Oh look, there's a perfect little room for the bodyguard.'

Along the back road from Alaró to Lloseta there is a series of small valleys which the road parallels, winding along only a single track wide in stretches. In two or three places the road is broad enough to park on, or there is space to pull in off the road, and some of the views from these spots are spectacular. It is here, too, I sometimes come to think after I've been being hyperactive, rushing from place to place following my nose instead of something smarter. I leave the car, climb down into the valley and simply walk where my feet take me and the terrain allows. And it was while doing this that I began to think about the Ninian I had known, began to consider what I thought he might have done or not done, began to try to put myself in his moccasins. As I've tactlessly made clear previously, the Ninian I knew was not a lovable person. He was an angry, litigious, aggressive, ill-humoured and bad-tempered man. He was a loner, with Hazel apparently his only point of contact with the rest of the human race. He looked for opportunities to cheat people, to abuse them, to pick fights with them. He had looked for trouble, and eventually had found it.

So why would a man like that have an accomplice? Or if he trusted anyone, wouldn't it be Hazel, and only Hazel? So was Hazel lying when she claimed no knowledge of his bugging capers? I thought not. Her responses when we found the bug and the tapes had been too passionately genuine to admit of artifice. No, Ninian probably had not had an accomplice.

By process of elimination this left the option that Ninian had sent evidence to a lawyer for safekeeping. Or to a bank, though he may not have trusted banks, as evidenced by his hideyhole postbox. But I wasn't convinced about the notion of his using a lawyer to safekeep evidence. One of Ninian's more prominent and less pleasant characteristics was that he was arrogant to the point of megalomania – he sued people not just because he was convinced he was right, but also because he was certain he would win, regardless of how weak a hand he might hold. So Ninian would not have had, in all likelihood, the same impulse to protect himself that a less self-aggrandising person might have when holding evidence that could prove potentially dangerous. Ninian wouldn't give credence to the danger, wouldn't admit that something negative could happen to him. He was in a state of arrested development. He was like those teenaged boys who drive motorcycles at top speed on winding roads in the rain. He thought he was invulnerable, immortal.

But somebody had violently disabused him of that idea, and like many others who out of hubris put themselves in the way of harm, he didn't survive to learn the lesson.

Which left me with one other fairly obvious conclusion. Ninian had no accomplice, had trusted nobody, had *not* taken steps to protect himself. He had in fact hidden the evidence, and although he had hidden it from Hazel, who knew nothing of his bugging activities, he hadn't succeeded in hiding his activities from his buggees, who had indeed apparently taken violent exception to being recorded.

By process of elimination, therefore – no tasteless pun intended – I became persuaded that Ninian had sent the package to himself. He'd send it to his postbox for safekeeping. He'd sent it prior to his murder but it hadn't arrived until after he was dead and after I had cleared the box. This was clearly the solution.

And how did I know this to be fact? Easy. Because at this very minute I was sitting in my *atico* flat holding the package in my hands. Once I'd figured out the probable location of the package, all I'd had to do was go back to the Santa Maria post office, make sure the postal *dueña* was looking the other way, and empty out Box 111. Easy peasie.

I opened it up. There was less to it than I had hoped, just one single tape. No papers or notes or other clues. And as with the other tapes, there were no markings or labels, though I noticed this one was rubbed and stained with sweat or grease as though it had been handled often. I put it on to play. At first, like the others, there was only background hiss and hum and clatter. Then there were voices.

First voice. 'I wish they'd hurry up with the drinks, I'm dry as toast. I don' know why we come here always, the service is so slow and the prices are too high anyway.'

Second voice. 'Relax. I see the waiter over there. Yes, he's heading this way.'

First voice. 'About time, too.'

Sound of clattering. Third voice – in Spanish – briskly. 'Here you are gentlemen.' More clattering, then an expectant pause.

First voice. 'Ahhhh. That's better. I needed that. God, my leg is aching. Damp again today. You think the salad's gonna be awright? Probly it'll be wilted this time of day. I don' want to have the runs tomorrow. My stomach is delicate. You know I had that operation last year. Remember? I'm not the same since. You know whad I mean?'

This was fascinating, absolutely riveting. I hadn't heard dialogue like this since the last time I was on a bus with a group of pensioners on an outing to Blackpool. But it was Solomon Meliá, the ostensible book-keeper, doing the complaining and I was willing to bet the other one was our sly Señor Fosas, who'd so far only uttered one line, the rest of the conversation having been a monologue of moans by Meliá. I sat quietly and waited for the script to improve. It didn't, at least not for a long time. They drank their drinks, ate some salad, with Meliá averring the whole time that it would give him wind tonight and cramps tomorrow. Finally they ordered some coffee.

'All right. Listen, Sol. Let's get the list wrapped up,' said Fosas, for indeed, it was he. 'I'm assuming you've done all the calculations.'

'Right, OK, I goddit right here.' Sound of fumbling and clattering, and then a sort of muffled thump. 'Right. You ready?'

'Go ahead.'

'I puttem in different currencies like they ast me to. OK?'

'Yes, yes. Let's just get it down so we can talk about the rest of it.'

'Awright already. You don' want anythin' else to drink, do you? I'm still dry.'

'No, Sol,' tightly. 'I don't want anything more to drink. Let's just get the list finished and then we can have something else.'

'Awright. If you're really sure you don' want somethin'?'

'Yes.' Studiedly patient pause. 'I'm very sure.'

'Right then. OK. Well the first one on the list is Orient 3. We agreed that before, didn' we?'

'Yes, Sol. We agreed that. How much does he get?'

'Thirty thousan' Swiss francs. That's a lot. Too much, I think.'

'No, Sol. It's not too much. He did a good job. We agreed on all the percentages up-front. Who's next?'

'Puerto Soller 221b. Forty-five thousan' pounds. But he hasn't finished his work yet.'

'That's all right. He will. I'll be checking in with him. Next?'

'Next comes Arenal 6. I'm not happy with him. He's down for thirty thousan' deutschmarks, but wha' did he do for that kinda money? It don' feel good to me.'

'No?' said Fosas. 'Well do you want to be the one to

tell him you're giving him less?'

'I didn' say that. I jus' said he didn' rate that kinda money.'

'Maybe. Maybe not. But if you don't want to tell him he's being cut back I can't think of anybody else to do it. You've seen him in action. Let's leave it alone, all right?'

'Awright. But you know how I feel, right? OK, we got Puerto Alcudia 57. He's supposed to get a hunert thousan' deutschmarks, but he's godda deliver somethin' better than he just did if we're gonna pay him.'

'Right. I agree with that. I'll ring him and make sure the work is best quality this time. It has to pass without a second look. Who else is left?'

'There's twenny-five thousan' U.S. to Pollensa 66. I guess that's awright wid you.'

'Yes. I have no problems there. Slick as oiled iced glass, that one. Who else?'

'You know goddamn well who else. Your baby in Portals. An' you wanted to start with twenny-five thousan' U.S. on that one. I'm not gonna decide. You're the one to fix that. I'm not touchin' it.'

'Yes. OK. You don't have to harp on. I know how you feel. Pollensa 66 is straightforward and I'll take the Portals situation in hand myself. It may be still open but you can forget about it. Now what about you and me? What's left on your calculations?'

'I tol' you up front. I get a hunert thousan' bucks off the top and that's it. I don't want to fool aroun' with percentages. So that's cut and dried. As for you, right now, based on no big overrun on expenses, I'm calculatin' you in whad you wanted, pesetas, at around thirty-seven and three-quarters of a million an' countin'. Make you happy?'

'I'll be happy when it's done. Until then it's all theory. I'm the one who's at risk here. It's my money, not anybody else's. Are there other expenses you haven't mentioned?'

'Naw. Nothin' that counts. There's some small stuff, but not much, and the delay's gonna cost us a little bit. I'll figure it up and tell you tomorrow afternoon.'

'Fine with me. Listen, let's get out of here. I'm getting itchy feet to walk and get some air. You can catch another drink further along.'

'If you say so, boss. Sir.'

'Oh, can the irony, Sol. Come on, we'll pick up the tab on the way out. And just by the way, what about Stella?'

'It's arranged now. We're sending her to Antigua.'

And then there were a few more bumpings and clatterings and then only a hiss of tape and the background noise of the restaurant. I let it run until it cut out, replaying the salient bits of dialogue in my head.

So I'd unkindly misjudged Ninian. The corny code wasn't his, it was theirs. But this was the tape he'd made the list from – the sums of money checked out, the towns obviously represented most of the people I'd tracked down, and what Ninian and I both seemed to know was who the speakers were. Perhaps my mystery was solved. He'd tried to blackmail Fosas – Meliá seemed out of the running, just an employee – and he'd paid the price. And based on my early assessment, bulky Sven was the most likely candidate to have done the job.

I mentally translated the amounts into Sterling so I could make comparisons, and the figures seemed to check out, assuming a gang structure. Fosas was the main man – the money man – and he was getting about £150,000 out of whatever the caper was. Meliá seemed some kind of accountant-cum-fixer, recruiter and general organiser, and he was winding up with about a third of the boss man's take. Then came Gewürz – I knew his name even if Ninian hadn't – and he did something technical for a sum around £33,000. And Holmes, another technical man of some sort, was going to get £45,000. His must be an important job. Our erstwhile friend Sven seemed to be being palmed off with only £10,000, but then I judged him to be muscle and not much more. Maybe Meliá was right about his relative value, but then if he was the one who took care of Ninian, even for a bonus, then he'd be worthwhile to have on the team. From Fosas's point of view, he needed a loyal thug just in case someone like Ninian turned up to spoil things.

Or someone like me.

There was another reference about which I hadn't a clue. While all the other references seemed to fall into place, the allusion to Pollensa was lost on me. I hadn't seen or heard of anyone connected to that town. Something for me to try to follow up.

And there was the other reference to Portals and an open situation that I'd need to try to figure out. My assumption was we were talking about Pascual Milagro and transport, but I didn't understand the Meliá's anxiety about that one. Everyone else seemed agreed to be getting a percentage, like Fosas, with only Meliá on a fixed sum. A small thing, but it didn't compute. Protection money, maybe? If that were the case it argued for Fausto Morell's involvement as well as Pascual's. Maybe that was why the matter was so delicate.

But, in a way, even that didn't matter. I'd liaise with the Commandant with this information. I thought I'd located and identified the principals in this outfit, knew who most of the others were, and was well on my way to solving the whole mystery. In point of fact, I felt I had best visit Vega as soon as possible. Surely I had all the points of the compass covered: my bugging device (well Ninian's actually, but mine by inheritance); Petra keeping an eye on the boat; and me continuing to check out the boatyard in Puerto Soller from time to time, the printshop in Alcudia, and even big Sven.

Altogether, I felt things were coming together. I went back to the hotel feeling tolerably self-satisfied, only to be met by all the spiteful ducks that dance attendance upon any hotel owner and peck him about the ankles at every turn. The pressure on the hot water was down, probably due to calcium buildup in the heat exchanger, some black fungus was trying to take up residence on the ceiling in the indoor Roman spa pool, mainly because I refuse to use chlorine and will only filter the water electronically and with oxygen so as to save our guests' eyesight. Regrettably, although these methods are fine for the water – even approved by the International Olympic Standards Committee – they don't kill off the stuff that likes to live on the wooden beams, so we have to get up on a ladder and sponge it off manually. Apart from that, the switchboard for our phone system – Telefónica's expensive kluge of 1970s technology – was ringing the staff room at 4 a.m. for no good reason, automatically and to the annoyance of the sleep-in night staff, which includes me a few nights a week. And the milk people had failed to deliver, so I had to go out and hunt down a case of semi-skimmed for tomorrow's breakfast. This was all telling me that I'd had my little adventure, my mini-holiday from reality, my boy's own fantasy, and that now it was time for me to come back to Earth with a bump. Welcome home.

Twenty

My sense of self-satisfaction with what I'd considered a coup didn't last long. By eleven the next morning I'd been disabused of the idea that I'd solved the case, or indeed had come anywhere close to solving it. I'd risen at seven, showered, shaved, fed the cat, had coffee and read the paper, done morning rounds of inspection to check the state of flowers, lightbulbs, or as yet undetected catastrophic occurrences in the middle of the night. Our hotel isn't huge, but it's big enough to remind me at times of one of my favourite old *Punch* cartoons. The Lord and Lady are breakfasting at the long table in the dining hall, the Lord reading the newspaper. 'Good grief, Emily,' he is saying to his wife, 'it says here the East Wing burned down last night.'

In any event, having satisfied myself that the East Wing was still intact, I had rung Commandant Vega and set up an appointment for 10 a.m., and had presented myself at his office door spot on time, a cassette player under one arm. I'd then gone straight to the point with a bare minimum of formalities and niceties, told him I had evidence that could wrap up the case, and played him the tape, skipping all the groaning and complaining from Meliá at the outset. One thing I didn't mention was where I'd obtained the tape. I didn't think it was relevant just yet. At the end of my presentation he pushed back from his desk and looked at me.

'So,' he said. 'What do you think this proves?'

I was taken aback. Wasn't it obvious? 'Isn't it obvious?' I said.

'Not to me,' he said. 'I'm hearing a lot of talk about money and it seems they're using a code of some kind, but that's something any discreet businessmen might do, especially if they had any reason to think competitors might be interested in acquiring information about whatever their deal is. It seems to me you're jumping to conclusions based on insubstantial premises and insupportable assumptions.'

'But you haven't seen them. I have.' He had a point, but so did I.

'That's irrelevant. Lots of crooks look like citizens and lots of honest citizens look like crooks.'

'All right. Fair enough, but you might change your mind if I tell you that this is a tape Ninian Mede recorded and probably was using to blackmail these people and that's the reason they had him killed.' I ended this peroration with a Perry Mason flourish. *Quod erat demonstrandum.* I looked at him with a 'case proven' look.

'But that doesn't prove anything either, save that you seem to have been holding out on me. How could Señor Mede blackmail anyone when they haven't said anything that could be construed as incriminating? Nobody threatens anybody. Nobody talks about a crime. I've heard more suspicious conversations sitting in church. Everything you've got, or even think you've got, is purely circumstantial.'

'Well, yes, I can see it's circumstantial,' I spluttered. 'But taken altogether, the circumstances and the facts create a logical set, a conjunction of probability, a common sense conclusion.'

'Maybe, maybe not. That's why stuff like this is called circumstantial, and that's why it's both meaningless and worthless.'

'Worthless to you, maybe.' I was beginning to become agitated. 'But something's going on, something went on, and a man is dead, worthless shit though he may have been.' And more to the point, I thought, but didn't say, now *I'm* the one in the firing line, probably from both sides. I was holding back on the one thing I wasn't going to tell *anyone* yet – that I knew the names of the men on the tape. That was my last card to play if things got really rough.

'Look,' he said, not unkindly. 'I recognise that you're under stress. You've been doing a lot of running around trying to scrape up evidence to get yourself exonerated, and to help me as well – I recognise that. But you're not experienced in these things, you don't have any backup, you're crashing around like a pig in the underbrush, and you're expecting too much of yourself. Slow down a bit, see what you can find out without trying to read too much into what you do find out, and most important, I repeat, most important, pass on everything you find out to me. Can I count on you to do that?'

That was a hard one for me. Logic told me he was right. Logic had usually been my friend, though at times a faithless and fickle one. Instinct was not something I trusted instinctively, but in this case I felt instinctively that instinct would serve me better than logic. I felt like a computer programmer caught in a reunion of flower children. Actually, I hadn't yet figured out what I felt, logically or emotionally. 'I'll do the best I can,' I ended up saying, lamely.

He seemed to think that was the best he was going to get out of me, and truth to tell I think he was a bit confused himself. 'Well, get along then, stay in touch, and let me know if anything develops.'

'Sure, I'll do that.' By then I just wanted to get out of there. And did.

Reviewing the conversation afterwards as I sat in the Café Lírico – still an authentic *local*, despite copious influxes of tourists – I began to realise how naïve I'd been. I'd followed a few people, projected my hopes of their ill intentions onto them, been impressed or intimidated by their macho-aggressive attitudes, and drawn conclusions from premises that now, by my own admission, were tissue thin. I still thought I was right about some of the more important aspects of the case, of course – my intellectual ego doesn't lie down that easily – but now I was also prepared to admit that it wasn't going to be as easy as I'd thought it would be, and that I'd just have to dig for some harder evidence. I'd been so eager to get to see Vega that I hadn't checked in with Petra this morning, so I thought I'd drive down to see if I could catch her. The fact of her blondeness, her twinkle, her straight nose and teeth and curvy everything else didn't enter into my decision, I do declare it.

Portals was even deeper in dust and noise than before, with trenches running in all directions and the usual ratio of supervisors to workmen – about five to one on any given site at any given time. Mallorquins are hard workers, but a cursory study of most public works projects would give the opposite impression. It seems to be the effect of spending public money. Everything is bigger, more expensive, less well organised and overstaffed. For some time now, our local town hall has had the intention of pedestrianising the narrow street alongside the plaza immediately in front of our hotel, a project in which I encourage them, as it would do away with the noise that can at times be heard in our downstairs front rooms. I've put double glazing on, of course, but those damned *motos* make a horribly penetrating noise and you hear them anyway. In any event, the project has been delayed for awhile, and I asked the mayor one day when it would be done. 'Oh, we're a bit short,' he said. 'We need another ten million or so to get the work started.' I was aghast at hearing a number like that. Ten million *short?* I am utterly convinced that my own small construction crew could do the whole job for less than three million. Regrettably, that's not how public projects work, though it seems a worldwide affliction, hardly specific to Spain.

I dumped the car in a residential area alongside a number of shiny machines belonging to other port crawlers. I always feel sorry for the people who live on the fringes of tourist areas. It must be grievously frustrating never to be able to get a parking place outside your own home, always to have noisy, disruptive traffic percolating though one's street. As I made my way down to the port area, I could see a black and silver Harley parked by the gangplank to Petra's craft. The hatch was partially open, so I figured someone must be visiting her aboard – the boy friend perhaps? A slight twinge of jealousy tickled at me, which simultaneously amused and appalled me. Why and how could I feel something like that? This was a woman not much more than half my age, with whom I'd only mildly flirted on one occasion, but who had flattered me into feeling only about a decade older than she – a woman on whom I had no claim whatsoever, but who simply happened to push some old hormonal buttons. And here I was feeling possessive and proprietary, like an old lion sniffing the spoor of a young pretender on his patch. Some of my hardwired atavistic responses I find baffling and distressing, whatever function they may have served my forebears ten thousand years ago. It's disconcerting to find oneself in the grip of such irrational and bewildering impulses. Not to mention distracting. Now I would have to make a concerted effort to think straight about this woman.

So in order to demonstrate my maturity, my independence from my hormonal impulses, and the clarity of my thinking, I hung around like a peeping Tom and watched her boat, admiring those curves, too, the long sweet teak ones. After about a half hour, her visitor appeared, a dark-haired round-headed man in his middle thirties, thick-necked and broad-shouldered though not tall, with a sharp curved nose that made him look birdlike. Predictably, I didn't like him on sight, though by this time my rational mind had downgraded us only to old rooster, young bantam. God, this stuff is ludicrous. Dawkins was right; we're all just pawns to our genes.

Petra appeared just after he'd cleared the hatch, climbed up alongside him and they conversed, apparently warmly, for a couple of minutes. She kept one hand on his shoulder in a gesture of intimacy. He started to leave, then turned back and kissed her in a way that was hard to parse, more than brotherly, less than loverly. Then he sprang onto the Harley, somewhat clumsily I noted to my satisfaction, and kicked it into life. In a moment he was gone. Petra still stood on the deck looking after him, but I couldn't see, from my vantage point a hundred or so yards away, exactly what her expression might be saying.

I was partially in cover beside another boat, and debated staying still so she wouldn't notice me, but then thought better of the idea. Curiosity, I suppose, as to what her response might be to finding out she'd been observed. I raised a hand and waved to attract her attention. She didn't react immediately. Shortsighted perhaps. Then she recognised me and smiled and beckoned me over.

'I was spying on you. You aren't the only spy here.'

'I hope I make you jealous,' she laughed. Pow. Spot on. How could she know about that stuff?

'Absolutely. That a new boyfriend?' Raised eyebrows and a tilt of the head.

'*Nej*, that's the old one. I'm glad he is not seeing you.' And she seemed serious about it. This was a mood shift. 'Are you watching us long?'

I wondered what she meant by that. Something I wasn't supposed to have seen? 'Long enough, I suppose,' I said noncommittally.

'He is here still wanting me to do things for him,' she said, still in serious mode.

'What sort of things?'

She ignored that. 'I didn't tell him about you.'

'Tell him about me? What is there to tell? I'm just a guy who came by to recruit you as a spy and who flirted with you.' At times I am so affectedly coy I make myself cringe.

'No,' she said, refusing to depart from her seriousness. 'You know you are looking for some trouble, and I say I will help and so maybe that is trouble too for me, *nej?*'

I let my demeanour adapt to hers. 'Yes, I suppose you're right. But I didn't want to involve you and I don't want to involve you and I don't want to put you in any kind of danger. I just thought you might be able to keep an eye on Milagro's boat for me, that's all.'

'I think maybe it is more complicated than that. Maybe you are not telling me everything so maybe I don't worry. But I maybe am involved already more than you think.' She did seem, if not exactly worried, at least subdued and thoughtful.

'Listen,' I interrupted. 'Do you mind if we talk down below out of sight. I'm feeling exposed up here.'

'Yes, yes. Of course. Me too.' We retired below into a roomy cabin with deep comfy down cushions, books in three languages, and a scattered patterning of vaguely indo-asiatic stencils on the bulkheads. It was totally unnautical, enchantingly feminine and inviting. Cosiest boat I'd ever been inside, more nest than boat, and a far cry from the smooth, sterile cabins one sees in so many megabuck gin palaces. It looked like somebody's home.

'Delightful,' I said, ducking away from the overhead beams and looking around.

'My father, he was what you call a blue water sailor, and he sometimes go many weeks to sea, but he always miss home and so he ask me to make him a space like our home.' She shrugged lightly. 'I like it too.'

'I can see why it's special to you and why you wouldn't want to give it up.'

'My boyfriend – my *before* boyfriend,' she said with a self-mocking grin, 'He offers me money for doing things, and before I said OK, but now he is wanting me to do some other things and it's hard because I need money but he is getting deeper into things I'm afraid about.'

'Things you can tell me about?' I asked.

'Not maybe yet,' she said, shaking her head.

Time for some active listening. The theory says that if you simply repeat things back to people they will tell you more. 'So you're caught between needing the money to keep the boat and doing perhaps something wrong for your,' and I put a lightly acidic twist on it, '*before* boyfriend.'

'Something like that,' she said, not taking the bait.

'But you did something before, whatever it was. And it didn't bother your conscience then?'

'Maybe you understand when you are new in a relation and you care about somebody and they ask you to do something and maybe you do it before you think about it. And you want them to be good and you want to believe they are not doing anything wrong, or maybe you try not to think about it too much, so what you do you do not choose to see, like maybe not being happy with your face and so you don't look in a mirror anymore. Something like that I did.' She looked down, twisting a ring on her left hand.

'But you still like him, care about him,' I said. 'I saw you kiss him.'

'My body still likes him, but my mind I'm not too sure.' She paused for a moment. 'And I cannot trust him more,' she said decisively.

'Which brings us back to the question – what are you going to do?'

'I am not going to do more what he wants. That I know.'

'Is there any way I can be of help?' I asked. I didn't want to press her on the boyfriend's scam, whatever it was. My life was complicated enough already. Or was he, too, connected with the bunch I was chasing after?

'I think probably no,' she replied. 'You are nice and I maybe can help you with Captain Martillo, but I do not know you too well yet and I cannot trust to tell anyone about Henry.'

'Perhaps we'll get to know one another better one day,' I said. Didn't I wish.

'Maybe,' she said, neutrally. 'But I can tell you only

right now that nobody is coming or going on the boat next door. I'm watching.'

'Are you here all the time these days?' I asked.

'Most of the day, always at night,' she said. 'I'm waiting to see if maybe my sister can lend me some money to sail home, but I have to pay some people first, and wait for good weather. I like it here so if I have to leave I would be sorry.'

'If I can think of any way for you to make some money I'll let you know. I might be able to make a few calls.' I knew I was sounding like those old farts who dangle film or TV contracts in front of naïve girls, but what the hell, I *would* make a few calls.

'Thank you. You are a kind man,' and she reached across and squeezed my hand. Then she smiled at me with real warmth and with a glint of something I wanted to think was physical interest in her eyes.

'Shows how little you know of me,' I leered.

'No, I am a good judge of men.'

'Except when it came to Henry?' I offered with a querying note.

'Yes, maybe you are right, but I did want to think Henry he is just weak, not really bad. But listen,' she said, seeming to come to a decision. 'I will tell you what happened. You know that man who was killed some days ago? You have maybe read about him?' She hadn't put me together with the hotel, and in truth I'd worked hard to keep the hotel out of the news reports as much as possible. 'That man I feel responsible about.' She stopped speaking, just twisting the ring again.

'Why is that? You're feeling guilty about something?'

'Yes. I am the one who partly caused it I think.'

I was surprised by this revelation. 'How? In what way?'

'It was me that pointed him out to them ...' She stopped again.

'To whom? "Pointed him out"? What does that mean?'

'To Henry, at first, but then to his friends. I didn't mean to.' She was borderline teary now, a side of her I hadn't seen before. 'It was one night here when it was warm and Henry and I are on deck and some men come to Milagro's boat to probably see Martillo, and I am just sitting and I notice a tall man hiding over close to where you was and watching them, and so I just say to Henry I think this man is watching those people and maybe he is police or something because I always think Martillo is doing things kind of funny crooked. And then Henry goes over to the boat and talks to somebody and comes back and doesn't say anything more, but two or three days later I read about the tall man being killed – they talk about in the paper how tall he is and I know it's the same man – and I think I am the one who puts the finger on him, I think you say. And I was angry with Henry and that is when we have the fight and break up.'

She stopped and pressed a thumb hard into her mouth, biting down on the taut skin of the joint. I shifted over and put an arm awkwardly over her shoulder, trying for something comforting but without any sexual overtones. Suddenly I had several salient questions to ask her about friend Henry, but right now seemed an inappropriate moment. Right now I felt I should give her some help with her obvious stress, perhaps with some direct hands-on therapy. Years ago I learned some powerful direct physical stressbusting techniques using shiatsu acupressure. I took her fist away from her mouth and worked on the points between the last two knuckles, the reset points, and then on the relief point up along the outside of the edge of the palm. Two minutes of that and then I shifted to the chi energy crossing sites under her eyes – their pure grey clouding with something like grief as I worked – tapping gently for about a minute. Finally, I turned her away from me and held the two forehead pulse points from behind, waiting – and it took a long time – until the irregular throbbing rhythm slowed and evened and I finally was rewarded with the sigh I'd been waiting for, the signal of letdown. She'd had herself wound up tight, but she'd be better now. No point in trying to deal with emotion by reason – hands on is often lots better. I propped her against the pillows again and closed her eyes with my two forefingers, keeping them closed with the gentlest of pressures. After awhile she sighed again and I could sense the emotional knots dissipating.

'Better now,' I said. A statement not a question.

'Yes. That was like some kind of sleepyhappy magic,' and she smiled drowsily. 'I think I go to bed now, OK?'

'I think you should,' and I squeezed her shoulder oh-so-gently right along the trapezius where Sven had rendered me paralysed the other day. 'Get some rest.'

'Thank you, Will,' she said. 'We have to talk some more, but not now.' And she offered herself for a kiss. This time we connected lips to lips. There was a poignant quality to it that was moving, and it seemed something like the kiss she'd shared with Henry, more than brotherly, less than loverly. But *loverly* all the same, if I'm allowed a Cockney word. I went home pretty sleepy happy myself.

Twenty-One

Fausto Milagro was my dilemma. I now knew, or at least was taking Petra's judgment at face value, that his brother wasn't involved in either the ring of blackhats – when I was young the Hollywood westerns always had the good guys in white hats battling it out against the bad guys in black hats – or Ninian's death. But Fausto didn't know I had ever even had any suspicions in that direction because he didn't know I'd seen him visit the boat, nor that I'd found out to whom it belonged. And since he'd never mentioned either the boat or his brother to me, I had to assume he either still was trying to protect his brother because he didn't know his brother was in the clear, or else that he knew something that I didn't know and that his brother was in fact involved with the gang. Either way it made for difficulties for me. Every time I spoke with him there was this lumpy awkward unmentionable subject between us and since each of us knew about it but felt we couldn't tell the other, we went to inordinate lengths politely to tippytoe around it like a pile of dung on the parlour floor, not saying anything that might call attention to it. It made for some stilted conversations, most of which I tried to conduct by phone so that he wouldn't see my face. Poker is not my game.

'Milagro here.' Clipped, military, formal.

'It's Will. I thought I'd better check in with you. You know I found a tape?' Another thing I didn't know was whether Vega had told him about the tape or not.

'No. What's on it?' So Vega hadn't told him, or else, of course, there was the possibility that Milagro just wasn't telling me that Vega had told him.

'Nothing important, I'm afraid. It was another tape Ninian had recorded. A conversation between a Spanish man and a foreigner in the restaurant. I thought it might have some evidence on it but mostly it just seems to be a discussion of some kind of business deal. I was hoping it was blackmail evidence that could tie them to Ninian's murder. I told Vega about it, too, but he doesn't think it's important either.' This last lightly, as though I had been the one not to attach much importance to the tape.

'Worth my listening to it?' Still all business. He sounded as if he were wearing the hat and full dress uniform today, with medals.

'Probably not, but it's here if you want to.' This was all pure bluff on my part. If he listened to even a minute of it he'd know it was the source of the information on the list I'd given him. At this stage I didn't want him to know I'd tied Fosas and Meliá to that list. I held my breath as I waited for his response.

'I'll consider it and let you know. Have to go now. In a meeting.' So that was it. Probably with superiors.

'Get in touch when you can then. Bye.' I breathed a sigh of relief as I dropped the phone in its cradle. I wasn't any wiser than when I'd begun that conversation but then again, neither was he, and at least I'd checked in and told him about the tape. The ball was now in his court.

Another thing concerning me was boyfriend Henry. I hadn't had a chance to ask Petra any more about him since she'd gone all sleepy on me, but I'd rung an acquaintance who is a member of the Harley Davidson club here on the island and he knew him and he'd told me that Henry's surname is Root, that his father was American and his mother Peruvian, and that he liked to be known as 'Hawg' – jumped up spiv that he is – *his* words, not mine. My acquaintance didn't like him and who was I to argue with his judgment? Some lovely women have the worst taste in men, I've noticed. Usually something to do with not feeling worthy. I'd have to investigate that theory with regard to Petra. Maybe I could be unworthy enough to appeal to her lack of self-worth, if that was the secret. Anyway, the most interesting fact I'd picked up was that 'Hawg' Root lived in Pollensa, so that made him the prime candidate for the role of missing member of the blackhat gang, the one who was going to get $25,000. The slick one, according to Fosas. So what had he done, or was going to do, to qualify for that amount of money? Would Petra know? She'd been forthcoming, but only up to a point. She might or might not know, but either she was still being protective of Root, or maybe was still unsure of me. On the other hand, he also might have promised her some of that money. In any event, it was something more to throw in the hopper for consideration.

Also, during my ruminations in the shower, that think-tank for weighty thoughts, the realisation had struck me of a glaring oversight on my part. There was a gap in my surveillance. I needed to go back to Puerto Soller and visit Holmes's boatyard again, this time not just from the outside. Several times when I'd been up to check on Holmes I'd seen the dog, and once I'd even gone up close to the fence to scrutinise him when I was pretty sure nobody was around. He'd seemed fairly benign, even forgiving of me, considering our first encounter. Or maybe he was just nearsighted, forgetful, or plain stupid. Anyway, as long as I stayed on my side of the fence he regarded me with neutrality. Even by a mother's standards, no one would deny he was an ugly-looking beast, and if his territory were invaded probably every bit as innately fierce as I'd thought. That he'd been trained not to bark made him even spookier. Dogs that attack silently should be always be considered dangerous. Certainly lots of barking dogs do bite, but many only yap to try to impress us, or other dogs. Can't bear 'em.

I'd got out my old guerrilla nightfighter's hand-to-hand combat notebook to refresh my memory on how to handle attack dogs. This is what you do. You crouch and brace as the dog comes at you, holding out your left forearm parallel to the ground, supporting it with your right hand and offering it to the dog. Then, as he leaps and bites, you thrust it as far back into his throat as you can, simultaneously whipping your right forearm around, palm down, to press on the back of his neck. At the same time, you throw yourself into a backward roll to lift his paws off the ground and take away his traction, using your forearm to push his head back as far as it will go. From this position the dog can be strangled until he passes out, or if you have the strength you can actually break his neck.

Screw that, I thought, and went over to our nervous neighbour to borrow a couple of Valiums.

I thawed out a couple of generous slices of *ternera* – only the best beef will do – ground up the Valiums and worked them into the meat, making two plump sleepy-doggy burgers. Then I went upstairs to change into my guerrilla nightfighter infiltration suit, the one I keep for special occasions. I had also decided I wasn't partial to repeating the sliding over the rocks lark to get around the fence, so I went down to our toolshed and got out the big boltcutters we'd had to buy last year when Joaquin managed to lose both sets of keys to the padlocks on the pumphouse. With luck, I could cut the fence in some discreet corner and it might go undetected for a long time, especially if I could wedge it cunningly back into place.

There was still some time to go until dark, so I watched the folk dancers on the church steps through the upstairs *sala* windows. It was another holiday today, the Feast of St Lazy, patron saint of all those who do not wish to work, or some such similar fiesta, of which there are so many in Spain. Calculating in all the saints' days and local festivals, I figure there must be, in addition to weekends, at least two weeks' worth of official holidays here. And if the holiday falls anywhere within two days of a weekend, then everyone takes what they call a *puente*, an extra day off bridge to or from the weekend. So depending on the year and how the holidays fall, one can add an additional six to eight days of *puente* holidays. Not bad if you're a salaried employee.

Nevertheless, I've commented previously on how

hard Mallorquins work, and they do, especially the women. During the Napoleonic wars when the French were in occupation here – one of so many nations to have held possession of this island – they had a phrase to describe how the Mallorquins worked: 'The children work like women, the women work like men, and the men work like *titans*.' That well may have been the case then, but things have obviously improved for the men since then and I've only ever noticed the women working like titans these days. And they're the ones who never ever get a day off. There is no *puente* for women's work.

In any event, while such idle thoughts were running through my head, the dancers were having a merry time gyrating in our church square. They were a group from another village visiting for the day, and wore the regional costumes of black and white with red sashes and cummerbunds. With the double-glazed windows closed, I couldn't hear the music from here, so they seemed to wheel and circle in graceful silence, making elegant shapes against the stone flagging of the square. Only a few people were actually watching, none of them with cameras. I recalled that shortly after we'd opened we'd had some big-wig head of a brace of airlines or chain of steel mills staying with us and something similar had been going on out there.

'Where are the tourists?' he'd asked. 'I don't see anyone taking pictures.'

'They don't do it for the tourists,' I'd explained. 'They do it for themselves. It's an expression of local history, local custom, local pride.'

'Ah,' he'd said. 'Not a show for tourists then. I understand.'

But after watching for another ten minutes he couldn't stand it any longer and got his camera and went down to take pictures of them.

After awhile the light began to fade and I decided it might be time to leave. I drove the winding back road through the almond groves, the white-blossomed trees now beginning to give up their petals, the pink still firmly in place, the whole sky flushing rose into mauve as the waning light reflected off a high layer of cirrus cloud. There'd been another shift in the weather pattern, another mood. It's one of the joys of living in a marine environment; the climate can ring its changes every four hours. As a visiting friend once said, 'You don't really get weather here, do you? Just samples.'

As I'd hoped, there was no sign of human life at the boatyard, though I noticed a disconcerting addition to the outside of the entrance to the offices. Attached to the wall above the door there was now a closed-circuit TV camera, though thankfully it seemed to be pointing at an acute enough downward angle so that I couldn't be seen out here by the driveway gate. I wondered what had happened to make them raise the level of their security. Perhaps my last break-in hadn't gone as undetected as I had hoped.

I parked in what had become my usual spot, tucked discreetly into the tiny side road up the way, with a broad view of the fence and the buildings, but poised to flee back up the hill if anyone came after me. In all the time I'd been checking on things here, I hadn't seen one single boat come in or out. There were just a couple of small sailing dinks moored at the quay, and still inside the shed, I hoped, would be the boat I'd come to investigate, the posh vessel I'd seen the first time I'd visited. For all I knew she was gone by now, but I wanted to follow up on a hunch.

After plotting the angles of coverage of the observation camera, I strolled down and rattled the gate gently. A moment later I heard the clunk of the dogflap and saw the silent dark shape streaking towards me across the entrance yard. Not a sound from the dog, only the scrape and scrabble of his paws on the gravel of the parking area. I waited until he was thirty feet away and then lofted the twin steakburgers over the gate so that they flopped a few feet in front of him. He ignored them and kept on coming at me, hurling himself against the chain gate, making it vibrate with a metallic chittering sound. Again and again he tried to push through to me, only to be prevented by the chain links. It seemed that however apparently neutral he might be behind the fence during the day, night-time was another matter. Not a sound came from him other than a husky panting as he sought a way to get at me, intent on ripping me apart just on principle. I was grateful that I'd opted for chemical discretion as the better part of valour. I didn't fancy having a wrestle with that hound, nightfighter costume or no.

After awhile he began to get the idea that he was unlikely to be able to burst open the gate to tear out my throat. Possibly he'd had this experience one or three times before. I backed off a bit to lower the level of provocation. After patrolling up and down about forty feet in each direction, he apparently concluded that while he wasn't going to be able to get out to chew on me, I likely wasn't going to be able to get in to invade his territory. At this point he turned back to investigate the meat, and after giving the burgers a thorough sniffover, began to devour them in great gulps. I'd counted on my observation that most owners of mean dogs here seem to like to keep them underfed, just to keep an edge on their meanness.

It was going to take awhile for the Valiums to take effect, so I walked back up to the car and tuned in on a concert on Radio Clásica. They play a lot of music picked up from the Beeb and it's always interesting to hear the announcers wrestling with the, for them, unpronounceable names: 'Kreestofear Hoagwud an' thae Academia uf Ancian Musik.' I'm not taking the piss here, I hate to hear my own murderous mangling of some Spanish words, but it's just that they play many Academy recordings and each announcer has his own way of twisting up the names. My heart goes out to non-native English speakers. Without having grown up with the language, how would anyone know how to pronounce certain of our letter combinations: the baffling 'o-u-g-h' sounds for example – plough, through, tough, cough or though. And hiccough. Not even to mention place or proper names, like Worcestershire, Cholmondoley, or Beauchamps Place, that Americans like me, *especially* Americans, who think they already speak the English language, find utterly confounding. There are literally hundreds of such examples. No language is easy, but English is a particular bitch, lovely though she be.

After awhile, I sauntered back down. The dog was still upright and moving, though describing staggered circle patterns as he tried to stay on his feet. It clearly wouldn't be long now. Up and to my left there was a patch where a carob tree overhung the fence, and some weedy long-stemmed grasses had invaded the gravelled yard from this side. It seemed as good a spot as any, given that I saw scant evidence of regular mowing of the fringes. Out came the boltcutters and I began work on the bottom section of the fence, clipping carefully near the crosswires in order to make a flap that would hang straight back down reasonably invisibly once I pushed it back in place. The dog had accompanied me, weaving along parallel to his side of the fence, and now he watched me blearily, head sagging, a few synapses still firing to tell him he should be ripping me apart, but the rest of him not in the game. Presently he lay down and put his head on his paws and began a stertorous drugged snoring. Those were virtually the first sounds I'd heard him make.

I was through the fence in a trice, however long that may be – one pull literally, but has anyone ever timed it? Or how about two shakes of a lamb's tail? How less poetic our language would be if I had to say I was through the fence in 2.74 seconds (though truth be told, that's about what it was).

After making a long circuit around the building to avoid the camera, and keeping an eye out for any others, I arrived at the back wall. The dog flap hung waiting and I was through that in less than a trice, maybe even a 'mo,' though even that understates the speed of my flashy nightfighter roll-under entrance. My fourteen-year-old son would have admired my cinematic stunt prowess, though doubtless he could have done it even better.

Once inside, the gloom seemed more pervasive than last time, and it took me a quiet couple of minutes or so to get the old visual purple cranked up to night vision levels. I didn't want to use the torch unless necessary, as I had no way of knowing if the inside was monitored by a camera as well. Just by its looming bulk in the almost stygian blackness, I could feel as much as see that indeed the boat was still here, but the reason it seemed darker in here now was that they'd finished painting her, and whereas she'd been white previously, now she was – well, if anyone would let me I'd use the word 'Cimmerian', a Homeric word for dark and gloomy that I only learned the other day and have been dying to try out. Anyway, she was as forbidding as any pirate ship. Creeping along in the inky darkness, I looked for the telltale blinking red light of a camera. After making a circuit of the boat, mostly by feel, I hazarded there was none and flicked on the torch. The repaint job seemed virtually finished. The matte black hull was smooth and dry, the woodwork varnished and gleaming, the brasswork glowing, and mooring lines braced in shipshape Bristol fashion.

Rounding behind her, I flashed the torch up onto the transom. 'Melanie,' it said, and underneath, 'St Kitts.' That was odd. We were a long way from St Kitts and she certainly hadn't sailed here from there, unless someone had persuaded Clare Francis or someone else equally intrepid to bring her across. Sweet and yar she was – maybe even a downsized recast of a Laurent Giles design, though more anonymous – but no way did I see this lovely thing doing a transatlantic run on her own. Among other things she was clearly such a valuable craft that I couldn't see an owner with an ounce of common sense risking her in the heavy Atlantic seas, however well insured they might have her. Besides, mere money could never replace a boat like this one. Then I twigged. Of course. She'd come over on the transporter. Maybe she was to go back on it. Maybe even with something extra built in under her planks. No, logically it had to be the other way around. She'd come from the Caribbean with something under those fragrant cedar planks, and then had come in here for a refit and a repaint, affording Holmes the opportunity to offload whatever had been put aboard her. And coming in on a transporter, she was much less likely to be inspected by customs or the drug dogs than if she'd sailed in under her own steam, so to speak. So that made some logical sense. The question now was, would she go back with something aboard as return freight? Money maybe? Offhand I couldn't think of anything illegal, apart from dirty money, that one would want to ship from Europe to the Caribbean, and the idea of shipping money by boat seemed pretty impractical anyway. After all, what are crooked banks for?

There was a ladder standing against the wall and I moved it over and leaned it against the hull, climbing up to take a quick shufti inside. Nothing to see, or at least nothing obviously apparent, as most of the interior work seemed to have been finished and all the planks laid and pegged down. They seemed to have only recently finished the painting, with pots of marine varnish, brushes, and a handspray still in evidence on the deck. I climbed back down the ladder and decided to call it a night. If my theory was correct, this was something for Commandant Vega. Even if it was too late to do anything about Melanie, he could keep an eye out for another shipment and swoop on the next boat they brought into the yard from off the transporter. No doubt this was a regular run.

Melanie, eh? Painted black. Somebody had a wry sense of humour. As I recalled, the name Melanie derived from the Greek *melas*, for black. That sort of felt like a Fosas touch.

And Melanie rang another bell. Where had I seen that name before?

Twenty-Two

I was using Hannah as a bounceboard again. I had told her about the failure with Vega, and my qualms about trying to have an honest discussion with Milagro, given my assumption that his hidden agenda was to protect his brother. And I was trying to figure out what Ninian must have had on them to cause Fosas and Co. to eliminate him, what evidence of his I'd either missed, or might not yet have discovered. And I outlined my theory about the drugs, and how they were moved, though I couldn't figure out a role for some of the participants I'd turned up, or thought I'd turned up. Truth be told, as Vega had made starkly clear, most of my theories were just what he said they were, suppositions and assumptions, empty speculation.

But dammit, Ninian was dead and the bastards had done it in my hotel. I felt involved, angry, and a bit of me was even worried it might keep guests away. Some of our loveliest guests are older folk, cautious and easily alarmed, natural worriers easily put off their stride, or hobble. And some of them have been people who come back and back to us, among other reasons because they feel safe and well cared for. A brutal bludgeoner loose in our place might well cause them to opt for a different hotel, unreasonable as that might sound. And I'd miss them if they stayed away. So, too, would our bank manager.

'There's something else that's not sitting right with me either,' I said. 'Something about Petra.'

'Pull the other one, Will,' replied Hannah. 'What is there *not* to be comfortable with about a – in your words – tousle-headed blonde with curves and a nice tan and good teeth? One who even seems to have evinced some interest in you, though I can't think why,' she added with her Giaconda smile. One of the reasons I can talk to Hannah about anything is that she hasn't a jot of jealousy in her, something I find admirable and incomprehensible in equal measure.

'Yeah well, that's it, I think. There's something of a too-good-to-be-true aspect to it. Something isn't right.'

'*Zum Beispiel?*' Hannah doesn't actually speak German, but she likes the sound of 'for example'.

'It just doesn't quite compute. It's nothing she's said, actually. All the words are well within the most Victorian bounds of propriety. It's the way she suddenly started looking at me. She's giving off some strong come-hither stuff with her eyes. Does that make any sense?'

'Yes. Why shouldn't she? You're an attractive man. Well, not totally *un*attractive anyway.' She put her tongue firmly in her cheek.

'Thank you so much for the reassurance, dear one. In fact, I seem to have detected some mild interest once or twice from maybe a couple of other women in the world – but women who have some miles on them, some wear and tear and history. Women who don't mind hanging out with a man who is probably more frog than prince. But the point here is that I'm well aware that my appeal is generally not to women in her age group. I'm beginning to think she has another agenda.'

'Oh, pshaw,' she pishtushed me. 'You've said yourself that you see lots of popsies hanging out – especially down there in the port – with men with snow on the roof, or even very little thatch at all.'

'That, my dear, is different. That's a form of commerce. *Quid pro quo* arrangements. Nothing to do with what she has been giving off, which is something I haven't run across for years now. Let me tell you about men my age; not that I need to, really. There's an adjustment we all have to make, no matter what kind of hot stuff we once were when young. We become *invisible* to younger women. Once upon a time we used to eye them and they eyed us, the classic mating game size-up. Then, as some of us grew up and got smarter, though not all of us by any means, we shifted our attention to older women, women like you, if I may say so, darlin' – with more sophistication, more substance, something more upstairs. Firm flesh and youthful vivacity have their charms, but they're transitory ones; they wear out, or off.

'Nevertheless, we continue eyeing whatever talent is available, partly out of habit, partly out of curiosity or speculation. But one day the time comes when we see something on the street and eye it up and down as in the past, and lo, there is no response whatsoever. And it's not just that she has seen us and hasn't responded, the plain fact is that she just hasn't seen us. We have become – as *I* have become, not the royal we – a member of the legion of invisible men. And so, however flattered I may feel by her attention, and however much younger it makes me feel to have those buttons pushed, the wiser part of me tells me that something is ringing false here, somebody has an axe to grind, something there is that I am not knowing about, as my Indian friend used to say.'

'Could be. Yes, put that way I do suppose you are a bit over the hill, superannuated, ready to be led to the knacker's yard.'

'Thanks a lot. Trust you to take the mickey. What do you really think?'

'Well, I think you shouldn't look a gift horse in the mouth. You remember telling me about the time you talked yourself out of bed with another smashing Danish girl, Ulrika something. Are you doing the same thing now?'

'Oh come on, that was a hundred years ago and in another country, as Marlowe's excuse went, though I hope the wench is in good health. Anyway, that was a time when I was a hot-blooded footloose bachelor too dumb to know my own luck. I was so overcome by the opportunity that I dithered and procrastinated until the moment had passed. But that was youth and inexperience, this is the recognition that although yes, it's possible to win the lottery, the odds are even greater of being struck by lightning, or maybe in this case even greater still of being struck by whoever struck Ninian. I'm just trying to exercise the caution and wisdom that are supposed to come as an antidote to my dotage.'

'All right, I'll concede the point, but you may be underrating yourself. There are young women who like older men.'

'That's also true. But this one doesn't strike me as one of them. No, I'm not going to question her motives to the point where I actually start examining those pretty gift-horse teeth, but I am going to watch my back.'

'That's an image to conjure with. You watching your back while doing whatever you end up doing trying not to turn down the gift-horse. In a mirror maybe? All this in her cramped cabin? May I watch?'

'Only if you watch my back for me, so I don't get distracted talking myself out of whatever opportunity presents itself. Oh stop it, this is getting silly.'

'*Getting* silly? The whole *megillah* has been silly from the start, except, of course, for poor old Ninian. I'll take your point, though, and actually I'm glad to hear that you're not so arrogant and vain as to think you could pull a bird like that all on your own.'

'Now you're being catty, but I'm glad you agree. Yes, I still like to think the stallion that lives inside me has races yet to run, but no, I don't have any illusions that he could run them every day.'

'That's my boy – *man*.' She winked.

'Funny. I just reminded myself of something Dorrie said to me once. We were standing on the shoreline out on the Formentor peninsula watching a big ship go by, a sleek white liner passing close to shore on its way across to Italy. People were dancing on deck, and the wind blew the occasional strains of music in our direction. The dancers swayed and swirled, and though they were far off they were – taken in the context of the ship, the sea, the moon, and the caress of the breeze – the embodiment of glamour. Then, as the ship changed course slightly, we began to lose sight of them. My attention moved to Dorrie and I looked over at her. A single big tear was coursing down one cheek. I must have looked puzzled, or worried, because she gave me a poignant smile and said, "Don't be concerned. It's only that sometimes I'm reminded that though I may be eighty-seven on the outside, part of me is still twenty-seven on the inside." I guess I feel the same way.'

'Ah well,' she said. 'You'll always be eighty-seven to me,' and she leaned over and gave me a quick kiss and a hug and then disappeared.

I hauled myself up out of the big squashy leather sofa where we'd been conversing and went down to the office to ring Vega. At least I could bring him up to date on the situation at Holmes's boatyard. We set up an appointment for an hour hence and so I took a quick tour to catch up on the maintenance schedule. Jaime was chipping the calcium deposits off the stainless steel plates in the heat exchanger. It's a never-ending job on Mallorca, dealing with *cal*. There's so much in the water that it gets everywhere and clogs everything – shower heads, kettles, dishwashers, drains, and – regularly – the heat exchanger for the hot water system. Pounds of it come out of that thing. It's no good, either, trying to soften the water chemically; you'd need your own salt mine to keep up with the usage. I have two of those electronic devices that are supposed to put a negative charge on the calcium ions and keep the particles in suspension, but it seems more like witchcraft to me than hard science; the machine sits there and its red light glows but I don't notice Jaime having to clean the exchanger plates any less often. However, if that's the price I have to pay for not having to endure Devon's weather – the endless grey drizzle that pervades that glorious landscape – then I'll sign the cheque right on the dotted line thank you very much.

Once I'd arrived at his office, Vega heard me out and made notes. He was clearly warmer towards this information than he had been in response to the tape I'd brought him. I had the feeling he was beginning to regard me more fondly, though mildly patronisingly, somewhat like a friendly neighbourhood dog who lollops up and wags his tail when you go by, bringing you offerings from time to time: old sticks, an abandoned shoe, yesterday's newspaper. This time, though, I think he felt I'd brought him today's edition.

'You said the name of this boat is 'Melanie'. How did you find that out?'

'I don't think you want to know.' I squinted slightly and gave him my *Fistful of Dollars* look.

'What I'm saying is that if you're running around breaking into places and behaving like a shamus in a movie, you better know that if anything happens I won't know who you are. Is that clear?'

'Of course.' But *I* knew who I was. I could hear the theme music in my head. 'The name is Stock.' Beat, pause. '*Will* Stock.'

He looked at me. 'I can see that nothing I'm saying is going to penetrate. I've met your sort before. All right, just be careful.'

'Of course.' Did Batman's mother ever tell *him* to be careful? Superman's? I rest my case.

'Ignoring that tone, I will say this is probably useful information. Or at least it's a plausible explanation for what we think has been going on in a general way. Some big shipments of drugs have been coming in regularly, and not from North Africa. As for these people, they've been known to us for some time, but we haven't paid them a great deal of attention or ever tried to associate anything specific with them. We just thought they were one more set of sleazeball business types. But in view of what's happened, your theory is at least worth checking out, though of course you realise that nothing, still nothing at all, links these people to the murder of Ninian Mede.'

'Of course,' I said, though this time in a less smart-alec way. I didn't know what had got into me today. I was all at sixes and sevens with my intentions.

Despite my cavalier behaviour, Vega and I parted on a cordial note and I thought that as long as I was in Palma I'd go over to my place to play some music and think. Hannah and Semiramis were on duty today, so I could relax and see if I could find one shred of evidence to back my hunch that Fosas and the others were behind Ninian's killing. That was the mystery that I most wanted to solve; all the rest of it was simply motive and mechanics. Vega had warned me once that I would be his fallback fall guy if necessary, and despite his recent amiability I hadn't any illusions about his sacrificing me, if called upon so to do for politically expedient reasons. The Spanish, at core, are a hard people. Hundreds of years of fighting to get back control of their country from the Moors bred into them a give-no-quarter attitude, a blood and bone and gristle toughness. It's in their character and it's in their language. We say we're between a rock and a hard place; they say they're between the sword and the wall. The point is graphically made with that sharply pointed image.

Once in the *atico* I paced around, couldn't settle, couldn't even decide among and between a Mozart piano concerto, the Benny Goodman small ensembles, or Stan Getz in Brazilian mode. If I smoked cigarettes I'd have been puffing away one off the other. I felt stymied, blocked, and abundantly dumb into the bargain. Something was there that I'd overlooked. Some key fact was either staring me in the face or sneakily peeking out from under the rug – in plain view were I to look harder, pay attention, change my focus, alter an assumption, open my mind to another possibility, think laterally, get smarter. But what was it? Something swam into view and then disappeared, tantalisingly, like a word you know but can't think of. Some fact, some detail that I hadn't paid heed to. It was on the tip of the tongue of my mind, but I couldn't retrieve it.

Then I tried to read, without success. Then I had a glass of wine, and that felt more the ticket. Sometimes a glass or two will grease the connections. Then I finally did put on the music. The Mozart was too sublime for rational thought, the Getz too sensual, but the Goodman was exactly the right combination of the intellectual and technical, melded with the seamlessly musical: all those endless filigreed variations on nostalgic Thirties tunes. And as Benny spun a cascading tracery of quicksilver notes around the theme of 'After You've Gone,' it suddenly came into focus; I had it.

Melanie was the name of one of the boats in the pile of title documents I'd found in Gewürz's desk.

So what did it mean? Well, it certainly tied him to the operation in a way I'd only speculated about previously. If he owned the boat – or boats, since I'd seen a whole stack of those papers – used for the smuggling, then he was directly implicated. He wasn't simply a technician, as I had thought, he must be a principal. Why wasn't he getting more money then? Or was he getting his cut off the other end, buying in the product and selling on to his partners at this end? I didn't know enough about how these things worked even to speculate, but it seemed a logical set-up. He owned the boats, Fosas put up the cash, Meliá organised – what? – distribution maybe? Sven was muscle, Martillo was the nautical end of things, possibly to move the boats, possibly to get the product from Mallorca to somewhere else, perhaps the mainland. Holmes offloaded the product in his closed shed and probably repackaged it for onward transmission. It all fit, and Pascual Milagro didn't rate in the organisational chart, so Petra was probably right about him.

So where did Root fit in? He was part of them, that was clear. But what did he do? I hadn't yet figured that one out. By default he must be somewhere along the distribution end, since he didn't seem to figure in importing the product. Petra might know but I doubted it, and anyway, she was currently on my Don't Trust list, more's the pity.

I got a pad of legal paper and drew some boxes and lines and charts. Usually it doesn't help me think any more clearly but it looks neat and tidy and far more organised than I am in reality. But it still didn't bring me any closer to Ninian's murderer, elegant solution though it might be as a schematic of the drug business. I began instead simply to make notes of all the things I still didn't know. They made a formidable list. Still, as I'm sure someone must have said in a more elegant way, if you know what you don't know, you're halfway to knowing what you want to know. I decided to go home and sleep on things.

Twenty-Three

Semiramis was trying to give everyone who uses the office a cold. Yesterday she'd been in and snuffled into the phone, caressed both computer keyboards with germ-laden fingers, and honked her way through a whole box of Kleenex, sneezing like a Gatling gun. Now Hannah was fighting it, I was fighting it, and even Alonzo, our stripey hotel cat, seemed less gruntled than his usual self.

So clearly logic dictated it to be a night to go and squat in the cold woods and listen in on Fosas. The bug was still in place, but the battery on the transmitter was getting low. If I wore an earphone and plugged into the record input I could make out conversations, but if they went through the machine and came out on the tape, I couldn't understand them. No doubt this was fixable, but the machine was a solid-state device with microchips inside and I've never understood how to deal with that stuff. At heart I'm a steam-driven person, comfortable with what I can see, what I can figure out by watching the wheels go around, or fix by using a spanner and lots of bad language when I bark my knuckles. It's always both impressive and disappointing to look inside a computer and see how little actual machinery there is relative to what it can do when it chooses to.

Consequently, I was hunkered down in the damp earth outside Fosas's house, one elbow resting on a stump, waiting and hoping that he would turn up and deliver a speech to my bug. 'I dunnit, Guv. I cannot tell a lie. It was me what done him in with my own shillelagh which I got hid under the bed. It's a fair cop. Take me away.' Only trouble with that scenario, of course, was that I was no longer recording and so matter what Fosas might say in whatever fantasy I constructed, I wouldn't have any hard evidence to present to Vega. My word against Fosas's claim of temporary insanity.

Nevertheless, I hoped I'd pick up something of use. I

wished he were more gregarious. He hardly had any visitors, so I barely had any conversations to listen to. I was becoming reasonably persuaded that this was all a monumental waste of time, and that he, like many Spanish men, held all his business discussions in restaurants or bars. The fact of the Ninian tape seemed to bear out this theory. On the other hand, he'd had Meliá over the other night, and presumably they must have talked business, as they seemed unlikely as kindred intellectual spirits. If I only could be patient enough – patience never having been my strong suit – perhaps I might be in with a chance, however slim. I'd just have to wait it out and hope the cold didn't take hold of my entrails.

The bug was voice operated and only supposed to transmit when there was a conversation to listen to, so I had optimistically hoped it would last for some days longer than Buster's original minimum ten day estimate, since that was predicated on a usage of two hours a day. To have had the batteries run down this much already was disappointing, but understandable, given Fosas's habit of turning up his music to the point where it triggered the operating mechanism. But pretty acceptable music it was, so at least my hours of waiting around in the cold were less miserable than they might have been.

I'd been there about two and a half hours, about my maximum for any given evening, and was about to throw in the towel when I heard the phone ring. The music level dropped almost to inaudible and I heard Fosas answer.

'*Diga*. Oh, it's you, Sol. What's on your mind?'

There followed a long pause, as I was only getting half the conversation.

'No, as far as I know it'll be in on schedule. I haven't heard anything to the contrary and they were supposed to call me if there was going to be a delay. And Holmes has all but finished, so Stella can leave as planned. Or rather Melanie, I should say. So what's your gripe?'

Another pause.

'No, Sol, I can't do that. It's all arranged and has been arranged for weeks. I can't change it now.'

Pause again.

'I'm sorry, Sol. We'll have to risk it. He can't have found out that much in such a short time.'

Much longer pause.

'Sol, Sol – I'm going to have to interrupt you. It's my decision to make and I've made my call on it. I'm sorry, but this is a matter of judgment and opinion and I'm going to leave things as they are. I'm sorry you disagree but we can deal with him later. Listen, Sol, I'm going to have to go now. I really can't talk about this anymore, especially not on the phone, so ring me tomorrow after you've cooled down and we'll meet and talk at the bar. All right? I'll take your viewpoint under consideration but I think you should plan on things staying as they are. Good night, Sol. Thanks for ringing.' And I heard the phone receiver go down.

That might be a nugget of pure gold, I thought, even though I hadn't yet figured out yet what it all meant. My cortical synapses were leaping about like rabbits, connecting all over the place, but my gut was beginning to churn over as well. That was the first thing that needed to be addressed: the emotional response. Who was this 'he' who was being talked about? Me? And what did he mean about him 'finding out that much?' And more to the point – the words that had caused my tummy to flip-flop in the first place, what did Fosas mean by 'we can deal with him later?' Portentous. Ominous. More chilling than the weather.

By this time the music had resumed its previous level and I didn't think lightning was likely to strike again tonight so I disconnected my earpiece and started tidying up the site, flashing the torch just once to make sure I'd scuffed the leaves into an innocent-looking arrangement and that the receiver was hidden well down out of sight. I was cold and stiff and tired, but also simultaneously scared and elated. That one short half conversation seemed to justify all the hours I'd spent out here lurking like a leftover spy from the cold war. Now, I thought, I could come in from the cold. Literally.

Apart from the possible threat to my precious hide – I decided as I reviewed the information during the drive home – the principle significant revelation had been that Stella was not a person, as I'd always assumed, but rather the boat I'd seen in Holmes's shed, the boat now renamed Melanie. So the nagging mystery of Stella's identity had been resolved. It made sense of those six empty letterplate spaces I'd seen the first time – S T E L L A. I wasn't yet sure how it fit, or why they'd changed the name, but it gave me one fewer person to have to track down, and something to check out via the police, who would have access to boat ownership records.

But something else set me to wondering. Sol Meliá had been upset, had been worried apparently – worried, it seemed, that someone, and the someone could be me, had found out things about their operation that might be threatening to them, and he seemed to want to have their timetable changed, or have some part of the operation put on hold, something Fosas wasn't prepared to do.

But I didn't know that much yet about their operation. I knew, or thought I knew, who was involved, and roughly what they were doing, but I still didn't have any hard evidence, and that was what stood between me and getting off the hook with the police. So, if I weren't the person Meliá was worried about, who was? My hope was that someone else knew the dirty facts about what they were doing and posed a threat. I had no desire to be on Fosas's list as 'somebody to be dealt with later'. He'd seemed too relaxed about the issue, too confident and unbothered. Even those few words had had a flavour about them of the bored assurance of a cat with his prey cornered. I kept trying to tell myself that it surely couldn't

be me he had in mind. But maybe Vega did know something I didn't know. Maybe he'd been trying to warn me.

The whole situation put me in mind of the business
about frogs and hot water. If you drop a frog into a pan of
hot water out he'll jump, lickety-split. But if you put him
into a pan of cold water and apply the heat slowly, he'll
stay there until he's poached. Part of me was telling me I
should have jumped long ago.

The next day I couldn't put off having a face-to-face
with Milagro any longer. It was something I'd avoided
pusillanimously for practically the whole past week, but
now – now that I needed something from him – I couldn't
avoid talking to him. I rang him and set up a meet down
in the Port where we'd last met. Perhaps I'd drop in on
Petra at the same time.

It was one of those unusual transitional days we get at
times in the early spring. The sky was as flat as a
painter's canvas, a pervasive milky light washing
everything in an unfamiliar, almost shadowless, way. No
breeze to speak of, the scent of almond blossom still
hanging over the fields, but most of the petals now on the
ground. Winter-flowering jasmine added a splash of
colour to sheltered corners, and our bougainvillea was
optimistically beginning to show some bud. Every year
Hannah prunes it hard and every year I become convinced
she's killed it – or at least I tell her so – but every year it
comes back gloriously and ostentatiously bright. Hannah
would aver that there are at least two messages in this
recurring pattern, but I'm not sure I want to face up to
either of them.

When I found Fausto he looked as bandbox fresh as
always, the handmade boots, the delectable lightweight
tweed jacket, a Gucci tie in a perfect half Windsor. What
he wears is the real thing, though I've joked to Hannah –
but certainly not to him – that I don't know why he
bothers. Right in the square in front of the hotel I can find
in the Friday market any number of Cucci ties, Hermas

scarves, Rollax watches, or other fine Channel products, all direct from Taiwan or wherever, right to Mallorca and offered at knockdown prices. Really, I know it's illegal and all that, but some of the imitations are quite good, and though I acknowledge that it's a rip-off of the original companies, I find most of their genuine products so overpriced that I have trouble summoning up much sympathy for them. Besides, I figure that anybody who is pseud enough to pay £5,000, or whatever they ask, for a watch as ugly as a Rolex, deserves to be upstaged by his gardener wearing a cheap copy. That company can spend any number of millions advertising those things as fashion items, but they'll never convince me that they are anything other than seriously unsightly. They do have my admiration, however, for having had the gall and the balls to promote those watches as something more than an accoutrement you wouldn't want to be caught dead wearing, save underwater and thus safely out of sight of the rest of us.

I plunked myself down next to Fausto and stretched out a hand to encompass all the new buildings and the roadworks going on.

'I suppose you remember all this when it was a sleepy fishing port.'

'No, not really,' he replied, following my gaze. 'I'm not even certain it ever was a fishing port. I think all this was just manufactured as demand for it rose. I do remember, though, when there was hardly a restaurant, in the true sense of the word, outside of Palma. Or at least it seemed that way as I was growing up.'

'Doesn't part of you resent all this, as a Mallorquin?'

'Not a bit. I'm no revisionist of history. All this development may have brought some inconveniences, but in my view the benefits vastly outweigh the negative aspects. We were a poor island, a poor people – with exceptions, of course, and I was lucky enough to have been born into one of the exceptional families. But I remember very well when the island had few roads, erratic electricity, a dodgy water system, inadequate drains and even limited food. The good old days are a myth. Don't even begin to think most Mallorquins aren't intensely aware of that fact, and grateful for how much better things are now.'

'Even when it sometimes seems that it's the foreigners who are making most of the profits?'

'That's a myth, too. Foreigners pay us monumental sums of money for houses that a few years ago we couldn't even give away, land that we hadn't used for anything but grazing or as orchards. They support our restaurants, our bars, our whole service industry, every kind of infrastructure necessary to keep them, and us, fed and housed and happy. And every time they buy something, however small, we make some money. Are we going to complain about that? You have to be a pretty blinkered nationalist to work up much enthusiasm for slamming down the portcullis. No, it's a more than fair trade. In fact, I think we've had the better of it all along. I will say that I like the idea of places like yours bringing the image more upmarket, and yes, I recognise that as the numbers of tourists increase we'll reach a point where the island can't support more visitors, but I think that's a self-limiting mechanism and that tourism can take care of itself. If we get too crowded, people will stop coming. If we get too expensive, people will stop coming, and if we get complacent and stop offering a good product, people will stop coming. No, I don't worry.' He stopped, glanced at his watch, and shifted mood. 'But listen, I find myself with a slight time problem. Tell me what news you have for me.'

I squared my chair around a bit so I was facing him. 'All right, I have to say I've been avoiding you somewhat over the past days.'

'Not that I haven't noticed,' he said with a lift of his shoulders.

'I have a confession of sorts,' I said as preface. 'No, not really a confession, it was something I saw pretty much by accident.' I still wasn't sure where I was going with this interview or how I was going to handle things. Sometimes I construct elaborate scenarios in my head and then when they play out the participants fail to adhere to my script, sometimes even myself included. So I just blurted it out. 'I saw you go aboard that boat out there.' I pointed. 'And later I found out it belonged to your brother. And still later I found out the captain may be one of the people on that list I found after Ninian's death, and that he may be implicated in the smuggling ring. And I'm also fairly certain, though this is almost incidental, that you've been using me as a stalking horse for information, but passing back the information to headquarters in such a way as to implicate me rather than your brother, or even Martillo.' I looked right in his eyes. 'This, you will understand, pisses me off.'

That stopped him, or at least slowed him down significantly. 'I see,' he said, stroking his chin. He looked at his watch again. 'I think I have to inform you of a few things I haven't vouchsafed to you until now. Let me make a phone call,' and he whipped out his mobile, dialled up and began gabbling in Mallorquin while I was left to ponder whether or not this man who spoke English as a fourth language had used the word 'vouchsafe' in a correct context. After awhile he finished, clicked the off button and turned to me.

'Everything you say is true. I didn't feel I could confide in you previously. Why should I have involved you in what is, for me, a family problem? Why should I have trusted you? This is, after all, a matter I haven't even yet discussed with my brother, though I see now that the issue no longer may be further postponed.'

I nodded, but said nothing. He paused, studied his immaculate fingernails for a moment, then continued.

'My brother and I are no longer close. What exists

between us is not a rift, but simply a separation of values. I am more a moralist, my brother more a pragmatist. In this case, however, his pragmatism may go beyond simple expediency; it may cross the line into the criminal. However, and this is the major "however" in my life at this juncture, I honestly do not know whether or not my brother is involved with Captain Martillo and his friends, or whether he is still the credulous, slightly naïve person I knew so well as a child. I have been giving him the benefit of the doubt, putting off the day of reckoning, avoiding confrontation – all the things I suspect you did vis-à-vis me.' As he said these words he paused again and looked up at me shrewdly from under beetling eyebrows. 'But now you have forced the issue and I must go *mano a mano* with my brother to make this evil thing become a right thing. I must know if he is a good man or a corrupt man. I must know if I must perhaps one day soon arrest my own blood brother and be a mortal threat to the peace of our dear mother.'

This was said in utter seriousness, but part of me heard an echo of Hemingway in the rhythms of his speech. Even worse, Hemingway at his most self-parodying, and so I took it with the same *granissimo* of salt I have often found necessary in reading the later works of Papa H.

'When will you do this thing? When shall you resolve this dispute of honour?' I asked, and then almost bit my tongue.

'Soon,' he said, not picking up on it.

'Then I will wait.' I said. 'But in the meantime,' I said, trying to break the cadence of these exchanges, 'there is a thing you must do for me. There is a boat called "Stella," and I must know her owner, her port, and her legal status. And there is a man, one so-called Henry Root. It would be a boon were you to find information of him. Can you do these things for me?' Stop this, dammit, it's getting farcical. This was communication on the level of 'best-consume-before-see-end-lid.'

'I would be honoured,' he said gravely.

'No, it is *I* who would be honoured,' I said, with as straight a face as I could muster.

He squirmed slightly, as though he finally recognised what we had been falling into. He went back to being Sloane, which he did so much better. 'I'll look it out, old man, and get back to you. Meantime keep the other little matter under your hat till I've checked it over. Will you do that?'

'Of course,' I said, with what I hoped was a trustworthy look.

He checked his watch yet again, threw a bill on the table to indicate that he was beholden to me, and made his exit, stage left. I sat for awhile deciding how much credence to give his story, and decided, on balance, that he was likely telling the truth. A rogue brother, or a weak brother, or simply an amorally selfish brother, could be a heavy cross to bear. I'd give him 72 hours before mentioning the matter to Vega. After all, I had my own back to protect.

And thinking of backs, and watching same, I was reminded, though I had hardly forgotten, that Petra's boat was only 150 yards away. I paid the bill with Fausto's money, pocketed the change – on principle I overtip in the interior, where nobody tips, and undertip in the tourist areas, where I figure the waiters are already spoilt and blasé – and went along to see what Petra was up to.

In point of fact she was up to about two-thirds of the way up the mast, wearing the same U of C sweatshirt, but this time with shorts. She was varnishing the crosstrees, secured by a webbing harness, but with her legs – her long, shapely, tanned legs, I noted – wrapped around the mast. Work on boats is as constantly Forth Bridgeish as work on hotels. No sooner do you finish than it's time to start again.

I called up to her. '*Hola*, Petra. Will you be down soon?'

'Hallo, Will,' she exclaimed with a grin. 'Stay you where you are, I am coming down soon,' and she seemed to speed up the painting. I leaned on the taffrail and admired her legs. Presently she finished and lowered herself down like a lumberjack descending a pine tree, hitching the web harness and sliding, braking with her plimsolled feet. She landed slightly flushed, smelling pleasantly of varnish and salt air and perspiration, a distinctly provocative combination, though I suppose the sweat pheromones had the largest say.

'You come down with me now,' she said lightly. 'I must put away things and change.' And she ducked down the companionway, leaving me to follow. As I reached the deck of the lower cabin I could see her through the hatchway in the far bulkhead, tucking the paint tins into a locker. Then she nipped into the tiny combination w.c. and shower, peeling off her top as she entered, and leaving the door slightly open. I didn't look away, partly because I'm not that much of a gentleman, partly because I had the feeling I wasn't supposed to look away. Not that there was a great deal to see, though we all know that partial nudity is more tantalising than total. She wet a cloth and gave herself a quick washover, her back to me, provocative flashes of warm flesh visible through the door ajar. Then she popped into a curtained-off space that was probably her sleeping cabin, was gone for a couple of minutes and then with a swish of the curtain she was back, smelling fresh and looking delectable.

'So, you have come to visit me,' she said, unnecessarily.

'So it would appear,' I replied, joining right in to belabour the obvious.

'May I offer you something maybe to drink?' she said, carrying on with the scintillating repartee.

'No, thank you. I just had something.'

'It is a nice day out there today, *nej*?'

'One of the nicest we've had recently,' I said. I

wondered how long we could sustain the Noël Coward roll we were on. Then she turned serious, as she had the other day.

'I have maybe a problem again with Henry. He is coming around once more and wanting me to crew with him on a boat. He is a good sailor, you know, and is also a good mechanic for fixing things.'

'And you don't want to do it.' I wasn't sure where this was going.

'No, it was what I don't want to tell you the other day but I have decided I should.' She paused and looked down and then it all came out in a rush. 'Henry is maybe still something half like a boyfriend but not like before. But when I first know him he take me one time to the mainland to get a boat and he is very secret about everything and we go at night and pick up a boat in the dark and sail for a long time with no lights and I think we are doing something not honest or maybe wrong and now he is asking me to go again, but I think no. What do you think?'

'I think you're probably right to be worried. And even more right not to do it.' She reminded me, though I didn't know how much was reality and how much wishful thinking, of those poor naïve girls you see in the papers from time to time who've been persuaded to mule drugs for a boyfriend and then get caught and do time for something they didn't even realise they were doing. And I suspected that was exactly what friend Henry was doing – moving drugs quietly at night. He needed help and so he took her along, but if he'd been caught she'd have gone down as well.

'So you think I am right to say no?' She looked relieved. She clearly was bright, but also clearly was still more involved with Henry than she was letting on, despite her flirtatious manner with me. I was feeling the tiniest bit manipulated, but because I found her attractive, I was disposed to give her the benefit of the doubt. My head told me that was foolish, but nobody ever said I wasn't a sucker.

'I think the smartest thing you could do is stay well away from Henry's activities. You've already told me you suspect he's tied to the gang that Martillo works with, and you even told me you thought he was the one who put the finger on that poor man who was killed. So why are you even asking me, really?'

'Sometimes I need to hear someone else tell me what my inside is telling me. Sometimes I have to act more cautiouslike. Or smarter.'

'Well, you probably recall what Henri Bergson said, "Think like a man of action, act like a man of thought."' This is pure tosh, of course, but sounds sufficiently pompously ponderous to qualify as an aphorism.

'I do not know Bergson's philosophy well. I read him only a little bit, but I never believe sayings that read the same backward and forward. They are maybe a little bit too much what you call "pat." Is that the word?'

Pow. Right in the kisser. 'Yes. That's the word. *Exactly* the word.' That would teach me to patronise her.

'So I should not go?' She looked touchingly helpless. I melted, quite unable to sustain rationality. It wasn't just that she was easy to look at or had a warmth that went right to my core, it was the combination of simple English over an obviously quick mind. Quite effortlessly, she puffed up my ego like a child's balloon.

'No, you definitely should not go.' Spoken just like Big Daddy.

'Thank you. Truly thank you. I wanted to hear that from – from *you* I think.' And she moved up close and gave me a hug and a warm buss on the cheek. 'Now I must make a phone call.' And she half herded me towards the ladder up the companionway. In the twinkling of a flirtatious eye, she'd moved from dependent supplicant to being very much in charge. How did she do that stuff?

'I'd better be going, too.' One has to salvage some

modicum of dignity from such dismissals. We left the boat together, walked down the quay, and then split in different directions, she to a public phone, and I over to my car. Just as we parted she once again looked up at me with those clear grey eyes infinitesimally ringed with jade, and again kissed me, this time square on the lips. 'I do really thank you,' she said, and walked away quickly.

I stood for a moment looking after her, still feeling partly manipulated, but also partly flattered. All in all, though, the result was that I felt pretty good, so what the hell. As I ambled in the direction of my parking place I caught something out of the corner of my eye. I slid my eyes left, but not so far that I'd be looking directly at what I'd seen. Standing still, looking down at me from next to one of the buildings up the hill, and placed so that he would have seen our recent parting, was a figure in black motorcycle leathers, a figure with a round head and a sharp beaklike nose. None other than friend Henry. Had he seen us? There was little doubt. Had she seen him? I couldn't guess. Just one thought was clearly running through my head. Oh shit.

Twenty-Four

'You are Will?,' came Petra's voice when I picked up the phone. It was sevenish in the evening and I'd just finished a bite to eat and a glass of wine that Chessie kindly had prepared. Hannah and Ben had gone out to try to find shoes for his size-a-month growing feet and so Chessie had fixed a tray that could have been a picture right out of a food magazine, an arrangement of neat oblongs of crispbread with Brie or paté or Mahon cheese, each one garnished with either a sprig of parsley or a smidgen of chutney, together with a photogenic cos salad with local olives and fetta cheese marinated in garlic brine with slices of pimento. Chessie has said she'll grow up to be a 'restaurant person', and if that's what she wants, that's what she'll do. Chessie is somebody who gets what she sets out to get – a formidable twelve-year-old-going-on-thirty-five.

She had accompanied the photo-shoot food layout with a glass of *blanc de blanc*, what we call blankety-blank local wine. (Where does that appellation come from anyway? It sounds like something stolen from the *Messiah* – 'King of kings, Lord of lords, Blanc of blancs.') The tray had been an excellent hunger-buster. Were I to put it on our menu I'd be tempted to resort to menuspeak and call it a 'repast', and add in a bunch of the other superfluous adjectives menu writers tend to use when they nestle epicureanly in front of their word processors, dainty fingers poised lovingly over a bed of choice polypropylene springily pliant alphabet keys, scanning the serried ranks of words arrayed in their cortexes (or more usually thesauruses) for just the *bon mot*, the apposite adjective, the Choice of choices.

'Yes, I am Will.' I tend to fall in with these locutions. 'It's good to hear your voice. What can I do for you?'

'You can come to see me,' she said. 'I am on the boat. I mean I am not on the boat now, because I am using the mobile of the people on the boat near my boat, but then I will go back. Can you come?'

'Yes, I'm free.' We had staff still on duty. 'Do you mean *right now?*' A faint alarm was ringing at the back of my head.

'Yes, if you can.' Her voice sounded slightly peculiar, but nothing I could place, and I didn't know her telephone manner.

'Are you all right?' One of those dumb questions nobody ever seems to answer honestly.

'Fine, fine.' The standard answer that didn't tell me anything.

'I'll be there in half an hour,' and I hung up. No need to prolong the conversation, or run up somebody else's mobile phone bill, larcenously expensive here. Telefónica has a trick for maximising profits. If you hang up the phone and watch the red indicator light, you can see that it stays lit for another second and a half before cutting off. My surmise – and though I've asked them, no one at the phone company has denied it – is that that extra time is charged on your bill, at least on a unit basis. If you take all those little seconds and a half and multiply them by every phone call made all over Spain every day, you have to be looking at some real money.

Portals was quiet and I even found a convenient parking place. My parking angel was on duty tonight. I walked out to Petra's berth and could see that her hatch was half open, with only faint light to be seen radiating from the portholes. There was no Harley in sight this evening, not that I had expected it to be. I stopped at the bottom of the gangplank.

'Petra. Are you there?'

'Is that you, Will?' she called from below. 'Come down.'

I ducked my head as I half squeezed down the companionway into the cabin, lit only by two candles in glass upright sheath cylinders. The light was dim and golden, with a wavering pulse of long shadows playing against the stencils on the bulkheads.

'Slide the cover and lock it, please,' she said. 'There is a draught coming.'

I slid the hatch closed and bolted it home with a click. It was difficult to see her clearly in the attenuated light but I saw the glint of a glass in her hand and heard a chime of ice as she gestured in my direction. She had tamed her hair a bit and some of it fell in a wavering curve across her forehead. Her eyes were dark in their sockets in this light, but her mouth was wetly reflective and the whiteness of her teeth showed against the darkness around her. She was wearing some kind of satiny jumpsuit, open down to the V of her cleavage. Her feet were bare.

'Come by me,' she said, and so I did, settling myself in beside her where she patted one of the fat cushions on the long bench she was snuggled up on, one leg curled under her. 'I'm glad you are here. But be comfortable.' She tugged at my jacket sleeve. 'Put that away. And you can put your shoes off too. You want to fix a drink?'

'No, thank you. I had a glass of wine earlier. I'll let you know.' But I did throw the jacket over to the other bench and slip out of my shoes.

'I'm glad you come to visit. I want to talk to you.'

'That's what you said, and here I am, all ears.'

'What is this "all ears"?' she asked. 'It is not an expression I know.'

'I'm sorry. I try to keep away from expressions like that when I talk to you, unusual words or slang, but sometimes I forget. It just means that I'm listening.'

'All ears. I like it.' She was clearly more than a teensy bit tiddly. I couldn't tell if she was fairly far gone, or simply relaxed. I didn't want her to go to sleep on me again, though that first time was more emotional overload reaction than anything else.

'What is it that you wanted to tell me?'

'Come here,' she said, which was a bit difficult as I already was about as 'here' as I could get. Then she looked around as though there might be someone else lurking in a corner. 'I need to warn you.'

'Warn me?' I said brightly, as though the notion of danger had never crossed my feeble mind.

'Yes. By Henry. I need to warn you by Henry. He knows.' And her conspiratorial manner deepened.

'He knows?' I said, with an inflection of interrogation.

'Yes.' And she said no more. Her eyelids drooped and I became aware that she was pretty well into whatever bottle she'd broached.

'Petra!' I said, sharpening my voice. This was the second woman to get drunk on me and I didn't like it either time.

'Yes?' she jolted out of her languor.

'What does Henry know?' I thought it was important, but I seemed to be losing her attention.

'He find out about you coming over, he see us on the quay,' she said, still not all there.

'So what? What does that mean?' I couldn't get her drift.

'He is being angry, jealous.'

Was she kidding? Was that all? And why? 'Why?' I said. 'There's nothing for him to be jealous about.' Mainly I was concerned about him finding out about me trying to link him to Ninian. A slight touch of the greeneyes didn't much worry me.

'Because I suppose he know about you visiting me and he assume things,' she said, gravely, nodding a bit.

'But you told him I was just passing by, looking at boats, harmlessly flirting with you?' The headline loomed in my head. 'Hotpants Hotelier Found Strangled on Nubile Blonde's Luxury Sloop.' Those idiots, they always get it wrong. It's not a sloop, it's a ketch.

'Yes, I tell him you are nice, harmless man but he don't believe me.'

Perversely, part of me immediately bridled at the 'harmless' bit. 'But you told me you broke up,' I said. I was mildly confused over what was really going on. 'You said you had a fight about him telling Martillo about Ninian Mede and you broke up.'

'*I* break up. For him, he didn't. And so he is still seeing me like a something belonging to him.' She shook her head. 'But I'm not, and I'll show him.'

'No, I don't see you as the chattel type,' I said, relieved that it seemed to be a lovers' quarrel rather than something that might compromise the intelligence that I was gathering on him.

'Come here,' she said, and she put an arm around me and pulled me down to her, reaching up to kiss me and squirming herself around almost underneath me, a slithery snake in a silk bag. At first I gulped some air, but then centred her mouth against mine and returned the kiss, deeply and sweetly on my part, boozily sharp on hers. She began to pull at my shirt, and took hold of my right hand and guided it to one of the warm round breasts pushed up against my chest.

Now far better wordsmiths than I have attempted to describe sexual congress. Whole tribes of writers have worn legions of verbs and nouns and adjectives to stubby nubs in attempting to find a new slant to describe the indescribable. My favourite subgenre is probably what George Axelrod called 'the-onward-and-upward-pulsatingly-and-throbbingly-and-afterwards-with-her-hair-spread-out-upon-the-pillow school of writing, though that has since been overtaken by a more graphic, even to say pornographic, literary genotype.

But what I've also seldom noticed described in these works are the realities of such issues as the instant proliferation of knees and elbows, seemingly totalling well beyond eight, and the awkward disposition of these extra appendages, or the effect of differences in rhythm and style, which is an especially vexing hurdle in new encounters, and of course the problem of size, and by that I don't mean of *that* thing, I mean of how people fit in terms of height and proportion. (I had always speculated privately about Ninian and Hazel in that department, as her nose must have come up somewhere between his navel and his armpit, at best, or worst.) Nor do the writers of romantic fiction spend much time on those unavoidable animal realities – stray hairs, sweat and spit, bits that are ticklish or oversensitive, or parts we're embarrassed about, ashamed of, or that get in the way: flabby bits, scars, cellulite, varicose veins, pimples, moles, wrinkles or pongs. Fictional heroines are as perfect and firm and smooth and airbrushed as any *Playboy* centrefold, and their heroes equally retouched to fit the mould of their fictional intent. In this case, it was the smell of the booze on her breath that brought me back to reality.

'Hold it. Stop!' I said, pulling away from her.

'No. Come here,' she muttered, burrowing into my chest.

'I mean it. We have to stop here.' *We?* Hell. *I* wanted to stop while my mind was still in control of me.

'What do you mean, stop?' she said more clearly, having pulled her head back from between my manly pectorals. She was looking at me half annoyed, half inquiringly.

'I mean that I'm not going to do this just because you're angry at Henry, because you want to show him you're a free woman. This isn't proving you're free, only that you want to punish him. Which says that you still haven't broken up with him any more than he with you. And I don't want to be just an instrument of your anger. If you really want to do this with me, then come to my *atico* some evening soon – come sober and calm and having thought it all through. Then we'll go to bed together in a proper bed. Is that a deal?' How much more virtuous could I be?

She squinted at me, and the grey eyes were more

awake now. 'You mean that? You are telling me *no?'*

'Yes. I mean it looks that way, doesn't it?'

'This is something new for me,' she said, cocking her head to one side. Then she seemed to stop and reflect. 'You know part of me is angry with you because I want to make love, but part of me tells me you are right, that I am wanting to make love to make revenge on Henry, and that is not a good reason to go to bed with a man. I'm sorry. I guess you are maybe right.' She squirmed away and began to rearrange clothing that had started to come loose.

And of course by this time another part of me was being heard from – 'No, no, I'm wrong, I'm completely wrong. Let's start over.' Oh, shut up, you.

'Yes, well, I may be right intellectually, but I'm also sorry. You are lovely and desirable and now I'm going to leave before I change my mind and we get totally out of sync. Are you all right?'

'Yes. I'm fine. I'm calming now.'

'Well, I'm not, so I'm leaving. I'll call you tomorrow – no, I can't tomorrow, I've got meetings I can't get out of all day and even in the evening. I'll call you day after tomorrow at breakfast time.'

She nodded and I got out, ascending the companionway with very mixed feelings indeed.

I didn't speak to myself all the way home.

* * *

'And so you talked your way out of bed again. What did I tell you?' Hannah raised one eyebrow archly. *She* can do that thing with one eyebrow. We were in our usual corner in the terrace bar again. I'd had to vent to somebody.

'Yep. I sure did. But the better part of me – that very small bit that you only see from time to time – thinks I did right. I couldn't say it to Petra, or didn't anyway, but it was the goddamn booze that actually put me off. I don't do well with drunken women, no matter how attractive they are. Besides, I made it a firm rule a long time ago not to take advantage of women who were chemically vulnerable, be it booze or drugs. And even more to the point, recognising the fragility of my ego, I also long ago tried to give up being used, whether as an instrument of revenge or as an animate dildo. Or even simply as a convenience. Placing some value on that loving act is a source of self-respect. It's no longer the indoor sport it was when I was young.'

'Oh, you're so virtuous you're going to turn into a smug bore, Will. I'm not sure I didn't like you better when you weren't so damned grown-up.'

'Grown-up being a code word for self-satisfied, complacent, self-congratulating and hypocritical,' I grinned.

'I suppose that's about right.' She smiled back and refilled my glass.

'Thank you. For the wine, I mean.' At times I have nothing against getting a bit tiddly myself. 'You think it wasn't hard?'

'Oh, I'm sure *it* was hard,' she said. 'And I know about hardness and lack of conscience. Was it only the booze that put you off? Anything else?'

'It would have been too easy, I suppose. That plus the alcohol. She was there on a plate and although it might have been fun to go ahead and to hell with it, I found I just didn't want to on those terms.'

'Your terms being an active choice of you and not as a substitute for somebody she's mad at.'

'Something like that, I guess.'

'Yes, well, you always did like to do things the hard way. What happens if she decides not to follow up on your terms?'

'Then I'll simply have one more thing to kick myself for.'

'Oh, I'll help if you want. I think you were dumb. I suspect it would have improved your disposition mightily to have something to feel all macho and conquistador about. There's nothing to cheer a man up like a little young tasty-cake.'

'Is that envy or reminiscence?'

'Just an observation, *mein caballero*. So, what are you going to do now? Wait for her call or haunt the docks?

'Well, if it hasn't escaped your attention my sweet *petit chou*, I may have the muscle boys on my tail at any time. As far as I know I've been discreet, at least about the murder enquiry, but if "Hawg" now knows of my existence, I'm less secure than I thought I was. For all I know he'll do me just for looking at his girl, sod the possibility of linking him to Ninian's murder. So, if you see a black Harley in the square, let me know so I can scarper out the back gate.'

'So what does he look like, this avenging Hell's Angel?'

'Give it up, Hannah. He's not your type. His head is too round.'

'That's a cavalier statement on your part. How do you know my type? Even I haven't figured that out yet.'

'Listen, Cookie, I've got to crash. My day she hath been long and adventurous, not to mention virtuous, but now I think I need to go and sleep it off.' I got up and stretched.

'And dream of tousled blondes.'

'OK, OK, so you know where to put the knife in. Just the one tousled blonde. Frustrating dreams full of regret, probably.'

'Well, don't say I didn't told you so.'

'I never did and you always do. Good night. Sleep well.' And off I tottered, leaving Hannah to do the nightly rounds. I hoped she'd let me know if she saw any suspicious figures in leathers lurking under the lampposts in the square.

Twenty-Five

The next day was a write-off. We get days like that at the hotel. First thing, the man came to inspect and recharge all the fire extinguishers. Just walking him around to show him where we hide them took an hour. Next came a meeting with some tour operators who want to put us in their brochure for next year, preferably, for them, at half price. Then came a photographer doing a recce for a shoot for an ad campaign, using the hotel as a backdrop. All he could do was complain about the light, with the sun too weak at this time of year, when in fact the actual shoot was planned for June, when he'd no doubt complain that the sun was too strong. Later we had – well, you don't want to hear it all; it's terminally boring. It went on like that all day: administration, bureaucracy, the tedious though consequential details that are the warp and weft of making a living. I went to bed early, dog-tired but still feeling virtuous. I hadn't had a free minute to think about my adventures, and probably was better off for the respite from them.

Early the next morning I awoke with a brain wave – residual fallout from a dream, I suppose. Like most people, I get these insightful dreams from time to time, but don't always know what's inner wisdom and what's errant nonsense, which is kind of silly, as I always thought being able to tell the difference was what inner wisdom was for. Anyway, when ideas are scarce you go with what you've got, and this notion was what I had, even though it seemed as if maybe I was drawing to an inside straight, something my Uncle Bill – the one who worked his way though college playing piano in a whorehouse, no lie – used to tell me not ever to do. Never.

But that's what I did.

It was still early, but I wanted to catch him early, before he had a chance to get his brain warmed up. I picked up the telephone and dialled Fosas's house. When I'd been up there ostensibly to use the telephone to call for help regarding my foot, I'd of course snaffled the number and noted it down on the palm of my hand, something daughter Chessie does all the time, and something I always tell her makes her look like a graffiti victim.

He answered sleepily. *'Diga?'*

'All right, Fosas, the game is up. I know all about you.' Influences there from every old gangster film I'd ever seen, so it came out Cagney by way of Peter Lorre's menacing whine, with even a touch of the soft palate pharyngeal Brando godfather. I was surprised he could understand me.

'Who is this?' he said, beginning to wake up.

'I told you. Somebody who knows all about you and your scam.'

'Who the fuck *is* this?' he snarled, now more awake. His veneer of gentlemanly polish was coming right off.

'And I also know about Meliá, about Gewürz, about the transporter, and I know about muscle boy Sven. You want more?'

There was a longer pause as he seemed to absorb this. 'What are you after? What do you want?' The man was nothing if not pragmatic.

'What do you think I want, stupid? Money.'

'Money?' he said, as if it were some alien concept, of which he had once heard but had no direct experience. 'What for?'

'Oh, do come off it.' I was having trouble maintaining my mixed accents. 'For keeping my trap shut, what else?'

'Listen. Who are you?'

'You asked me that before, birdturd. I didn't tell you then, so what makes you think I'm going to tell you now? Just answer the question, are you ready to come up with the money?'

'I fail to see what you are driving at. Who do you think you are ringing me at this hour of the morning with menaces?' He was beginning to recover some of his usual poise, or perhaps he thought righteous indignation might be called for.

'Oh, do shut up,' I said, more grumpily than menacingly. 'You're beginning to cheese me off. Don't try to flimflam me. I know about you, about your buddies in the gang, and I know about the boat. So spare us all the injured innocence. All I want you to do is cough up.'

'Or what?' There was residual defiance in his tone but he seemed to be getting the message this time.

'Or I roll up your operation like a Bokhara rug – like you'll see the inside of Guardia headquarters faster than you can count to one. I've got all the evidence I need and I've simply decided to cut myself in instead of turning you in. At least for now.'

'We should talk,' he said, now apparently convinced of my *mala fides.*

'Sure. And what happens when I come to talk to you? The same thing that happened to Mede?'

'Who?'

'Ninian Mede. As if you never heard of him. But leave that out for now. Let me tell you what you're going to do. Tomorrow, at noon, I want you to be in the car park at Es Vergé, the restaurant up above Alaró. You come alone. I'll be watching to see you do. Once you're there I'll get a message to you to tell you how much, when and where. Got it?'

'Listen. This is crazy. I don't know half of what you're talking about, but all right, I'll go up there tomorrow just to humour you. But don't expect you can get away with this.' He couldn't find the right tone. Some of him wanted still to play the innocent, but he was smart enough to know that wasn't going to wash, so some of him was being placatory, playing for time, but then slipping in a sly little bit of a threat as well. I was pretty sure I had him on the run.

'Just do as you're told. We'll handle the rest. And don't even *think* about doing a runner. You're being watched.' Might as well imply a colleague or two in case he thought he was dealing with a lone extortionist. I hung up.

I was sweating by the time the phone hit the cradle. This blackmail lark was stressful, though I hoped it would be even more stressful for him. It was right now that I regretted not being in the woods outside his house, listening to the bug. I'd have given a lot to hear his next few phone calls, but trying to hide up there in daylight was out of the question. I might go by and check the tape tonight, though I didn't have realistic hopes that anything more was recording.

Now, however, having set up a meeting, or at least a provocative opportunity for surveillance, I had to decide exactly what I was going to do. I certainly wasn't going to show myself, but I equally certainly wanted a look at him to see how he was responding, and, if possible, to find a way to prod him with another menacing message. Meantime, I thought I'd better make the rounds simply to make sure he didn't try to get the evidence out of the way, though I counted on that being impossible in the time I'd given him. Well, what the hell, it was another lovely day for a drive around the island, and it would give me a chance to work out a strategy for the endgame. Up until now I'd been improvising, but now at least I felt the pieces beginning to gel, the chickens falling into place, all my hard work coming home to roost.

By this time I could probably reach Petra at her usual breakfasting place, so I put in a call. She came to the phone after about a minute.

'Just a couple of questions,' I said without preface. 'Did Henry come to see you again yesterday? You don't have to explain. Yes or no will do.'

'Yes,' she said. 'But I think I need to tell you …'

'No explanation necessary,' I said. 'I don't want to hear one right now. We can talk about that later. Right now I just need to know if you know the name of the boat you were on with him that night, the night you told me about, sailing from the mainland.'

'Yes. I know. I looked. She is called Stella. Listen, I just want to say …'

I cut her off in mid-sentence again. 'And you docked her in Puerto Soller, right? In a big closed shed?'

'Yes. How do you know that?'

'No time for explanations now. That's all I needed to know. I'll talk to you again as soon as I can.'

'All right. And Will,' she said in a small voice. 'If you don't allow me to tell you, I want only to say I'm sorry. I truly am very sorry. Be careful.' And then she hung up.

She'd sounded different, not a bit like herself, but I thought I knew what she was sorry about, and that, too, would have to keep. There was another call I had to make.

'Milagro here.' Once more a brusque greeting. In person he was relaxed, personable, and charming. On the phone he was all business.

'Will Stock. Just a quick check-in with you about those two queries I had. Any joy?'

'Ah, yes,' he said, slowing the pace a bit. 'We did, in fact, have some joy regarding your friend Root. Do you know where he is?'

He hadn't actually told me anything yet. 'No, why?'

'Because there's a live warrant out on him from France. We didn't know he was here, damned single-Europe-free-passage-back-and forth regulations. In the old days we'd have had him the minute he tried to cross the border.'

I hadn't thought of Fausto as an unreconstructed Francoist, but I suppose most policemen are partial, at heart, to dictatorships. It makes their lives so much easier not to have to worry about all our ridiculous civil rights and freedoms.

'Well, he's here all right, I don't happen to know exactly where, though I'm told it's probably Pollensa. I can tell you though, that if you keep an eye on Punta Portals, down on the quay, and look out for a round-headed guy around thirty-five wearing leathers and bossing a black and silver Harley, you'll possibly pick him up.' Giving this information made me feel wonderful. I couldn't have ratted on a more deserving character.

'Duly noted. I'll pass it along. Dangerous, do you think? Should I send a squad if we spot him?' He was asking my opinion?

'I don't know. All I can say is that he's one of my two prime candidates for the Ninian Mede rub-out.' *Rub-out?* Who did I think I was talking to? I hadn't shaken off the style of my early morning Fosas call.

'Well, the warrant is for grand theft. No mention of violence, though that doesn't necessarily mean anything. If we see him we'll take precautions.'

'Personally, I'd be grateful. I have reason to believe he's onto me and may even be looking for me, so if you take him out of circulation, please let me know. Ring my mobile.'

'Will do. And *you* ring us if you see him.'

'Nothing would make me happier. How did you get on with my second request?'

'No answer so far, I'm afraid. I put it out on the wire but no one's come back yet with any information. She must have been foreign-registered because we'd have had an immediate answer if she were Spanish.'

'Try France, and let me know, please, if something comes through. I'm working on a hunch and I need to see if it might pan out.'

'A hunch about which you of course do not feel free to tell me,' he said, a bit pompously. This from the man who'd used me as lead ferret for most of this case.

'No. Nothing I can tell you. Not that I wouldn't,' I added disarmingly. 'It's only a hunch at this stage. Really not worth bringing you up to speed.'

'Of course not,' he said, manifestly – and correctly – not believing a word.

'I'll hear from you then,' I said, hoping I hadn't alienated him.

'Yes, I'll go that far,' he replied, slightly frostily. 'I owe you that at least for the information regarding Señor Root. We'll see how we get on.'

'All right. We'll be in touch then.' And we rang off, mutually.

I had one more base to touch before beginning my round of what I'd come to regard as the usual suspects. It took an age to get through to Commandant Vega. They tracked him through four offices before he came on the line.

'Ah, Stock,' he said genially. 'I was going to ring you this morning. Good news from your point of view. We think we have a credible suspect for the Mede killing. You may consider yourself off the hook.'

This was puzzling. How could it be that he knew as much as I did? I was working away to pin it on either Sven or Root, operating under orders from Fosas, or at a further remove, Meliá, and here Vega was telling me he'd narrowed it down to just one suspect.

'You're sure?' I asked, doubtfully, realising the instant the words escaped my mouth how insulting they would be to a senior professional policeman.

'Of *course* we're sure,' he said emphatically, instantly taking offence.

'I'm sorry. I didn't mean that to sound the way it did,' I put in hastily. 'What I meant was ...' I hesitated, then finally blurted, 'who did it?'

'I'm sorry, I can't tell you that right now. We're concluding our investigation and paperwork today and tomorrow and it's too early to release any details, even to you, though I acknowledge that you've tried to be helpful. Ring me tomorrow and I'll be able to tell you more.'

I was still trying to get my mind around this news. If

he had evidence pinning the murder to a specific person, it blew most of the theories I'd been working on right out of the water, though oddly enough it was neither incompatible nor inconsistent with the idea I'd had this morning. Maybe I'd been trying to make the package too neat. Perhaps I should simply put together the pieces that fit and leave the others aside until I could see whether there was a place for them.

'Thank you, I'll do that.' I paused. 'And by the way,' trying to keep a slight note of disappointment out of my voice, 'Congratulations.'

'Thank you,' he said, and rang off.

A cup of that intelligence-improving coffee was called for, since I was feeling distinctly stupid. Vega had been kind not to rub it in, but there had been a faint note of satisfaction in his voice as he had told me the news, the unspoken subtext being that they, the professionals, had cracked the case, and that I, the amateur, still hadn't a clue as to what had been going on. I drank my coffee and waited for some smartness to overtake me, which reminded me of the old joke about the man who kept buying smartness pills from his neighbour, who claimed to get them from a secret source. Finally, fed up with his continuing lack of smartness, he tells his neighbour he's not going to buy any more. 'They're horrible and bitter and I don't feel any smarter,' he says. 'And besides, they taste like dried rabbit turds.' 'You see?' says the neighbour, 'you are getting smarter.'

The more I considered, the more convinced I became that there must be a flaw in Vega's case. The one thing of which I was absolutely certain was that I knew more about Fosas and his gang than he did. Vega didn't even seem to know about Root, unless Milagro had rung him immediately after our conversation and that had been the reason for the delay in getting him on the line. No, on reflection that didn't feel likely, and besides, Milagro really did seem to unconnected with the Mede case. I decided I'd wait until tomorrow to talk to Vega again, maybe best in person. He didn't think I'd been able to help with the murder, but I was sure I could help him roll up the smuggling operation. There were still some mysteries to be solved.

But then another interior voice spoke up. The persona that was narked at Vega for being smarter than me, smarter than I'd given him credit for being. 'Why don't you see how much you could squeeze Fosas for?' it said. 'If you're careful, you could get away with it.'

Bah. Get thee behind me, greedy twerp. You don't remember, maybe, what happened to Ninian?

'Oh, all right,' said the voice. 'It was only a thought. You don't have to be so aggressive just because you didn't know what was going on.' I get very cross with some of those little interior voices. There are lots of people in there and not all of them are my friends.

So I rang Milagro again. He picked up on the first ring.

'Milagro here.'

'It's me, Will Stock again. Did you know Commandant Vega has a prime suspect for Ninian Mede's murder?'

'No, he hasn't said anything to me yet. You know very well that he has some reasons not to include me in his circle of confidants. I fear the situation with my brother has compromised his faith in my objectivity. But when I last spoke to him he said he thought one of his men had a lead and was working on it. Since then we haven't spoken. Why?'

'I just spoke to him. He thinks he has the case all but wrapped up.'

'Well, that's it, then. You're no longer a suspect. You can go home and forget about it all.'

'That's exactly what Commandant Vega told me to do, but you know very well why I won't be able to do that. By the way, have you spoken to your brother about the situation?'

'Not yet. I'm seeing him this weekend. We'll have to have a serious talk. By the way, I got that report you were waiting for a few minutes after we last spoke. I was going to ring you in a little while. That boat, the one you mentioned – Stella, was it? Reported stolen a few weeks ago in France, from Port Vendres apparently, one of those marinas just up the coast over the border. Mean anything to you?'

'Yes.' I stopped, as yet another small piece ratcheted into place. 'I mean, no. I mean I'm actually not sure yet. I'll have to think about it and see how it fits. Must go now.' And I hung up the phone almost rudely.

My head was whirling. The boat I'd assumed all along had come in on the transporter had in fact been stolen. And now I also knew who'd done it – Hawg Root, with Petra's assistance. But how did it jibe with what I already knew?

Then, all of an instant I had the epiphany, the eureka breakthrough. It was as though all the pieces of the puzzle had been shaken up as in a kaleidoscope, then suddenly rearranged to make a new pattern. I'd been wrong all the time in my assumptions, wrong about everything – well *almost* everything. I sat back and closed my eyes and ran through the new theory front to back. No doubt about it, it added up neatly. But how to test the hypothesis? Then, suddenly and all of a piece as these things seem to work, I had that, too.

I consulted my pocket diary and picked up the phone yet again. This time I dialled Gewürz's number. My hope was that Fosas wouldn't have rung him. I figured he'd have rung Meliá for sure, and then probably one of the muscle boys.

'Gewürz Associates,' came the lilting voice on the end of the wire.

'Give me Heinz,' I whispered hoarsely.

'Whom shall I say is calling, please?'

'Tell him Fosas,' even more abruptly.

'Oh, of course, Señor Fosas. I didn't recognise your voice,' she said cheerfully. 'Putting you through.'

'Yes, Roberto?'

'Listen, Heinz,' I rasped. 'I can hardly talk. Laryngitis.'

'I'm sorry to hear it, boss. Anything I can do? You need some medicine brought up?' So far, so good.

'No. I'm all right for that. This is what I want you to do. The papers for Melanie are all ready?' This was the critical bit. I'd give it away or not in the next sentence or two.

'You know they are, Boss. You've seen them.'

'Yes, yes, I know,' I whispered croakily. 'I'm just confirming they're all ready to go.'

'All set,' he said, seemingly without suspicion.

'This is what I want you to do. Right now. Drop everything else. You've got to take them someplace. Not here. Take them to Santa Maria post office and put them into postbox 111. Got that?'

'Yes. Santa Maria, postbox 111. Right away.'

'You can leave right away?' I threw in a consumptive cough for effect.

'Right away.'

'All right, do it. But don't ring me back to confirm. My line could be tapped. Just do and do it now. *Capich?*'

'I got it. I'm on my way.' And he hung up.

So was I on my way. I could have taken my time. I was lots closer to Santa Maria than he was. But all of a sudden I had that old longing for activity. I was bursting with the testosterone that gets us males into trouble, into fights and conflict and wars. It was a drive to *do* something. I felt it was all coming together and I was on a high. I'd been stuck in a waiting game for too long – now things were about to break.

After driving around Santa Maria for five minutes or so, I found a parking place where I could watch the post office, and facing the other direction from the way

Gewürz would come in. I had been there about twenty minutes when a green Range Rover with Gewürz behind the wheel came along the road at speed, then slowed as he sought the post office. He saw it and stopped, not even trying to park properly – inconsiderate bastard – jumped out with a brown envelope in his hand and raced into the building. He clearly was taking 'Fosas' at face value.

One minute. Two minutes. Three minutes. Four. Then he came out, looking slightly pensive. His hands were empty, but there was a air of puzzlement about him. He got in the big Range Rover and drove slowly away.

Just as soon as he'd turned the corner I hightailed it over the post office, went directly to Box 111 and opened it. Empty. Of course, I thought belatedly. I should have waited awhile. There's no way to deposit things directly in the postboxes, you have to hand them in at the counter to be put in the box from behind. He'd handed it in but they hadn't yet put it in the box. I went to the counter to beard the dragon who oversees the office. She was partially out of view, probably ripping up a personal letter or two or crushing a parcel underfoot. I rapped the counter for her attention.

'I'm expecting an envelope to be delivered to Box 111,' I said, waving the key.

'*You're* not Señor Mede,' she said, accusingly. 'He's dead.'

It had taken awhile but the news had finally percolated through to her. 'Yes, of course. I'm just picking up an envelope for his widow. It was to be delivered by hand,' I said patiently. Softly, softly.

'Well, you can't have it,' she said with finality. 'I have to hold it until I hear from his executor and then I have to fill out the PN-9484/M forms and turn the package over to him, and only to him.'

Oh shit, I thought. This was something I certainly could have, *should have*, foreseen. I'd let something important get into the official mill, and God only knew –

and even then I had my doubts as to the limits of His omniscience when it came to the Spanish post office – when it might emerge. Certainly too late for my purposes.

'Of course,' I said reasonably. Rule One: (there are several Rules One) Never argue with a bureaucrat. 'In that case, acting officially on behalf of the estate, I shall have to take down a description of the envelope to pass on to the executor and to Señor Mede's widow.' Fight bureaucracy with bureaucracy. 'You, of course, have the envelope here. You can confirm that, yes?'

'Yes. I received it just now. You almost must have seen the gentleman who brought it. I told him he shouldn't leave it here. I told him Señor Mede was deceased.'

So that was the explanation for Gewürz's puzzlement. I carried on regardless. 'If you are confirming that you have this envelope, I must ask you to show it to me so I can vouch that it is being kept safe, containing as it does valuable papers relating to Señor Mede's estate. The executor will expect me to have done that since I have been unable to secure the envelope itself.' All this time I was exuding sincerity and that special blandness that signals cooperation and understanding of the most unreasonable of rules and regulations – not that this one actually was unreasonable. It was my fault for not having been bright enough to come up with a better drop.

'I've put it away,' she said. Not uncooperative, just letting me know that I was being a pain asking her to go out of her way for me.

'And I'm sure you've put it somewhere very safe,' I said, with an encouraging nod. 'I'll mention that to the executor.' He was acquiring validity, dimension, and gravitas by the second.

'Well, I haven't actually had a chance to put it away yet,' she said, slightly on the defensive. 'But I was about to put it in the safe.' She reached under the counter and drew out the envelope, which had been on the shelf under the counter, thirty inches away from my nose but out of sight. She held it up for me to see.

'And that's the envelope that was just delivered?' I said, moving forward a bit.

'The very one,' she said.

'Thank you,' I said as I grabbed it out of her grasp. For a split of a moment we simply stared at one another, her mouth going round and her eyes opening wide in outrage. Then, wheeling quickly, I scampered out the door, which banged closed on her offended shouts. Such language. I try to get Semiramis to teach me all those words, but there are some she declines to pronounce, much less translate.

I bounded to the car, slammed the door and drove away as rapidly as I could without drawing attention to myself. I looked back to see if she'd come out to try to take my number and report me to the police. She hadn't, but as I turned my head back towards the road I saw something else, the Range Rover was parked on the opposite side of the street and Gewürz was staring straight at me. He'd clearly had his suspicions stirred by the postmistress's information and had circled back to see if he might spot whoever was picking up the envelope, and so, of course, he'd seen me emerge running, envelope in hand. That's the problem in dealing with thieves; there's no trust at all.

I hit the throttle hard as soon as I neared the edge of town and was thankful I'd brought the BMW. There wasn't much chance he'd follow me, or would catch me if he did. It would take him at least a full minute to turn around and I could cover a lot of ground in that time. Just to be sure, though, I swung a quick left into the lane that leads up to Hortus, Hugo Latymer's fragrant garden centre. I pulled out of sight behind a massive tractor and backhoe parked in the lane and waited for Gewürz to come by, which he did eventually, his posture and demeanour seeming to show he'd lost hope of catching me and was trailing back home. Well, small favours; at least he hadn't headed the other way up to Fosas's house, though no doubt he'd ring him.

It took me about an hour to get into Palma, get my business done with the contents of the envelope, and be ready to head for home. But as I was already on the far side of Palma, and as it was only a short run to Portals, I thought I'd pop up and check in with Petra. I'd cut her off short this morning and was feeling mildly guilty about it. She'd been trying to tell me something and I hadn't taken the time to listen to her. Now, with the most important elements of my duplicitous scheme in place, I had some time to spare.

Things were still quiet in Punta Portals when I got there. Off-season is always to be preferred, unless, of course, you enjoy pushy crowds – though true connoisseurs of pushy crowds tell me that the Tokyo underground is the *ne plus ultra* experience.

I was in a buoyant and larky mood as I strolled down towards the quay. The inside straight was looking good, and I was recovering from the ego blow of having failed to identify Ninian's murderer before Vega had. I consoled myself that I was almost certainly about to solve another puzzle altogether, one that the police didn't even seem to know about, much less have a handle on. So I was almost smiling as I made the turn to the quay, only to be disorientated by an unfamiliar configuration of the masts of the boats moored along the dock – a gap in the forest of masts and stays and shrouds. The anomaly registered with that mental device that recognises people moments before their identities penetrate up to our conscious minds. Then I got closer and the reality hit me with a jolt. My mind wanted to resist the truth my eyes were telling me. There was a sudden queasy, hollow feeling in the pit of my stomach.

The mooring was empty. Petra's boat was gone.

Twenty-Six

My night was restless. Ominous dreams, irrational worries, paranoia. In one 3 a.m. nightmare Petra had been murdered by Root either – or variously – because she knew too much, because she was informing on the gang, or out of misplaced jealousy. At the other extreme, in another cobwebby reverie she was the mastermind behind the gang, manipulating all of them just as she had at times manipulated me, but now had done a flit, flown the coop, leaving the rest of them to face the music and take the rap. Face the rap music? Even mostly asleep, I was amused by the images that dream evoked. On some dim rationally conscious level I think I knew the truth was probably somewhere between these extremes, but some part of me was hurt and disappointed, frustrated and even feeling – quite irrationally – rejected. The mind seems so often to refuse to accept the limitations of the body, age, or capacity. So from early on in life, part of us is always in mourning for lost opportunities, roads not taken, bad choices or wasted promise. Clearly, a bit of my self-image that hadn't caught up with reality had still been harbouring hopes of a romantic attachment of some kind. My lovely grown-up daughter Kate, now a writer in London, had once told me she wished me well in my private affairs, but please would I not bring home any popsies younger than herself. Petra had qualified within that caveat by some several years, but still was younger than anybody else I'd even looked at for a long time. So who did I think I was kidding? Well, as I said, these things ain't rational. All things considered, with the jolt of Petra's precipitous departure added to the anxiety about my arrangements for the morning, it wasn't the most tranquil of nights.

Dawn and strong coffee, however, brought a surge of energy and resolution. Today was the day I planned to pull the string on the neck of the sack. Today I hoped to catch Fosas out and reel him in. So the condemning man ate a hearty breakfast, made a few phone calls, and was early away. The earlier I could get up there, scout myself a hide, and get settled in to wait for Fosas to appear, the safer it would be for me.

Catriona had kindly lent me her car, as I wanted to avoid being identified by bringing mine into the car park up there. Sven had seen Balthasar and Gewürz the BMW. Fosas might or might not involve them, but I assumed he would cover himself one way or the other.

There were some errands to run for the hotel. Hannah is particular about where she gets supplies – sometimes over-particular in my view, but then we're back to Frank Lloyd Wright's principle that 'God is in the details' – so we buy our ham from one butcher, general *charcuterie* from another, some kinds of flowers from one shop, others from another, and so on. And I've long moaned to her about the carousel of bakery purchasing – bread in one shop, croissants in another, and *ensaimadas* in a third. At any rate, it was time consuming and by 10:00 I was already getting antsy to get up the mountain and in place. At last I dropped off all my purchases, got loose, drove on up, and entered the lower car park around 11:00, parking next to a big Jeep near the entrance. Few cars were there, and no evidence, I was relieved to note, of a motorcycle, though I wouldn't have expected Root to advertise his presence so blatantly if he were there.

I went along to the front left of Es Vergé and banged on the kitchen door. It's a rustic farmhouse restaurant with a history that reflects in microcosm what's happened over the whole island. Located only a few hundred yards below the Castell de Alaró, that Mecca for walkers, and accessible to cars only via a long, rubble-strewn unmade road that twists in a series of hairpin curves between terraces of pines, carob, and olive trees going back to Roman times, Es Vergé serves, lunchtimes and into the evening every day, absolutely scrumptious shoulders of lamb, braised for hours in a huge oven with garlic and herbs. (Skip the bought-in desserts, but do have a *cognac quemada* with your coffee, letting the alcohol burn off well.) The restaurant is run by a seamed and twinkly woman named Francisca, now in her eighties, helped by members of her family, most of them well into their seventies. Some years ago, walkers used to stop at the farmhouse to beg a glass of water, and that was no trouble at all in the days when walkers were few. Later, however, the numbers increased, and some would smell the family's Sunday roast lamb and knock on the door to ask if they might buy a meal. And so Francisca took up the habit of cooking a few extra joints and serving them on a trestle table set on the dirt floor of an adjoining barn. After that, simply by word of mouth, a fame of sorts began to spread, and twenty or thirty or forty people might turn up of a Sunday. Lunch was still served in the barn, more trestle tables were added, plus a rough wine and a few other items, like snails. The family prospered, and for those of us who knew of the restaurant it was a delightful outing with some of the aspects of a jolly catered picnic. Then, to the regret of many of us who live here and are protective of the few secret places still left untouristed, a guidebook wrote up the restaurant in such glowing terms that now one can hardly get up there weekends because of all the expensive 4 X 4s and rental cars cluttering up the stony track. Still, we're happy for Francisca and her family, and hope they are making a bundle.

After several bouts of knocking, one of the cousins, José Canyusea, finally answered the door – we've known most of the family for ten years – and I worked out a deal with him, using Spanish and a few words of Mallorquin, which is what the family mostly speaks. I gave him a 5,000 peseta note, a generous sum even if cheap for me in the circumstances, and briefed him on how he could identify Fosas. When he saw him arrive he was to take him a note, and he was to speak only Mallorquin, so that Fosas couldn't counter-interrogate him about me. If asked, he was to shrug and say I was an *extranjero. Nada más.* The note itself was simple. I had printed in bold letters:

FOR MY SILENCE I WANT $25,000 EVERY TIME YOU DO A RUN. USED NOTES. YOU WILL BE TOLD WHEN AND WHERE TO DROP THE MONEY. THE SHADOW.

'The Shadow,' for those too young or of a different culture, was a radio hero named Lamont Cranston who had the power hypnotically to cloud the minds of his adversaries in order to root out evil where it lurked in the hearts of men. (That's what they announced, every week.) I wanted to feel he'd have been proud of me; he was a model who shaped my youthful attitudes. I mourn the demise of that kind of radio drama. It was far more imaginatively intense than television is. As the small boy remarked when asked which he preferred between the two – 'Radio,' he said, 'because the costumes are better.'

That task done, I crept up into the woods above the car parks and found a corner where I could hunch down and still have a decent view of both parking areas, the original one above and the new enclosure farther down. I was wearing the nightfighter camouflage suit I'd worn to check out the boatyard, and though it looked mildly silly during the day, at least it blended into the leaves and pine needles and afforded me some cover. By this time it was 11:30 and I had a half hour to go. What is it about tasks requiring stealth and immobility that always seems to set off every tiny tic and tickle, itch and twitch? I hadn't been so antsy since I'd done my first parachute drop. And of course my bladder was telling me I had to pee, and it's no good arguing rationally against these urgings and pointing out that I had recently gone, which I had. It was a long twenty-five minutes.

Finally, though, a sleek black Lexus – I'd never bring

one of *those* up that road – pulled into the top parking area and Roberto Fosas got out, alone, and stood by the car, benignly gazing out across the expanse of the central plain of the island, a smudgy smear of sea cloud visible out beyond Alcudia Bay on the left. It seemed he was following my instructions. After awhile José emerged from the front door of the restaurant, looked around until he spotted Fosas, and trudged over on his patently painful waiter's feet. He spoke to Fosas briefly, passed the note, shrugged his shoulders and shook his head, and trudged back, seeming to limp on both feet, which is a trick in itself.

Fosas opened the note, read it at a glance, turned it over to see if there was anything else to notice, then folded it and stuck it in his breast pocket. He stood for a few moments looking back out over the view, showing no emotion that I could discern, at least not from this distance. Then he got back in his car and drove away down the hill.

All I could feel was anticlimax. I'm not sure what I had expected, perhaps a biblical grand gnashing of teeth and rending of garments and a falling down upon the ground? Or a stamping of angry feet and curses and invective hurled into the great chasm of the vista? Not a bit of it. The man had hardly reacted. My hopes of getting a reading of his reaction so that I could further provoke him seemed defeated, hollow, frustrated. The puff seeped out of me. I deflated as my nerves unwound.

But then they tensed again. I had to assume it was a ruse. Probably he'd posted Sven or Hawg to root me out. Probably they were just waiting for me to come out of hiding. If so, they were likely to be watching with binoculars from somewhere in the woods above me, the logical place for surveillance. I waited another strained ten minutes and then infinitely cautiously began to work my way across the slope above the car park. There wasn't much cover for me, but then there wasn't much cover for them, either, if they were there at all. I wasn't quite sure what I'd do if I saw one of them, so I kept as close to the restaurant side of the woods as I could, ready to bolt back to the safety of the clots of hungry people who were beginning to filter from the car park to the restaurant. After twenty tense minutes of hide-and-seek, I decided I'd misjudged Fosas on this one. He might be playing for time, looking to identify me so he could either take care of me on a ground of his choosing, or else – a remoter but more attractive possibility – he had simply wanted to know how much money it would take to buy me off so he might consider the cost effectiveness of it. He was, when all was said and done, a pragmatic businessman. If he calculated it would be cheaper to pay me off to keep me quiet, and that his scam could afford the extra overhead, it might well be that he would opt for an accommodation to my demands. That was what I was hoping for at this point, and that was why I had pitched my demand at a level that I felt he might deem affordable. If I'd judged it finely enough, he might go for the proposition. Then I could record him or expose him in some other way. One way or the other I was determined to nail him. This exercise had only been to draw him out, see if he'd take the bait. Looking on the bright side, his very presence had confirmed my theory.

The woods seemed clear. I came out of my latest hiding place and began a self-consciously relaxed amble in the direction of Catriona's car, half hidden behind the fat black Jeep Cherokee by the entrance. I was drawing a few looks from people parking and heading up to the restaurant. The suit itself was incongruous for the surroundings, so I suppose I looked like a member of the lost patrol, and on top of that I was sweating profusely, since the suit was made for night use and has a thin lining of Kevlar, that tough material developed by Du Pont for bulletproof jackets. One layer wouldn't stop a bullet, of course, but was meant to resist tearing on rocks or brambles, and also to serve as lightweight insulation against the cold. I ignored the looks; people always need something to stare at.

When I reached the car I dusted off the remaining leaf mould, twigs, and earth that still clung to the suit, reached in my pocket and went to insert the key. It wouldn't go in the lock. I pulled it out and looked at it to make certain I had the right one, there being three on the ring. It appeared to be the one I'd used previously, though since this was a borrowed car I didn't have the same level of confidence in my memory as I would with one of my own vehicles. Maybe there was a trick to it. I tried again, this time wiggling the key a bit as I attempted to slide it in. Still no joy. It was jammed. Puzzled, but not worried, I walked around the car to get in through the other front door. Just as I moved to insert the key I heard a quick crunch of gravel behind me and almost simultaneously felt something hard and pointed press into my back, right between the second and third ribs on the left side.

'Don't even think about moving, you son-of-a-bitch,' said an unfamiliar voice, an American voice, west coast at a guess, not that I was guessing its origins at this stage.

I didn't move. My jaw must have dropped in surprise, for I was suddenly aware of the drying sensation of the breeze in my mouth. I was filled with disgust that he'd got the drop on me so easily, gobsmacked that I'd been so foolishly careless. In one instant I understood how he'd done it. He'd got there earlier than I had – damn those errands – hidden somewhere below the drop-off to the next terrace down, nipped up when I went to the door of the restaurant and shoved something, a matchstick or toothpick, into Catriona's lock to jam it. Then he'd hidden under, or maybe inside, the Cherokee, and simply outwaited me. I began to blush for shame at my own stupidity. And that was followed by a wave of wild unreasoning anger, partly at him, but even more directed at myself.

'Hand over the keys,' he said, pressing the pointed thing against my back even harder. It felt as though it had caught in a fold of my suit. A gun? It didn't feel like one, but if it were I hadn't a chance. He'd picked a good spot for his ambush, hidden as we were between the two cars. I half turned to my left and pulled away so I could look at the weapon. Some wildly irrationally hopeful part of me was willing it to be a stick or a fake pistol. It wasn't. It was a big sharp mean-looking Bowie knife.

'Stand still, you bastard,' he growled, shifting the point of it along the line of my ribs to the spot where my ribcage rose. I was now half facing him and could see his round head, almost neckless, emerging from his dusty leathers. He looked in my eyes and must have seen fear because he smirked at me and I could see that one front tooth had a corner chipped off, the yellowed edge showing against his tongue. How could Petra have had the bad taste to link up with anyone with an ugly tooth like that, I thought absurdly. And that odd, almost spherical head. It would be like taking up with Charlie Brown, only a Charlie Brown with mean, piggy eyes and the general look of a fairground roustabout. 'Get in the car and slide over to the driver's seat. You're going to drive and this knife is going to be in your ribs.' And he gave a nasty chuckle as though he'd practised hard guy routines in front of a mirror.

One central truth was penetrating me as sharply as that knife might. Once I got in that car with him I'd soon end up like Ninian. There was a surreal aspect to it since, knife or not, part of me refused to take him seriously. Just at that moment though, he pushed the tip of the Bowie against me a little harder to make sure I got the point, so to speak. A once familiar bit of Shakespeare tried to surface in my mind – something graceful and wise about overcoming fear through action. I couldn't disinter the words, but got the message: if I didn't do something right now, this bastard was going to kill me. Drawing in a breath and leaning into his space, I screamed into his face as loud as I could, instantly stepping on his near foot with my right boot and simultaneously shoving him hard in the chest. I could feel the prick of the knife as he pushed it at me, but it lacked force as he was moving backwards. The thin layer of Kevlar wouldn't give to the point, wouldn't tear – bless those Du Pont boffins – and though I could feel the tip push at me, it didn't penetrate the suit, which must have surprised him. I shouted and shoved again and this time he went down, but started to bounce up almost immediately. Now I'd lost the element of surprise and I certainly wasn't going to hang around to battle it out with someone wider and stronger, probably rougher in experience, and lots of years younger. Before you could say Jack Robinson, this Jack was nimble and quick and jumping around the stakes of the wire fence along the terrace edge. I was out of there and down the drive.

If I took the straight route down, descending from terrace to terrace along the old donkey trail, I'd cross the road at least eight times as it snaked down before hitting flatter terrain. That gave me eight chances of flagging down one of the cars along the road, most of them still ascending. That might mean coming back along the grain of his chase, but I'd gain the protection of company. My children used to use this route – even after lunch and on full stomachs – leaping down from rock to rock and terrace to terrace like mountain goats, while we adults effected a more stately descent in the car, usually reaching the bottom well behind them.

My progress was more mountain walrus than mountain goat, but even Fosbury-flopping I could make a quick passage down. I glanced back to see if Root was following, but he'd ducked out of sight. I managed to get down three terrace levels without pursuit and was beginning to look around for cover where I might go to ground. Then, as I crossed the road for the third time I saw a car heading my way and rushed to flag it down.

The startled driver, a mild-looking farmerish man with an apparent wife and three children in the car, took one look at this frantic sweaty crazed maniacal apparition in a dirty camouflage suit and accelerated away in panic. That knocked one smart little scheme on the head.

Then I did see someone who'd want to pick me up. It was Root, at the wheel of the Cherokee, skidding down the road at a ferocious clip, blowing his horn at the oncoming cars, waving them out of his way – determined to get me once more in his sights and skewer me on the tip of that big Bowie. The prospect goaded me to sweatier, if not more noticeably speedy, efforts.

Twice he got close enough almost for him to be able to pass me and cut me off, but each time he met someone coming up who took exception to his road manners and kept him blocked long enough for me to get a better lead. At one point I saw the bastard waving a white handker-chief across the window, which in Spain is the signal for 'Medical emergency. I have a sick person on board. Please get out of the way,' a signal Spaniards respect and give way to. Luckily for me, most of the drivers coming up the mountain were foreigners and the message was lost on them; they only saw a rude bastard in a big black 4 X 4 trying to muscle them out of the way and so, of course, some of them took perverse pleasure in frustrating him in his efforts to pass them on the narrow file.

I made another halfhearted attempt at flagging a car down, but only succeeded in frightening yet another set of innocents on a Sunday outing. I must have looked truly deranged by this time. My prime hope now lay in getting to the bottom before Root did so I could hide in the better cover at the foot of the hill. Up here there was apparent cover, but it was thin and scattered, and as long as Root knew approximately where I was I'd stick out like a cherry in a peach bowl.

Heaving and blowing like a grampus, I passed the first house-sized rock that marks the transition between the unmade road and the wider, tarmac road. Bad news. That meant Root could go faster down here. I was soaked with sweat that stung the small cut the knife had made even through the Kevlar. Considering what it might have been, I wasn't complaining.

Then my goal was in sight, the group of huge rocks that mark the steeper part of the ascent to the castle. Once there, the cover would be thicker or I even might keep the rock between me and Root, circling as in a children's game until someone turned up to afford me help, or rescue, or a ride out of there. Cars had to slow there to pass so I figured it was a good spot to hide, or make a stand, or even jump on the back of one of those 4 X 4s and hunker down to cadge a ride down to civilisation. Looking back, I could see Root's fat wagon stalled by a queue of three small rental cars, and even all the way from here I could distinguish the general content, if not all the individual words, of his shouts. He had a rich line in invective.

With renewed energy I lurched and reeled and wove my way down the last few hundred yards towards the great sentry rock. No doubt it has a name, but I've not heard it. Once I circled round it, I'd be out of Root's view and I could look for cover. I hoped I could lie low long enough to get my wind back and then maybe work my way down to Alaró, where we've got friends whose telephone I could use. Just a few minutes more and I'd be out of Root's reach. At my back I could hear his insistent horn and fulminating curses as he strove to clear past the drivers who were the last few obstacles between us.

With faltering steps, I reached the rock and scrambled into the pull-off area on the town side, now safely out of Root's line of sight. My gaze swept the area, searching for cover. No one was about. Almost immediately, I began to breathe more easily. But then my eye was caught by one of the cars parked over by the trees and with sickening dawning realisation I recognised it, though I was too exhausted immediately to pull all the implications together. It was Sven's car. The white Mercedes. Then I fumbled my thoughts into place. He was the backup man, just waiting here for me. Root had lost me temporarily, but had herded me straight into Sven's clutches. All he'd had to do to serve was stand and wait. I felt like some small furry thing trapped at the blind end of a cul-de-sac tunnel.

A wash of resignation enveloped me. For once, I didn't even feel stupid, or at least not entirely so. I'd done well in getting clear of Root, and realistically this had been my only way out, or at least the clearest way. I might have gone down the other side of the hill to Alaró, but for all I knew Fosas had men posted there as well.

All these thoughts seemed to run together in confusion. I swivelled to see if I could scrabble off in a different direction but saw them both, Sven and Gewürz, moving towards me from where they'd been standing out of sight behind some trees. I twisted to run in the other direction, though with little confidence that in my puffed state I'd be able to outdistance them, but overdid the twist, wrenched my foot on a rounded rock, and sat down with a dusty and inglorious thump, feeling my already overstrained ankle give way with a sharp pang.

Sven walked over and just looked down at me.

'You look like shit,' he said matter-of-factly. Probably he had been hoping for more challenging prey.

'I could say the same about you,' I managed to gasp out, meanwhile massaging my painfully twisted ankle.

We could have carried on this clever verbal fencing for a number of turns, dialogue to make Tom Stoppard envious, but there was the sound of tyres sliding on gravel and the black Cherokee nosed into the pull-off space, the motor dying with a disgruntled squeak, and then there was the sound of heavy footfalls as Root leapt down from the cab and advanced on us. The Cherokee was now blocking the sightlines from the road, which meant that I was effectively isolated with my three captors.

'So,' he said with a malicious grin, 'we meet again.'

I actually laughed. Despite my shit-scaredness, this was right out of a Victorian melodrama. All he needed was a moustache to twirl. But of course I'd done the wrong thing. His sneer turned to scowl and he reached for the Bowie tucked into a leather holster dangling from his belt. He took out the knife and wiped it on his leg. It gleamed enough already, I thought, or do polished knives slide in more easily? He advanced on me with measured, purposeful strides.

'Laugh? I'll cut a smile in your throat, you son-of-a-bitch,' and he made a great roundhouse swipe of the knife at my neck. I rolled away at the last second as the blade swept past my jaw, all laughter gone from my thoughts, all my future shrivelling into a curled filament of bitter chance. As I rolled, I managed to grasp one of the sharp rocks that were scattered across the clearing – too small, I thought, a puny defence against his knife, but I tucked it out of sight down by my side. Now I was half on my back, and he kicked me hard on the thigh, put one foot on my throbbing ankle, and leaned forward over me, knife poised. Suddenly I had no place more to go. The only way of stopping him would be to smash the rock into his face, but I'd have to wait until he'd committed himself to his knife-thrust. I'd have but one chance. I wriggled to free my arm. The knife drew back for a second strike, the final slash that would leave my blood staining the rocky ground, my life draining away in a matter of seconds. I saw the sunlight glint off the blade, and watched it almost hypnotised, seeing it framed cinematically between the rock, the sky, and his shoulder.

Then suddenly a great ham of a hand reached into the frame, grasped his wrist, and twisted until the knife fell with a resonant clatter onto the dry and stony surface.

'Stop it, Hawg,' said Sven in a gruff voice. 'I don't get involved in killink people. Vee get paid to cotch him, not kill him.'

'I won't charge extra to kill this bastard, Sven. Leave me alone and I'll take care of him. You don't have to be involved. You can piss off now.'

'Just cool down, Hawg. You don't get told to kill him. Vee don't kill nobody yet and I don't vant to do nutink till the boss come.'

Even lying there helpless on the ground listening to these two apes discuss my fate, I wondered at part of that remark. But I still had other concerns. The outcome of the continuing debate was by no means yet clear. Given a halfway persuasive reason, I feared Sven might capitulate to Root's arguments. He certainly didn't seem to be objecting to my prospective murder on moral grounds. It seemed more a matter of following orders, or price, maybe on a piecework basis, or perhaps he was even taking a not-my-job-man attitude.

'I don't give a shit, Sven. This is personal now.' And he started to reach down to pick up the knife.

'No, I don't tink so. Not a good idea.' said Sven, putting one big shoe on the handle. They stood there and stared at on another. My future, were I to have one, seemed in the balance.

Then a movement in the corner of my eye caught my attention, and coming round the end of the broad dark rock, whom should I see but Fausto Milagro. He was wearing a sky-blue jacket with brass buttons that made him look like an oversized version of Peter Rabbit. Accompanying him, with a pistol unsheathed, was Commandant Vega. They both wore grim expressions.

'I think that will be enough, gentlemen,' said Milagro offhandedly, but with a distinct undercurrent of menace. Vega said nothing. The leveled pistol spoke for him.

The rest was just business. Gewürz and Sven and Root were bundled into the Guardia car, with Root, the smallest of the three, having to sit ignominiously on Sven's lap. Vega and Milagro had seen Fosas come down, but had let him go by. They'd pick him up later. I couldn't walk on my twisted ankle and so a passing motorist was flagged down, given the key to Catriona's car, briefed about the jammed lock, and then posted off to fetch the car down for me.

In the end, I couldn't even drive on the foot, so Milagro stayed on to take me home while Vega ferried the prisoners to the Palma holding tank. I probably wouldn't have been able to drive even with an intact ankle; all I did for at least ten minutes was quietly tremble in the shade of the rock. Perhaps it was true, I reflected, that God does sometimes temper the wind to the shorn lamb. Gradually, though, I began to come back to myself. As we were about to get in the car I found myself staring at the sky-blue jacket with the brass buttons, and Fausto caught what must have been a mildly quizzical look on my face. Uncharacteristically, he blushed. 'No, not my usual attire, old man. But I have to go undercover at a convention of TV weathermen this afternoon and I thought this would do.' The whole notion of Fausto undercover with all those earnest hamsters in sports coats tickled my imagination into a shower of whimsical fancies, but I refrained from comment.

On the way back, after explaining the scam to him, I asked him how he happened to be there at the propitious moment.

'Well, I knew you were finally onto something when you gave me those ship's papers to check for authenticity,' he said. 'And when they turned up duff, and when you didn't want to tell me where you were going, I checked with Paco and we decided to have you followed.'

'For which I am sincerely grateful,' I said gravely. No joke. My near death experience had left me both stirred and shaken.

'Let me tell you just a couple of things,' he said. 'We have some rules in the Guardia, and if you will persist in doing this sort of – what you'd call a "caper" – you'd be wise to pay attention to them.'

'And they are?' I asked, appropriately chastened.

'First, just as your mother always told you when you were young, always let people know where you're going when you go out.

'Second, just as your platoon sergeant always told you when you were a bit older, never go into a dangerous situation without backup.

'Third, just as I've been trying to tell you even though you're old enough to know better anyway, don't always try to be such a fucking hero. You'll live longer.'

I got the message. He was right on every count. I looked sheepish and nodded. Nevertheless, it was hard to suppress an internal smile.

Postscript

Son Ben and I were sitting side by side up in the bistro, each of us with a left foot wrapped in bandages and propped on a chair. He'd twisted his practising skateboarding We must have looked like two components of a Russian doll. He'd probably still fit inside me, but the squeeze would be tight these days, and he's still growing.

Hannah had furnished us with drinks, a wine for me and a shandy for him, and now was settling herself opposite, glass in hand.

'But don't expect me to go on spoiling you just because you're both gimpy,' she said, floating us a bantering smile. This, of course, was pure balderdash. Anyone who hangs around Hannah gets spoilt. She's famous for it. 'All right,' she said. 'Let's start at the beginning and work through it. You've only told me in dribs and drabs so far. But you're saying Root didn't kill Ninian?'

'No, and neither did Sven, but hang on and I'll come to that in a minute.' I'd glossed over the climactic encounter with Root. Some things are better left alone.

'So why was he after you, then?'

'Partly because he was under orders from Fosas, something that's still being confirmed now he's been arrested, partly because he thought I was blowing the whistle on them all, which was correct, and partly because he thought I was after Petra, which was …,' I hesitated and grinned.

'Also correct,' she finished for me, with an arch lift of the eyebrow, that one eyebrow.

'At any rate, that's neither here nor there, especially now,' I said. 'You wanted the main story, not the subplot. It turns out we were all mistaken in our assumptions – they weren't into drug running after all. It was a different scam entirely.'

'Which was?' put in Ben.

'Boat theft, but in a sophisticated form. The way it worked was this. Meliá had contacts to a bent boat broker in the Caribbean who would bird dog a wealthy purchaser, usually an American who was looking to berth his boat somewhere down there more or less permanently. They'd find out what he was looking for and offer to locate that model for him, mentioning a price that was well under market value, but not so ridiculously low as to attract attention. They'd usually spin a tale about knowing of a distress sale situation or some similar come-on to keep him on the hook for awhile, anything up to a couple of months.

Then Martillo, who knows the French coast well and speaks French, would go on a scouting tour, find something as close as possible to that make and model and find out as much as he could about the owners – how often they took the boat out, where they lived and so on. He could get a lot of that information simply by chatting up other skippers in a casual way. And they only chose super-luxury boats – top quality makes, but not of a size to be able to go transatlantic by themselves. Or at least not easily. That was the secret.

Once they had something spotted, and generally with a buyer on the hook, then Root would go in at night, cut it out, and sail it away. Usually Sven accompanied him on these trips, but on one occasion Sven was ill and so he pressed Petra into service, keeping her in the dark, obviously, about what he was doing. Nevertheless, he raised her suspicions, as she finally felt able to tell me.'

'I've got something to tell you about that situation,' said Hannah. 'But later. I want to hear how the scam worked.'

'So Root and Sven would bring the boat back here to Mallorca. You can cover a fair amount of sea in a night of sailing, enough to get well clear of the port where they'd picked up the boat. They worked the Spanish ports sometimes, but mainly concentrated on the smaller ports just along over the French border. One clever wrinkle was that they usually tried to make their pickups on days when there were regattas or at weekends when there were lots of boats around. In the case of Stella, the boat I saw up at Holmes's yard that later metamorphosed into Melanie, they stole her only an hour after the owners had brought her in and tied her up and headed off for home.

'After that it was simple. They brought each boat into Holmes's place, stashing her in the closed shed. She was repainted and refitted in various ways to change her general configuration and appearance. Once that was done, Gewürz, with all the facilities of his printing business at hand, counterfeited a full new set of papers giving her origin in one of the islands of the West Indies and then she was shipped off to the Caribbean on a transporter. Because she was too small to have sailed across the Atlantic on her own – or at least without a great deal of both skill and luck – no one questioned that she hadn't been based in the Caribbean all her life, so to speak. After all, that's what the papers indicated.

'And here on the Mediterranean side, once the boat had gone, a description was of course circulated and harbour police notified, but no one ever thought it necessary to circulate the description as far away as across the Atlantic. Or if they had, that was covered, too, since once she left Holmes's place, she would have been virtually unidentifiable as the craft that had come in. It was a masterly simple stratagem, with low costs relative to the profit, a low level of risk, and minimal penalties if caught. It's even difficult to establish jurisdiction, since they stole the boats in France, converted them here, and resold them in various countries across the water. Even after extradition to France, none of these characters is looking at more than two years in jail, maximum, even less if they're lucky and can get an influential lawyer or a pliable enough judge. It all seems hardly worth my while.'

'How did you finally figure it out, Dad?' asked Ben.

'Luck, mostly, and one of those funny insights you get from time to time when you're worrying away at a puzzle. I didn't do any better than the police, actually, though I did run across some information they didn't have. We were all blinded by our assumptions. My primary assumption was that Ninian's murder had something to do with the investigation that Fausto Milagro was carrying out regarding drug smuggling, and that Ninian had found out some incriminating evidence and was trying to blackmail the gang. But that was a red herring in that Ninian, in fact, hadn't actually figured out the scam, however much evidence he had, so he couldn't have been blackmailing them, and so of course couldn't have given them a motive to kill him. Hell, they didn't even know he was recording them. In fact, we still don't know for certain *why* he was recording them, but assume he had blackmail in mind, though I don't wish to malign the dead. Maybe he was just nosy.

'Meantime, Fausto Milagro, in the wake of the murder, and knowing of Ninian's recording activities, but also knowing that his brother's boat was being used as a centre for some illegal activity he hadn't yet been able to find out about – but which he assumed was drug related – concluded that his brother must be involved. So Fausto took it upon himself to divert any possible police attention away from his brother by fingering me for the murder at the beginning, and then when Vega didn't swallow that bait, deciding that he could use me as a stalking horse to find out more about the scam. He didn't actually want the murder suspicions against me to stick – he's dead straight as a cop – but he hoped that perhaps he might derail the other investigation long enough for him to figure out the scam, get his brother out of harm's way, and maybe even catch the real killer.

'Commandant Vega, however, wasn't taken in by Captain Milagro's machinations, which is why he took over personal direction of the case, even though he, too, had similar ideas about using me to get inside the ring that he'd assumed was responsible for Ninian's death. He kept the threat of arrest hanging over me in order to motivate me to continue hunting and pointing for him. I was his pawn, set to hare along like a truffle hound with one eye on the doughnut and the other on the clock, a task at which I was reasonably successful. What he hadn't anticipated was the nature, the sophistication, or even the extent of the operation. He, too, had simply assumed it to be a straightforward drug-smuggling operation based around Pascual's boat, probably with Pascual's full knowledge. But *his* further assumption – though of course not something he would have told me – was that Ninian was involved and that the murder was simply another instance of a falling out among thieves. He never believed in the blackmail theory.

'As it played out, both of the policemen were mistaken one way or the other, so I wasn't alone in having misread some of the clues. And just by the way, it appears that Pascual Milagro actually is in the clear. Whatever was going on around the boat was all Martillo's doing, not Pascual's. Petra was correct in her assessment of that situation, even though it seems it was Fosas's intention to try to recruit Pascual, which is why there was an allocation of money for a mysterious recipient in Portals. That was a dead end because Fosas never got far with Pascual, who apparently may be a little flaky, but not corrupt.

'But you asked how I tumbled to how it worked. It only came clear to me when I suddenly realised that none of the facts *quite* fit the assumptions – close, but no cigar, as the saying goes. But then, simply by standing my assumptions on their heads, all the facts fell into place. Once I'd realised they were changing the name of the boat, and once Petra told me about that trip with Henry, which led me to suspect the boat was stolen, I could see how it all might work. But I didn't have any proof, which was why I had to lay my hands on the ship's papers and give them to Fausto Milagro to check to see whether they were genuine or counterfeit. Once I got them out of the post office in Santa Maria it only took two phone calls for him to find out they were phonies. They were fine for a cursory examination, the kind you usually get in the Caribbean, but wouldn't stand up to close scrutiny by professionals. The international documentation requirements are too stringent. That, by the way, is what that transporter guy was upset about when I first saw him with Gewürz and Sven. He'd refused to accept Gewürz's papers because he didn't think the first set was good enough to pass muster. I still don't know his name.

'It's all pretty improbable stuff,' said Hannah. 'I mean I still find it hard to make the leap from Ninian's murder to a boat theft ring. Could they actually make it justify the time and effort?'

'Absolutely,' I said. 'A decent boat in the categories they were moving would go out for between two hundred thousand and up to half million or more dollars. The costs of the operation never exceeded a quarter of their selling price, leaving several hundred thousand to be split up, with the lion's share to Fosas himself. Do it four or five times a year and he'd be laughing. And indeed, they all must have been laughing, though one of them, apparently, suddenly started doing his sums and demanding more money, presumably with menaces. There's even some indication that he was trying to strike out on his own. My guess is that it was Root, but then I have to admit to a mild bias against him. Whichever of them he was, he was the subject of the phone call I overheard the other night up at Fosas's house.'

'All right,' she said. 'I think I'm ready to have you tell me about who did Ninian in and why, but first there's a phone message I think you should listen to. Are you up to hobbling along to the office?'

'I'll give it a go,' I said, though reluctant to move from

my comfortable chair. 'Is what I'm to listen to a secret?'

'Just go listen to it yourself. I haven't heard more than the beginning. Once I realised who it was I saved it for you.' She winked, and my tummy gave a sideways lurch. I hoped I knew who it was.

Once in the office, I punched the playback button. The connection was patchy but her voice was clear enough.

'My dear, dear Will. I try to tell you I am sorry but you cannot listen yesterday. I have to go away. My sister send me the money to pay my debts and run away from Henry. I have to tell you, and I am ashamed, that last time after you are on the boat he come later and he hit me and hurt me until I tell him you are following them all because they are selling drugs or something. But then I cannot stay there more and so I am calling from a marina on the coast on my way to Holland first and later back to home I think. That is best, *nej?* Home is where you can be free from fear. Mostly I am calling because you are a good man and kind to me and I like you. I am thinking about you and thinking maybe if you ever come to København we – well, I don't know, but we can talk and maybe be friends. I must go now but I thank you and send you a – what do they say there? *Abrazo?* A hug. Good night and bless you.'

That was all there was. I felt better, while at the same time I felt, well, something hollow in my gut. My fantasies had been misplaced, inappropriate, but my instinct about her had been right. She had used me for her own purposes, but no more than I had used her. There seemed to be good will and essential benevolence, if that's not too strong a word, on both sides. The words she had left me with were simple but they tied up a loose end and put a healing touch to a sore spot. And who knows? Some day I might get on a plane and fly north. I could always use another friend.

I limped back upstairs. 'Well? Better for that, I hope?' asked Hannah.

'I don't really know. I think so. I'll let you know in the morning,' I said, thoughtfully, even perhaps a bit ruefully.

'Well, in the meantime you can put us out of our misery of suspense. Tell us who did it and why.'

'All right. But you may be surprised, or even disappointed. It seems it's a firmly justified rule of thumb among police forces the world over that about two thirds of all homicides are committed by the nearest and dearest of those who are killed, if that's not too ironic a notion. And so it was in this case that Captain Gumersindo Pososeco, an assistant to Commandant Vega, and whom I never met, first looked in Hazel's direction in a totally routine way. Regrettably for his ease of solution of the crime, she had an irrefutable alibi, having been observed by no fewer than fifty-four people in the restaurant during the time when the murder, according to the forensic evidence, took place.

'As I was on the spot, however, and as I had no similarly puncture-proof alibi, and as the police were ignorant of the relationship – distant acquaintanceship – between Ninian and myself, I became the default suspect, an idea also promulgated by Captain Milagro for the self-serving reasons I've described previously. Bit by bit, however, Vega came to the conclusion that I was in the clear, though of course he wanted to keep me worried and dangling. And running for him, sniffing out clues. Milagro had exactly the same idea, just with less pressure.

'However, though I wasn't aware of the fact, nor even was Commandant Vega, the able Captain Pososeco had simply pursued the usual mode of enquiry, starting with the person closest to Ninian, and having eliminated her from his list, moving on to the next closest person, and so on. It was inevitable that the list would reasonably quickly move to an investigation of Manuel, which it did. From then on, once his whereabouts at the time of the murder had been checked, the matter progressed to a swift

– in police terms – conclusion. Captain Milagro gave me a copy of the confession, so perhaps it would be best to hear the end of the tale in Manuel's own words. This is what he told them:'

'Meester Mede he say he want me to make dinner for heem an' Missus Mede for *aniversario*. He want I bring dinner to Stock's Hotel for big surprise to Missus Mede. So I use my day off, my only free day, and I whark five *horas* to make perfeck dinner – I make everything special, good, *perfectissimo*. An' so I bring dinner in beeg box to hotel an' Meester Mede he meet me outside an' let me in with he key an' we go upstairs to library room. Then he say he want to taste food before I bring to hotel kitchen, so I open my paté an' the pot with *estofado* stew an' he taste an' he say they need salt. More salt! Pfui! They *not* need salt. Are perfeck already. An' then he taste my *tumbet*, my lovely *tumbet*, with all the delicado *vegetales*, an' he say again it need salt. It not need salt an' so I tell heem again I whark five hours to make perfeck dinner an' I not put salt on. An' he tell me I muss do what he say an' I say I do many theengs for heem I no whant to do but I not put salt on *aniversario* dinner. For years he is boss me aroun' an' the people are laugh at me because I don' fight him back an' I do like he tell me. But I yam a man and I have the pride in my whark. I am chef. I not ruin perfeck food. So he say he fire me an' I say I not care, I can go many other restaurant. So he say he put own salt on dinner, an' I say you not ruin my perfeck dinner an' he jus' laugh an' start to walk away an' I get so angry I pick up piece of metal on table an' I hit heem. I hit heem so hard I can. I keel heem. Then I take my beautiful food an' I go home. I *not* sorry.'

'Then there's a stenographer's note to say he stopped and simply shrugged.'

'And so that was really the end of the story?' asked Hannah.

'Yep,' I replied. 'Justifiable homicide.'

If you enjoyed *The Bloody Bokhara*, you might be
interested in reading the first chapter of the second
book in the Will Stock Mallorca Mystery series,
The Chewed Caucasian

One

The stones felt cool as they slipped between my fingers. They didn't look like anything special, roughly-faceted and lumpily uneven, dusty, dull, and unprepossessing. But in the attenuated light from the half closed shutters they glowed a faint green and rang some kind of bell deep in my memory. I scooped down into the box, wrist deep, plucked a medium-sized stone from the bottom and held it against the light.

'Emeralds,' I said. 'Uncut and unpolished.'

'Pfawagh...' expostulated Mariela, her azure eyes going big and round. That's her all purpose sound for 'Get out of here, pull the other one, you gotta be joking.'

'I'd lay odds,' I said, scraping at the surface of the stone with a fingernail. It was actually only a half-educated guess on my part, but the undivided attention of an attractive woman brings out the know-it-all in me, and I certainly had Mariela's undivided attention right now.

Besides, it all just seemed to fit.

She'd brought me the package from Karamazov's room after he failed to show up for three nights running. After the second night, I'd checked the address he'd given us but it turned out to be a phoney, nonexistent. An inspection of his belongings had revealed no clues as to where he might have gone – no papers, nothing at all personal apart from six pairs of Italian handmade shoes, marked 'Osolemio.' The clothes he'd left were an eccentric mixture of cheap Russian polyester blends in those unlikely peasant browns they affect, plus three lightweight silk Armani suits, one of which he'd worn on his first night here, and which had draped oddly on his stubby frame. There wasn't a scrap of identification in his room or in his clothes. I was stymied, baffled. There had seemed nothing with which he might be traced until – when she went in to clean the room – Mariela noticed a scrape mark on the inside wall next to the water tank at the top of the bathroom utility cupboard, put her hand up to explore the space at the back of the tank, found the package, and brought it to me.

We'd inspected the brown-paper-wrapped parcel, but it was devoid of markings. Searching for a label, I'd then cut the plastic tape and slid out a wooden box, heavy for its size and well crafted, about the size of a box for ladies' shoes. The slideable boxtop was positioned in two grooves along the side of the uprights. There were some words in the Cyrillic alphabet marked on the bottom that looked like a possible clue, but although I once studied Russian for a fruitless year, the only thing that's left is '*Vy govorite po-russki?*' 'Do you speak Russian?', which may be the least useful sentence any non-Russian speaker can know, since of course if the person to whom you direct this question does, he will, and then where are you? So I tilted the box and showed it to Mariela, who *is* fluent in Russian. 'Made in Tbilisi,' she said, with a dismissive flare of the nostrils. Mariela's Bulgarian, and the Russians are not among her favourite people.

That was when I slid the top of the box back, revealing the stones – only the stones, no handy little tag stating ownership. These were clearly like those corporate bonds that have no identification, sort of bearer baubles, redeemable by the possessor anywhere such things may be traded.

I could see no obvious way forward, but had a strong intimation that we might not be going to see Comrade – are we all still good comrades? – Karamazov again. Probably the best policy at this point would be to keep stumm and put the stones somewhere very safe. Would the hotel safe be secure enough? For now, we'd better keep this between us, Mariela and I.

Totally on impulse, I picked up two of the larger, oblong stones off the top of the pile and held them out to Mariela, putting a finger to my lips in a childish gesture of secrecy. The azure eyes got even rounder. She hesitated momentarily, then reached out and plucked them from my fingers, and with an oddly sensuous movement of her tongue across her lips, popped them into her mouth. I closed the box and pushed the wrapping back into place. I had a feeling that impulsive gesture of generosity, or perhaps something closer to bribery, might just cost me dear. After all, who was I to be so magnanimously open-handed? The stones weren't mine to give away. Theoretically Karamazov might come back to claim them at any time.

Or perhaps one of his brothers – he'd mentioned having brothers. *That* was a prospect I didn't fancy.

I waved Mariela away, stuck the box under my arm, and went to the office to stash it in the safe, poor fragile receptacle that it might be for something of the value I calculated. The stones must weigh a fat kilo and a half – over three pounds. So we'd be looking at a lot of money even at only $25 per carat, a price I seemed to remember from Lord only knows where, probably a chat with my friend Simon-the-diamondcutter in Amsterdam. Five carats to a gram, times about 1500 grams in the box, times $25 as the uncut price, possibly more depending on quality – I was holding almost $200,000 worth of stones under my arm, a value our little safe hadn't seen since the Duchess dropped her tiara in my lap with such insouciance. And once cut these stones might treble their value. Quintuple it? I really had no idea.

But let me digress. My name is Will Stock and I'm the owner, together with Hannah, my best friend and ex-wife next door, of Stock's, a small luxury hotel in the wine country in the centre of Mallorca, the unspoilt, unexploited bit. We get a fairly cosmopolitan clientele here, lots of different nationalities – which makes for some interesting mixes in the evening up in our bar bistro – but we hadn't had many Russians visit us so far. Ivan Karamazov had been something of a rarity. He'd turned up unannounced and without a reservation, which is also something unusual for us, since our off-the-street trade is practically nil, given that we're hidden away in an untouristy *pueblo* and with only a discreet brass plaque to identify us, nothing more. And we're also usually mostly booked out, so it's even a rarity for us to have a vacancy for the unexpected visitor. This time, however, we'd happened to have space in our Cafe Olé Room, the coffee and cream one with the half tester bed, and Karamazov's four night booking had just filled an empty slot neatly. After all, hotel bedrooms are like airline seats; empty rooms after midnight, just like aeroplane seats after takeoff, are worthless, no matter what their prices may have been a few hours earlier.

I put the box in a plastic bag and stuck it at the back of the safe. Then I went up to go through Karamazov's clothing with the proverbial 'fine toothcomb.' When young, only ever having heard the phrase, it had puzzled me as to why people might want to comb their teeth. Mine had seemed reasonably kempt just as they were.

First of all I laid out all the clothes on the bed and concentrated my attentions on the suitcase, a cheap man-made fibre job, with tacky fake brass hinges and a plastic handle. The pattern was imitation Vuitton, but it wouldn't have fooled anyone, most especially a shrewd bellhop, who sees any amount of pretentious luggage in a given day. Paradoxically, of course, it's the possessors of fake quality designer gear who tip better than those who buy the real thing, possibly because the owners of the real stuff have so little money left over after spending it on the conspicuous acquisition of genuine 'name' accoutrements. But Karamazov had checked in late, and as we don't have bellhops or concierges, I'd carried the bag myself, and noted its relative lightness. He'd probably stashed the stones in the attaché case he'd carried, which was now missing, along with its owner and presumably all of his papers.

I tapped all the surfaces of the suitcase, which

seemed a somewhat feckless undertaking, given that they really weren't thick enough to have hollow caches in them. I didn't know what I was expecting; with these tolerances any more hidden emeralds would have to be in splinters. Then I examined the outside seams, but they looked intact. A bit threadbare, but untampered with. Lastly, I ran my fingers over the lining. Our fingers can detect changes in thicknesses too slight for the eye to see. A sheet of 80 gram paper can seem like a blanket compared to a sheet of 60 gram paper. Here, I had more luck. Up in the right hand corner of the lid there was an almost imperceptible lift to the lining, and I spotted just the tiniest bubble of glue along the join. Slipping a fingernail into the corner, I slid it along, pulling the lining up and away. It came easily, and there was a business card tucked into the space that had been created. I extracted it with two fingers. It looked like an ordinary commercial card:

> Banco Baleares
> Sucursal Plaza Peyton
> 07000 Palma de Mallorca
> Tel. 971 705000

No person's name, which seemed peculiar. The bank I knew, not one of my favourites. A bank with a sleazy reputation. I couldn't recall ever having seen that *sucursal*, branch, but then if I go that way I'm usually on my way to stuff my face at a Basque restaurant nearby, so I wasn't surprised. What could Karamazov have to do with them, I wondered.

I went over all his other belongings but didn't turn up anything I hadn't seen before. Frankly, the game was beginning to get boring. I knew I'd have to get in touch with the police, probably the Guardia Civil, those stalwart guardians of our freedom here in Spain. It wasn't something I was looking forward to. I figured it could keep until tomorrow, so I folded all of Karamazov's clothing and packed it in his suitcase, sticking down the loose flap of the lining with a bit of Pritstick. Then I stuffed it all in the office to await the morning.

The next day dawned looking as though it would turn out hot. We were into the second half of June and although there was a constant breeze, the midday sun was already strong. We had fewer guests than usual, since what we regard as 'our people' visit the island less during the hotter months, when the roads and the restaurants and other facilities are more crowded. Since we only welcome children from the age of twelve – having discovered that small children don't mix well with silk curtains and good antiques – we don't get the family holiday trade, for which I am thankful almost every day. We're a very boring hotel, actually, offering virtually nothing by way of entertainment or diversion, and so appeal only to those people who are seeking peace and quiet, civilised comfort, and unpretentious quality and taste.

After what seemed like a thin breakfast, I determined to gird my loins and ring the local Guardia office. Even though it worried Maribel, who fusses over me like a mother hen on a productivity contract, I'd had only fruit and yoghurt since I'm determined to lose some weight this month. For a long time I took psychological refuge in a description in a book I read awhile ago which referred to a stag that was 'thickening through the middle as do the virile males of most mammalian species as they grow older', but now I've had finally to admit to myself that whatever form my virility might still take, chubbiness is probably not one of them. So it's time to notch in the appetite a bit. Diets are rubbish. The formula is simple: eat less and you'll lose weight.

I sighed as I dialled. I'd already decided to hold back on the information about the emeralds. After all, they could always turn up later if I felt it to be appropriate.

'Good morning, this is Stock's Hotel. I wish to report a missing guest.'

'Thank you for calling the Guardia Civil.' This was a

new wrinkle; they'd been taking American telephone charm lessons. 'Where is the guest missing?'

I was a bit stumped by this one. 'Well if I knew where he was missing, he wouldn't be missing, would he?' I reposted blithely. Mistake. The charm fell away like a moulted snakeskin, fraudulent carapace that it was.

'Don't be a goat's bottom, Stock.' He knew me. And I now knew the voice. It was the crosspatch older one who bitched if we were ever even a day late in bringing in our monthly guest registry reports, not that he ever did anything with them except shove them in a file drawer.

Better to be obliging; a little accommodation, not to mention cringing obsequiousness, wouldn't go amiss. 'I'm so sorry if I sounded rude. I think I misunderstood your question. It's just that we've never had a guest go astray before. I need expert advice and you have so much experience I naturally felt you'd know what to do.' This with a straight face, even.

'Well, now that you put it that way, perhaps I might be able to help. You'd better come down here.'

'I'll be there in five minutes. Beat, pause. *Sir.*' In for a Peseta and all that. Actually, they don't have a larger denomination, so the old saying doesn't translate.

The Guardia building is down on the *carreterra*, the old main road, the one with all the seedy shopfronts and sticky-floored bars and neglected or abandoned buildings. The Mallorquins are pretty good at concentrating the unsightly elements on the island into specific locations. Fat German tourists are concentrated on the beaches of Peguera and Arenal, British lager louts are mostly corralled into Magalluf, and here in our town we keep the ugly elements along the old *carreterra*. Maybe that's why the Guardia is here.

There isn't much love lost between me and the Guardia. There're two officers in the headquarters in Palma for whom I have respect, even gratitude, though that's another story, but the local bunch and I have always been chalk and cheese. They think I'm a smart alec snob who thinks he's better than they are, and I think they're a lot of uneducated, small-minded, arrogant, bully-boy hicks. Which is to say that we pretty much have each other's numbers.

The Guardia building is split in two, with a passage through the centre and an office on either side as you enter. The younger ones hang out on the right hand side. Three were in attendance today, one jug-eared and still spotty youth polishing the patent leather tricorn hats they wear for special occasions. They all seemed to be practicing looking tough whilst listening to the unintelligible gabble on the shortwave radio. Am I the only person who can never, ever understand what anyone says on these things? I'd never make it as a taxi driver, and I had to quit private flying in congested airspace because I couldn't understand what they were telling me to do and once started to fly the wrong way round the traffic circuit at Exeter airport. My ears still burn when I recall that one. But these young patent-leather-heads seem always to understand and be cheered up when their patrolling cohorts report that they've trapped some poor innocent driver whose papers were nine hours out of date and carted him off to be drawn and quartered, or only halved if they're feeling lenient.

The left hand office is for the older officers, the senior man and his grizzled, silent adjutant, the one who remains ever nameless but whom I think of as Officer Menace. It's quieter on this side, but smokier, too. There's a room off this office that leads to the back, and I've long speculated that that's where they keep the instruments of torture left over from the Inquisition. Sorry. Just joking. But it's a reflection of how I feel whenever I visit. Anyway, it was in the left hand office that I now found myself.

'Good morning, Sir. You are, I hope, well?' I bared my teeth in a simulacrum of a smile.

'I'm fine, Stock. Sit down. So you've lost a guest.' I think he thought he was going to enjoy this.

'Perhaps just misplaced him, so to speak. It may all just be quite excessively responsible on my part, but he hasn't come back for three nights and I felt I should report it to you.' I gave him my sincere look, the one I learned selling encyclopedias door-to-door. I'm not sure it convinces anymore, if indeed it ever did.

'I never thought I'd see you suffering from an excess of responsibility, Stock,' he said, clearly already doubting my motives. Was I really so transparent?

'Even leopards are allowed to change their spots, as we say in my language.' I was continuing with the bland sincerity.

He looked at me a little oddly. 'We have an expression like that in Spanish, but it's just the opposite.'

'Ah well,' I said, 'same strokes, same folks.' I half-lidded my eyes. He could make of that whatever he might.

'Yes,' he harumphed a bit. 'Well, let's get down to business here. Enough of this idle chitchat. What's the name of the missing guest?'

'Ivan Karamazov,' I said. 'A Russian national, checked in four nights ago, stayed over one night, left in the morning and hasn't been seen since.'

'Hasn't been seen by *you* since,' he corrected me pedantically.

'You are, as usual, absolutely right, Sir.' I think I was having more fun than he was. So far.

'Right. Well, I have the forms just here,' he smiled, and reached down and pulled up an enormously thick bundle of papers. This is where he knew he had me. Now it was his turn.

And so I shall draw a veil over the next two hours – the tedious, repetitive recording of irrelevant facts and pointless detail. Besides, how was I to know the patronymic of a guest's grandfather on his mother's side?

At one stage I pointed out, almost pleadingly, that really all they needed was the man's name and a description so they could put out an APB, but my implacable interlocutor just smiled and plodded on. 'I've started so I'll finish,' was the way he put it.

At last he let me go. I'd signed all the forms in triplicate after waiting almost an hour for one of the young ones to finish typing it up. I hadn't heard any typing noise for a long time after my *bête noire* had taken the papers across the passageway and then gone off to have a coffee, and so I finally went over to check, and found the young group all just sitting around, lasciviously discussing the details of a rape report. They love that stuff.

'But I didn't know it was for *today*,' said the jug-eared one reproachfully. 'He never told me that.'

'Surely just an oversight on his part,' I remarked. 'The right hand office not knowing what the left hand office is doing.' Bastard.

In due course it was all sealed and stamped and I was released, only a decade older. I walked back home along one of the narrow streets that lead to the square, detouring around a pile of firewood that had been dumped in the road in front of one our bakeries that still uses a wood oven. It's bothersome to have an obstacle of that size to negotiate every day, but everyone seems to appreciate that wood-fired bakeries are dying out, so we all do what we can to support any baker who is willing to take the trouble to make a fire every day and maintain it for all the hours required. This is a town where one can still see, on Sundays and fiesta days, women carrying huge trays of meat along the street to be roasted in the bakery ovens, since they are the only ovens large enough to accommodate the multiple joints required for dinner for an extended family of thirty people. Of course, too, many people here don't even have ovens in their homes.

Late that afternoon I decided it was time to tell

Hannah about the emeralds. Sooner or later I tell her everything – something to do with trusting her judgement. We'd poured ourselves some wine and had settled into chairs in the patio courtyard. It was a pleasant seventy degrees under the rubber tree and the patio was fragrant with the aroma of jasmine, while the dappling sun on the white petunias made a vivid counterpoint to the rosy bougainvillea that was bushing out – late, and I always rib Hannah about her hard pruning – along the arch over the gate.

'So you and Mariela are going to scarper off to Rio with the emeralds, are you?' Hannah likes her sly witticisms.

'Oh absolutely. Mariela and the new baby, and Veronica. We could even celebrate Veronica's seventh birthday up on Sugarloaf. Of course Tony might like to come along, too.' Tony is Mariela's Danish husband, a big guy who's somewhere between a hunk and a hulk.

'Well, it's an image to conjure with, anyway,' she said, chortling softly into her wine.

'As a matter of fact, she tried to give me back the emeralds this morning. You know what a straight arrow she is. She came up and said, 'Here, I think you should put these back,' and spat them into her hand like two lime gobstoppers. I wonder if she'd kept them in her mouth the whole time. A funny place to hide valuables.'

'To each her own. I'd be afraid I might swallow them and then where would I be?' She wrinkled her nose.

'You mean like that young man who was given a tryout for a new job in the Coleman factory, and he worked out so well that within three days he had passed mustard.'

'Oh yuck, Will. Next you'll have me making references to where there's muck there's brass. But seriously, what are you going to do about the emeralds?'

'Seriously, I haven't the foggiest.'

'You can't just sit on them, you know. Karamazov –

or *somebody* – is bound to come back for them.'

'Don't think I'm not aware of that. What I'd like to do would be to get them out of our hands and out of the hotel, publicly and visibly. But I still wonder whether that would get us off the hook with either Karamazov or your *somebody*.' I scratched the top of my head and looked fruitlessly at the fleecy clouds overhead for inspiration.

'There is, of course, the other option,' she said, shrugging lightly.

'What? You mean put them back and pretend we never found them? Yes, I've thought about that one, and you just might be right. If K or his associates – or his *brothers* – are linked to the Russian Mafia, I really don't want to be anywhere near any of their booty. Those guys are pure poison.'

'So you'll put them back and try to forget about the whole thing?' She gave me a querying look.

'I just might. The downside, of course, is that I have to ask if I want to put the emeralds back and then have to worry that somebody else might find them. They weren't exactly expertly hidden. It's unlikely that anyone would snoop up behind the tank, but within the realm of possibility.'

'Just check every day to see if they're still there. You're basing hypothetical problems on total supposition.' She was right, of course, but there was something that was blocking me from following her common sense advice. I wasn't sure what.

'Yes. That's probably the best idea. Just let me sleep on it and see how it feels in the morning. By rights I ought to turn them in – probably to my great buddies the Guardia. But I know what a can of worms that might open up in terms of questions and suspicions. On the other hand, I loath the idea that some crook, including maybe even Karamazov himself, might be going to waltz in here, and waltz out again with a boxful of valuable stones. It just goes against my grain somehow. You and everyone else have always counselled me to live and let live, and I do bloody well try, but there's also the moral aspect to it; I just hate to stand by and watch those cockroach Mafia types getting away with things. It corrupts us all, as in that old adage about democracy going down the drain if enough good people just do nothing. But yes, on the other hand – or is that the third hand? – I don't want to be in the line of fire, nor do I want you or the children to be in danger if someone comes looking for those stones. Doing the right thing is often enough a hard choice, but even more so when what the right thing may be isn't all that apparent.'

'I know what your feelings are, Will, and I agree that this isn't an easy one. I'll go along with whatever you decide, but I have to say I'm partial to the idea of turning the whole thing over to the Guardia and walking away from it. That has to be the safest option.' She shifted in her chair a bit to ease her arthritic back, the original reason for us coming out to Mallorca.

'That's my worry – finding a solution that's both right, morally speaking, and safe. If I were sure dropping the stones off at Guardia headquarters was the safest option I'd opt away in a minute. My concern is that if somebody comes back here to get the stones, be it Karamazov or anybody else, I don't think they'd take kindly to the news that I'd turned over to the police something they consider to be their property. They might just decide to disagree with my decision, violently.'

'All right, I'll accept that as a valid concern as well. Let's agree mutually to sleep on it and decide in the morning.' With that she rose, picked up our empty glasses to drop off in the kitchen, and traipsed away to her flat across the square. I fooled around in the office for awhile, but my heart wasn't really in it. After about half an hour I wandered upstairs to the bistro to cadge a sandwich off Pepa, and then went to bed early to read. Even that was unsatisfactory; all I had was a lousy thriller, some dumb thing about a bloody carpet.

The next morning I rose to quaff down one of Maribel's mugs of hot strong *café con leche*, fed Alonzo, the hotel cat, about a quarter pound of the ham that he likes so well – distaining the catfood we try to inflict on him – and then went to the front door to pick up the daily paper.

It was all over the front page.

MANGLED BODY FOUND NEAR CALA RATJADA

The horribly lacerated remains of what appears to be a middle-aged Caucasian man were found early this morning on a farm outside Cala Ratjada. The victim had fallen, or been placed, into an almond shelling machine which had chewed and torn his flesh until the machine had broken down as a result of the blockage caused by the man's bones. The police are treating the incident as murder, since experts have indicated that there is little likelihood the man could have fallen into the machine by himself. Safety devices on the apparatus had been disabled. There are so far no hints as to the victim's identity, as no papers were found on the body. The only possible clue to finding out the victim's name is a pair of handmade Italian shoes found beside the machine, with the maker's mark 'Osolemio.' Anyone having any knowledge of the possible identity of the victim is requested to get in touch with the Guardia Civil.

Oh shit, I thought. Here we go again.

About the Author

When young, George Scott was deeply impressed by the aggrandising puffery to be found on the inside back covers of contemporary novels, generally portraying their (male) authors as steely-eyed, rock-jawed, pipe-smoking he-men who raced cars and worked as steeplejacks, yet who were sensitive and profound and practised brain surgery, spiritual healing, or high-energy particle physics in their spare time. Having now had a chequered enough history as a door-to-door investment peddler, prizewinning documentary film-maker, manager of a Liverpool rock band (no, not that one), high flying ad-biz exec, carer for elderly people, presenter of stress alleviation seminars, would-be launcher of earth resources satellites, occasional writer of busybody newspaper columns, sometime rallye driver, and now night porter in a small luxury hotel, he finally feels qualified – having also obtained a few university degrees, his pilot's license, and a third language – to allow himself to be described inside a back cover, not a bit steely-jawed or rock-eyed, but with one or two experiences to serve as spurs to the imagination.

Book Ordering Information

The Bloody Bokhara is available through all good bookshops. In case of difficulty, individual copies are available through:

Scott's Hotel Brochure Line, UK, 0113 274 9720, or by writing to:

> Scott's Hotel
> c/o Alternative Mallorca
> 60 Stainbeck Road
> Meanwood
> Leeds LS7 2PW

The fax number for ordering is 0113 274 2204
The email address for ordering is booksales@scottshotel.net

The price of a single copy is £5.99 plus £1.50 shipping and handling in the UK, a total of £7.49, payable by UK cheque made out to *Will Stock Booksales*, or by sending your Visa, Access, or Mastercard number, with expiry date.

For foreign postage within the EU, add an additional £.50 for a total of £7.99. For all other countries, add an additional £1.50 for a total of £8.99.

Discounted advance orders of *The Chewed Caucasian*, the second book in the *Will Stock Mallorca Mystery* series, are available in the same way. Telephone, write, or email, but simply subtract £1.00 from all prices. The book will be sent to you as soon as it is published, sometime in the spring of 2000.

Trade enquiries regarding *The Bloody Bokhara* should be addressed to the publishers:

> Eyelevel Books
> Oldbury Grange
> Lower Broadheath
> Worcester WR2 6RQ

The Hotel

Stock's Hotel regrettably seems to be booked solid for the next five years, but the author warmly recommends:

> Scott's Hotel
> Plaza Iglesia, 12
> 07350 Binissalem
> Mallorca, Spain
> Telephone (34) 971 870100, Fax (34) 971 870267
> email: information@scottshotel.net
> website: www.scottshotel.net